# EAGLE WOMAN

by
Don Mahanay

PublishAmerica
Baltimore

© 2005 byDon Mahanay.
All rights reserved. No part of this book may be reproduced, stored in a retrieval system or transmitted in any form or by any means without the prior written permission of the publishers, except by a reviewer who may quote brief passages in a review to be printed in a newspaper, magazine or journal.

First printing

ISBN: 1-4137-5145-8
PUBLISHED BY PUBLISHAMERICA, LLLP
www.publishamerica.com
Baltimore

Printed in the United States of America

# Dedication

To Karen, my wife of forty four years

# Acknowledgments

The author would like to thank Karen, his wife, who typed much of the manuscript from a handwritten note book and helped with many hours of editing, his daughter, Christy, for her help in typing from the same handwritten manuscript. Also, for the many hours she spent with him both on and off an Indian reservation where she lived and worked, discussing different Indian beliefs. He would also like to thank his daughter, Ann, who helped with putting everything together when we had trouble with our computer, as well as his daughters, Kathy and Laury, for their support and belief in him.

# Chapter 1

Maria was on the bus to her grandmother's. "This time he's gone too far," she said to herself, sitting next to the window, looking out toward the mountains. The land was extremely desolate in that part of Arizona. Nothing but greasewood on the low desert. *When we get near the reservation the land will change to grassland,* she thought as the bus rumbled along.

She had placed a carry-on bag in the seat next to her so no one would sit in it. The bus was only half full and there were plenty of empty seats, so no one needed to sit next to her.

As the bus rolled on, her thoughts drifted from one thing to another.

She had ridden this bus many times in the past and she had always tried to sit next to someone for company and have someone to talk to for the long trip. But on this trip Maria didn't want to talk.

Her face was swollen and was turning blue by now. It was feeling sore and the numbness had worn off. She put her finger in her mouth and felt the loose tooth. This was the third time in the last year Jack had beaten her up.

He had been out late last night. When he arrived at four o'clock this morning drunk, he had gotten mad because Maria was in no mood for his advances. Jack grabbed her by her hair, dragged her out of bed and hit her a few times, then flopped down on the bed and passed out.

Maria took a shower, put on some makeup, got dressed, and

packed a suitcase of jeans, shirts and underwear. Putting an extra pair of shoes and some socks in a carry-on bag, she then took a cab to the bus station. There she waited until the bus to the reservation left with her on it.

It was mid-morning now and Maria wished she had some coffee and something to eat. *This was a good sign,* she thought. Maybe, she was calming down. She sure didn't have an appetite earlier.

*He is such a dope,* Maria thought. *I would have done anything for him if only he didn't get so mean.*

The bus pulled into a rest stop. The bus driver got up after they parked. "We will meet back here in fifteen minutes." Everyone started getting up and heading for the restrooms. Maria stopped at the vending machine on her way back to the bus and got herself a cup of coffee and picked up some Danish from another machine.

Back on the bus, everyone was awake now and Maria was enjoying her Danish and coffee. *I never thought that vending machine food would taste so good,* she thought. Then she felt a sharp pain from the tooth Jack had loosened when he hit her that morning.

*I wish I could fix that Jack,* she thought. *If only there was a way I could get even, I'd fix him. If it's the last thing on earth I do, I'll fix him.*

The bus arrived in Flagstaff and Maria was enjoying the sights of the buildings. It was still a ways to the reservation but this was the last town or city she would be going through before getting to the reservation. When Maria first got on the bus in Benson, the bus driver put her suitcase at the end of the storage compartment so he wouldn't have trouble finding it. There wouldn't be very many people getting off at the reservation so he liked to keep the baggage separate from the people who were going further.

The bus finally came to the bus station in Flagstaff and made its stop. "It won't be long now," she said to herself. *It'll be nice to see Nana,* Maria thought. *She's eighty-seven now, I wish I could have seen her more often after I married Jack. But, whenever I mentioned going to see her, Jack would throw a fit and after awhile I just gave up trying to go, just to keep peace with that bastard. God, I've got to quit thinking like this. I've got to get my mind on something good, so when I see Nana I'll be in a good mood.*

The bus started loading up again. There were a lot of People meandering around the bus but not many got on. Maria started counting, only thirteen. *Thirteen,* she thought, *unlucky,* then the bus driver got on and she sighed a sigh of relief, *fourteen*.

The bus was soon in the prairie land where it was all grass with no trees. Maria's mind wandered back to when she was a kid and she would ride her horse on the grassland. Sometimes she would stay out all day riding that beautiful land. Sometimes she would go to the rocky area where the canyons were with a few cedar trees here and there. Many times she would take her little sister along with her, but most of the time she rode alone. As the bus rumbled along she gazed out the window, it was grass as far as the eye could see and in a little while Maria was fast asleep.

The bus rocked a little as it pulled in front of the grocery store when one back wheel went over the curb, and then a small jerk as it came to a stop. This was sufficient enough to wake Maria and she lifted her head to see the small, family-owned grocery store. This was it, the reservation, the place she new as home when she was a child. Somehow it didn't look the same. Of course she thought, nothing does, not even the reservation. It changes, too, but not as fast as the rest of the world.

Stretching she got to her feet, picked up her carry-on bag and made her way to the front of the bus and then stepped down the two steps to the ground. Four of the other twelve travelers were already walking away or getting into cars where their friends had come to meet them. Maria's suitcase was on the blacktop with one other. The rest of the passengers would stay on for the next stop. Most of the passengers didn't have baggage, they just used the bus to go to town, and then home, after shopping in Flagstaff or drinking in Flagstaff. Liquor had always been a problem on the reservation, as long as Maria could remember. Maria picked her suitcase up and started towards the store when a cow walked in front of her and stopped to look at her own reflection in a car window. Maria had an urge to hit the beast with her bag to make it move, but resisted the urge and walked around it instead. It was almost dark now and the Indians brought hay down to the highway next to the store to feed their cattle, so there were several cows and steers roaming around the parking lot.

There were several pickups there, some still with hay in them. If a tourist or someone just traveling on this highway through the reservation was unlucky enough to hit one of their beasts, it was always their prize blue ribbon cow. The tourist would have to pay big bucks for it. Just one of the ways the Indian had at getting back at the pale face.

Maria reached the front door of the store and stepped inside where there were several people getting groceries. In the back of the store was a lunch counter with eight stools. Two tourists were having coffee. Maria went over and sat down, she was starving. After ordering, she sipped her coffee and had a hamburger that she had to chew on the side of her mouth without the loose tooth. After a second cup of coffee, Maria picked up her bags and headed for her grandmother's house that was only about three blocks away.

Reaching her grandmother's house she could see the lights on. Maria was nervous now. She hadn't seen Nana for five years.

Maria stood there for a minute then walked up to the door and knocked.

An old lady came to the door dressed in traditional tribal clothes. "Yes," she said.

"Nana?" Maria asked

"Maria?" The old woman replied.

"Yes, it's me, Maria."

"Maria!" The old woman said in a delightful voice. "Maria, Maria," and the old woman put her arms around her granddaughter. The two women stood in the doorway hugging each other.

"It's so good to see you, Nana," Maria said.

"My prayers have been answered," Nana replied. "Come in, oh, come into the light and let me see you."

The two ladies stepped into the house with Maria carrying her two bags. She set down the bags in the living room and they walked right into the dining area where there was a light burning brightly.

Nana held Maria at arms length so she could study her face and eyes. She could see the bruises on Maria's face, but she didn't mention them. "It's good you came to Nana," she said.

"Oh, Nana, I've missed you," Maria replied. She was studying the old woman's face, the same as Nana had studied hers. This is something Nana had taught her as a child.

Maria had stayed with Nana much of her childhood. She had gone to school on the reservation. After school, Nana had spent many hours teaching her the secrets and ways of the tribe. Some, Maria kept in her heart, but most she rejected as superstition, though the studying of the face and eyes Maria believed to be a true science.

Maria had studied Jack's face and eyes and had seen the truth, but he was so charming and handsome that she didn't trust her own instincts and, of course, she was so in love. *If only I had believed what I knew, there would have been no Jack in my life,* she thought.

Maria saw a hurting in Nana's face, but it wasn't because of something Maria had done. She couldn't quite tell what it was. If Nana had been a white woman she would have asked her what was wrong, but this wasn't something you asked an Indian, according to tribal tradition.

The two ladies sat at the dining table and talked, then Maria had to excuse herself to go to the bathroom. Looking in the bathroom mirror she couldn't believe her eyes. Her face was black and blue and swollen from Jacks beating. *God, I must have scared Nana, looking like this,* she thought, as she lightly touched the bruises. They sent stings of pain through her under the light touch. *I shouldn't have come to Nana, looking like this… Well, it's too late now, I'm already here.*

Maria walked back out to the dining area table. Nana poured them each a cup of something she had taken off the stove.

As the two ladies sat down, Maria had a strong urge to ask Nana what they were drinking, but knew better. This would have been impolite under the circumstances. Nana wouldn't have criticized her, she would have just replied, warm water, Indian style. In fact it was warm water for Nana, but for Maria, it was a mixture of dried berries, Yucca roots, dried saguaro flower, and some other desert plant seeds, all ground to a fine powder. This concoction all dissolved quickly in the warm water.

Maria sipped her drink that had a tangy sweet taste. Quite nice she thought, but in a little while Maria was getting sleepy.

Nana took her to her old bedroom. Everything was the same except her old dream catcher wasn't there. Maria put her bags down, gave Nana a hug and they told each other goodnight.

Maria got ready for bed. When she went to bed she noticed that the bedding was fresh, like they were just washed. How did she know I was coming? Maria thought. That was her last thought before she was fast asleep.

# Chapter 2

The next morning Maria awoke late. She lay there, not knowing where she was at first. Then the memory of the last day came back to her. Maria lay there in bed on her back looking at the room she used to call her own. Now there was a dream catcher hanging where her old dream catcher had hung. She knew it wasn't there last night because she had noticed that her old dream catcher was missing. Maria just figured Nana's superstition had caused her to place a new dream catcher in her room after she had fallen asleep. Maria got up and was greeted by a cheerful, "Good morning."

"Good morning, Nana," Maria returned.

"Did you sleep well, little sparrow?" Nana asked.

"Very well," Marie answered. Nana used to call her little sparrow when she first came to live with her.

"Are you ready for breakfast or do you want to take a shower first?" Nana asked.

"Can I have coffee first, a shower second and then breakfast?" Maria asked.

"Why, of course you can, little sparrow." She brought Maria and herself a cup of coffee. They sat and had small talk, and then Maria went to take a shower.

When Maria got to the bathroom she looked in the mirror to check her bruises. To her surprise they had almost disappeared. She then checked her tooth that Jack had knocked loose. It had tightened up. *That was some concoction Nana gave me last night,* she thought. *Of course, she always took care of me.* Maria took her shower and dressed.

Maria joined Nana in the kitchen where she was fixing breakfast. "Smells good," Maria said.

"I hope you like it," Nana answered.

"That was some drink you gave me last night," Maria said.

"You liked it?" Nana asked.

"I like the results," Maria answered.

Nana just smiled and put the food on the table and both sat down for a nice breakfast.

"You always were a good cook, Nana," Maria said.

Nana nodded, "Thank you."

"I always loved to have breakfast here, you always make such a good breakfast, and I just love it."

"What are you wanting with all that flattery?" Nana asked with a laugh.

Maria laughed with her.

They sat a little while in silence. "I noticed you hung a dream catcher in my room last night."

"Yes," Nana said. There was a small pause. "You were dreaming, so I hung the dream catcher."

"You think it caught my dreams?" Maria asked.

"You stopped thrashing and kicking and quieted right down," Nana answered.

"I don't remember dreaming," Maria said thoughtfully.

There was a pause. "You know they are a spirit don't you?" Nana asked.

"What's a spirit?" Maria asked.

"Dreams." Nana said.

" Dreams are spirits?" Maria asked.

"Yes," Nana answered.

"I noticed you took my old dream catcher down. You know the one with the pink and white feathers. I loved it, it was so pretty. It had those pearl colored beads on white leather straps. What did you do with it?" Maria asked.

"You remember your old dream catcher?" Nana said with a smile. "It was pretty. Well, after a dream catcher is no longer used, you have to let the spirits go, or there wouldn't be any dreams anymore."

Maria thought all this was simple superstition, but she would never say this to her Nana. "How did you set the spirits loose?"

Nana went to get the dream catcher from Maria's room. She cleared away a spot and laid the catcher flat on the table, smoothing the feathers and strings of beads in the same direction they would fall if it was hanging from it's top loop. "When you make a dream catcher for someone you know, you should decorate it to the personality of the person you are making it for. That way it works better. Like the catcher you had as a little girl. I used pink and white feathers and white leather, because the dreams that a little girl would have, would like that color and they get sucked right in.

But to answer your question, when you want to release the captured spirits you cut one or two of the cords around the small center circle. Like this one or this one," Nana pointed to the cords that she was talking about. If you like we can cut your new dream catcher and leave it in your room tonight and you can find out what your dream was.

Maria thought it over a minute, took a couple sips of coffee, then said, "I think I'll pass."

"Nana?"

"Yes, little sparrow," Nana answered.

"I was wondering if I could stay with you a little while?" Maria asked.

"You can stay as long as you want. I'd love to have you stay with me, just as long as you want to," Nana answered.

"Thank you, Nana," Maria said as she reached across the table to pat Nana's hand. Maria studied Nana's face and especially her eyes. Maria knew Nana wanted to ask her what was going on, but she also knew that Nana would never ask. "I've left Jack for good his time."

"You're welcome to stay with me forever, if you want to." Nana said. "If you need anything just ask me."

Maria knew Nana meant it. If she wanted her to put a curse on Jack she would, but she didn't want to get Nana involved, and besides Maria didn't believe in curses. But she new Nana did.

Nana got up from the table and started cleaning it, and so Maria got up and started helping her.

"What's... what's your plan for the rest of the day?" Nana asked.

"I haven't made any plans yet," Maria said. "I was hoping to spend time with you, of course, and look up some old friends here. I'd also like to find a job here if I can."

"Why don't you wait and take a break from the job? Relax with me. I have plenty here and if you need spending money, I can help you with that." Nana said.

"Thanks Nana, I just might take a break from the job thing. I won't need any money. I have my own checking account. Jack's name is not on it," Maria said. "When we first started having trouble and he was drinking so much, I started putting money away that he doesn't know about. I wanted to be prepared for an emergency like this one now. Nana, I'm leaving him this time, I mean it, I'm leaving. I'm making a promise to myself right now." Maria closed her eyes and tilted her head toward the ceiling. "I promise I'm not going back to Jack. Ever."

"If you still mean that after two weeks, you can go to the council of the squaws elders and get a tribal divorce," Nana said.

"I can?" Maria asked, all excited!

"Sure, We have our laws here that the white man can't interfere in. And, I am chief squaw now," Nana said with pride.

"You are the chief squaw now?" Maria asked with surprise.

Nana nodded her head with a smile. This is a great honor in her tribe, a lifetime honor. She will be head of the women of the tribe now until her death. When the chief squaw dies, the tribal squaw members which number fifteen take a secret vote who they want to be their leader. It has to be one of the fifteen members. The elder squaws, which everyone of the tribal members refer to as the Women Council rule over the women of the tribe. They make the laws that the women have to abide by. After they pass a law, it goes to the men council. If the men council doesn't veto it, then it goes to the tribal chief, who is always a man. If the chief passes it, then it becomes law for the women. If the chief vetoes it or fails to do anything in thirty days then it doesn't become a law. All the laws that pertain to women have to start with the Women Council.

All laws that pertain to both men and women have to start with the men council. If a law that pertains to both men and women conflict with a law that pertains to women only, the law that pertains to both men and women prevails. If the men council passes a law that pertains to men and women that conflicts with an existing law that pertains to women only, because they didn't like the law for women. The men council would be in big trouble, because the tribe's chief had passed that law for the women or it wouldn't have been law. It didn't matter whether it was an old law or a new law. The tribe's chief protected any law that passed through him or any of the chiefs that came before him. In the past, a few men lost their lives for trying that scheme. The Women Council carries a lot of weight with the tribe, but not as much as the men council in most things.

Whenever anyone is voted into either council or when they installed a new chief of the Women Council or the man chief of the tribe. The whole nation of the Socike Indians comes to the reservation for a big celebration that lasts two weeks.

Maria realized that she had missed the celebration of Nana's installation as the women chief. "When were you installed as chief?" Maria asked.

"Fall of last year," Nana replied.

"Oh, I'm sorry I missed your celebration," Maria said, looking down and shaking her head slowly.

"You had your own trouble at that time." Nana replied.

*That's right, that was when I was in the hospital after Jack beat me up and I lost our baby,* Maria thought. She was four months pregnant and was in the hospital two weeks and almost lost her life along with the baby's. That was the first of October, which was the fall season for the Socike. They didn't use the white man's months, only the spring, summer, fall and winter.

But, how did Nana know she was in the hospital then? Maria wondered. She knew a lot of things that Maria didn't understand how she got the knowledge. Maria started to ask how she knew but thought better of it.

Going back to what we were talking about earlier. "How can I get a divorce so easy? I remember, before I left the reservation, Jamie Whitecloud wanted a divorce and she couldn't get it."

"Yes, yes, but Jamie Whitecloud was married to a Socike Indian. It is harder to divorce a Socike than a white man," Nana said.

Even though Maria is a full-blooded Socike, the Socikes considered her as an outsider now because she is married to a non-Indian. If a Socike man marries a non-Indian he is still a Socike and his wife has a chance of being initiated into the tribe. The woman's husband doesn't have that option. This started with their ancestors when they raided other villages and killed the men but would carry off the women and children to be slaves or wives.

"If you are sure you want a divorce then we will have a ceremony for you. It will last about an hour and then we have a celebration that can last as long as we want it to. You come dressed in any clothing you want. We first all sit in a circle, all of the elders of the Women Council. The elders eat and drink of cooked dear meat and ooka drink. We pass the meat and drink among us. Deliberately not giving you any food or drink. That signifies you are no longer in the tribe. Then we give you a freshly cut forked willow branch. You take the willow branch hold it like a wishbone of a turkey and pull the branch apart. It has to come completely apart. This signifies you and your husband are no longer one. You remember your friend Lolo Songa?" Nana asked.

"Yes" Maria replied.

"Well when she got to this part of her divorce. She had a broken hand and couldn't pull the branch apart. We didn't know what to do. But Lolo wanted that divorce so bad she took that branch in her good hand grabbed the other end in her teeth and pulled." Nana started laughing. "She got it to break but couldn't quite get it apart and wound up chewing it apart." Nana was really laughing now.

"Maria started laughing with Nana. "You're kidding?"

Both women were cracking up "No, no it really happened!" Now both women were in tears they were laughing so hard.

After a bit Nana gained her composure. "After this you throw down one part of the branch. Then you give me the other. The elders form a circle around you. They help you undress down to your underwear. So don't wear fancy underwear. If you don't have plain, we will buy you some."

"Don't worry all my underwear are plain. Mostly plain and holy."

"Anyway," Nana continued. The elders dress you in traditional Socike dress, including moccasins. Then all the council form a large circle. You go to each one and hug them. They will hug you back. After this, you are divorced and back in the tribe in good standing." Nana gave her granddaughter that look of being so proud of her.

"I really appreciate this, Nana, and I want to do that as soon as I can," Maria said.

"Oh I forgot, after the hugs, we celebrate. Your friends will come, probably all the women of the tribe will come and we will have singing, eating and drinking. You can stay as long as you like. When you go, then others will start leaving, but some will stay and celebrate all night. But no one will leave before you do. That's our way," Nana said with pride.

Nana continued, "The reason I asked you what plans you have for today is I have to go to a council meeting early this afternoon. I'll be back after dinnertime. You're welcome to help yourself to any food here. The refrigerator is full and the cupboard has canned food. If you go somewhere I'll leave the door unlocked. No one bothers my house everyone knows who I am and even the kids don't bother with someone on the council. Especially the chief of the squaws."

Maria smiled, "I really thank you, Nana," and gave her grandmother a hug. "I'll probably go to Rita's house. She wrote me several letters this last year."

"Rita," Nana repeated. "I've seen her several times in the past year. I always liked her, even when you girls were teenagers. You two were a handful. She's staying with her parents now."

"Yes, I know. It'll be nice to see her and her parents again. I haven't seen them since I got married. I know Rita got a divorce last year. Is she seeing anyone else?" Maria asked.

"I don't know dear, I don't see her very often." Nana Answered.

By this time they had the table cleared, dishes washed and everything put away. The two went to the living room.

"I've got to start getting dressed for the council meeting Maria. But tonight, if you are here early, we will talk some more. If you are not, we will talk more tomorrow." Nana said.

Maria agreed.

# Chapter 3

"If you don't have anything planed for tomorrow, maybe we could go riding," Nana said.

"I'd love to!" Maria said. She knew Nana meant horseback riding. Nana would ride in a car or bus, but never for pleasure and only if a horse wasn't practical or wasn't available. In most Indian tribes the men would ride horses. But, with the Socike women, they rode as much as the men from the beginning of time. In their history there were great women warriors that rode as well as any man. There was even a woman warrior called the Eagle Woman because she was so fast. She still, to this day, is honored for having killed more enemies than any other warrior in the history of the Socike nation, man or women. Eagle Women rode a large coal black stallion that was bigger and faster than any of the other brave's horses. She rode faster than any other brave and would ride up to the fleeing enemy and club them with her war club with ease. Because she had this huge fast horse she could reach more fleeing enemies than any of the other Socike braves. With this distinction she was feared by the other tribes and they were more anxious to flee than fight which gave her a big advantage.

Legend has it, she was five feet tall and was beautiful. In reality she was over six feet tall built like a man and was not beautiful. In those days it was a terrible shame to a brave and his family if he was killed by a squaw brave (woman brave).

Every year the socike nation celebrated the Eagle Woman and that was coming up next month. Maria was looking forward to the celebration. She would get to see many of her childhood friends and their families.

Nana left the house dressed in her traditional Socike dress. She had to walk about six city blocks but she was used to walking.

Maria watched her go around a corner then she left for her friend Rita's house. She only had to walk about three blocks. But, she wasn't used to walking that far and realized how out of shape she was. When she reached the porch she felt like sitting on the steps instead of going to the door but she didn't. Maria knocked lightly on the old door. After a moment it opened slowly.

"Yes?" Then Rita recognized her friend. "Maria!"

Maria smiled.

"Maria! When did you get here?"

"Just now, I walked over," she said, teasing.

"No, I mean when did you get to the reservation?" Rita asked excitedly

"Yesterday evening, I'm staying with Nana," Maria answered.

"I'm so rude!" Rita said, "Come in."

The two ladies made their way through the living room to the kitchen, where they both sat down at the table.

"Mom and dad, left for Flagstaff this morning. I took them to the bus stop. You know, our grocery store," Rita said.

"Yes, I was there when I came in yesterday," Maria said.

"You took the bus, didn't drive, huh?" Rita asked.

"No, I don't have any wheels." Maria answered.

"Well, I do. Today anyway," and Rita dangled a set of keys in front of Maria. "Want to go down to Roy's for lunch and a couple of drinks?" Rita asked.

Roy's was a small bar and grill just off the reservation where some of the locals went to let down their hair. It wasn't a real bad place, but there were a few fights among the cowboys, both white and Indian, that hung out there.

Maria thought about that awhile undecided.

"Aw come on, we'll get something to eat, catch up on old times, enjoy a couple of hours together?" Rita asked, and then waited for an answer.

"Well I'd love to, but I need to get back early this evening. I want to have supper with Nana," Maria said.

"Great," Rita said jumping up with the keys, and ran to her bedroom and grabbed a jacket. The women went to Rita's folks' car and started the forty-minute drive to Roy's.

Maria caught up on her friend, Rita's, life on the long drive. She had gone through the same divorce procedure that Nana had told Maria about. She warned Maria that if she went through with it, that she also needed to get a legal divorce through the Arizona law.

They arrived at Roy's, it was eleven forty-five. *Just in time for lunch,* the two ladies thought.

Maria stepped out of the car. There was a southwest breeze and it went through her hair. She felt a sort of freedom with this cool wind on her face. That and with all the talk of divorce she felt free and safe here by the mountains. Maria slowly looked around, she saw the prairie and a few trees. "God this is beautiful. I hope I never leave this beautiful country where I grew up," Maria said to herself.

"Come on," Rita said as she reached the door of Roy's. This snapped Maria out of her daydream. She walked briskly through the door.

The ladies stood there inside Roy's until their eyes got used to the dim light after being in the bright sunlight. In a minute they could see clearly. They made their way to a table out in the open where they could see what was going on in the rest of the bar. There were half a dozen men and three other women. The jukebox was playing a country western song. One couple was dancing. All the men were at the bar and the two other women were sitting at a table by themselves. There were three drinks on the table, so either the other person was in the bathroom or on the dance floor.

A waitress came over to Maria and Rita's table, "Menus?" she asked.

Maria said, "Yes, please."

"Just a hamburger, fries and a tall draft," Rita said. Then started eyeing the men at the bar.

The waitress looked at Maria, "What to drink?"

"An iced tea, please," Maria answered. The waitress turned on her heals and was off. *This is a mistake,* Maria thought.

The waitress was back in a minute with Maria's ice tea, menu, and Rita's beer. Maria looked the menu over.

"Trust me, go for the fries and hamburger. Everything else tastes like hamburger anyway," Rita said.

Maria scrunched up her face and gave a slight shrug, then laid down the menu.

The two ladies had caught the attention of two men at the bar.

Maria kept her eyes on Rita and their table, but Rita kept looking up at the men at the bar.

Soon one of the men at the bar sauntered over to the table. "Care to dance ma'am?" he asked Rita. Rita got right up and they headed for the dance floor.

*Kind of early in the day for that.* Maria thought. She caught a movement to the right of her that kind of startled her. It was the waitress picking up her menu.

"Decided yet?" she asked.

"Yes, I'll have the hamburger," Maria answered.

The waitress just turned on her heals and was off with the menu.

*Now there goes a woman of few words,* Maria thought. Then she turned her attention to Rita and the cowboy dancing.

"Howdy!"

Maria jumped. There stood another cowboy. "Would you like to dance?" he asked.

"It's a little early, don't you think?" Maria answered with a question.

"Well a—, your friend doesn't seem to think so," the cowboy said.

Maria just kind of ignored him after that.

"Mind if I sit down?" he asked.

This got her attention. She turned, "We are waiting for lun..." Maria saw he was already sitting. "lunch."

"Well let me buy you lunch," the cowboy said.

"You don't even know me," Maria answered.

"You're right. I'm Dale, and you are?"

"Hungry," Maria said, and started watching Rita and the other cowboy. *From the looks of them dancing it looks like she knows that cowboy quite well,* Maria thought.

At the end of the song Rita and the cowboy walked over to the table. "I see you've met someone already, Maria," Rita said.

"Maria, that your name?" the cowboy that was sitting at the table asked. "I'm very glad to meet you."

"Look, I only came in for lunch. I don't want to be rude, but that's all I want. Understand?" Maria said, staring at the cowboy's face now.

It couldn't have gotten quieter at that very moment at that table. The guy looked embarrassed, got up from the table and went back to the bar.

The first cowboy thanked Rita for the dance, held her chair for her and she sat down. He then followed the other cowboy back to the bar.

"Kind of cute don't you think?" Rita asked.

"Which one?" Maria asked.

"Why both," Rita answered.

They both giggled. "Do you know that guy you were dancing with?" Maria asked.

"I do now," Rita said with a grin.

Just then the waitress showed up with their food. Other people started coming in for lunch and the place filled up pretty fast.

The hamburgers were good and Maria even tried a french fry or two of Rita's.

"You know I don't like any of their other dinners here, but they sure make a good hamburger." Rita said.

Maria nodded because she had a mouth full of hamburger.

The waitress came by and picked up Rita's empty beer glass. "Need another? More ice tea?" she asked.

Rita said, "Yes," and then asked Maria if she didn't need something stronger.

"No, iced tea is fine," Maria replied.

In a short time the waitress had cleared away the dishes and Maria and Rita sat there talking, each with her own drink.

"This place has really filled up," Maria said looking around. "Maybe we should leave to give other people a chance to get something to eat?"

"Naw it'll clear out shortly," Rita said. "Then it will only be those cowboys there at the bar that are looking to get lucky." She then let out with a loud laugh.

"I think that beer has gone to your head," Maria said.

This happens to many people especially of Indian decent. Many Indians have a low tolerance for alcohol.

Rita ignored Maria's remark and started trying to make eye

contact with the cowboys at the bar.

Maria knew she had to put a stop to this or she'd be in for a real argument after a little more beer. "I've got to get back, Rita, I want to be with Nana when she gets back from her meeting."

"We have plenty of time. Here, have a drink," Rita said as she scooted her beer over to Maria.

Maria took the beer but put it aside so Rita couldn't reach it.

"Well, drink up," Rita said.

Maria stood up, "Let's get going."

"Aw, sit down, relax," Rita said with a slur.

The cowboy that danced with Rita earlier got off his stool and headed for the table.

Maria stood up and got right in his face. "Look buster, get away from us. I'm having enough trouble with my friend without you interfering. So go back to your perch and leave us alone."

"Why'd you do that," Rita asked.

"Look, I got to get back and I don't want to hang around a bunch of drunks," Maria said in a firm voice. "Now give me your keys. I'll drive us home."

"Aw, just one more beer," Rita protested.

"One more beer and you'll go?" Maria asked.

"Yes, I promise," Rita said, as she made a cross over her chest with her finger. With that she waived the waitress over and ordered a beer.

Maria went to the restroom and when she returned Rita was dancing with that same cowboy. *Oh, great! Now I'll never get her out of here,* she thought. They stayed on the dance floor through two dances and her beer sat on the table, untouched. Rita's purse was on the floor next to her empty chair. Maria picked it up and took out her car keys.

When the song ended Maria jumped up, ran over to Rita and the cowboy. Grabbing Rita's hand she headed off the dance floor. Rita followed unwillingly, but not putting up much of a struggle. Maria headed out the door and over to Rita's folks' car, pulling Rita all the way. Maria opened the passenger door, pushed Rita in and threw her purse on her lap. She slammed the door, then headed for the driver's side. Jumping in she hit the button that locks all the doors, because Rita was trying to get back out. Maria had no trouble getting the car started. She then gunned the motor a couple of times slammed it in gear and threw gravel all over as she left the parking lot. When they hit the black top the speedometer was showing fifty.

"Better fasten your seat belt," Maria said to Rita. By the time Maria got her own seatbelt fastened they were going sixty-five.

Rita looked at how fast they were going and gave up on the idea of getting out. She laid back, settled down and then fell asleep.

Maria reached Rita's house and pulled into the driveway and stopped right in front of the garage. She then woke her friend up and got her into her house. Rita was sick now so Maria helped her into bed then walked home.

*Boy, that's the last time I go out with Rita to a place that serves liquor,* Maria thought. She had heard of people who got drunk on one beer, but it was the first time she had witnessed it. But that ordeal had gotten Maria's problems off her mind and she reached Nana's house a little before Nana.

# Chapter 4

Another member of the council came home with Nana to borrow some herbs, which Nana had picked last summer.

"Maria, this is my friend, Hanna. Hanna, this is my granddaughter, Maria."

Both ladies said hello to each other. "I promised Hanna some summer blue teal," Nana said, and went into the root cellar through a trap door to get the Teal. The cellar was dark, but for a small light bulb hanging from the center of the ceiling. The wall was lined with railway ties and the floor was dirt.

"I see you have a dream catcher." Hanna said to Maria, pointing to the dream catcher Nana and Maria left on the table.

"Nana and I were talking about dream catchers this morning," Maria said fingering the dream catcher.

"Did she talk to you of Red's dream catcher?" Hanna asked.

"Red's?" Maria asked.

Hanna started stuttering and Maria saw she had gotten very scared or nervous.

Nana showed up with the blue teal herb. Hanna took it and left immediately.

"She must have been in a hurry," Nana said with a slight laugh.

Maria was puzzled, and then agreed, "Yeah."

Nana and Maria talked about different things and then Maria asked about a red or Red's dream catcher.

Nana got very quiet and no one said anything for awhile. "Where did you hear about Red's dream catcher?" Nana asked.

There was a long silence and Maria was nervous. Then she answered, "Hanna saw the dream catcher on the table and I told her that we had been talking about dream catchers. She asked if you had talked to me about red or Red's dream catcher. Nothing more was said about it."

"I see." Nana then went to the trap door and went down in the root cellar after a few minutes she returned with a dusty wooden flat box. Nana laid the box on the table. It was dusty and she made no attempt to dust it off.

"This is Red's dream catcher. The squaws and the Men Council are the only ones who are supposed to know about it. This is something that is not supposed to be talked about by anyone outside the council. Hanna should not have mentioned it." Nana said.

"Hanna, I think, well, I think it just slipped out, I think it was a quadra," Maria said. "You do not have to show or tell me anymore. I am not in the council. I know that certain things are mica."

Quadra is the word that the Socike nation used for a spirit either good or bad that whispered to them or made them do it. Mica is the word they use to describe sacred to their tribe, nation, council or even individuals.

"Yes, this is mica! But, it's part of your heritage," Nana said.

"My heritage?" Maria asked.

"Yes, yours, and you should know about Red's dream catcher." Nana opened the box. Inside there lay a traditional Socike dream catcher that was all black. It had the traditional willow branch made into a loop, wrapped with black leather. Not a metal hoop like the other tribes use for their dream catchers. The net was even black. The feathers were vulture's feathers black with no white. Everything was black and Maria could tell that it was old. She noticed that none of the strings were cut. All old dream catchers that Maria ever saw as a child and as a teen, growing up on the reservation, had the string cut in one or two places right where Nana had shown her to cut to let the dream or spirit out. But, this one had the whole net intact.

Maria didn't touch the dream catcher because this would be considered bad manners and disrespectful to Nana. It was Socike tradition not to touch something that someone was showing you, but didn't hand it to you or invite you to touch or pick it up.

"Do you remember Red Yellowhair, my brother?" Nana asked.

"Yes—s"

"Well" Nana went on. "When he was about fifteen he started having these awful dreams. Mama put several dream catchers in his room, but they didn't do any good. The dreams got worse. They bothered him so much he couldn't concentrate on his schoolwork. He started drinking heavily and, in a short time, he was committed to an asylum, an insane asylum. This all took about three weeks from when he first started having his dreams. In the asylum he got so bad that he repeatedly tried to kill himself. They had him in a straight jacket and kept him in it twenty-four hours a day. The drugs they gave him didn't work. He begged us to bring him poison so he could die and have peace. He begged his doctors and nurses to kill him. He was in constant torment."

"As a little girl, I went with my mother every week to see my brother. I loved my brother, but he scared me. It was the worse thing I had ever seen or heard of. He was skin and bones, his body was twisted and he cried and screamed constantly. The doctors told us not to come and see him until he got better, but Mother insisted on seeing him every week."

"After one visit like this, I went to the sacred mountain of knowledge and prayed. I got a vision of this dream catcher you see here. I was only nine years old and this all frightened me very much, but I obeyed the God of knowledge and made this dream catcher. I cut the branch for the hoop from the top branch of the tallest willow tree I could find. I got the vulture feathers from a dead bird by a road. The black leather my mother's brother gave me. The netting I turned black with the hull of green black walnuts."

"When mother took me to see Red that week, I wore a coat and hid the dream catcher under my coat. When we were let in his padded room he sat in the corner. When the attendant wasn't looking, I slipped the dream catcher under one of the pads."

"The next visit the doctor wanted to see us before they would let us see Red. We were taken to the doctor's office. There he threw the dream catcher at us and told us that they had found it in Red's room that morning. That they were helping him and they didn't want any interference from our silly superstitions. He said that he was afraid that Red seeing that thing with feathers would cause him to slip back into a state of hysterics, that Red hadn't screamed for a week now and, as far as he knew, he hadn't cried either."

"Mother looked at the dream catcher, then at me and then she smiled, but the doctor couldn't see her smile. She turned back to the doctor with a straight face and nodded."

"The doctor went on, 'We've cut his medication in half and have him even talking. I just hope and pray that you haven't made him regress, from your silly superstition. Now if you leave that thing out of his room and away from him you can see him.'"

"When we saw Red, he was sitting quietly and even smiled at us."

Each visit he was better than the one before until he was able to come home. You know the rest, how he got married, had two sons. He never had another bad dream as long as he lived."

"After about five years he was able to talk to me about the dream. He told me that a monster would twist him in knots and bite him. It was very real to him. He said that the monster would do other things, but Red couldn't keep from crying when he tried to tell me about them. So I never did hear all about his dreams."

"About a year before his death, which was when he was eighty-one, he confessed that he kept poison powder made of caster beans in a bag around his neck in case he ever started having those dreams again. He had gotten the poison his first week out of the asylum."

"The Socike law says that after the person who the dream catcher was made for dies or if he or she no longer believes in the dream catcher, then the web must be cut to let out the spirit dream."

"I refused to cut the web on Red's catcher because it holds such a bad dream. I was taken to the Men Council and ordered to cut the web. I refused again. This has all been discussed in both the men and the Women Council many times. The last time I was ordered to cut the web. I brought the dream catcher and gave scissors to the chief of the men. He refused to cut the dream catcher. No one else would cut it. I was told that I was responsible for the dream in the catcher and I should release it, but I have refused. Both the men and Women Council are afraid that whoever lets the dream spirit out will be haunted by it, like Red was."

"I'm not afraid of the dream haunting me, I just don't want this dream spirit loose to ruin anyone's life like it did Red's. But, the law says all dreams should be released after the death of the person it was made for. Therefore I, the women chief, have been breaking the law now for ten years. This is not good. But, what to do? So both the women and the men council discuss what should be done with Red's dream catcher at least twice a year."

"There you have it. That's Red's dream catcher, what do you think?" Nana asked.

"I think that's quite a story!" Maria said.

"And, it's quite a problem. I really don't know what to do, I don't like breaking the Socike law, but I can't turn that monster loose either." With these words Nana closed the lid to the box and fastened it. She picked up the box, sighed, and then took it back down to the root cellar.

*I thought I had a problem, but poor Nana, I know she would rather die than break the Socike law*, Maria thought.

Nana returned and sat down at the table.

"I'm sorry, Nana," Maria said. "I'm sorry you have this burden on you. I wish there was something I could do."

"There's nothing any person can do, only God knows the answer," Nana replied.

Maria and Nana talked, had dinner and then talked until they both were ready for bed. The dream catcher that was hung in Maria's room the night before was once again hung in her room.

Early the next morning, Nana woke Maria. "Do you still want to go riding today?" she asked.

Maria fought to open her eyes. "What...? Riding?" she murmured with her eyes still closed.

"Do-you-still-want-to-go-riding, this morning?" Nana asked again.

Maria got her eyes open. "Aaa, I guess."

"Then you need to get up so we can get an early start," Nana said.

After her shower, Maria stepped into the kitchen in her robe where Nana was cooking breakfast. "Smells good," she said.

"I hope you're hungry, but get dressed and by the time you get back out here breakfast will be ready." Nana said.

Nana started the eggs to go with the fried corn and Indian tortilla. She then set out a small glass of goat's milk and coffee. By the time she had the breakfast on the table Maria was back, dressed in jeans and a western shirt.

"Looks and smells great!" Maria said.

"I see you remember how to dress for riding," Nana said.

"Oh, yes, I remember, no dresses or skirts for Socike squaw braves," Maria said with a grin.

The two women sat down and ate breakfast. They talked a little but not much, because Maria knew that Nana was anxious to get started.

After breakfast they did a fast clean up and set the dishes in the sink to soak, intending to wash them when they got back.

Nana brought out two scarves. A black one and a gray one. She rolled the gray one up, tied it around Maria's head to keep her hair in place. Its being gray meant Maria was of the clan of the Giant Eagle, the same clan of the famed Eagle Woman.

Maria looked in the mirror and lightly touched it with her fingertips. It felt good to wear the clan's color again. As a child she wore the gray headband almost every day, to show the other kids what clan she belonged to.

The other kids didn't wear their colors as much because they didn't have such a famous ancestor. But still, at ceremonies every child would wear their colors. The teens, especially, wore the colors of their clan. This is because no one in the nation is allowed to marry someone in their own clan. So, if you were wearing the same color as a boy you thought you might like, you wouldn't flirt with him. You would have to find a boy with another color.

Nana tied the black scarf around her head. This signified that she was head of her clan. If a clan's color was blue then the head of the clan would wear a darker blue than the rest. Nana took an eagle feather and stuck it in her headband. She pushed it half way down passed the headband. This was the way the Socike Indians wore their feathers. This way they didn't come out with every gust of wind.

Maria longed to put the famed eagle feather in her headband like she did as a child on special occasions and when she rode horses. Nana told her as a child that if she should fall off a horse the spirit of the eagle would keep her from hitting the ground too hard if she was wearing her eagle feather. But she knew there would be no feather for her today because she was out of the tribe until she went through the ceremony of her divorce.

Nana grabbed a bag. "Come on," Nana said, taking her

granddaughter by the arm, leading her out the door. It was still early in the morning and cold outside so they both took jackets and headed for the stables with a brisk walk.

When they reached the stables the sun had just come up. A young Indian man dressed in blue jeans and a western shirt and a western hat with a leather band covered with silver studs came out to meet them. "Jode, this is my granddaughter, Maria," Nana said.

"Hello" Jode said.

"Would you saddle one of the better gelding for her?" Nana asked.

"Yes, Pupa," Jode answered.

*Pupa* is the Socike word for female leader.

Jobe went back to one of the rear stalls and brought back a saddled chestnut colored horse with saddlebags.

Nana took the reins and looked him over good. "He's a good one, Jode."

"Yes, Pupa," Jode said.

Nana took something out of her sack and put it in one saddlebag, then put the rest in the other side of the saddlebags sack and all.

"What's his name?" Nana asked.

"Nekey," Jode answered

"Nekey," Nana repeated. "Bright Star. Okay you be good to my granddaughter, Bright Star." With that she handed the reins to Maria.

Maria took the reins and looked at Nana with a puzzled look.

"You go on ahead, Little Sparrow, I'll catch up with you in a minute," Nana said. With this she walked over to an inside wall and picked up a strap, then headed for the corral. She walked through the corral and back behind the stables.

"Is she going to be alright?" Maria asked Jode.

"She will be just fine. You'd better get going or she will be so far ahead of you, you'll never catch up," Jode said.

*I'll show him*, Maria thought. She had spent hours bareback and in the saddle as a child. She hooked the stirrup on the saddle horn and checked the cinch to make sure it was tight enough. With this done she unhooked the stirrup.

Jode had taken this all in, and had a silly smirk on his face. *Thinks she knows horses, huh*, he thought.

Maria noticed the smirk on his face and turned her attention back to her horse. She then whopped Nekey on the rear, "Yeah." With this, the horse bolted foreword in a full gallop. Maria held onto the saddle horn and pulled herself up on the side of her horse almost in a fetal position, she then straightened her legs hitting the ground in a graceful arc, swinging up into the saddle in one smooth motion. In the short time it took her to do this Nekey was in a dead run.

Jode was staring at Maria and her horse with amazement and great admiration, now a ways off and getting further with each second. "She's her grandmother's granddaughter all right."

Maria got to a small clearing on the riding path where the trail turned. She pulled her horse to a stop and turned to see if Nana had started yet. Nana was nowhere to be seen, but a big black horse was coming at a dead run across the field with what looked like a big boy or a young man by the way he was riding. He was almost to a stone fence, which is why one had to take the trail to get here. Maria watched with apprehension as the rider came closer to the fence. She thought the horse was going to run into it because it was way to high to jump and, in a minute, would be too close to turn. In the last split second the horse and rider went into the air in a jump that looked like they were flying. The horse was stretched out with it's front legs folded up close to the body and the back legs tucked up close to its belly as they sailed over the fence, as if in slow motion. The rider was laying so low on the horse's back that it looked like, in that moment, there was no rider at all, just a horse. Maria sighed with relief as the horse landed on the other side of the fence. She had never seen a horse and rider like this, she was wishing that Nana was here to see this. Maria had seen a wide gully between her and the rider, but paid no attention to it as the rider had lots of room to ride around it. As the rider came closer he made no attempt to turn his horse and go around the gully. In the next moment the horse and rider were in the air. Maria gasped, The gully was way to wide to jump, and then the horse and rider were on the other side still in a dead run. Maria was transfixed, as if watching a movie. She had never seen anything like this. The horse was large, but not that large and the rider was small, but not that small. But together they made jumps that were, otherwise, impossible. In a few moments the horse and rider were right in front of her at a dead run. This snapped Maria out of her trance, they were going to collide. In the next moment the horse and rider were past her.

They had jumped some rocks directly behind Maria and kept going. *That was Nana!* Maria thought. She jerked the reins and spun her horse around. With a quick kick they were off up the trail. When they passed the rocks that Nana had jumped, they took a quick right and Nana and that beautiful, black horse came back into sight. Maria was riding as fast as she could, even taking the ends of the reins and popping Nekey on the rump to spur him on. But Nana was getting further away.

There was no way to catch up, her only hope was if Nana slowed down. In a few moments she noticed that Nana and her horse were getting bigger. Encouraged, she spurred her mount on, Nana's horse had stopped. Right before she got there, that big black stallion reared up and paws the air. *Oh, my God he's going to throw her.*

When Maria reached Nana, Nana was laughing. "He likes to run," she said to Maria.

"Are you alright?" Maria asked.

"Of course, I'm alright." Nana answered. "Why do you ask?"

"I thought he'd throw you when he reared!" Maria answered.

"Baroka?" Nana asked. "Baroka would never do that."

Baroka? Maria thought, Baroka? She knew that word, but couldn't think what it was.

Then the black stallion pawed the ground. "He wants to run some more." Nana said and took off up the trail.

Maria noticed that Nana was riding without a saddle. She didn't even have a bridle on her horse only a strap in the mouth and around the chin. *How does she do that?* Maria wondered. I'd better get going or I'll never catch her and off she went further up the trail with Nana getting smaller. Maria was at a steady gallop when she came onto a mesa. There was the black stallion, but Nana was nowhere to be seen.

When the black Stallion saw Maria's horse it reared up and pawed the air, sending a chill through Maria, it was so huge! "Easy," Maria said to both horses. "Easy Baroka, Easy," The Black horse reared again, causing Maria's horse Nekey, to vault, jumping to the side about five feet. This surprised Maria causing her to grip her saddle tightly with her legs. Being the horseman or horsewomen she is, she didn't have to grab the saddle horn, but sat straight and tall in the saddle. "Easy, Nekey, easy." she said and patted the neck of her gelding to settle him down. She was to the right of the stallion, so she pulled the reins to her right to turn her horse away from the stallion to get a little further away. Maria slid off her horse then took the reins and held them up close to the bit so she would have better control, should he spook again.

The black stallion was standing still now with just the strap in his mouth hanging to the ground. "Guess you don't like us to get too close, huh, Baroka?" Maria asked. "Baroka, Baroka, now I remember what that name means. Ghost, your name is Ghost, well it fits you well!"

"Do you think so?"

This startled Maria, and she whirled around to see Nana standing there. "You scared me!"

"I'm sorry, I didn't mean to scare you," Nana said. "Do you remember this place?"

Maria looked around and then it hit her. "This is where we used to have picnics. We must have taken a back route."

Nana nodded, "yes, they put in this back trail four years ago."

"Nana, I had no idea you could ride like that," Maria said. "You always just rode with me, never faster and usually behind me."

"Well, little sparrow, I went with you to teach you. I can't teach you anymore. If you go further in your riding skills you must ask the spirits to help you. If you ask, they will help. The more you practice and the more you go to the spirits for help, the better you become. There is no end, practice and ask, it is a never ending chain."

Maria nodded, "I sure need to practice after seeing you this morning."

"Aw, this morning Baroka just wanted to run, so I let him run," Nana said.

Maria and Nana walked around looking at different sights. They stood at the edge of the mesa and looked out at the valley. The sky was clear and blue, all but one small cloud that was way up there. They could see a hawk circling, looking for something to eat. In a moment it took a dive for a rabbit, but the rabbit went into a burrow and the hawk went back up and started circling again.

Maria sat on the grass. "This is beautiful," she said.

"I'm glad that you still think it is beautiful," Nana said. "See that mountain over there?"

"That one?" Maria pointed to a mountain to their right.

"Yes. Do you know what mountain that is?" Nana asked.

Maria studied the mountain. She then noticed a road down in the valley that went into the mountain. "That's Eagle Woman's mountain," Maria said.

"Wanna go there for lunch?" Nana asked.

"Sounds good to me," Maria said.

Both women mounted their horses and headed off the mesa with Nana taking the lead. The trail was steep and Maria wondered how Nana managed to ride so easily without a saddle when she was having a hard time, even with a saddle. The trail was so steep that if it wasn't for the saddle Maria was sure that she would surely slide right over the horse's shoulders and head. Nana seemed to ride so easily without any sign of strain or discomfort that she actually looked like she was part of the horse herself.

When they reached the valley they started a steady gallop. Maria was feeling more sure of herself in the saddle now that she was off that steep trail. They rode along beside a tour bus, at least it was what the Indians called a tour bus. It was actually a truck with seats bolted to the bed and a canvas stretched over the top to block the sun from them. The tourist started taking pictures and waving at them. Maria and Nana were about one hundred feet from them when the tourist started shouting at them, so the two women put their horses in a dead run and pulled ahead of the bus. The bus was headed for the bottom of a canyon that ran through Eagle Woman's Mountain. Maria and Nana were headed up to the top of the mountain. Then the women veered to their left and the bus took a road to the right. When they got to where the mountain started up Nana took the lead and her great black stallion went up the steep trail with little effort. Maria followed, falling a little behind as they rode because her horse was not as strong and it took more effort for him. Nana would stop whenever she got too far ahead and let Maria catch up.

After what seemed like hours to Maria, of a hard climb, they reached the top of Eagle Woman's Mountain. The view was breathtaking. It looked like they were part of the sky when you looked back from the direction they came. When they looked in the opposite direction it looked just like they were on flat ground.

They rode over to the edge of the canyon and looked down. They could see a house with cars parked nearby. There was this square patch of green, and Maria wondered if the green patch was corn, a staple that the Indians grew a lot in this part of the country. Then they saw a tour bus and Maria wondered if it was the same bus that they had seen earlier. Everything looked so small from up there it reminded her of toys.

Maria and Nana walked their horses over to a shade tree growing out of the rocks. The two horses were getting used to each other and were not so skittish now. So the women just dropped the reins and let them dangle to the ground. This gave the horses the feeling of being tied and they wouldn't wander off.

Both women walked over to the edge of the canyon where the reservation had erected a guard rail with a sidewalk next to the rail. This was the place where Eagle Woman had single-handedly wiped out an entire enemy tribe. There was a monument there for her. It was a four foot granite rock with one flat side with a bronze plaque stating, "This is the place the legendary Eagle Woman ran twenty braves of an enemy tribe over this cliff killing them and their horses. Saving the Socike tribe from further raids from this enemy."

What had actually happened was the Toto tribe was a vicious band of Indians that raided other tribes killing everyone they could find. They sometimes would wait until the braves of a tribe would go out on a hunting trip. Then they raided their camps killing everyone that didn't run away and hide. The only ones that would be at their camps would be the men too old or sick to be on the hunt, the women who were not classified as braves and the children.

The Toto and the Socike had been bitter enemies for generations. Both tribes killing the other whenever they would happen to meet. This kept the two tribes small where neither would have enough people to become a nation.

It was during the winter when the days were short and a snow storm had come up. The Socike brave were on their way back from an unsuccessful hunting trip when they came across the hunting braves of the Toto.

Eagle Woman led the attack and the Toto braves turned and rode away trying desperately not to be killed by a woman. All of the Indian tribes knew of the women braves of the Socikes and it was the Toto's belief that if they were killed by a woman they would be a woman in their next life, through all eternity. The Toto treated their women as bad as they did their slaves. Because of this, they were terrified of being killed by a woman. They also knew of Eagle Woman's big black horse and of her reputation of being able to bash in any brave's skull with one swing of her war club.

The Toto rode away not out of fear of the Socike, but of the fear of being killed by a woman. Now if Eagle Woman would have been alone they would have taken a chance, and fought because of their numbers. But being pretty well matched brave for brave no one in the Toto tribe wanted to take the chance of being the one Eagle Woman would kill. So they ran! She rode in front because she had the fastest horse, the way she did in all of their attacks. Because of the snow storm, the Totos didn't know they were that close to the canyon and rode over the edge.

Eagle Women saw them go over, so she could stop before she succumb to the same fate.

When the Socike braves reached her, she had dismounted and was doing her victory dance and chant.

The next day, the braves went down into the canyon, butchered the horses, and took them back to camp. There, they hung the meat in trees where it stayed frozen until they took it down to use.

That evening the Socike chief bestowed a great honor on Eagle Woman by proclaiming that she would be the women's chief and govern all the women of the tribe. This was the beginning of the woman chief of the Socike. Actually, she had saved the tribe from near starvation by driving those men and horses over the cliff. It had been a hard winter with little game to eat and from the dead horses they had enough meat to last the whole winter.

For the women who were not braves, their duties for the next few days was to smoke and dry some of the horse meat.

The braves, both men and women went out to find the Toto camp. When the war party found the Toto camp, Eagle Woman led the charge. The braves rode in and killed all the men except one. They captured all the women and children. Normally they would have killed all the men. But when Eagle Woman rushed forth on her black horse one brave that stayed in camp sick when the other braves died, ran towards Eagle Woman. Instead of fighting, he dropped flat on the ground and worshiped Eagle Woman. This pleased her so much she spared his life.

The Socike braves rounded up the rest of the Toto horses and drove them along with the women, children, and the one man back to their camp. This took some time because the Toto were starving and weak, their hunting having also been unsuccessful this winter. Leaving three braves to watch the captive women and children and the one man, the rest returned and packed up all of the Toto possessions and hauled them back to camp.

The Socike's fed their captives with the horse meat the women had prepared for all the tribe. Then they gave some of their possessions back to them. This impressed the women captives because they were being treated better than they would have been by their own men.

They then put all the women in one group, each with their own children, if they had children. The Socike then made a circle around them. All the Socike men who were not married, starting with the oldest got to choose one captive woman for a wife. If she had children he had to take them, too. He had to provide for all as if they were his own. After all the unmarried men chose, then starting with the youngest married man they could choose. If he took a second wife he had to care for her and her children and still treat his first wife good and equal. That day, Eagle Woman took the captive Toto man for her husband, because she was not married.

Taking captives for wives did two things for the Socike. It put new blood in the tribe and made the tribe grow very fast so they eventually became a nation. The second thing was, they didn't have to guard slaves.

Maria read the monument out loud. Nana and Maria looked at each other in that knowing way. The way that each knew what the other felt for they were descendants of Eagle Woman. But Socikes tradition was that they shouldn't talk to others of such things.

"Are you getting hungry?" Nana asked.

"Why... yes... I am, a little hungry." Maria answered.

Nana went over to Nekey (Maria's horse) and pulled out the two sacks she had brought. Bringing it over to Maria, she motioned to a table with benches that was there for the tourists.

Sitting down on the bench, Nana put the sack on the table. Nana took two bottles of water out of one sack. They had been frozen when they started out that morning and now they were still nice and cold. The other sack had a trail mix that they sold at the local grocer and two pieces of beef jerky bought at the same place.

The food and drink was good and the women enjoyed their meal immensely. "This really hit the spot, Nana," Maria said.

"I'm glad you enjoyed it. I thought we could use some eats," Nana said.

"It was great, I'm sure glad you thought of it," Maria said. "By the way, have you seen Rosa? The last time I heard from her was about eight months after I married Jack. She had come to see me and showed up drunk."

"That's about the time your little sister was drinking heavily. One weekend she left without a word and I haven't seen her since," Nana said. "But, I will see her when she quits drinking. The great spirit of knowledge has promised me that."

"I sure wish I could see her," Maria said. "I worry about her a lot."

"I know you do. But she will be alright," Nana said.

"How do you know?" Maria asked. But as soon as she said that, she had regrets that she asked, it wasn't polite to Nana. Asking her how she knew.

Nana smiled, "That spirit hasn't lied to me yet. It told me that you would come back to the reservation. It didn't tell me how long you'd stay, but it told me three years ago that you would be back."

Maria reached across the table to put her hand on Nana's hand. "I'm so glad to be here with you, Nana. I've missed you terribly."

"And I've missed you, too," Nana said.

About this time tourist started taking pictures of the two women, this was because Nana was wearing traditional Socike clothing with her headband and Maria was wearing her headband. The two women looked the part of Socike Indians.

The women gave each other an all knowing look and headed for their horses. Maria started off mounting her horse on a dead run like she did for Jode, the stable hand, and soon disappeared over a rim and down the trail.

Nana mounted her horse right after Maria mounted hers. The big black stallion reared and pawed the air, giving a loud whinny. The stallion gave a high and long leap in the air and Nana was off right behind Maria.

The tourists were stumbling over themselves to get this picture, but it all happened so fast that none of the tourists managed to take a good picture. They all stood there in amazement, wondering if they had actually seen what they had seen.

When they reached the stable Maria was aware that she was going to be sore from all the riding, but it was going to be worth it. This had been a wonderful day, she couldn't remember when she enjoyed a day so much. Jode took Maria's horse to wipe down, but Nana wiped down the black stallion. That was a job that she trusted to no one else. As soon as she was finished the two women walked home.

After they reached home the two women each took a turn in the shower. Both helped make a large meal and both sat down to eat. They spent the rest of the evening visiting and enjoying each other's company.

# Chapter 5

Early the next morning, Maria awoke before Nana. She got dressed and started to fix breakfast for her and Nana. She noticed she was pretty sore from all of the riding they had done the day before. Maria touched her posterior lightly and felt a slight sting from the bruise left from the saddle. *I can't believe I'm that far out of shape,* she thought. She went back in the bathroom dropped her jeans and panties held a mirror around to her back side to get a look at the bruises.

"What are you looking for," Nana asked.

Maria dropped the mirror and made a small screech. "You scared me," she said as she pulled her pants up. "I thought you were asleep!"

"I was asleep, but now I'm awake," Nana said. "Pretty sore? Huh," nodding and looking at Maria's rear, even though her jeans were covering it now.

"Yeah," Maria affirmed.

"Want some salve for it?" Nana asked. "It's pretty greasy but it will sooth it some."

"I don't want any salve but I was thinking about that drink I had the first night I arrived," Maria said.

"I could give you that drink, but you would go to sleep and sleep for at least six hours. What do you think?" Nana asked.

"I think I'll suffer through it, without anything. Thanks anyway," Maria said.

"I'll give you the drink tonight when it's time to go to bed," Nana said.

Maria nodded, "I'd like to make you breakfast this morning, would that be alright?"

"Sounds great to me," Nana said. "Do you want me to fix the coffee?"

"I already have it started. It should be ready in a minute," Maria said.

"I'll just set at the table. We can visit while you make breakfast," Nana said.

The coffee was ready in a minute just like Maria had said and both women got themselves a cup. "I hope it's not too strong, Nana," Maria said while she fixed eggs and hash browns. "You like onion with your hash browns don't you, Nana?"

"You remembered," Nana said.

In a few minutes Maria had breakfast on the table and each of them a fresh cup of coffee. The two sat, ate, and talked a lot. They were about ready to start clearing the table when there came a crash from the other room. Both women jumped and looked at each other with a question on their faces.

"What?" Maria asked.

Nana got up and rushed into the other room.

Maria followed. "What is it?"

"This shelf came right off the wall," Nana said. "I guess the nails holding it up weren't long enough."

Maria saw a shelf hanging by one end. There was some broken glass, books, and some wooden trinkets on the floor. Maria started picking things up.

"I'm going to fix that shelf right now," Nana said. She went outside and was back in a minute with a hammer and a can full of nails.

Maria held up the shelf while Nana nailed the bracket back that had come loose. "I bet it won't come off now," Nana said, after driving four big nails into the bracket that had come loose. Maria and Nana put what wasn't broken back on the shelf.

They then went back and finished clearing the table. After getting wash water in the sink, they had just gotten started doing the dishes when a knock came at the door.

"Are you expecting anyone?" Maria asked.

"No, but it's probably one of the council women, they sometimes come around on Friday morning. Would you get it for me?" Nana asked.

Maria went to the door, opened it. "Hello...?"

Jack O'Reily stepped through the door. "Thank God you are alright. I've been so worried about you. You left without a word. I was so afraid something bad had happened to you. You should have called me, at least. You know, to let me know you were alright," Jack said.

A fear went through Maria. Then she said to herself, I am a descendent of Eagle Woman. I am afraid of no one. But she couldn't help, but shake a little. "You weren't worried about me when you hit me the other night, Jack."

"Aw, honey, I'm sorry. It wasn't my fault, I had been drinking. I promise nothing like that will ever happen again," Jack said.

"That's what you always say, but it does happen again, and I get the crap beat out of me, and it's never your fault. Well, Jack, it is your fault, no one else puts that booze down your throat. You're the one who picks up the bottle," Maria said, glaring at him.

"Honey, I know you are angry now. I know you're saying things that you really don't mean," Jack said, stepping close to Maria to put his arm around her.

Maria stepped back, "Don't touch me," Maria snapped. "I'm through being your punching bag."

"O, it's my fault, always my fault. You don't ever start it?" Jack said in a perturbed voice.

Nana, hearing all, this came into the living room and stood there saying nothing.

Jack saw her but said nothing to her. "Aw, honey I don't want to argue with you. I love you."

Maria crossed her arms over her chest and stared at Jack.

"Didn't I drive all the way up here for you? Doesn't that prove something?"

Maria didn't say anything.

"Well, didn't I?" Jack asked again. "Aw, Maria don't be that way. I told you I was sorry."

"Why, I even went to a see a minister about our problem. I'm even willing to start going to church with you, honey," Jack said.

"Our problem?" Maria asked.

"Yes our problem, you know, the arguments we have. How you always make me lose my temper. But that's going to change. Now it's a long way back so we need to get started. Tell your Nana goodbye and let's get going."

Maria felt sorry for Jack. She looked at him in a tender way and forced a half smile on her face. "Jack, I do feel for you, but you need help. Help that I can't give you."

Jack interrupted, "Me?—Me! I need help? Why is it that I need help? Why is it always me? Nothing wrong with you? Right? It's me. It's always me. What about you? It's never you? It's always me, never you?" Jack was shouting now.

Nana broke in, "You are shouting, Jack."

"Mind you're own business Nana!" Jack yelled.

"Don't yell at Nana," Maria broke in.

"I'm not your Nana and this is my house, so it is my business," Nana said.

Jack was looking at Nana now.

Nana stood up straight with her shoulders back, looking like the proud Indian she was. "I am Maria and her sister's Nana. I am Mrs. Yellowhair, Anita Yellowhair or Pupa to everyone else."

Jack squished up his face and said in a high, squeaky voice. "Mrs. Yellowhair, Anita Yellowhair or Pupa." He then laughed and turned to Maria and laughed even louder, trying to get Maria to laugh with him. "Come on, Maria, that's funny!" Laughing again, "That's the problem with you, you're too damn serious. You never want to have any fun. You're just a stubborn Indian, like Nana!" he said, putting the emphasis on, "Nana."

"Look Jack, I'm not going back with you, so why don't you just leave." Maria said this with a very light voice. "Please leave now. I'll call you next week."

This took Jack by surprise. He looked at Maria with disbelief. *How could she do this to me? After all I've done for her*, Jack thought. "How can you do this to me? If it wasn't for me you'd be here on this backward reservation. You ungrateful—" Jack screwed up his face and mocked in a high voice, "Please leave now— I'll show you leave. You go get your bags now!" Jack shouted, *"Now.* I'll leave, and you're going with me. Now get your bags!— Now!"

Nana got right in Jack's face, "You go, Maria is staying. Now you go!"

Jack grabbed Maria by the wrist very firm and started dragging her towards the bedroom to get her things.

"I'll get the police," Nana said, heading for the back door. She didn't have a phone and she knew Jack could get between her and the front door.

Jack reached Nana just as she was headed out the door. He grabbed her by the shirt collar and yanked her back so hard she fell behind the kitchen table, hitting her head on the edge of it. Jack slammed the door shut.

Maria screamed, "Nana!" then ran over to her and kneeled down by her. Maria felt for a pulse, but couldn't find one. "We've got to get help, Jack!"

"Oh... she didn't fall that hard," Jack snapped.

"Jack, she's a fragile old lady. She needs help," Maria pleaded.

"She'll be alright. Now! Go! Get! Your! Stuff! And let's go!" Jack yelled.

Maria jumped up and headed for the front door. Just as she was opening it, Jack, running full speed, rammed into the door with full force, banging it shut. Maria was thankful she wasn't halfway out or have her arm in the way when he hit the door.

"What are you doing? I told you to get your bags. See what you've done! You caused Nana to get hurt, and you still insist on playing your stupid games."

"Jack, we've got to get help for Nana, she's hurt bad. Please Jack, please!"

"If I go get help for your Nana, then will you get your bags and come with me?" Jack asked.

"Yes, yes, I'll go with you, just get help for Nana." Maria pleaded.

"You go get your bags then we will get help for your Nana." Jack said.

Maria's heart sank, she knew Jack wouldn't do anything for Nana. "Okay, Jack, I'll get my bags."

Maria went into her bedroom and slowly closed the door trying not to make a sound. She then ran on her tiptoes to the window and opened it slowly. She had to pry the hook off the screen and work with it until she got it open. Maria got one leg out the window when Jack rushed into the room. He got to her just in time to grab her by the other leg. Maria tried to kick loose, but Jack hung on. He dragged her back inside and slammed the window down.

"I trusted you!" Jack yelled. "I trusted you!" Jack slapped her so hard it knocked her off her feet.

"Jack please," Maria murmured.

"Please what? I trusted you and you betrayed me." He grabbed her by her hair and dragged her out into the living room. "I try to be nice to you and what do you do?" Jack shouted. He pulled her up and got her on her feet. Jack still had hold of her hair in his left hand. He was turning one way then the other, like a short pace. Jack clinched his teeth then turned to Maria. He punched her in the stomach knocking the wind out of her. Maria folded over with pain and fell to the floor.

Jack sat on the sofa. *What to do, what to do,* he wondered. Jack decided to check on Nana. He watched Maria as he walked over to Nana. Maria was still rolled up in a ball with pain. Jack could hear moans of pain coming from her. *She'll stay put while I check on this old woman,* he thought. Jack stood over Nana, staring down at her. She wasn't moving. Then he saw the blood leaking from her head. "Oh, my God," Jack felt for a pulse. He couldn't find one. "She's dead."

Maria heard him say, "She's dead." She tried to move, but the pain was too great.

Jack walked back to the sofa, he was getting scared. *They will think I killed her,* he thought. "You killed Nana, Maria! You know, you killed her. You and your stupid games. You killed her as sure as I'm sitting here." He sat on the sofa with his head in his hands trying to think.

Maria was hurting too much to do anything.

Jack sat there trying to think what to do now. *I know they'll think I did this.* "It wasn't my fault." Jack yelled, "It wasn't my fault." He looked up to see what Maria was going to say about his statement. No Maria! "Maria, Maria! Where are you?" No answer.

Jack jumped up to look for Maria. *Where the hell did she go?* he wondered. "Maria, you better not be hiding from me." He was starting to panic. *I can't let her get out of here,* he thought. He ran from room to room looking in each one. No Maria. Jack was running back and forth in a panic. "I can't let her out of here," he murmured to himself. He noticed the hammer and nails and picked up a hand full of nails and the hammer. He knew she was still in the house. He hadn't heard a door open. He knew the windows were still shut. He checked every room and had left every inside door open. Yes, she was still there, but hiding.

Jack went to the back door first. He quickly drove a nail through the edge of the door into the jam. Pushing his bottom lip out and nodding his head, "Well done" he murmured. Then to the front door and nailed it shut. Then to each bedroom, nailing every window shut. The bathroom was next. Off to the kitchen and then back to the living room. He had done it, now all of the windows and doors were nailed shut. *She's caught like a rat in a trap,* he thought. Jack took a deep breath and relaxed.

"Lucy..., I'm home," Jack said in a high loud voice. With a big grin on his face he started his search.

Maria had crawled to Nana's bedroom and slid under the bed. She had seen Jack's feet when he had come in to check to see if she was there. She also saw him again when he came in to nail the windows shut. She couldn't actually see him do the nailing, but she heard him doing the hammering in there and elsewhere in the house.

Maria didn't understand what Jack was doing with the hammering. She tried to consider what he was up to, but her stomach hurt so much it was hard to think.

"Maria, Maria," Jack called. "Look, don't make me come looking for you. I forgive you. Now come on out." Jack waited. Each second that passed made him madder and madder! He hit a cabinet with the hammer hard, making a loud crack! He was furious now. "Alright you asked for it. You're going to pay for this."

Jack headed for the bedroom where Maria had been spending her nights. He turned the bed over then ransacked the closet. In a rage, he smashed a dresser with the hammer.

Maria was shaking with fear. She could hear Jack turning the furniture over in her bedroom. *I can't stay in here any longer,* she thought. He'll be in this room next. Shaking, she crawled out from under Nana's bed. Peaking around the door she could see the hall was clear. She had slipped her shoes off so her footsteps wouldn't be heard.

Maria ran to the back door. Grabbing the door handle, turned it and yanked. The door knob slipped out of her hand and two finger nails broke off. Pain ran up her hand from breaking her nails below the quick. There was a snap of the door knob. Maria froze.

Jack heard something, but didn't know where it came from. "Your making a noise, I can hear you," he said in that mocking high voice.

"Here I come, ready or not."

Maria saw the nail driven into the door. That's why it didn't come open. She ran on her tiptoes to the front door. There was the nail in the door. Panic set in. She rushed to the window, nailed. Maria's heart sank. "I've got to fight," she said to herself. *Weapon, I need a weapon. What can I use for a weapon?*

Maria ran to the kitchen. She could hear Jack turning Nana's bed over. Maria's thoughts were going too fast for her to think straight. *A weapon, a weapon, what kind of a weapon? What can I use? A weapon.* She picked up a knife, made a few practice swings with it. *No he'd take this away from me and kill me with it.* She grabbed a skillet, made a couple practice swings with it. *This is it.* She held it with both hands, *wham,* she thought. "This is where I'll make my stand," she said to herself. "Now calm yourself, take deep breaths." Her heart was racing as she heard Jack turning things over in Nana's bedroom. *He'll be out here in a minute,* she thought.

Jack came out into the hall. He was so mad, that he threw the hammer at the wall across the living room. It stuck in the sheet rock like it was a hatchet thrown at a block of wood.

This made Maria jump. She tried taking deep breaths. Her knees were weak. She wished she could run, but she had no choice. She had to stay and fight. She stood next to the counter straight, her chin up and determined.

Jack went into the living room to get his hammer. Then he saw Maria standing in the kitchen. This stopped him in his tracks right in the middle of the living room. He turned, *She's standing like a deer in the headlights of a car,* he thought.

Maria was standing up straight with both arms to her side. The counter blocked the view of the skillet in her right hand. Maria could feel sweat on her face. She was hot because of her adrenaline.

Jack forgot his hammer in the wall and started walking towards Maria.

No one said a thing. They were staring at each other. Jack walked slowly toward Maria.

Maria tensed, but stood her ground. Jack got three feet away looking her in the eyes, tilted his head and smiled, still not seeing the skillet.

Maria brought the skillet up in a swinging motion grabbing it with both hands. Taking one step forward still into the swing, hitting Jack on the side of the head, knocking him off his feet and down. The skillet went flying from Maria's hands.

Maria took off for a window in the living room. She pulled and pushed, it was nailed. Picking up a chair she broke the glass. Then she used the chair to push out the screen, taking the chair and pushing it back and forth across the bottom of the window to break out most of the glass that might cut her. She then tossed the chair to the side and started crawling out. Maria was straddling the windowsill with her body on the outside. Thinking she was free, she gave an extra effort to get all the way out, when she was jerked back into the room.

Jack had a hold of her ankle. The next thing she knew she was on her back on the floor and Jack was on top of her. Maria was hitting and trying to kick with her knees. Jack was too heavy. He straddled her and his hands were around her neck. Jack put all the pressure he could on her throat.

Maria was not struggling so much now. Jack said in a sarcastic voice, "Maria they say dead men tell no tales. You know what? Neither do dead women." After Maria stopped breathing Jack kept choking her until he was sure she was dead. He thought of taping a plastic sack over her head, but he had no idea if there was any tape or plastic sacks in the house. He took one last look at Maria to make sure she was dead.

Jack pulled the hammer out of the wall, went to the front door and pulled out the nail. He then went in the bathroom and got a towel to wiped down every place he might have touched. Then he looked out the front window to make sure no one was there, and when he was confident that the coast was clear he went outside to his car.

# Chapter 6

Jack had made a clean getaway. He was on interstate ten between Phoenix and Tucson and had just passed the rest stop that Maria's bus stopped at, but he had no way of knowing that.

It was getting late in the afternoon and he hadn't eaten all day. "God show me a place to eat," Jack said. "I know I need a place they won't notice me. I can't risk a place where a waitress might take notice of me and tell the police. You know God, I had to do that. Those evil women had made a mockery of your laws and your ways. Your word says, 'Women, obey your husbands,' doesn't it?" There was a pause in Jack's conversation to God, "And that old woman, you know she was evil. She even talked to birds and animals. Doesn't your word say kill the witches and sorcerers?"

Then it came to Jack that there were three fast food places ahead. "That's a perfect place to eat," he said to himself. "Thank you, God!" Jack believed that God had told him this was a safe place to eat.

There it was up ahead. Jack could see those tell-tale arches from were he was. Pulling off the highway onto the long off ramp. He was looking for the busiest place and finally decided on the hamburger. *It'll feel good to get out and stretch,* Jack thought. He walked in and it was crowded with three lines waiting for service. *No one will remember me in this crowd,* Jack thought. He was feeling very confident while he was standing in line, but after a few minutes Jack noticed people were looking at him. *Why the hell are they looking at me?* He wondered.

*I must be imagining it.* Then it was Jack's turn to order. *That girl is staring at me,* he thought. "I'll have a number three." The girl typed it into her register. "What drink?" "Coffee" Jack said and then paid for his meal.

The girl brought back his hamburger, fries, and coffee. "What happened to you?" She asked Jack.

"What do you mean?" Jack shot back.

"Your head, it's all bruised and there is blood in your hair," she said. Other people by him were looking him over, now curious to hear the answer.

Jack raised his left hand to his head and a twinge of pain hit him. He felt on up, his hair had dried blood caked on it. He hadn't felt pain because of all the adrenaline in his blood. "I...," he paused, "I fell..." He grabbed his tray and headed for a table. *God this is wrong, I wasn't supposed to attract attention. What have you done to me?* He thought People walked by and they all stared at him. One little boy was holding onto his mother's hand and pointing at Jack's head as his mother pulled him along. "What have you done to me?" Jack murmured to God.

Jack grabbed his meal and drink and headed for his car, cursing under his breath. When he crawled in, the first thing he did was grab the rear view mirror and turn it so he could see his head and face. There was blood from the whack of the skillet Maria gave him. "God! How could you do this to me? Haven't I always obeyed you? Haven't I proclaimed your name to the infidels? Oh Lord, if you will keep me out of prison I will always obey your laws." He was pleading with God now. "I've got to get some place and clean up." Tucson was coming up. Jack couldn't think of any place that would be safe. There were a lot of cops cruising the streets of Tucson, especially the west side where interstate ten went through. No it'd be safer to stay on the highway. There was a large truck stop east of Tucson. Jack thought he'd try there.

Jack drove on, putting his hand up to his face, trying to hide the blood whenever a car passed him. It seemed like forever before he saw the truck stop on the north side. He pulled off the highway on the right and went down to the underpass to the stop sign. He checked for traffic then proceeded under the highway to the truck stop. There was no place in front where he could wash up inconspicuously, so he drove around the back and saw a water spigot.

Jack pulled up close to the building and stopped. He checked to see if there was anyone around to see him. It was clear, he got out and looked around again and then turned on the water. It was cold to his face and hair. Jack took a comb out of his glove compartment and combed his hair and checked his face in the mirror. He'd done a good job washing away the blood and even thought of going into the restaurant part of the truck stop. Then he thought, *Why should I take the chance?* He just drove on to his home in Benson feeling much better about the drive. *I'm home free,* he thought. Going inside, Jack started thinking about an alibi. He took a shower and changed his clothes. He thought of burning his old clothes, but he couldn't do that in town. "I need an alibi," he said to himself.

Jack got into his car and drove down town to the Horseshoe Café. Once inside he sat at the counter. The waitress came over, not even making eye contact; she laid down a menu and a glass of water. "What do you want to drink? She asked.

Jack noticed she was new. He didn't know her from Eve and she didn't know him from Adam. This wouldn't do, he had to get the attention of someone he knew, but how?

When the waitress didn't get an answer she put down the pad she was scribbling on and looked at Jack. *This was better*, Jack thought.

"Is the coffee any good or did the cook make it with horse apples again?" Jack asked.

The waitress was new at the Horseshoe, but she wasn't new at waitressing. "Oh, it's made with horse apples alright, but I think you'd like it," she said with a smile. Jack didn't like her smart remark and his face turned red with anger.

Anita, a long-time waitress at the Horseshoe saw Jack getting mad at the new girl. She came up behind him and put her hand on his shoulder, "Giving Angie a hard time, Jack?" Jack turned and saw Anita. That was his alibi!

"You know..., gotta give the new help a hard time to break her in right." Jack said.

The waitress left and brought back a cup of coffee and set it in front of Jack.

"What happened to you, Jack?" Anita asked. "Maria hit you?" This last question agitated Jack and he could feel his face getting red, but he tried not to show it.

"She's not guilty this time," he said. "She's up at her grandmother's at the reservation." He pointed to his head, "this happened when I was fixing the screen door. I had it propped open and it slammed closed hitting me. Damn near knocked me out. I had blood all over me."

"Looks like a doozie," Anita said, looking at the swollen cut on his head. "Well take it easy, Jack," and walked back to her own customers.

Jack looked at the menu, then ordered and had a nice and very late lunch. *Well I've got it made now,* Jack thought, as he drove home. He felt good, he had gotten rid of that disobedient wife and rid the world of a heathen, maybe a witch. God should bless him because of this. "Lord, if you keep me out of prison, I'll always praise you," he said to himself again.

# Chapter 7

Rita woke up late and felt terrible. The alcohol poisoning was hard on her and she knew she should never drink. After eating something to make her feel better, she decided to go over to Maria's grandmother's house, so she could apologize to Maria. She really felt bad that she had gotten drunk when she was with her.

Rita walked over to Pupa's house and knocked on the door. As she waited she kind of swayed back and forth. She knocked again. "I might have known they wouldn't be home." Rita would have called first, but she knew that Pupa never had a phone in her house. "Oh, well." Then she got the idea of going around back to see if they were in the backyard. She spotted the broken window and screen and went over to the window and looked in. Furniture was turned over and things were thrown around. "Oh, my God," she said and ran all the way home.

She was breathing so hard she could hardly get out what she saw to her parents. Her mother called the reservation police. Then Rita, her mother and father drove over to her friend's grandmother's place.

They were there before the police and the father went in first. Rita was right behind him. They had just reached Maria's body when a young Socike policeman showed up and ushered them outside, told them to get in their car and stay there. He was on his way to the station when he got a call on his radio to investigate what had happened at Pupa's house. He saw Maria and checked her for any signs of life. He could tell she was dead immediately. Getting on his radio he called for backup and looked around quickly. Then started putting police tape around the area, including the street in front of the house.

It didn't take long for reinforcements to arrive. There were not a lot of serious crimes on the reservation, so all available police came to the house. They began to tromp around the house, contaminating the crime scene until the Captain arrived. He put a stop to that. Calling all of his men into the street, he instructed Bob Yazzie, the young officer first to arrive, to stay. He then picked officer Robert Tsinnijinni and Orlando to stay. The rest he instructed to go on their regular duties, but to call him if they saw anything suspicious.

Captain Yellowhair walked over to the car with Rita and her family in it. He introduced himself and the other officer. He then asked a few questions and left officer Tsinnijinni to take their statement.

He then instructed officer Orlando to check the outside of the house. To look for footprints or anything else that might be a clue.

Captain Yellowhair turned to officer Yazzie to come with him into the house.

Officer Yazzie pointed to Maria, "There she is. I took a quick look around, but I didn't see Pupa anywhere but things are tore up bad, she could be here someplace."

"Well, let's take this one step at a time," Captain Yellowhair said. They walked over to Maria. There was some blood on her and the floor from the cuts she had suffered from the broken window. The Captain kneeled down by Maria's body and felt her. She was cold and rigor mortis had set in. He could see the cause of death and left the body the way it laid. "Did you move the body?" he asked the young officer.

"No, sir,"

The Captain stood up and looked around. Officer Yazzie started to walk into the kitchen.

"Stay with me, "Captain Yellowhair said.

Officer Yazzie froze in his tracks. Captain had worked for law enforcement for thirty years now, most of it in Los Angeles, some in Tucson, and the last five years on the reservation. Bob was anxious to learn from the Captain and waited for him to tell him what to do.

"Did anyone else come in here?" The Captain asked.

"No, sir, no one came in the house, except Rita and her father who found the body and they didn't go any further than right here," Bob answered.

The Captain took out his flashlight from his belt and started down the hall. The first bedroom he looked in and shined his light in the corners. "Big foot print," he said as he shined his light on a print on the rug. They went on down the hall to the next bedroom, it had furniture scattered about.

"Shouldn't we look under the turned over beds for Pupa?" Bob asked.

"We will shortly, but let's take a quick look around first and make sure nothing is overlooked" the Captain answered. They headed for the dining area at the end of the hall. When they reached the dining area they could tell that a struggle had taken place. Because of overturned chairs and the table being at an angle. The tablecloth was pulled down one side barely hanging on, if it hadn't been for the sugar bowl and the salt and pepper shakers, it would have been on the floor.

The two men walked over to the table. Behind the table, hidden by the cloth and the table itself, was Pupa lying in a fetal position.

"Pupa!" The two men said at the same time. The Captain kneeled down and felt her. There was a gash on her head where she hit it on the table when she fell, but she wasn't cold and there was no rigor mortis. She sure looked dead. Captain felt for a pulse on her wrist. No pulse. He then felt her neck.

A small pulse. He got excited. "Get me a blanket out of my trunk or get yours!" He said to Bob.

Officer Yazzie took off to get the blanket.

Captain Yellowhair got on his radio and called for the paramedic helicopter from Flagstaff. He also called for a doctor from the reservation hospital, which was not much more than a clinic with six beds. The doctor was a retired family doctor who took care of cuts, bruises, and the normal sickness.

Officer Yazzie arrived back with a blanket and small pillow. The two men slid the pillow under Pupa's head. Then covered her with the blanket, tucking it under her, trying to keep her body's heat in.

"Is Pupa any kin to you, Captain?" Officer Yazzie asked.

"Maybe, way back. But, I don't know any common relatives."

Yellowhair is a common name on the reservation. Captain looked around some more. "Bob, come here."

Bob left Pupa and went in the kitchen. He looked where the Captain was pointing. It was a skillet in the corner of the room with blood on it.

"We need a camera down here before we start collecting evidence," Captain said.

Bob got on his radio and called the station. "Get us a camera and evidence bags, big and small, down here right away."

*He's going to make a good detective yet,* the Captain thought. Just then the screen door slammed and Bob and the Captain jumped. Spinning around they saw officer Tsinnijinni.

"I've got their statement, Captain. Do you want them to stick around?" Tsinnijinni asked.

"No, you can let them go. Be sure to tell them if they think of anything else to call us." Captain said.

"Do you know them?" The Captain asked Bob.

"I know Rita from high school. I'd never met her parents. She was a good friend of Maria, the victim," Bob said, nodding toward the dead woman in the living room.

"What relation was Maria to Pupa? Do you know?" Captain asked.

"She is Pupa's granddaughter. She lived with Pupa ever since she was in grade school."

"When's the last time you saw Maria?" Captain asked.

Bob thought for a minute. "It's been five or six years. I didn't even know she was back on the reservation."

The two men went back to look at Pupa, she hadn't moved.

"Doc should be here soon," Captain said.

They then went into the living room and looked at Maria again. "No wedding ring," Captain said. "Do you know if she was married?"

"No, I really don't" Bob answered. "That's something we need to ask Rita."

Captain nodded.

The doctor and the camera and evidence bags arrived at the same time.

Captain shook hands with Dr. Cook. "Thank you for coming over, Doc. It's Pupa, she's over here. Doc and the Captain went over to Pupa.

Bob took the bags and camera. Setting them on the floor he followed Doc and the Captain over to Pupa. Doc first looked at the wound on her head. He then felt for a pulse. Next, he pulled back an eyelid and shined a pen light in it, then the other eye. By this time he had Pupa on her back. He tucked the blanket back around her. "We need to get the paramedics from Flagstaff here," he said as he looked up at Captain and officer Yazzie.

"They've been called," Captain said.

"Good," Doc replied.

Officer Yazzie picked up the camera, walked over to Pupa and took her picture. She had been moved a little and he made a mental note of how she was lying on her side in the fetal position. He then took chalk out of his pocket that he had gotten out of his car when he went out and got the pillow and blanket. He marked the spot where Pupa's head, butt and feet were when they first saw her. This was so he could draw an outline of how they found her. He then marked around each table leg so they could put it back the way it was.

"You look like you know what you're doing," Captain Yellowhair said.

"Shouldn't I be doing this?" the young officer asked. Thinking that the Captain was being sarcastic.

"Yes, yes, you are doing an excellent job so far. I'll let you know if you miss something." Captain said. Doc Cook stayed with Pupa. Captain and Bob moved the table so he would have more room. Doc took out his stethoscope and listened for a heart beat. He also listened for breathing. After about four minutes, he looked up.

"Well?" Captain asked.

"Well, she's breathing. For how long, I don't know. We need that MEDEVAC." Doc said.

Captain got on his radio, "How far out is that MEDEVAC?" He asked. There were a few minutes of silence. "Twenty minutes? Thanks, out." Captain looked up, "How do you want to handle this Doc?"

"Well, I think the safest way would be to have one of your officers meet it at our pad and then instruct the chopper to follow him here. She's warm and the less we move her, the better."

"You're the boss," Captain said.

"Get Tsinnijinni to meet the MEDEVAC," he said to Bob.

Bob gave the instructions to officer Tsinnijinni then came back in to finish his photo taking. The two officers walked the house together, looking for clues and taking pictures. Captain laid a ballpoint pen that he knew was six inches down next to the footprint on the rug. Then Bob took the picture. They continued through the house.

After about thirty minutes the MEDEVAC helicopter landed in the road right in front. Two men rolled in a gurney. Doc Cook stood up, explained the situation and the two men put an oxygen mask on her then wheeled her to the chopper. As soon as they got her on board they were off.

"Thanks, Doc," the Captain said. "I really appreciate you coming out so soon."

"Well, I'd have to make it sometime anyway. Do you want to do the chalk thing before I start?" He nodded to Maria. Doc was also the coroner.

Bob took his chalk and did the drawing. As he was doing this he realized that he once knew this woman and now she was dead. *Why would anyone do this?* He thought.

Captain Yellowhair saw that this was starting to bother Bob. He went over to him, "Let's stay focused."

Bob nodded. The two men went on about their work.


The next morning all the officers were at a meeting the Captain had called, "I appreciate you all coming this morning as some of you have been on night duty and want to get to bed. I want you all to know that Pupa is still alive. There was a rumble among the officers of joy.

The Captain put up his hand to quiet them. "She is alive, but in a coma. We don't know if she will ever come out of it. So we can't count on her to come to, and tell us who did this. I talked to the Chief this morning. He was very concerned that this happened. As you know, Pupa was a direct descendant of Eagle Woman, plus being the women's Chief. Some of you may not know the young lady who was killed was Pupa's granddaughter. That means we have one murder of a descendant of Eagle Woman and one descendant brutally beaten. If Pupa dies, then we have two murders of Eagle Woman descent."

"We must solve this." The Captain continued, "Maria O'Reily was strangled by someone with their hands. It was a man with a shoe size fourteen or fifteen. All windows and doors were nailed shut when this happened. The nail in the front door was pulled out before he left. Right now that's all we know, except that one of the women may have gotten in a hit with a skillet.

"Now, today I want everyone of you to talk to everyone you see. I want you to ask them if they saw anything suspicious yesterday. I want you to ask if they saw anyone acting strange or out of place. Write down anything they tell you, get names, phone numbers if they have one, and their address. You may tell them what happened to get them thinking. Today is the best day to get information. Officer Yazzie and officer Orlando will go to Pupa's neighbors and see if anyone saw or heard anything."

"I'm going over to see the young lady who discovered the disturbance." Captain said, "Now let's roll."

Captain Yellowhair was on his way over to Rita Small to visit with her about her friend, Maria. He had read officer Tsinnijinni's statement that he had taken the day before. He wanted to get additional information.

Captain pulled up in front of Rita Small's parent's home at about nine a.m. It was a modest two-bedroom house with a detached garage. It looked like ninety percent of the houses on the reservation except it had a garage. Most homes there had driveways but no garage.

Captain walked up to the front door and knocked. Rita soon answered the door and invited Captain Yellowhair in.

"Ms. Small, I know you gave officer Tsinnijinni your statement, but I have some questions for you."

"Okay," Rita said.

"You told officer Tsinnijinni that Maria was married."

"Yes."

"Do you know her husband?" Captain asked.

"I don't know him, but I've met him a couple of times," she answered.

"When's the last time you saw him?"

"It's been four or five years." Rita answered.

"Five years?" Captain asked, kind of wrinkling his brow.

"Yes, Maria came up here and Jack came up here after her to take her back home. She hadn't been here but two days," Rita said. "That's when I met him the second time. The first time was at her wedding." Rita said.

"When was the last time you saw Maria?" Captain asked.

"That was four or five years ago. The time I just described. I know she hadn't been back since then, because she told me she hadn't when we went to lunch together two days go," Rita said.

"You went to lunch with Maria two days ago?" Captain asked.

"Yes."

"Were did you go to lunch?" Captain asked.

"At Roy's," Rita answered.

"Did anyone else go with you?" he asked.

"No, she and I went by ourselves," Rita answered.

"Do you remember what you talked about?" Captain asked.

"Well we talked about her upcoming divorce she was going to get while she was here. We talked about old times we had when we went to school together here," Rita said.

"Tell me more about her upcoming divorce. Was it going to be one through the courts or one through the Women Council?" Captain inquired.

"One through the Women Council. But I advised her to also do the paper work through the courts. That way the state would recognize it," Rita answered.

"How did Jack feel about the divorce?" Captain asked.

"He didn't know she was planning to get one. You see, Jack is a wife abuser. He beat Maria the night before she caught the bus up here. She didn't even tell him she was coming. She just left without telling him," Rita said.

"So, she died on the fourth day after she left?" Captain asked.

Rita thought for a minute, "Yes."

"Is there anything else you can tell me?"

Rita thought, then shook her head and uttered, "No."

"Your folks, they never even saw Maria, is that right?" the Captain asked.

"My dad was with me when we went into Pupa's house and saw her laying there dead. My mother had stayed in the car." Rita said.

"But they never saw her alive..., recently, I mean."

"No," Rita said, shaking her head.

"I thank you for your time. If you think of anything else, please call me or officer Tsinnijinni," Captain gave Rita his card with his name and phone number on it.

Captain Yellowhair drove over to the crime scene. Parking across the street and outside the police tape, he sat in his police pickup. He saw two squad cars that belonged to officers Yazzie and Orlando. They both were parked on the other side of the police tape. In a minute, officer Orlando came out of one house and went up to another.

Captain Yellowhair leaned back in his seat and thought. Why would anyone try to kill these two women? Most people here on the reservation had great respect for Pupa. Maria had just gotten here…, she had come up here unexpectedly, according to Rita Small. If that were so, no one here would have known she was here unless they saw her arrive. All the windows and doors were nailed shut. Even the front door was nailed shut. Then the nail was pulled out far enough to open it. Maria's checkbook and money were left in her purse. Nana had money in her pouch that she carried with her most of the time. Furniture was turned over, even the bed. Nothing was left in its right place, like someone was looking for something. "Or, someone," he said to himself.

*The only suspect we have now is Jack O'Reily and I don't even know if he was here,* Captain thought. He had sent the skillet off to a crime lab that he'd always had good luck with. It and the footprint were the only good clues he had, and he didn't want any mistakes. They'd check for fingerprints and DNA on the blood. They'd also check for anything else the skillet might tell them. The results would be back in about a month. Captain put his pickup in reverse, backed up enough to be able to turn around. He gunned it making a U-turn and headed for the hospital in Flagstaff. It took awhile, but it gave Captain Yellowhair time to think.

Captain Yellowhair walked up to Pupa's room. Officer Bob Reeze was sitting next to the door. He stood up to greet the Captain. "Captain."

"Bob," the Captain replied. "Any change?"

"Not that I know. But Doc is in there now," Bob said.

Captain walked on in and shut the door behind him. Doc was bent over Pupa. Captain waited until he was finished. Doc turned, he heard someone come in, "Captain."

"Doc," the Captain replied.

"Well, she's still not awake, but she looks better than yesterday." Doc said.

"Got an educated guess if or when she'll come around?" Captain asked.

Doc shook his head. "Something like this, your guess is as good as mine. I've talked to Dr. Goodshaw here at the Hospital and he is of the same opinion as I, wait and see."

Captain walked over to Pupa's bed and looked down. "Who did this to you, Pupa? I sure wish you could tell me." Captain turned to Doc. "I'll keep a guard at her door until we find out who did this."

"I'll let you know if there's a change," Doc said. "Dr. Goodshaw said he'd let me know of any change if I'm not around, he's a good man. Are you headed back to the reservation?"

"Very soon, I just had to see Pupa with my own eyes. What about you, need a ride back?"

"No, I'm going to stick around for awhile, then go home."

"I appreciate all the work you put into this. Well, keep in touch, Doc," Captain said and nodded to the doctor as he headed out.

Captain headed for his office next. When he arrived he checked to see if anyone had called in about the homicide. They hadn't. He then called officers Yazzie and Orlando on their radio. They had canvassed the neighborhood, but no one had seen anything.

Captain sat at his desk. "I've got to interview Jack O'Reily," he said thoughtfully to himself. He looked through a directory for the name of the police Captain of the city of Benson. *City*, he thought, *more like a small town with its population of four thousand.* Anyway, there it was Bill Blight, Chief of Police of the City of Benson, Arizona.

He sat and pondered... Bill Blight, I met him in Phoenix at a police convention two years ago. Seemed like an okay guy. Stocky, but not too heavy, about five feet eight or nine. Captain got a good mental picture in his mind before he dialed the number in his directory.

"Benson Police Department," the female voice on the other end said.

"This is Captain Yellowhair calling for Chief Bill Blight."

"Just a minute please," the voice came back.

"This is Chief Bill Blight."

"Chief, this is Captain Yellowhair from the Socike Nation Reservation. I don't know if you remember me, but we met at the convention in Phoenix a couple of years ago."

"Yes!" It came to Chief Blight who he was talking to. "I remember you had worked with my old buddy, Mike Jay in L.A. What can I do for you?"

"I'm investigating a homicide up here. I need to know if you know Jack O'Reily."

"I know him and his wife, Maria," Chief answered. "We've made at least six domestic violent calls to their house last year."

"Maria was a Socike Indian. She was up here visiting her grandmother when someone strangled her yesterday morning." Captain Yellowhair said. "I'd like to interview Jack O'Reily tomorrow."

"I'll email you everything on the investigation. I'd like you and your men to keep it quiet about Maria's death for now. If Jack is the culprit or knows about it, it'll give him time to stew. In the mean time, if I could get your men to check and see if he is in town. If he is and you have the manpower, I'd like you to keep an eye on him until I get there tomorrow. If you could check around and find out if anyone saw him yesterday and if so when? That would be a great help," Captain said.

"We'll do it and I'm looking forward to working with you," Chief said.

The Captain hung up the phone and leaned back in his chair. "Think," he said to himself. Is it possible that anyone else would have a motive to do this? Sure wish Pupa would come out of her coma. Maybe she could shed light on this.

Officers Yazzie and Orlando came into the station and the Captain called them into his office.

"What did you find?" The Captain asked.

Orlando went first, "Almost everyone was home, but no one noticed anything. No stranger or strange cars. I'll go back this evening to the people who weren't home. I left my card with everyone I talked to. Those that had kids, I even talked to them. That's it," he shook his head.

Officer Yazzie said, "Same thing with me."

"Well, try again this evening. Be sure to talk to the kids. They notice what goes on in their neighborhood," Captain said.

"Tomorrow I'll be gone. But I'll have my radio. So if you find out or even suspect anything, call me. I'll brief Sergeant Blackwood. So report to him anything that might come up you don't feel you need to call me on. He'll decide if you should call, okay guys?" Captain asked.

Both officers nodded affirmative and Officer Orlando said, "Yes, sir."

After taking care of some other business and briefing Sergeant Blackwood, the Captain went home. He packed some clothes and headed to Benson. He hoped he'd make it to Tucson before he had to stop for some sleep.

Captain Yellowhair pulled into a large motel on the interstate early in the morning, he had exceeded the speed limit, but he figured this was an emergency. He had made it to Tucson now to get some sleep before he headed for Benson. He walked into the lobby and noticed a bar to the right with some soft music playing. He could see a couple sitting at the bar, talking. To the left and a few feet further was the front desk. Captain Yellowhair rang the little bell that was on the counter.

After getting the direction to his room and the plastic key that motels use now, he decided to have one drink at the bar before retiring. He sat at a table where he could slouch down and enjoy a rum and cola. His thoughts kept going to Maria and her killer. He had to get the killer. *There is just no option*, he thought.

Captain Yellowhair was full-blooded Socike, but he wasn't cursed with the problem of alcoholism as so many of his tribal people were. After he finished the one drink he went to his room and retired for the rest of the night.

Captain Yellowhair awoke at a quarter 'til eight. That drink put him out like a light. He lay in bed, thinking of a dream he had. It was very vivid. Eagle Woman was on her black stallion at the edge of a great cliff. She was far away where he could barely make the figures out, but he knew it was Eagle Woman. Then he began to move closer so the figures were getting bigger and clearer. It was like he was looking through the zoom lens of a camera and he was zooming in on the picture. Then he was so close that he could see the features of her face. She looked straight at him and smiled. That's when he woke up.

Captain Yellowhair was not especially a superstitious person. He had been out in the world too much to believe in all of the old Socike beliefs. But, he had seen enough of them on the reservation not to dismiss all of these beliefs. He sat on the edge of the bed, wondering what that dream meant, if anything.

After breakfast and a call to Chief Blight, Captain Yellowhair was on his way to Benson. It'd take him about forty-five minutes to get there. There's not a lot of scenery on the way to Benson. Interstate ten is the only practical way to get where he was going. It's a gradual climb until you get to skyline road, then for the last five miles it's downhill. Benson lay in the San Pedro Valley. It's a small town of about four thousand that was started by the railroad back in the old Wild West days. But, it was still alive and doing well.

Captain Yellowhair pulled up in front of the police station. He was anxious to talk to Jack O'Reily and was hoping that they knew where he was.

Captain Yellowhair walked into the station; Chief Blight was talking to an officer and recognized Captain Yellowhair, even though he was in his civilian clothes.

Chief excused himself to the officer and walked over to the Captain. "Captain Yellowhair," and he put his hand out to the Captain.

"Chief Blight," Yellowhair said.

"How was your drive down?" Chief Blight asked.

"Oh, I was so anxious to get here I didn't have the time to enjoy the ride," Captain answered.

"Is this the first time you've been to Benson?" Chief asked.

"Oh, no. In my younger years I used to drive down to Bisbee to visit a young lady and I'd stop here to get something to eat," Captain answered. "Did you get a chance to read the email I sent you on this case?"

"Yes, I did. It's got me very interested. You know, when we talked yesterday I told you we have arrested Jack several times because he liked to hit Maria. I've got an officer that's keeping an eye on his place right now, and he's home. If you don't mind I'd like to go out there with you," Chief Blight said.

"I'd appreciate that. What I'd like to do is go out and tell him his wife is dead. Then ask him to come down here to look at these pictures," Captain handed the chief some pictures he had taken at the crime scene.

The Chief looked at one of Maria. "This should never have happened," he said.

Both men walked to Chief's office. In a couple of minutes both came out and walked to Chief Blight's squad car. They headed to Jack O'Reily's house.

They walked up and Captain knocked on the door. It was a few minutes before Jack O'Reily answered the door.

"Mr. O'Reily?" Captain asked.

Jack nodded, "Yes."

"I'm Captain Yellowhair and this is Chief Blight. We need to talk to you. Can we come in?"

Jack opened the screen door for them. "Yeah, come in."

Captain and Chief stepped in.

The two men instinctively saw Jack's bruised face and both looked around the room.

Captain Yellowhair spoke first. "Mr. O'Reily I'm the police Captain of the Socike Nation. Do you know where your wife, Maria, is?"

"Yes, she's at her grandmother's on the Socike reservation. I took her to the bus station to catch the bus there," Jack answered.

This surprised Captain Yellowhair, he knew that Rita had told him that Jack didn't know that Maria had gone to the reservation. But he recovered quickly, "I'm afraid I have some bad news for you,"

"What, what bad news?" Jack asked.

"I'm sorry to tell you this, but your wife, Maria, is dead."

"Dead?" Jack asked.

The Captain didn't answer for a few minutes then, "Yes...," and waited.

Now this wasn't Chief Blight's way of doing things, but Captain Yellowhair had a reputation of solving crimes from his days in L.A., so he bit his lip and said nothing.

Then very slowly from Jack's lips, "How did it happen?"

No one said anything. Silence.

"How did she die?" Jack asked again.

"She was killed, Jack." Captain said, staring him right in the eyes. "Killed by a cowardly son of a bitch. Killed by a coward, Jack."

Jack didn't know what to say, he'd never dreamed he would be told of Maria's death like this. *He knows,* Jack thinks, but kept it to himself. He finally got the words out, "How was she killed?"

"I told you, Jack," Captain said. "We have some pictures to show you, and some papers for you to sign down at the Benson police station. Will you follow us back to the station or would you like us to drive you there?"

Jack looked at Chief Blight for some sign of what was going on. Chief Blight didn't show any expression at all.

Captain Yellowhair staring at Jack. "Jack! What will it be?"

Jack was starting to panic, he never had much of a conscience, but this form of questioning by Yellowhair was getting to him.

"Yeah, I'll follow you," Jack said.

"Good," Yellowhair said. With that, Yellowhair headed for the door.

Chief Blight followed. When they got to their car they stood outside until Jack came out.

The two officers got in their car and Jack got in his.

"I couldn't keep my job if I brought news of a man's wife dying like you did," Chief said to the Captain in his car on the way back.

"I didn't give him any news he didn't know already," Captain Yellowhair said.

"I know, but I still couldn't get away with it," Chief Blight said.

"That's one reason I moved to the reservation. I do things my way," Yellowhair said.

"That'd be nice to be able to do that here," Chief Blight said. "That's some bruise Jack has on his head, isn't it?"

"Yeah, Maria did a job with that skillet," Captain said.

"You think it was Maria. It couldn't have been her grandmother that used the skillet?" asked the chief.

"I don't think she had the strength to put that bruise on Jack's head," Captain answered.

They pulled up to the station.

Jack parked across the street.

"You want to talk to him alone?" Chief asked.

"No, at this stage there's not much more I can do until we have more evidence," Yellowhair answered.

The two officers waited for Jack at the steps of the station and the three went in together. The chief then took the lead and led them into a small room with a table and six chairs.

"Have a seat, Jack," Chief Blight said.

Jack sat down and looked at one officer then the other.

Captain Yellowhair liked to keep any suspect waiting for what would come next and he did this very effectively with Jack, in just about forty-five seconds, but it seemed to Jack like five minutes before Yellowhair spoke.

"Jack, in homicides most officers like to keep the bloody details from the victim's loved ones. But, I'm not that way. I think a man has a right to see what went on, don't you?" Captain Yellowhair leaned down, placing his knuckles on the table across from Jack, staring him in the face.

Jack looked down at the table, not wanting to make eye contact with Yellowhair and nodded his head.

"Is that a yes, Jack?" Yellowhair asked.

Jack nodded his head again and said, "Yes."

Yellowhair laid a large manila envelope in front of Jack. "Here's what happened, Jack."

Jack waited a minute then started to pick up the envelope.

Captain Yellowhair placed his hand on the envelope, pinning it to the table, keeping Jack from picking it up. "You don't mind if I take a picture of you getting to look at the evidence do you, Jack?" He kept his hand on it until Jack answered. Then he nodded to Chief Blight.

Jack said, "No, no, I don't mind."

Chief Blight got close with Captain Yellowhair's camera and took a picture of Jack picking up the envelope.

"Sorry, Jack, I'm not too good with a camera, better take another." Chief Blight moved to get a different angle of Jack holding the envelope. He made sure he got a couple of the bruise on Jack's face and head.

Jack blinked because of the flash on the camera. He couldn't see well enough to see the pictures that tumbled out of the envelope on the table. When his eyes could focus again he saw Maria's bloody body face up. *This is wrong,* Jack thought, *I didn't hit her hard enough to cause her to bleed.* He stared at the picture.

Captain Yellowhair or Chief blight couldn't read Jack's mind, they just had to play it out.

Jack looked at the other pictures. They were all of Maria from different angles. Even three of her in the makeshift morgue Dr. Cook put together.

"This is terrible," Jack said. No one said anything. The two officers were waiting for Jack to say more. "Was she shot or stabbed?" Jack asked, thinking this question would throw them off.

"She was strangled, Jack." Captain Yellowhair said.

"Strangled? Then why all the blood?" Jack asked.

"That blood came from the attacker, Jack. He had a wound that left that blood on Maria. Captain Yellowhair said. He walked over to the side of the table where Jack was sitting. Captain touched the wound on Jack's head. Jack winced. That's quite a cut and bruise you have there. Where did you get it?"

"I got that from the screen door. You can ask Angie, the new girl at the Horseshoe Café, and Anita, they know," Jack said.

"Oh, were they there when you got hit?" Captain Yellowhair asked.

"Well, uh, they weren't there, but they saw me at noon after the morning it happened, and they asked me how it happened," Jack answered.

"What day was that, Jack?" Captain asked.

"Friday," Jack answered.

"What screen door?" Captain asked.

"What do you mean?" Jack asked.

"What door, your door? Front or back?" Captain asked.

"Oh," Jack said. "Yes, my front door," Jack answered.

"And, you were at the Horseshoe at noon, Friday?" Captain asked.

"Yes, at noon," Jack replied.

"Were you there in the morning?" Captain asked.

"No, I was at home Friday morning. Fixing my screen door," Jack answered.

"That was your front door?" Captain asked.

"Yes," Jack answered.

"Did anyone else see you there?" Captain asked.

"No, I was by myself until I went to the Horseshoe at noon," Jack answered. "Then I went there for dinner about seven and Angie saw me there then, too."

"Jack, I appreciate you coming in. Do you have any questions?"

Captain Yellowhair asked, looking him right in the eyes.

*Think,* Jack thought. "Do you have a suspect?" he finally came up with.

Captain staring at him had Jack unnerved.

The Captain just nodded his head.

Jack didn't know what to say. "When can I get the body back for burial?" Jack asked.

"The body back?" Captain asked, "Do you mean Maria's body back?"

This really shook up Jack. "Of course, that's what I mean."

"Well, we will let you know, Jack." Captain Yellowhair said. "Do you have any more questions?"

"I guess not," Jack stuttered.

"Again, I'd like to thank you for coming down." Captain said.

Chief Blight was wondering what was going on and started to say something, but thought he'd let Yellowhair play it out.

Jack got up and started to leave. As he reached for the door, the Captain said, "Jack?"

Jack turned and it was apparent that he was agitated, "What?"

"Jack, can we get a blood sample from you?" Captain asked.

"A blood sample?" Jack snapped. What do you need a blood sample from me for? I didn't leave Benson."

"We need a blood sample from you, to eliminate you as a suspect, Jack," Captain says.

Jack thought for a minute, "No, I was here. You don't need any blood from me."

"You're going to make me get a court order to get some blood from you?" Captain asked.

"I'm going to get a lawyer, and we will see what you'll get." Jack said and walked out.

"I guess I over did it." Captain said. "I'll check out his alibi, but I know he's guilty. What do you think?"

"I think he did it." Chief Blight said. What proof do we have without the blood sample? You know no judge will make him give blood on what we have."

"This is what we have," and Captain Yellowhair listed them. "He said he took Maria to the bus stop to catch the bus to visit her grandmother. I have a witness that will swear he didn't know where

Maria went, at least until he found her. He didn't ask the normal questions that a grieving husband would ask. He didn't ask about Maria's grandmother because he thinks she's dead."

At that time a woman came into the room. "I'm sorry to interrupt you, Chief, but there's a phone call for Captain Yellowhair."

"Can I get it in here?" Captain asked. Chief pointed to the phone on the desk.

"Captain Yellowhair," Captain said into the receiver.

A voice on the other end said, "This is Bob. Doc called me a few minutes ago. Pupa came out of her coma, but she's too weak for any questions. I tried your radio, but I couldn't reach you." Officer Bob Yazzie said.

"I'm down in a valley here. That's probably why," Captain said. "Did Doc know when he thought we could talk to Pupa?"

"He said we'd just have to wait and see. But get this, that Flagstaff hospital has already transferred her to our little hospital on the Rez. Can you believe that? They brought her over by MEDEVAC." Bob said.

"Why did they do that?" Captain asked.

"Insurance, she doesn't have insurance. Doc said he'll keep us informed," Bob Yazzie said.

"Good, I'm planning on being back tomorrow, late," Captain said.

"Should we keep an officer at the hospital? Sergeant Blackwood wants to know." Bob asked.

Captain thought for a minute. "No, I can't see we need one there anymore. I'll see you tomorrow." Then he hung the phone up.

"Where's this Horseshoe Café?" Captain asked.

"Do you want me to go with you?" Chief asked.

"Sure, if you have the time." Captain said.

Captain Yellowhair followed Chief Blight to the Horseshoe Cafe. They parked around back, so they came in the back way. Both men sat in a booth.

A young blonde waitress came up. "Hi Chief," she said, then she turned to the Captain, "Hello."

Both men acknowledged her. "Is Anita here now?" Chief asked.

"I'm not good enough for you…? Yes…, she's here. I'll get her." The blonde said.

Chief smiled, "Thanks."

Anita walked over to the booth where the two men were sitting. "Now, Chief, whatever it is, I didn't do it."

Chief smiled, Anita always joked with all her customers. Through the years as a waitress she found she received a lot more tips by being funny than by being serious. "Do you have a minute, so we can talk to you?" Chief asked.

"Sure, Chief," she sat down in the booth next to Chief Blight. She then acknowledged the Captain.

"This is Captain Yellowhair from the Socike reservation. He is investigating the homicide of Maria O'Reily." Chief said to Anita.

Anita's eyes got big as she stared at Chief Blight and then at Captain Yellowhair. "Maria O'Reily, when? Where? Jack was in here yesterday and the day before." She said.

"Yes, he said he was here the day before and talked to you." Captain Yellowhair said, "Do you know about what time he was here?"

Anita thought for a minute. "Well, it had to be after four o'clock. I'd have to say between four and five."

"It couldn't have been before four?" Captain Yellowhair asked.

"It couldn't have been much before four if any, because Angie's shift didn't start until four and she was his waitress. We usually don't get started before our shift starts." Anita said.

"Are you sure he wasn't in earlier and then came back later?" Yellowhair asked.

"If he was, I didn't see him," Anita said, "I hadn't seen Jack or Maria for almost two weeks and then he's here two days in a row."

"What time did he come in yesterday?" Chief Blight asked.

"Oh, he came in with the noon crowd," she answered.

"And that would be between what time and what time?" Captain Yellowhair asked.

"The noon crowd starts about a quarter 'til twelve. People wanting to beat the noon rush. It'll usually stay busy until one or one-thirty then it lightens up again," Anita answered.

"So you are saying that Jack O'Reily was here yesterday at around noon but, the day before— Friday—he was here after four?" Captain Yellowhair asked.

"Yes, that's right."

"Was there anything unusual about his visit?" Chief Blight asked.

"Not at first. He was giving Angie a hard time, which is like Jack. When I butted in, he was friendly. Now that's unusual," Anita said.

The two men looked at each other as if to ask if either had a question. "Thank you, Anita. This being Sunday, would there be a chance of Angie being here?" Captain Yellowhair asked.

"I'm sorry, but Angie quit here and went to work at Hank's Cafe out by the interstate," Anita said.

"Thanks again, we will check out there," Captain Yellowhair said, wanting to get going.

"Can you tell me when, where, and how this happened?" Anita asked.

"I'm sorry," Captain Yellowhair said. "I get busy on some of these cases and I tend to streamline it. How well did you know Maria?"

"I knew her as well as anyone. Jack tried to keep her at home, except to let her work. She'd slip down here for a break once in a while, and we'd talk. Funny thing, even with all the manipulation she still loved him," Anita said.

Captain Yellowhair saw tears welling up in her eyes. He sighed, "Maria was strangled at her grandmother's sometime Thursday evening or Friday morning. Her grandmother lives on the Socike reservation. That's why I'm involved."

"Nana," Anita said.

"I beg your pardon?" Captain said.

"Nana, that's what Maria called her grandmother. Is she alright?" Maria asked.

"I'm sorry, I can't say any more about this case." Captain said.

The two men got up and headed for Hank's Cafe. They found Angie waiting tables. They decided to have coffee and talked briefly with Angie. She confirmed that Jack hadn't come in until about four-thirty, because she was fifteen minutes late on Friday, which was her last day at the Horseshoe. She mentioned that at first he was really sarcastic, but after Anita came over he was alright.

They thanked Angie for the information and headed back to the station. When they were back in Chief Blight's office, the two men sat and discussed all of the evidence.

"We've got enough evidence to get a court order to get the blood test from Jack now. Do you want me to call Judge Roder for a court order?" Chief asked.

"Yes, let's do it," Captain said.

One call to Judge Roder's home and Chief found out that he was somewhere between Bisbee and Wilcox. He wouldn't be back until tonight. "I can call Judge Little in Wilcox, but he's such a stickler on details."

"I know, I had to deal with him on a drug dealer two years ago. Wait until tomorrow and get Judge Roder, if you don't mind working on this with me," Captain said.

"My pleasure," Chief replied. "I'd love to get Jack in here. Maria was a good woman."

"I brought my uniform. I'm going to check with Jack's neighbors, then I'm headed home. Where can I change?" Captain asked.

"Last door down the hall is a small locker room. Feel free to use that. I'll get that blood sample from Jack, and then let you know. What lab are you using?" Chief asked.

Captain told Chief the lab's name and then went to the locker room and changed into his uniform.

Captain Yellowhair pulled up across the street from Jack O'Reily's house. He noticed he wasn't home, or at least his car wasn't in the drive. He had pulled up in front of a red burnt adobe home with green trim. It was right across the street from Jack's house.

Captain looked the place over and then got out and walked up the sidewalk to the house. He knocked on the door and waited. In about a minute right before he was going to knock again, the door opened slowly.

"Can I help you?" a voice from a little old lady asked, standing in the doorway.

"Yes ma'am, you can. I'm Captain Yellowhair from the Socike Tribe police department." Captain said, tipping his hat.

"Yellowhair?" the lady repeated.

"Yes ma'am, Yellowhair," Captain said.

"That's a strange name. I've never heard of a name like that before," she said.

"It's quite common on both the Socike and the Navajo reservation," Captain said.

"Really? I didn't know that." she said.

"I'm here in Benson investigating a homicide of a neighbor who was a Socike Indian."

"Oh, what neighbor is that?" the little old lady asked.
"Your neighbor across the street. Maria O'Reily," Captain said.
"Maria... she's dead?" she asked in surprise.
"Yes Ma'am," Captain said. "I'm sorry to say she is. She was killed on the reservation."
"Oh no!" the lady exclaimed.
"Ma'am, I'm checking with the neighbors about some things. Do you know when Maria left Benson?" Captain asked.
"Yes, I do," she answered.
"You do? When?" Captain asked.
"It was Tuesday," She said.
"How do you know that?" Captain asked.
"Jack came over here looking for Maria, Tuesday morning. He thought she might be staying here. She did that once in a while when he came home drunk. She came over here and stayed for two days once. He sure got mad when he found out. Called me everything but a white woman," she said.

"Are you telling me Jack O'Reily came over here last Tuesday morning looking for Maria? He thought she was here?"

"Yes, and he wasn't very nice abut it. I threatened to call the police before he would leave," she replied.

"Do you know if Mr. O'Reily left town from then to now? I'm asking if there was a period of time you know of that Mr. O'Reily wasn't at his house for any length of time?" Captain asked.

"I'm sorry, I don't know how long he was away. He comes and goes at all different hours," she answered.

"Did you notice if he was home Friday?" Captain asked.

"I'm sorry, I was visiting my daughter in Tucson, Thursday evening until Saturday morning," She said.

You could read the disappointment on the Captain's face, but he tried not to show it. He filled out a form that he had with him, getting her name, phone number, and address. He then asked if she would be willing to go to the Benson police station and make the statement that she had just given him. She agreed and they made an appointment to meet there in two hours. He then thanked her and went to the next neighbor.

All the rest of the neighbors were a disappointment, but none of them remembered seeing Jack's automobile in his drive Friday.

However, none could be sure that it wasn't there.

Next, Captain went back to the Horseshoe because it was the bus station, also. There he got the name of who would have been on duty from eleven p.m. Monday until seven-thirty Tuesday. They told him that person was Mary Smith and she would be in today at two-thirty.

Captain Yellowhair then went to the police station to meet Betty Brown the lady who had the appointment to meet him and give her statement. When he got there she was already there waiting. Chief Blight sat in on her statement.

After Betty Brown left the station, Captain and Chief Blight sat and talked about the case. "I'm going over to the Horseshoe to talk to Mary Smith, before I leave for the reservation. She was on duty Monday night and Tuesday morning, she handles the bus tickets. My guess is that's when Maria left town... Anyway, I'm hoping this Mary Smith has a good memory," Captain said.

"If Maria caught the bus, then Mary Smith will know. They are cousins," Chief Blight said.

"If Maria caught a bus, and Jack was nowhere around we'll have enough to haul him in for questioning. Now, that's my guess. I believe Betty Brown. I think that Jack didn't know Maria was leaving town. I'll call you and let you know what she says." With that said, Captain Yellowhair left for the Horseshoe.

Yellowhair walked in the Horseshoe from the front door this time. Somehow it looked different coming in the front way. He asked the lady at the register to see Mary Smith. She left and in about a minute, a very attractive light-skinned woman with coal black hair came over to him. "Are you Mary Smith?" Captain asked.

"Yes, I am," she said.

"I'm Captain Yellowhair from the Socike tribal police."

"How can I help you?" Mary asked.

"I understand that you were on duty here Monday night from eleven until seven-thirty Tuesday morning, is that right?" Captain asked. Just then, two women and two men came in the front door of the café.

"Why don't we step into the dining room?" Mary said, leading Captain into a small room to the left with five tables. There was no one else there. Mary sat at one table and motioned with her hand for Captain Yellowhair to have a seat. "Yes, that was my shift," she said.

Captain was taken by her beauty, he couldn't believe that such a beautiful woman lived out of Hollywood. What was a clumsy silence for the Captain, was a power trip for Mary. She was quite aware of her beauty and she used that power to her advantage.

Captain got his focus back in a few seconds. "Did Maria O'Reily catch a bus here that morning?"

"Yes—yes she did. You're down here checking on Maria?" Mary asked.

"Yes! It is about Maria. Can you remember if she was alone when she caught the bus?" Captain asked.

"Yes, she was alone," she said.

"Are you sure?" Captain asked.

"Oh yes, she was alone after her husband dropped her off and brought in her suitcase," Maria said. She sat over there in that front booth." Mary pointed at the booth they could see through the door of the dining room. "Jack brought in her suitcase, kissed her and said, "Tell your grandmother hello for me."

"Then they were getting along good?" Captain asked.

"Oh, yes," Mary said.

*This can't be right,* the Captain thought. *I know something's wrong.* "Was there anyone else here in the cafe at the time?" Captain asked.

"Well, let's see," Mary thought for a moment. "There was Jim, the cook. He always has the early shift. Connie was the waitress on, with me. Oh, yes, Nita came in."

"What is Nita's job here?" Captain asked.

"Nita, she's kind of an assistant manager, slash waitress," Mary said.

"Are any of those people here now?" Captain asked.

"Nita is," Mary said. "Jim gets off at eight in the morning and Connie is on a two-week vacation. She's somewhere in Kansas right now."

Captain had been taking notes in a little pocket note pad.

"Would you mind asking Connie to come in here?" Captain asked.

"Sure, are you through with me then?" Mary asked.

"Yes, I have no more questions," Captain said.

"Would you like some coffee?" Mary asked.

"Thank you, that would be good," Captain said.

An older lady came in the dining room with a cup of coffee. "You must be Captain Yellowhair." She put the coffee in front of the Captain. "Cream? Sugar?"

"No, thanks, I like it black," Captain said, "Are you Nita?"

"Yes, I am."

"Nita...?" Captain asked.

"Nita Smith" She said.

Captain jotted it down. "Are you any kin to Mary Smith that I was just talking to."

"No, just same last names, no kin," she said.

"I understand you were here Tuesday morning when Maria O'Reily caught a bus to the Socike reservation."

"Yes, I was here when the bus arrived." She affirmed.

"Did you see Maria or Jack O'Reily?" Captain asked.

"I saw Maria sitting in the booth. I didn't see Jack." She said.

"Did you see Maria come in?"

"No, she was already here when I arrived."

"Can you give me Jim's address?"

"Sure, I'll get it." Nita left, and then came back with Jim Beed, the cook's, address.

Before Captain Yellowhair left, he asked Nita if anyone else had been there when Maria came in to catch the bus. She confirmed that there were only three other people there when Maria waited for the bus that morning. With the directions Nita gave him, Captain found Jim's apartment. He was no help, he hadn't even seen Maria that morning because he was busy in the kitchen.

Captain drove past Jack O'Reily's place once again and saw his car in the drive way now. He pulled his car around the corner and parked. Captain Yellowhair pondered the situation. *He's guilty, I know he's guilty. But why the two conflicting stories? Mary said Jack dropped his wife off at the Horseshoe and knew that she was going to the reservation. But Rita, on the other hand, said Maria told her that Jack didn't know that Maria went to the Reservation. Betty Brown's story matched Rita's. Of course he could have still been the one, but what was the reason for the two conflicting stories?*

Captain thought for a minute of just driving back to the reservation and not sharing his new information with Chief Blight. That way he would have no trouble getting the judge to sign a court order to get Jack's blood to compare with the blood on the skillet. He pondered this for a few minutes, then drove to the station and shared his new information with Chief Blight. Captain was a great believer in the do unto others. He had always been above board with his investigations. He had no qualms with tricking or lying to the bad guys, but he was very up front with anyone he was asking to do a favor for him.

"Well, don't worry about it. I'll get that blood sample," Chief Blight said. "I'll keep you informed on what's going on here, please do the same."

"I will, and again, I appreciate the help, Chief," Captain said.

The two men shook hands and Captain Yellowhair was on his way back to the reservation.

The drive seemed much longer than it did when Captain was a teenager and drove to Bisbee to see a girlfriend. There was that big truck stop to the north of the road where he used to stop and get a piece of pie when he made the trip down this way. Captain recalled to himself, he used to think he was getting close to Bisbee when he'd reach this spot. Funny how things change as you get older. This place had to be fifty or sixty miles or more from Bisbee.

This part of Arizona was desert, but not like parts around Yuma where there were sand dunes. But it had greasewood growing or the famous jumping cactus. So called (jumping) because if you got near it, you seemed to end up with a piece on you. It was usually because while you were looking out so the plant wouldn't stick you, you usually wound up kicking a piece that had fallen off the plant and getting it stuck on your foot or leg. Or if you watch out for the many pieces on the ground, you wound up walking into a plant. The people who lived here would stay away from these plants. But the tourists would get stuck a lot when they would go after the cactus wood that seemed free, because it was laying out there at no cost. The cost was usually getting some painful pricks from some nasty spines. It was almost irresistible because of the price of this cactus wood in the local tourist traps.

As he drove, Captain Yellowhair wondered if he was like the tourist and went after Jack like they go after the cactus wood and he just wasn't looking around at anything else, just like the tourist. He was starting to doubt his conviction that Jack was the one. Especially after Mary Smith had told him that Jack had dropped off Maria to catch the bus and knew she was going to visit her Grandmother. He tried to think of anyone else that would have done such a thing. From Yellowhair's experience, he knew it was possible that this was a random act, but wasn't likely.

Just then he got a call on his radio. It was Sergeant Blackwood. "Captain?" Came the voice over the radio.

"Captain Yellowhair here, over," Captain said.

"Captain, this is Sergeant Blackwood, do you read me, over."

"Affirmative, I read you loud and clear," Captain said.

"Captain, we have a problem. Pupa is missing. Doc called me, they've looked all over the hospital and she is no longer there, over."

Captain Yellowhair went weak. He couldn't believe what he was hearing. Was Pupa the target and he took the guard away? "Sergeant, call in every officer, no one goes home until we find her. I want every house around the hospital interviewed for anything anyone saw. Put roadblocks at both ends of the highway. I want everyone on the street looking for her. Check by the stable, check her home, and check the Women Council. I'm driving straight through, but I'm not even to Tucson yet. Keep me informed, do you read me? Over."

"Affirmative, will do, out" Sergeant said.

Yellowhair pushed the accelerator down a little more. *How could I have done that,* he thought. He was headed west on interstate ten just before the curve where it turned to the north. It was a long way to the reservation. Captain was biting at the bit. He wanted to get there and find out what had happened to Pupa. *What happened here?* He thought. This whole investigation was going to crap. I was so sure it was Jack O'Reily. But what happened to Pupa? Why am I getting two stories about Jack knowing his wife went to the reservation? If he didn't know, how did he know she was there? And if he didn't know, why was Mary Smith lying about him knowing that Maria went to the reservation. All of this was bothering him.

He sailed right passed Tucson. Picacho Peak was coming in view, Captain Yellowhair noticed the mountain that looked like a saddle. It was a landmark that you couldn't miss whenever you drove this route. Captain was needing a pit stop, so he pulled into a restaurant parking lot at Picacho Peak. After entering, he sat in a booth ordered a sandwich with coffee. It was going to be a long trip.

Captain Yellowhair was sitting there eating when it came to him.

If Jack O'Reily made this trip then most likely he stopped at least once or twice going up and coming back. As soon as he could get the film developed he was going to get officers out on this highway, showing Jack's Photo and seeing if anyone recognized him. It was a long shot, but worth the time, he thought. He needed that blood test. If that didn't match the blood on the skillet then he had really screwed up. It was possible that he had read the crime scene all wrong. It could have been Maria's or even Pupa's blood on the skillet. Captain Yellowhair gulped down the rest of the coffee, paid his bill and headed towards Phoenix.

This stretch of the highway was the most desolate, lots of greasewood and sand, lots of sand.

Captain's mind started to wonder what made him come back to the reservation. It was in an area like this. He had been investigating a murder of a sixty-four-year-old woman. There were tracks that led him to a camp of two young men. There were all kinds of evidence that these two men had been at the crime scene. They even had some articles from the lady's house. He had been quite sure that these two men killed the women.

The two men swore that they hadn't killed anyone. But, all evidence showed that they killed her. Both men had a record of house burglary, each man had articles of the women on their person. To Captain, it was an open and shut case.

The two men were convicted and spent two years on death row, when someone else confessed to the murder. After much more investigation, it was proven that the first two men were innocent. After that, Captain decided to go back to the reservation. He thought there he wouldn't have to do murders anymore. *But, look at me now*, he thought. *Even on the reservation I get this thing thrown in my lap. I've got to get this right.*

Captain stayed on the highway right through Phoenix. He still had a long way to go. Flagstaff would be the next city of any size. First though, he had to drive over some steep hills.

This seemed to be the longest drive he had ever made, even though as a teenager he used to drive even further to visit with a young lady that lived thirty miles further than Benson. She lived in Bisbee, an old mining town southeast of Benson. He'd head off Friday night, stay until Sunday morning and head back.

Captain thought of those times with fondness. There was a little town five miles south of Bisbee, called Naco. It was on both sides of the American and Mexican border. Sometimes on Saturday night, they'd go to this sleepy town and go across the border. There, they would party with some friends on a strip where there was nothing but bars on both sides of the street. It would go strong until wee hours in the morning. People from all parts of that area would slip over the border to party there.

He had read that after the AIDS scare, that place had dried up and he wondered what had ever happened to his friend. They had split up like so many young people do in those circumstances. There was a great physical attraction, but they had never taken the time to really get to know each other's minds.

Captain Yellowhair went to college in flagstaff and she was wanting to be a nurse. He wondered if she had pursued her dream of being a nurse. With that thought, he started to nod.

His head jerked up and his eyes went wide open. For an instant he had drifted off to sleep. His car was headed for a slight curve and he did what he was trained not to do. He jerked his car back too quickly and, at eighty miles an hour, Captain Yellowhair rolled his car over six times. His car came to rest at the bottom of a ravine with one headlight shining straight ahead and the other headlight shining straight up like a beacon in the darkness.

# Chapter 8

Sergeant Blackwood was at his desk when he received the news of Captain Yellowhair's death the next morning from the Arizona Highway Patrol. He had been up all night with his officers, looking for Pupa. He sank into his chair. "God, what is going on?" He thought out loud. This can't be happening. I don't have the experience to complete this investigation.

His men had been up all night looking for Pupa with absolutely no sign of her. No one had seen a thing. It was as if she had disappeared from the face of the earth. He had let two of his officers who had been working the longest go home at about two a.m. He was going to have to start letting the other officers go get some rest. "God help me. This was not supposed to happen," he said aloud.

Sergeant Blackwood sat and thought for a while. Then looked up Benson's chief of police number and called Chief Blight. After getting Chief Blight, Sergeant Blackwood explained what had happened to Captain Yellowhair.

Chief Blight filled him in on what he knew about the investigation. He also informed him that he wasn't going to be able to get a court order to get blood from Jack O'Reily anytime soon. It seems that Jack had hired an attorney and he was pulling a delaying tactic. Chief Blight said this didn't mean that they wouldn't get the blood sample, but they would have to wait to get a hearing with the Judge because Jack O'Reily was accusing the police of harassment after the death of his wife.

Sergeant Blackwood thanked the chief and promised to keep in contact.

After hanging up, Sergeant Blackwood sat at his desk pondering all of the things he knew about this case. It didn't take him long before he decided he didn't know much.

Now, Sergeant Blackwood had two options. He could back track what Captain Yellowhair had done and try to move this investigation forward. The down side to this was that they would, in all probability, move a more experienced man in to take Captain's place. He would have to start over again, doing the investigation the new man's way.

The other option Blackwood had was to go through the motions, keep things together until a new man moved in.

Sergeant Blackwood chose the former. First he called in every man except two. Those, he left on their job of checking every vehicle that left the reservation.

When he got the men together he informed them of what had taken place and that the most important thing now was to find Pupa. "I want each of you to go back to your regular shift. You can't do anything unless you get some rest. When you get home, I want you to do me a favor. Call every relative you have and any friends and see if they had seen Pupa or if they had seen something unusual. Call me on my radio if you get anything, I'm not interested in their theories, just facts," Sergeant said.

"You are all dismissed except those of you who investigated the crime scene," Blackwood said.

Officer Bob Yazzie was the first to arrive at the crime scene, officers Robert Tsinnijinni, and Yata Orlando stayed behind.

Sergeant asked each officer to explain what had taken place at the crime scene and what their assessment of the crime was. After this, Sergeant Blackwood dismissed Tsinnijinni and Orlando, asking Bob Yazzie to accompany him to Pupa's house.

Sergeant Blackwood and officer Yazzie went to Pupa's house. They noticed the police tape was down on one side of the door. Both men looked at each other with a question.

They entered her house. The scene was surprisingly eerie to Sergeant Blackwood. He hadn't been in here before. Blackwood dismissed it as being in Pupa's house and it being in such a shamble, this leader of the female population of the great Socike Nation. Just being in her house was a great honor to anyone who entered.

In the Indian nation of the Socike, the women were honored, especially leaders of the women. Sergeant Blackwood was honored just to be in this house. He soon got over his awe and got to work.

"Bob, I want you to show me how you and Captain Yellowhair went through this house and point out each item, object or anything that you or Captain Yellowhair thought was important or out of character. Besides the furniture being out of order." Sergeant Blackwood said.

Officer Yazzie nodded, and went about pointing out the bloody footprint and everything else that he took pictures of. After that, they had gone through Pupa's house and all around the outside, seeing if they could find any new clues. But with all their efforts, nothing turned up.

Bob Yazzie went back to his duties and Sergeant Blackwood went over to Rita's parents' house since she was the one who called the police in the first place.

# Chapter 9

That night Jack O'Reily woke up in a sweat. *That's the strangest dream I've ever had,* Jack thought. It was of a giant flying mammal. It looked a lot like a pterodactyl but with huge eyes and sharp, spiked teeth in its pointed mouth. It appeared in a blue sky just as a speck that just kept getting larger. When it reached Jack, it landed in front of him and stared at him with those large eyes. It then opened its mouth and snarled at Jack with saliva dripping from those pointed teeth. Jack could feel the sweat pouring off his face.

Jack got out of bed. "Man, that was intense," he said out loud. Jack got a beer from the fridge and drank it to help him get back to sleep.

After going back to bed, Jack started to dream again. This time he was standing in a beautiful meadow, the greenest grass he had ever seen, with small white flowers dotting the landscape. Jack felt good and turned his face and eyes toward the blue sky with fluffy clouds. Then he saw a black speck that looked like a small bird. It kept getting bigger, it was that horrible creature he had in his earlier dream and he was coming fast and Jack knew he had come to eat him. Jack turned and tried to run, but his legs would hardly move. He struggled to run, but it was like his feet were in gummy mud where he had to pull his foot out each step. He was terrified and struggled to get away from this awful creature. Then the pain hit him as the beast struck with one of his mighty claws and ripped his back open. Jack could feel the flesh being stripped from his shoulder as the animal bit into his body. He tried to scream, but there was no sound. The pain was so bad he couldn't stand it. He wanted to die, but he wouldn't die and the pain wouldn't let up, it was like an excruciating cramp that was getting worse.

The beast turned Jack over and bit into his stomach and ripped out his intestines. Jack could see his intestines being ripped from his body and he could feel the pain. It was worse than anything he had ever felt in his life. The beast kept tearing and eating his flesh. With a loud scream Jack awoke utterly terrified. He could still feel and smell the stench of the beast's hot sulfur breath. The pain was still there. He moved his hand to feel the torn flesh and then he realized it had been a bad dream. He was alright, the throbbing pain was slowly subsiding.

Jack crawled out of bed, he was so tired, it had seemed so real to him. Jack sat in his recliner pondering his dream. That beast, what could it be? He remembered a picture he had seen entitled, "Hell." *That's it, that's where I saw that beast before! It was from that picture!* Jack sat there thinking of the time he had seen that picture in an art gallery with his mother as a young boy. It also had some animals that looked like toads with human arms and legs. His mother had taken him there so he could be exposed to the "finer" things in life. She also took him to symphonies and even once to the opera.

His mother, his dear sweet mother... she was so beautiful and he loved her so. She was slim and very light-skinned, always wore her hair down passed her shoulders and was always clean and neat. Men would turn as she walked down the street. He was so proud to be with her. Even at the young age of eight, Jack knew how beautiful his mother was. People, both men and women, would say she should be a movie star.

Jack's father was very jealous and Jack woke up to their fighting many times. His mother frequently wore sunglasses to cover black eyes her husband gave her.

On Christmas Eve, Jack's father killed his mother. His father went to prison and Jack was shuffled from one foster parent to another. When he got older, Jack ended up in reform school where he stayed until the age of nineteen. Jack had taken a vow to kill his father, but someone else beat him to it while his father was in prison.

Jack sat there thinking about his mother and what she had wanted for him. He didn't even come close. *I guess that's why I don't think of her much anymore,* Jack thought.

Jack sat there and he felt himself fall asleep. He jerked his head up. He started to walk around, he didn't want to fall back to sleep. He was really afraid of that dream. Jack washed up, shaved, and put on clean clothes and headed down to the Horseshoe Restaurant. As he walked in, he caught Mary's eye, so he took a sharp left into the vacant dining room and sat at one of the many empty tables.

In a minute, Mary came in with a cup of coffee. She sat it down in front of Jack, looked around to make sure no one could see them, then leaned down and kissed him. "I miss you so much," she said.

"I miss you too, but for now we must be careful. Those cops have a one-track mind and that's framing me for the murder of Maria. They're too lazy to find the real killer, so they concentrate on me," Jack said.

"I know," Mary said, as she looked at Jack fondly. "You really look tired. What's wrong?"

"Oh, I had trouble sleeping last night" Jack said, "I had these bad dreams when I did sleep."

"Are you going to the street dance tonight?" Mary asked.

"Yes, I'll see you there?" Jack asked.

Mary smiled at Jack, "You bet."

Benson's street dance was actually a time when the whole town was out of their homes and on the street meeting people that lived in town or around the area. It gave people a chance to catch up and talk to people they hadn't seen for a while. It was like a big family reunion but much bigger. Oh, they had a dance going on in a small parking lot with a mariachi band with a few people dancing, but the whole downtown area was full of people standing around talking. Some had their drinks in their hand, and there were young kids running back and forth. Just a time for people to get out and mingle.

Mary and Jack stayed there talking for about thirty minutes, then Mary had to get back to her other customers. Jack finished his coffee and left.

Jack spent the rest of the day doing things around his house trying to stay awake and not think of the dream. That evening, he went to the street dance and listened to the mariachi band playing their Mexican music. Jack had brought a beer from home and was taking small sips and thinking of the last week's events. He had hired an attorney who had stopped the police from getting the blood sample they wanted.

Also, he was getting Maria's body released to the local funeral home here in Benson.

Mary walked up behind Jack and gave him a loving poke in the side. It startled him so much he jumped, swung around and almost punched Mary before he caught himself. The look on his face scared Mary, she muttered, "I'm sorry," and turned and started to walk away.

"I'm sorry," Jack said and grabbed her arm to turn her around. "You just startled me. My mind was miles away." He then smiled at her.

Chief Blight took all this in from a short distance. He was standing in a crowd and neither Jack nor Mary saw him. *This is why Mary's story of Jack knowing Maria was at the reservation was different from everyone else's,* thought Chief Blight. The rest of that evening Chief stayed in the shadows and kept an eye on Jack and Mary, who also kept out of sight as much as possible. He saw them kind of swaying together to the music, but not dancing. Later, they separated and each took a different car.

Chief decided to swing by Mary's house on his way home and see if Jack's car was there. At first, he didn't see it, but after a closer look he saw it parked back behind the house under a huge tree. "Bingo," he said, then drove home.

Jack and Mary stayed together at her house. Jack dismissed his dream as something from all the stress he had been through in the past week.

After falling asleep, Jack started dreaming. He was in the middle of the same meadow with the short grass and small white flowers. There was a light warm breeze and Jack was standing there watching the light fluffy clouds floating by. He felt great, no problems.

The clouds started to move faster... then turn gray. Then they turned a very dark gray, almost black. Lightening flashed. Jack looked for shelter. There was nothing. No place to get out of the storm. Then a loud boom and a bolt of lightening hit near him. The lightening was so bright it blurred his vision. Hail started hitting him with great force. The hail got bigger and when they hit him it shot such pain through him. He tried to run and cover his head with his arms, and then lightening hit him on the foot burning his foot and lower leg off. Jack fell and the hail was hitting him with such force, and with each thud he screamed with pain. But no sound came from his lips. The hail was beating him to a pulp. His skin was starting to look like hamburger. Jack tried to scream. No sound came out, and then a sound came, a loud scream.

"What's wrong with you, Jack?" Mary was screaming at him.

Jack was awake and screaming.

"Jack! Jack! What's wrong?" Mary kept repeating.

Jack finally came to his senses. He awoke, holding his foot. In a few minutes he realized it was just a dream and he stopped his screaming.

Mary was out of bed leaning over Jack, screaming, "What's wrong?"

"I'm sorry, it, it was a dream," Jack said.

Mary was almost crying. "Dream? I've been trying to wake you for fifteen minutes, Jack! What's going on?"

"I don't know. Last night and tonight I've had these terrible dreams," Jack answered. He then swung his legs around and put his feet on the floor and sat on the edge of the bed.

"Is there something you're not telling me?" Mary asked.

Mary knew she asked the wrong question. "I mean, are you feeling alright otherwise?"

Jack didn't answer. "I'd better get going." He got up and started putting on his clothes.

"Don't go. Stay with me a while," Mary whined.

"Better not," Jack uttered, and finished getting dressed.

"You used to not want to leave so soon," Mary fussed.

"Oh, for crying out loud," Jack scolded. "You know the police are trying to frame me."

"Just a little longer?" Mary asked in a seductive way.

Jack just got up, dressed, then drove home. When he got inside he made some coffee. He wanted to be wide-awake. He didn't want to fall asleep. The dreams were just too bad and to real. Jack drank cup after cup of coffee. He was getting sick from all the coffee. Jack got some bad stomach cramps and in a few minutes he was worshiping the porcelain God. After he upchucked three times, he sank back in his recliner.

Jack was dead tired, worn out physically and mentally. In a few minutes he was fast asleep again.

The dream started again. Jack was standing in the same green meadow with the white flowers. Jack knew this was going to be bad. He didn't know what would be happening, but it would be bad. He tried to find shelter, but there was no place to go. He ran in one direction, then another. Jack had no idea what was coming or where he could hide. Then he saw one black dot in the sky. Jack stood and stared in fear. The dot started getting bigger, and then he noticed three other black dots.

Jack watched as the biggest dot got bigger and started taking shape. It was the same beast as in his first dream. The other dots were the beast that looked like toads with human legs and arms. They had wings like bat wings that flapped slowly as they flew. Jack tried to run, then the first beast was on him with his talons in his back. They sank deep into his body. Jack tried to scream. The pain increased. Jack was lying on his stomach with this creature on him, his wings spread out with a fifty-foot wing span. With one flip of his leg, he flipped Jack up about ten feet into the air. He landed fifteen feet in front of the monster on his back. The fall knocked the wind out of him.

The smaller beasts were on him in seconds. They each were strong, and Jack could feel them pulling him apart. The pain was excruciating. Each beast was trying to pull off an arm or leg so they could eat it. The smaller beast had a toad-like mouth and didn't have the teeth to tear the flesh like the large beast did.

Jack could feel his left arm being pulled out of socket and the muscle tear from his shoulder. Just when he thought the pain couldn't get any worse, he felt a burning, searing pain in his right leg.

His eyes turned to his leg and one of the smaller beasts had driven a red-hot iron stake into his right leg. Jack could smell his own flesh burning. *Why don't I die? Why don't I die?* Jack thought. He tried and tried to scream, but couldn't get the sound out. Then it came through, his scream came, and he was awake.

His eyes were on his right leg and he could smell the burning flesh. He watched as his pant leg slithered out of the hole in his leg. He couldn't move his right arm. It was out of joint.

Jack screamed. "What's going on?" He still had so much pain in his shoulder and he had just seen the hole in his leg fill in.

It was supposed to be a dream. "My God, My God, what have I done?" Jack screamed. He still couldn't move his left arm. He had this racking pain in his left shoulder.

Jack checked the clock. He had been asleep for two hours. His shoulder was killing him. He couldn't sit still, he tried to get relief by holding his left arm with his right hand.

After trying to get relief for about an hour, he gave up. He got into his car and drove himself to the local hospital.

After hearing his story about a bad dream, that threw his shoulder out of joint, the doctor shrugged and had Jack lay on a gurney.

After taking some x-rays, the doctor gave a nurse some instructions that Jack didn't understand. In a minute she came back with a hypodermic and proceeded to give Jack an injection. "What is that for?" Jack asked before he let her proceed.

"It's to relax the muscle around the shoulder so the doctor can pull it back into place," she said.

Jack nodded and let her continue.

After the shot she said, "It might make you a little woozy."

This last statement upset Jack, but he was in too much pain to say much. Jack lay there and was almost asleep when a nurse came back and gave him another shot. In a few minutes, the doctor came in, pulled on his arm and it was back in place. This was a great relief to Jack.

In a short time Jack drifted off to sleep. He was standing back in the green meadow with the white flowers. Jack tried to run then suddenly one of the beasts that looked like a toad with human arms and legs was standing in his way. Jack turned and was running in the other direction. His steps slowed, he couldn't get going and then he saw the other two small beasts holding a woman between them.

The woman was standing up straight with both arms stretched out perpendicular to her body. She looked like a cross. Each beast was walking, holding onto each of the woman's wrists. They were stretching the woman's arms and making her walk with them.

The woman called to him, "Jack!" They got closer, "Jack! Why did you do this to me?" She asked.

"Who are you?" Jack asked.

"Don't you recognize me Jack?" The woman called back.

*It's Maria*, Jack thought, but didn't say a thing. All this went on while they were getting closer.

"Jack, you bad boy, you did this to me," she said.

Jack still couldn't see her face clear, but he could see she was twisting and turning, trying to get away.

"Why did you do this to me?!!" She screamed, "You did this to me! You're worse than your father!"

Jack could tell she was in pain from the beast pulling on her arms. Then he recognized her… It was his mother, his dear sweet mother. "Mama!" Jack screamed, and he tried to go to help her. Jack tried to run, but his legs wouldn't move. Then the beast behind him slammed a steel hook into his back. It was like a giant fishhook and it was held to the ground with a chain about eight feet long. Jack's legs were working alright now, but this steel hook in his back wouldn't let him go forward.

The beast brought his mother closer. She was screaming obscenities at Jack now.

"Mama, don't say that!" Jack said, and he was crying. He was crying, not because of the pain, but because his dear, sweet mother who never swore was swearing at him.

"Mama, I love you!"

The beasts started tearing the clothes off of Jack's mother. She was screaming because the beast was so rough with her. "Jack you did this! Why are you doing this?" She cried to Jack.

"I'm not doing that to you. These beasts from hell, they are doing that to you!" He screamed back to her.

But she paid no attention to what Jack said. The beasts had all her clothes off of her now. They were trying to get her to the ground, but neither would let go of her wrists.

The beast that was behind Jack hopped over to help the other beast.

Jack tried to go help his mother, but couldn't because of the hook imbedded deep into his back! The chain that was fastened to the hook with the stake in the ground wouldn't let him get any closer. The pain from the hook was all that he could bare, as he tried to pull loose.

The beast reached the other two in about three hops. He then grabbed the woman's ankles and the three yanked the woman up and off her feet like she was a blanket. All this time she was still cursing Jack.

The beast slammed her to the ground, which knocked the wind out of her and she was silent for a few seconds. They were holding her on her back like a cross.

In a minute she recovered and started accusing Jack again. Jack was crying and begging his mother to forgive him. "I'm sorry, Mama, I'm sorry!" he was saying.

Then Jack saw the black spot among the dark clouds moving across the sky. He knew it was the big beast. In a minute, the beast swooped down and landed on his mother's lower legs.

The small beast holding her ankles, barely got out of the way of the big beast. The big beast looked at Jack, growled at Jack then turned his attention to his mother.

Jack's mother was screaming. Jack felt sorry for his mother, but he was terrified of this beast.

The beast bit his mother in the stomach. She screamed. The beast tore the stomach open and pulled her intestines out.

Jack screamed. This beast was eating his mother. The beast looked at Jack with some of the intestines of his mother hanging from his mouth.

The beast smiled at Jack and then took another bite. He was devouring Jack's mother and she was screaming because of the pain.

The doctor was trying to get Jack awake, giving him four different shots to counteract the first two drugs, because he was screaming.

After about forty-five minutes, they manage to get Jack awake. Jack screamed a couple of times after he was awake, thinking the doctor and nurse were the beasts. He was embarrassed lying there with everyone around him. He knew he had made a spectacle of himself.

After this fiasco, the doctor had a talk with Jack. He recommended Jack see a psychiatrist, a friend of his, and gave him a card with the doctor's name, address, and phone number on it.


A little while after Jack had left Mary's house, Chief Blight was on her porch, knocking at her door.

Mary thinking Jack had returned, opened the door without looking first. "Jack!" Then she saw the chief and knew she had made a big mistake.

He opened the screen door and took a step forward. "May I come in? We need to talk."

After a short conversation, he convinced Mary to dress and follow him down to the police station for more questioning.

# Chapter 10

Sergeant Blackwood had a problem. There was going to be a funeral for one of the respected officers of the Socike tribe, Captain Yellowhair. There would be people from all over the nation. Socikes that didn't live on the reservation would be there and all the clans of the Socike nation would be represented. The reservation would be so crowded that he would need all the officers for traffic control and intervening in arguments that would get out of control.

Sergeant Blackwood was pondering what to do about the ongoing investigation of the missing Pupa, when a woman from the Women Council came into his office. "Can I help you?" he asked.

"Yes, Sergeant, Pupa requests your presence at our meeting this afternoon," she says.

Sergeant Blackwood jumped up out of his chair, "Pupa?"

"Yes, Sergeant, and may I remind you that you are talking to a representative of the Women Council. Please lower your voice," she said.

The reality came to him of the importance of this woman and quickly apologized, "I'm so sorry, I guess I got excited to hear that Pupa wanted to meet with me. We have an ongoing investigation to find Pupa. She has been missing for several days, now," he said.

"She's not missing. She has been on a mission. Please come to the meeting this afternoon and she will explain everything then," she said.

Afternoon to Socike, meant one o'clock if no other time was given. At one o'clock, Sergeant Blackwood was at the women's meeting hall. When he walked in, there she was standing, while the other women were sitting in a circle.

"Welcome, Sergeant Blackwood," Pupa said.

"Thank you, it's good to see you alive," Sergeant Blackwood said.

"I feel you have some questions for me. Why don't we go into the private council room," Pupa nodded toward a door that led to a small room.

Sergeant agreed and they walked to the smaller room. There was a table with six chairs. They both took a seat across from each other.

"You may ask me anything you wish," Pupa said.

"Thank you, Pupa," Sergeant said. "First, I'd like to know where you went after you left the hospital, and did you leave of your own accord?"

"I did leave of my own choosing. I was on a mission to undo a broken Socike law. It's no longer broken," Pupa answered.

"Would you like to expand on that?" Sergeant asked.

"Not at this time," Pupa said.

"Are you alright, Pupa?" Sergeant asked.

Pupa smiled, "I'm fine."

"Do you know what happened to your granddaughter?" Sergeant asked.

"Are you asking me if I know she was murdered?" Pupa asked.

"Yes."

"Yes, I do know that."

"Do you know who did it?"

"Yes, I do" Pupa said.

"Can you tell me what happened?" Sergeant asked.

Pupa went into detail about what had happened. It seemed although she was in a coma she could hear everything that was going on in the house and also what went on in the hospital.

Sergeant Blackwood sat there entranced with the story Pupa was telling him.

"When he pushed me and I fell, I couldn't move or speak, but I did hear everything that was said and went on. I know it was Jack O'Reily, Maria's husband, who murdered her. I was there," Pupa said.

Sergeant sat there, not saying anything for a minute. Then he got up and nodded his head. "I thank you for all the information. I greatly admire you for your courage. You do know we will need your cooperation to prosecute him?" Sergeant Blackwood said.

"I'll do whatever you need for me to do, so you can do your job, but don't be surprised if the spirits do it for you," Pupa said.

Sergeant didn't know what she meant, but he nodded. "I still don't know what you were doing or where you were, but I have no choice, but to drop it."

They both left the room. Pupa went back to her circle. Sergeant left to go back to his office.

Sergeant Blackwood called Chief Blight in Benson. A young lady answered the phone, "Benson Police."

"This is Sergeant Blackwood at the Socike reservation calling for Chief Blight."

"One moment."

Sergeant could hear the transfer.

"Chief Blight," the voice on the other end of the line said.

"This is Sergeant Blackwood. I talked to you the other day about Jack O'Reily."

"Yes, I remember, I was about to call you," Chief said.

"Well, you can pick up Jack O'Reily for the murder of his wife, Maria. I have an eyewitness," Sergeant said.

"You have a witness you say?" Chief came back with.

"Yes, Pupa, Maria's grandmother, she showed up with this amazing story of being there and hearing everything that went on." Sergeant conveyed all the details to the chief.

"Well, that certainly is interesting, but we won't need your witness, Jack O'Reily is in here right now confessing to the murder. In fact, we can't shut him up. He keeps telling everyone he did it. We have him in a cell and he's yelling to anyone who comes within earshot that he did it."

"His attorney just left and he couldn't shut him up," Chief said with a chuckle.

"Did you get a signed confession?" Sergeant asked.

"We've got two signed confessions. One he brought in of his own handwriting. One we took of his rambling, then had him sign it. I've never seen anything like this before," Chief Blight said.

Captain said his goodbyes to the Chief, then sat in his chair, contemplating the events of the day. This has been some day, he thought. Just then the phone rang. It was a representative of the chief of the Socike nation. He informed Sergeant that Captain Yazzie would be arriving today and he was taking Captain Yellowhair's place. *Another Yazzie in the force,* he thought.

That afternoon Captain Yazzie arrived. He walked in and Sergeant Blackwood's first impression was he was a very confident man. The two men hit it off and spent the afternoon getting Captain Yazzie informed on the O'Reily case. They also discussed the upcoming funeral of Captain Yellowhair.

The next morning Sergeant Blackwood introduced Captain Yazzie to the other men on the force.

Captain Yazzie got up and addressed the men. "Not all police stations do things the same way. Until I get to know you better and you get to know me better, keep doing things the same way you did under Sergeant Blackwood. In fact, Sergeant Blackwood is second in command and I want you to use the chain of command for all things.

"We're going to be quite busy in the next few days. Sergeant Blackwood has informed me that all of you are veterans of this type of celebration."

The Socike celebrated the death of anyone who achieved leadership as a police Sergeant or Captain. For a council member that died there would be a celebration. How high of status he has, determined the length of the celebration. Captain Yellowhair's celebration would last three days.

People had already started arriving on the reservation. The ones who came early usually stayed with relatives. The ones who came later were ones who usually had campers or stayed at motels near the reservation. Some stayed in their cars or pickups. Most drank a lot and all came to the releasing of the spirit.

It was on the third day of the celebration and the women of the Socike nation all dressed in their traditional dress, if they were women braves they dressed in their war garb. The leaders of the men dressed in their leadership dress, lots of fur and feathers.

The two days before, the men had built a traditional wood platform fifteen feet off the ground. There was a wooden ladder bound to the platform. Wood was then stacked underneath the platform in between each layer of wood, green pine tree branches with their needles still attached were laid. They stacked this clear to the bottom of the platform.

Early in the morning, before dawn the body of Captain Yellowhair was moved to the platform.

When the sun rose, any passerby could see a body wrapped in a white garment. In the old days, the young people of the tribe had to weave this garment from fibers of the witch plant. But, in these days they just used bed sheets.

At about seven in the morning everyone would gather around this platform that was traditionally out in the bareness of Skull Hill. This was a rock hill and in the late afternoon the wind always blew.

This morning the air was very still. Ten men leaders and one woman of the Women Council and one person who had no particular status in this clan took torches, lit them in the starter fire and a single drum started a steady beat. The twelve circled the platform, when the drum stopped they threw their torches on the stack of wood with the pine needles.

The pine needles were like gasoline and soon the whole pile of wood and platform were burning.

There was the sound of light drumming, beating a funeral march. The crowd started a kind of dance march in a clockwise circle around the fire. This went on until the flames got too hot and this made the circle spread out. After the circle spread out so far, the drummers stopped. The crowd stopped their dance and then people started drifting away. After a while, the only ones left were the direct blood relatives of the deceased. After the drums stopped no sound was uttered by the people. Until then some of the people would hum. This gave off a buzz from the crowd that sounded like a beehive. But, after the drums stopped the only sound was the crackling of the fire. This was the releasing of the spirit. When the people heard a sound like a crow call or bird sound of any kind, they assumed that it was the spirit of the deceased.

Afterwards the people would discuss whether a sound they heard first was the spirit of Captain Yellowhair, because some would hear a dove call, others heard a sparrow chirping, some heard a far off crow call. That morning most, but not all, heard a hawk scream. The ones that heard the hawk were convinced that it had to be Captain Yellowhair.

The rest of the day people gathered in small groups and discussed that morning. Some of the visitors started home in the early afternoon, others left later in the evening. And some waited until the next morning to leave.

By the following day everything on the reservation was back to normal.

# Chapter 11

Captain Yazzie was in his office when Sergeant Blackwood came in to discuss the O'Reily case.
"Captain?" Blackwood said.
Captain Yazzie nodded.
"I called the Flagstaff police to see if Jack O'Reily had been transferred there yet. They don't have him. Do you know anything about it?" He asked.
Captain Yazzie shook his head. "No, I haven't heard anything. I wonder why he hasn't been transferred there. That's where they will try him or, in this case, take his confession and sentence him. You'd better call Benson and see why he hasn't been shipped to Flagstaff," Captain said to Sergeant Blackwood.
"I'll get right on it." Sergeant Blackwood said.
Captain Yazzie was unpacking his office supplies and some keepsakes when Sergeant Blackwood came back in.
"I got in touch with Chief Blight of Benson. He said that Jack O'Reily is in Yaford hospital in Bisbee," Sergeant said.
"Yaford?" Captain asked. "He's trying to make everyone think he's crazy?"
"That's what I thought. So, I called the hospital and talked to Dr. Gonzales. He says that if he's faking it, it's the best act he has ever seen," Sergeant said.
"Why's that?" Captain asked.
"That's what I asked. He says that Jack is kept in a padded cell and

a straight jacket twenty-four hours a day. That's because he keeps trying to kill himself. According to him, he beats his head on anything to keep awake. He claims he has such bad dreams that he gets injuries from them. Three broken ribs, dislocated shoulder, dislocated knee, and three broken fingers," the Sergeant said.

"What do you think?" Captain asked.

"I think I'd like to see with my own eyes what he's doing. This doesn't make sense. If he's found to be insane and not competent to stand trial what has it gained him? After he gets treatment and the doctor declares him sane, he would go on trial for the murder then," Sergeant said.

Sergeant went on, "If he had waited until the trial, then the jurors may have found him not guilty by reason of insanity, unless he plans on after they so-call cure him, claiming he was insane at the time of the murder. That's it! He's faking it, so later he can claim he was insane at the time."

Captain Yazzie pulled his mouth down at the corners and tilted his head to the side and kind of shrugged. "You may be right," he said, "If you were there, do you think you could prove he's faking it?"

"I don't know. But if I don't try, we'll never know, will we?" Sergeant Blackwood said.

"Let me call the doctor down there and set up an appointment for you to go talk to him and see his patient." Captain Yazzie said. He picked up the phone and asked the desk officer to get him the phone number of Yaford hospital in Bisbee. As soon as he got it, the Captain made the call.

Captain looked up at Sergeant Blackwood, "He hasn't come in yet. He should return my call as soon as he comes in. Why don't you go home and pack. I'll call you at your house when I hear from him."

Sergeant nodded to Captain Yazzie and left.

About two hours later, Sergeant Blackwood got the call from the Captain.

"I was surprised, he had no objection to you watching or interrogating him. He said anything short of hitting him was fine. The doctor didn't seem to know what was wrong with O'Reily. I think it'd be to our advantage if you spent some time with him. Video all of your conversations, or at least record them with O'Reily, so later they can't come back and say he was tortured," Captain said.

"Will do," Sergeant came back. "It might take me a couple of days to crack him," Sergeant said.

"Take all the time you need, but keep me informed," Captain said, "If we let this guy get away with this, we'll all look like the Keystone Cops of Socike land."

This last statement put pressure on the Sergeant, but he didn't let it show in his voice, "I'm on it," he said.

"Take your time getting down there, he doesn't expect you until tomorrow afternoon, and take your time coming back, we don't want another accident like Captain Yellowhair," Captain Yazzie said.

"Will do. I'll call you tomorrow evening to let you know how the afternoon went." With that, the two men hung up.

Sergeant Blackwood was on his way. He wore civilian clothes, but drove a Socike police car and he was enjoying this part of the drive. The high grassland had kind of a blue green color to it this time of year and all the livestock on it were fat and healthy. *They will make some good steaks,* he was thinking when he noticed the sign, ten miles to Flagstaff.

As a young man he spent a lot of time in Flagstaff. There is a college there and he had really enjoyed the company of a young coed. In fact when he took some law enforcement classes, he wound up marrying one of the coeds.

The time went by fast as he drove right through Flagstaff and the steep hills between Flagstaff and Phoenix. Then came the desert. Sergeant Blackwood just didn't like the desert. It was never as it seemed. You could be out there and you'd swear there wasn't a living thing within miles of you, but then you'd spot a lizard there watching you, or a snake in the shade of a bush. At night, it came alive with all kinds of things. Though he was fascinated with every living thing, he always felt the desert was a deceptive thing. A lot like the crooks he had to deal with.

He didn't mind the drunks he'd pick up and usually take to their home, or traffic violators he dealt with on the reservation, but he also had the thieves and the domestic squabbles he had to take care of, too.

Thieves are deceptive because they don't want you to know what they are up to. Domestic violence is deceptive because someone who is supposed to love you is causing you harm of some kind. Sergeant Blackwood knew there was a lot of desert to drive through before he got to Bisbee and he wasn't looking forward to this long drive.

He tried to get his mind off the desert by turning on the radio. He got a western station and kept time with the music by tapping on the steering wheel.

Sergeant Blackwood saw the fast food signs ahead and decided to take a break from the driving. He had driven right through Phoenix and was almost to Tucson. It was time to get a place to stay for the rest of the day and that night, but now he needed a bathroom break and some food would be nice. He pulled off the highway and had to make a decision which fast food to go to.

In a minute he was in the same place that Jack O'Reily had stopped for a food break on his way back to Benson after he killed Maria. Sergeant Blackwood had no way of knowing that, but as he sat there eating he felt the hairs stand up on the back of his neck. He instinctively put a hand to the back of his neck and wondered what made him feel this way.

After the food break, he stopped at the same motel that Captain Yellowhair stopped at the night before he went to Benson.

Sergeant Blackwood had recognized the name of the motel. He had talked to Captain Yellowhair when Yellowhair was staying here when he came down to Benson on the investigation of Maria's murder. He remembered the name and was even wondering if he was staying in the same room. He thought of checking with the front desk to see which room Captain stayed in. *That's silly*, he thought and went on to his room.

Sergeant got a good night's sleep. He even slept in, which was very unusual for him. He did get up and dressed in time to have the complimentary breakfast. As he sat in the dining room, he revisited the events of the last few days. Pupa's disappearance, Captain Yellowhair's death, then out of the blue, Pupa's reappearance. *What did she mean by, "Don't be surprised if the spirits do it for you," pertaining to doing my job.* Did she know that Jack would confess to the murder of her granddaughter, Maria? Or did she mean the spirits would punish him instead of the law? This was a great mystery for Sergeant Blackwood.

Then his mind wondered to Captain Yazzie coming to head the

police department just in time to help him with everything. Even making this trip possible.

He had been sitting at his table for about thirty minutes now, and he noticed that he was not conducting himself as he was trained as a policeman. He thought if someone were to ask him who else was in the room eating, he wouldn't be able to tell him. Sergeant Blackwood took a fast glance around the room now thinking like a policeman. He noticed there was one single woman about thirty years old, eating by herself. She had a white shirt and blue jeans, no glasses on. At the far end of the diner was a couple in their sixties, he guessed. Both of them wore glasses and she dyed her hair that gray color. She had a white shirt and blue shorts on. He wore khaki shorts and a blue shirt. No one else was there at this time.

*Now I'm back in officer mode,* he thought. But in a minute his mind drifted back to the events of the past few days. He was one of the people who had heard the hawk scream at Captain Yellowhair's funeral though he hadn't told anyone else he heard it.

As a child, his own mother and grandmother had taught him the ways of his people. But as a young man in college he rejected most of their beliefs. As he got older and started seeing things that happened on the reservation, he started to wonder about some of the old beliefs. He had seen things that had no rational explanation. Sergeant Blackwood was wondering if Yellowhair's spirit really went into that bird.

*Oh, snap out of this,* he thought and finished his coffee, and then went upstairs to get his things and check out.

The sun was well up and the highway skirted the west side of Tucson then it took almost a ninety-degree bend to the east and skirted the south side of Tucson. In a few minutes, he was driving east with the sun in his eyes. Sergeant flipped down his sun visor to block the glare and turned on the air conditioner because the car was starting to get warm.

To his right were some high power lines stretching across the desert and, behind them, the mountains. In a few minutes, the power lines would make a turn and go right across the highway. Some people called the power lines an eyesore, but he thought they fit right in with the desert. They looked innocent enough, but they were carrying thousands of volts of electricity that would kill you in a minute if it could.

After he passed under the power lines he saw a sign advertising a cave, then the road started a gradual climb. In a minute he was passing the Eka trees.

Eka was the name the Socike had for the small twisted cedar trees that grew in the rocks. The word 'Eka,' meant determined. This tree grows where nothing else can grow. They seem to grow right out of the rocks. What actually happens is a seed finds its way in a small crack where a small amount of dirt has accumulated and when the rain comes, it germinates. Somehow that small seed becomes a tree, and after many years it's impossible to dig it out of the rocks.

Sergeant Blackwood knew the elevation was higher here because these trees didn't grow on the lower desert floor.

In a minute, he passed a hill and in a small valley between two hills there was saguaro growing, the huge cactus that grows in some parts of the desert of Arizona. You see pictures of them in every souvenir store in Arizona, New Mexico, and Southern California. He was surprised to see them because they only grew where the temperature didn't get too cold or to hot. That meant that this small valley had controlled temperature. The Indians knew if they were out there, they could live in a place where the Saguaro grew. In fact, the land where Saguaro grows is called blessed by the Socike. They can get food from the fruit and a man could stay in the shade of one if he needed to. This stately cactus can grow to sixty feet tall, but a twenty-foot cactus is considered very large. Sergeant Blackwood admired this cactus because, by the time they are noticed they are very old. These slow-growing cactus grow larger than any other.

He'd had always thought of police work kind of like that. You go around gathering the evidence putting it together slowly, bringing the perpetrators to court and then justice, a slow growing process.

The highway was still climbing and in a few minutes he was driving through grassland with Yucca dotting the landscape. He knew in a minute he was going to have to make a decision to go south through Sierra Visa or go straight going through Benson then south through St. David and Tombstone and then Bisbee.

Sergeant Blackwood noticed a sign that read, 'Eelevation Four Thousand Feet.' Then came the sign, 'Sierra Visa, Ft. Huachuca turn off,' and he decided to go that route. After the elevation sign, the highway started a gradual decline, then the turn off and the road started a climb again.

Shortly after this there were signs advertising another cave. Right after, this road started a long decline. He could see a high valley to his left. Sergeant Blackwood wondered if the far distant mountains were in Mexico or the United States. He knew they were close to the border.

This was a long stretch of grassland with ocotillo covering the countryside. At the bottom of the decline in the road, the ocotillo stopped and there was Huachuca City then a steep hill to upper Huachuca City. About five more miles down the road was the city of Sierra Visa and Fort Huachuca.

The state had built a bypass road around the city so he took it. Another hour and there was Bisbee that old mining town built right on the side of a mountain. In its early days it had been a wild place to live and many a miner lost his life trying to hang onto his mining claim or in a barroom fight. As he drove through the downtown of Bisbee the old brothels and some of the old saloons were turned into tourist traps now. He passed a street sign, 'Brewery Gulch,' a narrow street that was notorious for brewing beer and its bars. The old police station wasn't a block away, then he was out of the main business part of Bisbee and passing one of the biggest man made holes in the ground he had ever seen. He couldn't see the bottom of this open pit mine as the road curved around the north and east side of this old mine.

Then there it was, Yaford. That big gray building on top of a hill, it gave Sergeant Blackwood chills as he drove towards it.

He saw a small hamburger and hotdog stand with tables and chairs outside on the right of the road. He thought he'd better get something to eat before he went to the asylum.

Pulling into the small, dirt parking lot he got out to stretch. It felt good to get out of his car and walk around. Sergeant Blackwood got a hamburger and sat at one of the tables and enjoyed the warm sun.

The sky was as blue as any sky he had ever seen. Then he saw a hawk circling overhead and thought of the funeral of Captain Yellowhair when he heard the screech of a hawk. Seeing this hawk circle overhead was a good omen for Sergeant Blackwood.

He sat there enjoying his lunch and studying that overpowering gray building of Yaford. *I don't know who designed or built it, but it looks spooky to me*, he thought.

The building was perched on the side of a mountain with the peak of the roof about twenty feet below the top. It was constructed of gray cut stone with gargoyles on each corner and above each side of the front door and one gargoyle above the back door.

The building was constructed in the eighteen hundreds for Dr. Yaford, a rich doctor during the heyday of Bisbee. He chose Bisbee because there was no law there to stop his unorthodox practice. It was so close to Mexico that when he ran out of patients he would recruit men to get them from Mexico, whether they needed a doctor or not and whether they wanted to come or not.

The doctor did a lot of experiments and lost a lot of patients. He then went into psychiatry and the experiments really started up.

It was Dr. Yaford's son, Dr. Yaford, the second, who treated Red, Pupa's brother. But Sergeant Blackwood knew nothing of Pupa's brother. He just had a little knowledge of the history of Yaford.

It stands on that hill, looking like some evil haunting castle out of a Dracula movie. Many people in Bisbee believe it still has the ghost of its patients and staff walking the halls, not to mention people swearing they have seen the ghost of Dr. Yaford standing at the window looking out.

Sergeant Blackwood looked at his watch. It was after one o'clock. *Well, I was supposed to get here in the afternoon. I guess I'd better get over there*, he thought.

Sergeant Blackwood drove up the mountain to the hospital parking lot. There weren't a lot of automobiles there. But he did notice a shiny red Mercedes convertible. *Must be one of the doctor's cars*, he thought.

The place gave him the willies as he started up the front steps. He heard a hawk screech. That made the hair on his neck stand straight up! Sergeant Blackwood looked up and there sat a red-tail hawk on top of the building, looking down.

*Could that be Captain Yellowhair?* He wondered. Sergeant took two steps backwards so he could get a better look. Out of a whim he saluted the bird and it flew off.

Sergeant Blackwood continued up the steps, feeling better about going in after seeing the bird.

After going through the front door he walked over to a desk where a middle age woman was seated behind it, doing paper work. "I'm

Sergeant Blackwood from the Socike Police," he announced.

The woman looked up from her work. "Yes, Dr. Gonzales is expecting you," she said. "He's the third door on the right." She pointed down a hall, then went back to her work.

"Thank you," he said. *Not very talkative*, he thought as he walked towards the open third door on the right where a heavyset man sat.

"Dr. Gonzales?" Sergeant asked.

"Yes," he answered.

"I'm Sergeant Blackwood."

"Yes, yes, come in. Please have a seat," the doctor said. "I'm Dr. Gonzales." The two men shook hands and exchanged pleasantries for about five minutes. "You're here to study Jack O'Reily?"

"I'd like to talk to him," Sergeant Blackwood said.

"Right now he's sleeping. He should wake up shortly. He never sleeps over forty-five minutes to an hour," Doctor Gonzales said.

"How long has he been asleep?" Sergeant asked.

"Actually, I was informed that he fell asleep at one fifteen. It's one thirty-three now, so, eighteen minutes. I have him monitored twenty-four hours a day now. Would you like to see him sleeping? It's quite interesting."

"Interesting, him sleeping?" Sergeant asked.

"Yes, I'll show you." With this, Dr. Gonzales got up and headed for the door.

Sergeant followed him down the hall and up one flight of stairs, they then entered a dimly lit room with a woman in a nursing uniform sitting at a small table with a light on the table. She had a journal and was taking notes. The doctor introduced her to Sergeant Blackwood. The room itself had a rail in the center, boxing off a square about ten feet by ten feet with two rows of bleacher benches around the rail. In the center of the rail was a glass ceiling on the room below. It was a teaching room for medical students. It was put in so students could observe operations performed in the room below.

However, the room below was now converted to a padded room and there was a man in a straight jacket strapped to the floor on his back, his arms and legs stretched out in spread-eagle fashion. He was twisting and turning.

The doctor handed Sergeant Blackwood some low powered binoculars and said, "Look at his face."

Sergeant Blackwood put the binoculars to his eyes and then jerked back and took them from his eyes.

"Something, isn't it?" The doctor asked.

"What's going on?" Sergeant asked.

"We don't know," Dr. Gonzales answered. "We are going on the hypothesis that it's all in the dreams he is having."

"Does he look like that when he's not asleep?" Sergeant asked.

"No, only after he's been asleep from five to twenty-five minutes. The longer he stays asleep the worse it gets."

Sergeant gingerly put the binoculars to his eyes again. It looked like bugs were moving under his skin on his face. Actually, it was facial muscles going into cramps and knotting up. You could tell that the pain was extremely intense. This seemed to be going on inside his mouth also. His mouth was open and his tongue protruded out and took a sharp bend to the left.

It was all that Sergeant Blackwood could take. He brought down the binoculars and it took all the courage he could muster not to leave the room. He stood there in a cold sweat.

No one said a word. In a minute, Sergeant brought up the binoculars again. He noticed his tongue was outstretched like before, but bent to the right. Then all at once he made a lunge up, stretching the straps that secured him to the floor and let out an awful screech. His eyes popped open and then he fell back flat on the floor. Sergeant almost dropped the binoculars.

The woman who had been taking notes looked at her watch and wrote down the time. She then picked up a radio, "He's awake."

Sergeant looked at Jack's face through the binoculars, it's normal now except he was crying and mumbling.

Sergeant handed the binoculars back to doctor Gonzales. "Wow, that's amazing."

"Isn't it? We've had over thirty visiting doctors and nurses, just to witness him sleeping." The doctor said, "About a third leave the room after the first look, only about half come back for a second look."

"I know how they feel," Sergeant said.

In a minute, two orderlies came in and unstrapped Jack, then strapped his arms around him in typical straightjacket style. Jack lunged for the wall with his head down, and hit the wall with his head and bounced back. The orderlies were on him and put shackles on his ankles so he couldn't run.

"He was trying to break his neck." Dr. Gonzales said, "I thought he'd quit that."

"Good thing the walls are padded," Sergeant said, "How does he do that thing with his face?"

"I have no idea. I've never seen anything like it. Neither has anyone else that's come to see him. You see a lot of drunks and homeless people in your line of work, don't you?" the doctor asked.

"Yes, I've seen a lot on the reservation." Sergeant Blackwood answered.

"Have you seen anything slightly resembling that?" Doctor asked.

"No, can't say that I have. I know Jack drank a lot from studying his rap sheet. I've never seen anyone or heard of any cases of alcohol doing this to anyone," Sergeant said.

"You're starting to believe that he is insane, aren't you?" Doctor Gonzales asked.

"After seeing what I saw I've got an open mind to that now. I'd still like to talk to him," Sergeant Blackwood said.

"You will, just as soon as he calms down, that'll take about an hour. Then I'll talk to him about the dream he just had, which will last thirty minutes to an hour, depending on how Jack cooperates. He doesn't like to talk about it, but I make him. You can watch and listen if you like," the doctor said.

"That's why I made the trip, to observe and talk to him. So I appreciate you letting me do that." Sergeant Blackwood said.

"I've got other patients to see. If you wish, you can stay here and observe him for an hour or you can go and come back in an hour. Whatever you want," Doctor Gonzales said.

"I'd like to stay right here if you don't mind." Sergeant said.

"That'll be just fine, when you see the orderlies come and get Jack in about an hour, come on down to my office. We'll wait until you get there before we start."

Sergeant thanked the doctor and settled down to watch Jack. The lady taking notes, who the doctor had introduced as Jane Weiman, sat only about four feet away from Sergeant Blackwood. She turned to him, "Sergeant Blackwood, I'm going to have a cup of coffee brought up for me, would you care for a cup? Or maybe you'd like tea?" She asked.

"Coffee would be great," Sergeant said.

"Good, they bring up cream and sugar with the coffee." She then picked up her radio, pressed a button, and asked for two cups of coffee. "This is the only time I get to order from the kitchen and have it delivered. They don't want me to leave Jack. If I take a bathroom break I have to call for someone to take my place until I'm back. Otherwise, I'm here watching Jack there," she nodded toward the glass.

"Can he hear us talking?" Sergeant asked.

"Not unless you scream at him and then you can barely hear down there."

"How long is your watch?" Sergeant asked.

"Two hours on, two hours off. Four hours during an eight-hour day. Doctor Gonzales doesn't want us to get too bored and miss something." She said.

"When did you start watching him?" He asked.

"You mean today?" She asked.

"No, I'm sorry, after he arrived?"

"Oh, I've watched him from the first day. It's boring, most of the time, but he's different from any of the other patients," she said.

"How so?"

"All the other patients you have to watch out that they don't hurt you. You know, we house some of the worst criminally insane people in the western states here. But, oh Jacko here, you just have to make sure he doesn't kill himself," she explained.

"Jacko?" Sergeant asks.

"That's the name the nurses have for him. Jacko instead of Jack," she said.

"How many patients do you have in the facility?" Sergeant asked.

"A little over three hundred now," she said. "There's been more, there's been less."

"Three hundred, I didn't have any idea you had that many here," Sergeant said.

"Oh, yes, we've got the whackos," she said.

Strange choice of words for a nurse he thought, but didn't say so.

In a few minutes their coffee came. They both sipped their coffee and watched Jacko, as she called him.

Jack didn't really do much, he sat on the floor up against the wall, his head would jerk up against the wall once in a while. He'd shake his head. Then he'd work himself up on his feet and hobble around. That's all he could do in the straight jacket and his feet shackled with straps.

"Why are you taking notes of Jack's action and why's he on twenty-four hour watch?" Sergeant Blackwood asked.

"Jacko, here, is a study. I'm here for a project to help me get my Doctorate," Jane said.

"Oh, soon I'll have to call you Dr. Weisman," Sergeant Blackwood said, "I'm impressed. Your accent, where are you from?" Sergeant asked.

"New York City, I've been a mental patient nurse there for ten years and decided to go for my doctorate," she said.

"When did you come to Bisbee?" Sergeant asked.

"A nurse friend of mine who works here, called me when Dr. Gonzales arrived. When I heard, I caught a plane right out." She answered, "You know he's the most famous psychiatrist in Mexico. He came here a year ago and his methods are a little different than what they do here in the states, at least in most of the hospitals here in the U.S. I wanted the experience with him, also, so when I go into practice I'll have studied with one of the most famous doctors in the world."

"He's that famous?"

She nodded her head, "Yes."

"Why does Jack keep jerking his head?" Sergeant asks.

"He's trying to stay awake. When he goes to sleep he has such bad dreams that he doesn't want to go back to sleep." She answered.

"He always dreams?" he asked.

"Always."

Just then two orderlies came in and got Jack.

"I guess that's my cue to go down to Dr. Gonzales's office," Sergeant said.

Jane nodded and Sergeant got up and headed down to Dr. Gonzales's office.

Dr. Gonzales's office door was open and Sergeant Blackwood walked in. Dr. Gonzales got up from his chair behind his desk and walked around to the front of the desk where Jack was sitting in a chair facing him, "Jack, this is Sergeant Blackwood from the Socike reservation," Dr. Gonzales said.

Jack looked at the Sergeant, "I did it, you know. I killed Maria and her grandmother. I hit her so hard it broke her neck."

"Jack!" Doctor Gonzales interrupted. "We've told you many times that Maria's grandmother isn't dead. She was in a coma, but she's all right now. You didn't kill her."

"Liar! She's dead and she's the one sending these demons when I sleep!" Jack snapped back.

Dr. Gonzales turned to Sergeant Blackwood, "Have a seat."

Sergeant sat in the chair next to Jack.

Jack gave him a look, "Are you here to arrest me?" he asked with a hopeful tone in his voice.

"He's here to talk with you, Jack, after we finish our talk," Dr. Gonzales said.

"Can I have this thing off while we talk?" Jack asked.

"I'm sorry, Jack, but you know we've taken that restraint off you eight times and eight times you've tried to kill yourself," Dr. Gonzales said. They were talking about his straight jacket and shackles Jack had on.

Jack sighed and settled back for his usual talks with Dr. Gonzales. After about an hour Dr. Gonzales asked Sergeant if he wanted to talk with him now.

"Yes, I would," Sergeant answered.

Jack spoke up, "I need to go to the bathroom."

Dr. Gonzales called for the orderlies to come in and take Jack to the bathroom. Two very muscular men entered the room and helped Jack to his feet, then took him out of the room.

"Jack doesn't give them a hard time, in fact, he doesn't give anyone a hard time. He just wants to get rid of his dreams," Dr. Gonzales said to Sergeant Blackwood.

"What makes him dream?" Sergeant asked.

" If I knew that, I'd be world famous," the doctor said.

"I understand you are, world famous," Sergeant said.

"I am known," the doctor admitted, "But, world famous, I don't think so."

"Do you think you can cure him of his illness so he can pay for his crime?" Sergeant asked.

"I don't know," Dr. Gonzales said looking at Sergeant Blackwood intensely. "But don't you think he is paying more now, than anything you and the law could do?"

"If he's not putting on an act, I'd say he is," Sergeant replied.

"I've seen a few phonies in this business," Dr. Gonzales said. "I'd bet my reputation that this is not an act. My God, man, he's woken up with broken bones. Besides that, if I found him insane and later found him sane, you would still try him."

"But if they found him insane at the time of the murder he could get off," Sergeant said.

"Yes, that is true, but he has told me he hadn't started with the dreams until a few days after the killing," Dr. Gonzales said.

"You would say, he wasn't insane at the time of the killing, but maybe he is now?" Sergeant asked.

"From my talks with him, I'd say, if anything, the killing gave him the dreams not the other way around," the doctor said. "If anything, he's gotten worse since he's been here. His dreams are more intense and he can't function with his preoccupation of the dreams. You'll be able to talk to him as soon as he comes back," the doctor said.

The two orderlies came back with Jack and sat him in a seat. Doctor Gonzales nodded to Sergeant Blackwood.

"Jack, I want to talk to you about Maria, your wife," Sergeant started.

Jack looked straight at him and interrupted, "I killed her, and her grandmother."

"Jack you can have a lawyer present, if you like," Sergeant Blackwood said.

"Don't want no damn lawyer," Jack said.

"Okay, do you mind if I record this?" Sergeant asked.

"Record anything you want," Jack said and then turned his head away.

Sergeant pulled out a small tape recorder from his shirt pocket and started it. "This is Sergeant Blackwood with the Socike Indian police. I am at Yaford hospital in Bisbee Arizona with Dr. Gonzales and Jack O'Reily. This is an interview with Jack O'Reily." Then he gave the time and date. He sat the recorder down on the edge of Dr. Gonzales' desk.

"Jack, did you kill your wife, Maria?" Sergeant Blackwood asked.

Jack turned, and looked straight at Sergeant Blackwood. "I told you I killed Maria and her grandmother."

"How did you kill Maria?" Sergeant asked.

"I was fighting with her and I choked her until she quit breathing. I wanted some plastic to wrap over her nose and mouth to make sure she didn't come to, you know. But I couldn't find any, so I just made sure she wasn't breathing," Jack said matter-of-factly. He had repeated this story many times.

"I accidentally killed her grandmother before I killed Maria. She was going to the police and I yanked on her shirt so hard she fell and hit her head," Jack said, staring down at his feet now. "She's the one who turned these dreams loose on me. She's a witch you know or was a witch. She's deader than hell now." Jack said as he turned his head to look at the Sergeant.

"What do you mean, she turned the dreams loose on you?" Sergeant asked.

"When she died she got Satan to turn loose this evil beast on me. She is one of his disciples now. She was a witch when she was alive, but now she must really have powers from Satan," Jack said.

"Jack, why are you confessing to Maria's murder?" Sergeant asked.

"I thought if I confessed my sins, God would make Satan take away these dreams," Jack said.

"You think Maria's grandmother caused these dreams because you killed her?" Sergeant asked.

"Yes," Jack answered.

"What if I told you that Maria's grandmother isn't dead, that you only killed Maria, not her grandmother?"

"Chief Blight and Dr. Gonzales told me she was still alive, now you, what are you trying to pull?" Jack asked. "I was there, she was dead. She wasn't breathing, her heart wasn't beating, she's dead. So don't try whatever you're trying. I know she's dead." With that Jack turned his head away.

Sergeant Blackwood and Dr. Gonzales looked at each other both with a puzzled look and both men kind of shrugged.

"Jack," Sergeant Blackwood said.

Jack turned towards him.

"Jack, Pupa, Maria's grandmother, was in a coma after she hit her head. Her heart was beating very weakly. We thought she was dead, also. But, Rigor Mortis had not set in. But, with Maria, Rigor mortis had set in. Maria was dead, but Pupa was not, Sergeant Blackwood said, "It's that simple. I'm not saying she won't die from what you did, but she's not dead now."

Jack stared at Sergeant Blackwood. "I think you are lying," he said in a faint, weak voice. "She's set her demons loose on me and they won't quit until you execute me and I pay for my sin."

Sergeant Blackwood was finished with his questioning. The three men sat in the office, no one saying anything. In a minute Jack nodded off to sleep.

"There he goes again," Dr. Gonzales said. He called in the two orderlies that were in earlier. They immediately grabbed Jack and half carried, half dragged him to his padded cell to strap him down.

"He'll start dreaming in a minute." Dr. Gonzales said. Do you want to observe? Sergeant nodded his head, yes. The two men made their way back to the observation room where they had been earlier. Jane was still there, taking notes. Her relief was there also getting ready to start her two hour turn.

In a few minutes, Jack began to squirm and pull against the restraints.

"He's starting to dream," Dr. Gonzales said.

Jane and Sergeant Blackwood both acknowledged the doctor's remark.

In a minute Jack's face was so distorted from the strain that he was no longer recognizable as a man. In fact his face looked to Sergeant Blackwood more like a flat face bulldog than a human. This was something that most people couldn't imagine in their worst nightmare. To Sergeant Blackwood it was upsetting. To Dr. Gonzales and Jane it was intriguing. This was their work after all. They believed this was a once in a lifetime study.

Jack slept for about one hour and all this time he was straining and moaning, he finally woke with a bloodcurdling scream. The sweat poured from his pores.

"Interesting," Dr. Gonzales said, "You know Sergeant Blackwood, one time he actually sweat blood after his dream. Every time he drops off to sleep, he dreams. It's amazing."

Jane agreed with Dr. Gonzales. She had decided to take on another two hour shift and let her relief off for now.

Sergeant Blackwood was actually feeling sick from seeing Jack's torment, "Well, this is why I made the trip here and I thank you, Dr. Gonzales, for all your cooperation," Sergeant said.

"My pleasure," Dr. Gonzales answered back.

"Nice to meet you, Jane," Sergeant said to Jane.

"Nice to meet you," She answered back with a smile.

With this, Sergeant Blackwood headed back to the reservation to give his report to his new captain.

# Chapter 12

Bob Atkee, Jack O'Reily's landlord just found out where Jack was and that Maria was dead. Jack was behind in his rent and Bob knew he would not be getting any more rent now.

Bob hired Old Roster and his two boys to pack Jack's things away, and clean up the house so he could rent it again.

"Now you boys be careful with that stuff. Mr. Atkee hired us to do a good job. All the small stuff needs to be packed in these boxes," Roster said to his boy. They had just entered the house where Jack and Maria had lived for the past three years. "The large stuff we'll just store as it is."

"What is old man Atkee going to do with all this stuff, Pa?" The older boy asked.

"You call Mr. Atkee, 'Mr. Atkee,' boy. I don't want you being disrespectful to him. He's being nice, giving us this job," Roster said. "Now get busy and pack these boxes and tote them out to the truck when they're full. All the trash you put in that barrel over there." He pointed to a plastic barrel that Mr. Atkee had brought over earlier.

The two boys got busy picking up the small stuff and Old Roster went around looking for money that might be hidden and anything else he thought he'd get away with helping himself to.

After a short time the older boy asked his father again, "What do you think Mr. Atkee is going to do with this stuff?"

"He has to store it for three months, then he'll probably sell it. Why do you ask?" Roster said.

"No reason. I just wanted to know," the older boy answered.

The boys worked hard and Roster supervised. Soon they had everything in the truck except the bed and what Roster helped himself to, which they put in the cab. The two boys picked up the mattress and carried it out to the truck. Then they came back for the box springs, "Hey, Pa, what's this?" the younger boy asked.

Roster got up and went over to the box springs. There was a black hoop with feathers attached and a web inside the hoop. "Why, that's a dream catcher," Roster said. "Ugly one," He picked it up, "Maria was Indian, I suppose some superstition she had, maybe I can sell it… No, it's broken, see here? That web is broken, right next to the center." Roster put his finger on the two cut strings. "Nobody will give anything for a broken dream catcher. Might as well stick it with the rest of that stuff to go in storage.

After they finished unloading Jack O'Reily's furniture and the box of small things into the rented storage space, Bob Atkee dropped by to pay them. He looked at the box of stuff and the black dream catcher on top. "Funny things these renters keep," he said, and closed the overhead door.

# Chapter 13

Pupa was sitting in her home thinking of the loss of her granddaughter. It was weighing heavily on her mind. She had talked to the Women Council about reinstating her granddaughter back into the clan as a member, because she had intended to divorce her husband before he killed her. She put up a good argument for it, but was unable to get the three fourths vote she needed for reinstatement to take it to the Men Council for approval.

People on the reservation were all back to their own problems now, and as far as Pupa could tell she was the only person who was concerned about Maria's spirit. Pupa didn't want her granddaughter's spirit to roam the land, not knowing how to find her ancestors.

It is the long-held belief of the Socikes, that if a body was not burned and then their ashes left on the land, their spirit would wonder forever, trying to find their ancestors. Some believed that their bodies would have to be burned on the reservation with the big fire to signal to their ancestors that a person had died, or the ancestors would not look for them, even if their bodies were cremated at a funeral home and their ashes were left on the reservation it would do them no good without the big fire to signal the ancestors. Pupa didn't know what she believed on this subject, because there was a good argument on both sides of these beliefs. She was taught as a child as all Socike children were, that when one of the tribal members died, at their funeral their ancestors would come and help them into the new world and help them to pick out an animal or bird so they could travel in the human world in the body of that animal or bird. In the later years it became a popular belief that all who died would take on a body of a bird. The idea that they may take over a body of an animal instead of a bird was mostly scoffed at, because who would want to be an animal when they could be a bird and fly. Pupa remembered that when she was a child her grandmother told her that the spirits could come and go into different animals and birds as they saw fit. But she emphasized that the ancestors that went on before them would come and help them with the spirit world. This weighed heavy on Pupa as she sat and pondered all of this.

It had been several weeks since Pupa had talked to Sergeant Blackwood. She was satisfied with the punishment that Jack O'Reily was going through and she had received her granddaughter's ashes from the Benson funeral home. But, she was at a dead end as to what to do with the remains. On one hand, she could place the ashes anywhere on the reservation and hope her ancestors would find her. There was no law against that. But there was no way that she could have a large bonfire to signal her ancestors like they did at the funerals. This would be against the law, and even if it wasn't, she could never pile the wood that high by herself. She could never get the men to help her without the consent of the chief. She pondered about asking for a meeting with the men's Chief, but knew she would be turned down without going through the Men Council. She had talked informally to some of them about her granddaughter's ashes, and in their opinion, they thought that Maria would be alright if Pupa just left her on the land. One even suggested placing her ashes still in the cardboard box on Skull Hill so when they burned another body that the ancestors would find both spirits. But, this was not good enough for Pupa, without knowing for sure that Maria's ancestors would find her.

It was way past Pupa's bedtime by now, but she wasn't sleepy. Reaching way back in her kitchen cabinet Pupa pulled out a tin canister about the size of a fruit jar. Prying off the lid, she reached in and pulled some dried leaves out and crumbled them into a small pan, added some water and put it on the stove to simmer. After simmering for about fifteen minutes Pupa took the pan off the burning burner and placed it on a burner that wasn't lit. There she poured in some cool water to cool down the concoction. After she had it just the right temperature, she poured herself a cup and went into the living room and sat on the sofa to enjoy her drink. "I know the white man calls it a sin, but it takes the edge off of the hurt, and it makes me sleep," she said, as she lifted her cup as to make a toast.

After she finished her drink, she went to her bedroom to get ready for bed. Looking around her bedroom, it seemed strange because there was no dream catcher anywhere to be seen. She had always had a dream catcher in her room, usually two or three as long as she could remember. After Maria's death, she removed all dream catchers in case Maria tried to come to her in a dream, but with no results. Pupa wasn't afraid that Maria's spirit would get caught in one of her dream catchers, but she was afraid that they might scare her and she wouldn't come to her Nana in her dream. Pupa sat on her bed and removed her shoes. Starting to get up she felt a little faint and sat back down. She lay down on her back with her knees bent and feet still on the floor, to rest a minute.

In a few minutes, she heard someone in her room and sat up straight to see a figure standing about five feet from her. The light was dim so she couldn't make out the face. "Nana?" a voice said.

"Maria? Is that you?" Nana asked.

"Yes, it is me, I'm scared, Nana!"

"Don't be afraid, Maria, I'll help you." Nana said.

"I can't help it, it's so dark and I'm so alone." Maria said. With that said, she turned and started walking away.

"Wait!" Nana yelled, got up and started after her.

Maria went out the front door and Nana followed her.

"Wait, Maria, please wait." Nana cried and tried to catch up with her.

Maria kept walking as if she didn't hear Nana and by now she was across the street and disappearing around the corner of a house.

Nana was running as fast as she could at her age, trying to catch up to Maria. She rounded the corner of the house where Maria had disappeared. "Maria, Maria," she frantically yelled, looking all around to find her. Just then, a huge dog lunged at Nana's throat and bit down hard. She struggled to stay on her feet, but the dog was too strong and forced her to the ground. Nana was on her back with the dog on top of her with a strangle hold on her throat. She had her hands on both sides of the dog's face, trying to work her two index fingers in his eyes trying to make him let go. She couldn't get her breath and was starting to pass out. Nana gave one last effort to push the dog off when she woke up in her bed breathing heavily. "Oh God," she said.

Pupa sat up on the edge of her bed, still breathing heavily. She was still dressed, except for her shoes that she had taken off before she laid down. Getting up, she walked into the kitchen where the clock was to see how long she had been asleep. She figured it had been about two hours. It had all seemed so real. *What did it mean?* she wondered. Wandering back to the bedroom she finished getting dressed for bed and brushed her teeth. The drug that she had drunk before, was making her extremely sleepy and she laid down across the bed and fell asleep.

Pupa woke to a pounding at her door. She dragged herself off the bed and got her robe to answer the door. *Wonder who could be knocking this early?* She wondered as she opened the door. Hana was standing there, smiling at her. "What are…?" Pupa said. She was going to ask, what she was doing there that early, when she noticed that the sun was high in the sky. Pupa put her hand on her forehead to shield her eyes from the sun. "Come in, come in Hana," Pupa said as she opened the door wider for Hana.

The two ladies stepped into the living room. Pupa remembered that this was Friday, the day members of the council sometimes came by in the morning to visit. "I'm sorry for my appearance," Pupa said. "I didn't mean to sleep this late. While I'm getting dressed, why don't you make some coffee.

"Sure," Hana said. "I was worried about you, when you didn't answer the door right away. This isn't like you to sleep this late, are you okay?"

"Yes, I'm okay, Pupa said. I just overslept. What time is it, anyway?" Pupa asked.

"It's almost ten o'clock," Hana answered, using the white man's time. She spotted the pan on the stove and took a sniff of what was in it. "I see why you overslept now." Then she finished making the coffee and went to the living room to sit on the sofa.

In a few minutes Pupa came in, combing her hair. "That Ica drink is powerful stuff. I haven't slept this late in twenty years," she said. Pupa took a few more strokes with the hair brush, then put it on the end table and sat down in the overstuffed chair across from Hana.

A perking sound was coming from the kitchen by now. "I'll get the coffee," Pupa said as she got up and headed to the kitchen.

"Rose and Rita should be here soon, at least they were planning to come over, when I talked to them last night," Hana said.

"Good ," Pupa said, from the kitchen. It seems like forever since we all had a good visit. In a few minutes, she entered, holding two cups of coffee. Handing one to Hana, she was about to sit down when a knock came from the door. "Must be Rose or Rita," she said as she went to the door to answer it.

Pupa opened the door and there stood a woman four foot three inches tall with a big smile on her face. "Shosho!" Pupa exclaimed.

"Shosho?" Hana said as she got up from the couch and started towards the door.

"Come in, come in," Pupa said excitedly, and stepped aside so the woman could come in.

Stepping through the door, Shosho gave Pupa a big hug and then stepped over to Hana and gave her a hug, also. Stepping back a step she turned enough so she could talk to both women. "I thought I'd catch you with some of the council here," Shosho said, looking around the room to see if anyone else was there. "Am I too late for the morning social?" Shosho asked.

"No, we are just getting started," Pupa said, taking the arm of her friend and setting her down next to Hana. "We were just about to have coffee. Here, take this one. We haven't even gotten started yet. I'll go get me a cup and the cream and sugar." This said, Pupa headed for the kitchen.

"I don't need the cream or sugar," Shosho said.

"I thought you liked cream and sugar in your coffee?" Pupa said, more as a question than a statement.

"I used to, but when Black Feather was going to school we were so strapped for money I learned to drink it without cream or sugar. Now I prefer it that way." Shosho said as she lifted up her cup.

"You are looking good," Shosho said to Hana.

"You, too!" Hana replied. "What are you doing back? How long are you going to be around? Is Black Feather with you, or are you traveling alone? What have you been up to, since you left?"

"Yes, what have you been up to? We haven't heard from you, for at least two seasons." Pupa said, as she entered with her cup of coffee and the cream and sugar. Shosho had called some of the council members every month or so and they would share their conversation with Pupa and other members of the council.

"Well, Black Feather and I went to his clan in New Mexico to live right after our wedding here. Lets see, that's been one year and two seasons ago."

"We know that. We were at your wedding, remember?" Hana said laughingly.

"Yes, I know you were there," Shosho said in a good humor tone. "As I was about to say, before the interruption." She nodded toward Hana, laughing. "We stayed there two seasons, then moved to Albuquerque. There, Black Feather finished his schooling and got his master's degree. That is where we live now. Black Feather is here to interview about the Principal's job at the high school. If he gets the job, then we will move here. He's getting the interview Monday morning. So we will be here until Monday." Shosho took a sip of her coffee.

In the next few minutes not only did Rose and Rita show up, but also White Bird, Sylvia and Rosebud, which some called Bud to keep her straight from Rose. They were all glad to see their old friend, Shosho, who was once a council member until she fell in love with a six foot three inch school teacher named Black Feather and got married. Shosho was the youngest woman to ever be on the Women Council in the history of the council. She was chosen because of her bravery. There was a house on fire with a mother, father and two small children in it. They were asleep in their beds when a faulty furnace started a fire. The whole family had been asleep when the smoke overcame them. Shosho saw the flames and, at great risk to herself, she entered the burning house four times, each time carrying or dragging an unconscious person out. This was all witnessed by a woman in a wheelchair and her two granddaughters. The council was so impressed that they made her a member of the Women Council. This was what the Socike nation was all about, being brave and helping each other in their troubles, also in the past being great warriors.

There were more people than Pupa usually had over on Friday, so she had to drag out chairs from the kitchen so everyone would have a place to sit. This was a social event and no one tried to make it anything more. No council business was ever discussed at these gatherings. The women were so relaxed at these gatherings that they did a lot of joking with each other, even drawing Pupa into the joke once in a while. But, when they did this, they were very careful not to offend her. After all, she was Pupa, leader of the Women Council. Each woman took turns making coffee and serving it. Sometimes someone would bring a snack. This morning both Whitebird and Sylvia brought something.

Shosho was so glad to be with some of the council members, she could hardly contain herself. She had a smile on her face constantly. She missed being a council member and having a say on what went on at the reservation.

"Shosho, ever since I got here you've had a smile on your face. Are you that glad to be back or does that Black Feather have something we don't know about?" Rosebud asked.

This made Shosho blush. You could see the red on her cheeks, but she smiled even bigger.

Rita piped in, "Well, Bud, we've noticed you don't smile too much any more. Maybe Shosho will talk to Black Feather and he can give your man some hints." With that the whole room started laughing.

"No, have him talk to my man. I think he forgot why he got married," Rose said. With this everyone laughed even louder.

Shosho said, "I always liked these gatherings on Friday morning at Pupa's, but I don't remember them being this lively.

"They usually aren't, you just do something to bring life to the party, Shosho," Rosebud said.

"What are you saying, Bud? She is the only one that has life left in her," Rose said. "The rest of us are so old, that Geronimo was our heart throb."

Whitebird got up and went to the kitchen and brought back some queto, that had been warming in Pupa's oven. She passed them around the room. Queto is a round flat thin corn bred with whole corn and red peppers mixed in. The Socikes ate this a lot with their coffee or tea. After Whitebird was finished, Sylvia got up and went to the kitchen table to get her treat which was titi, an Indian soft candy made from the fruit of the prickly pear cacti. This, she passed to everyone.

The ladies ate their treats and did a lot more talking. About twelve noon the ladies started leaving one at a time until only Shosho and

Pupa were left. "Pupa, I'm so glad to see you. I hope Black Feather gets the principal job so we can move back," Shosho said.

"If that's what you wish, I hope that you get your wish, also. It would be nice to have you here with us," Pupa said. The two ladies stood there studying each other's eyes. "I see that all is well with you, Shosho, I am so glad to see that."

"Pupa, is there anything I can do for you?" Shosho asked. She could see the trouble in Pupa's eyes, but because of the Socike tradition Shosho couldn't ask Pupa what was wrong. Instead she asked if there was anything that she could do for her, which was perfectly acceptable.

"No, not at this time, but I thank you for asking," Pupa said.

"Pupa, there is something that I need to tell you," Shosho said.

"What is it, Brave one?" Pupa asked.

"First I want to tell you how sorry I am about Maria's death. I heard that she died fighting as a brave should, and I'm sure you are very proud of her, even in your days of grief," Shosho said.

"Thank you, I am proud of her," Pupa said.

"I also wanted to tell you that I have been seeing Rosa," Shosho said. "We sometimes..."

"You've seen Rosa?" Pupa interrupted.

"Yes, we sometimes have coffee together. When I told her we were coming here she asked me to ask you something," Shosho said.

"What... what did she want you to ask me?" Pupa asked.

"You know Rosa has a drinking problem?" Shosho said while Pupa nodded her head. "She wants to know if you will see her, if she is sober when she comes to see you?"

"Of course, I'll see her. Why would she think otherwise? I'd see her if she wasn't sober. I've been praying to see her before I die. Please tell her to come and see me. Or if you would tell me where she is, I'll go to her!" Pupa said.

Shosho looked Pupa straight in the eyes. "I told her, that was what you'd say. She doesn't want you to go to her just now. She wants to come to you, when she's sober. The weekend before I left, Rosa entered a clinic to help her kick the dependence on alcohol. She will be there two months. During that time she can't have any visitors. The rules are very strict about that. They have a seventy-five percent success rate. Rosa is very determined to lick this beast that has a hold on her. I'm convinced she is determined enough to be one of the seventy five percent success stories. She told me to tell you if you agreed she would be here after she finishes her time in the clinic, at the end of this season, in two months," Shosho said. She smiled even bigger because she was saying months to Pupa, and knew Socikes used four seasons, never months unless they really needed to be more precise. Then they would sometimes use the white man's months.

Pupa was so excited, she laughed, she cried and just about hugged Shosho to death! "I can hardly believe what you are telling me. The spirits told me that I would see her again and I believe she will come," Pupa said. Then she hugged Shosho again.

Shosho hugged her back and the two stood there laughing!

"I've got something to do, but I'll be back before the two months. I won't miss the chance to see Rosa!" Pupa said.

Shosho waited to see if Pupa was going to say anything more about what she had to do, but Pupa said nothing more. Shosho was a full-blooded Socike so she didn't ask her anymore. That would be very bad manners, to do so.

The two women said goodbye, and Shosho left to find her husband at the high school. He went to look around to familiarize himself with any changes that had occurred in the high school in the last two years.

Pupa sat down on her sofa and thought over everything that Shosho said. She would be so glad to see Rosa. "I'm going to the Great mountain to give thanks to the great spirit that protects us," Pupa said to herself. She then went to her kitchen and made a small lunch of Indian corn bread. She couldn't eat much because of the sweets of the morning and of the excitement of knowing that Rosa would come and see her in two months.

As soon as Pupa had finished her lunch, she took a box out of her closet and set it on her kitchen table. Opening it up she pulled out some writing paper, ink, and a large turkey feather that had the stem at the big end cut off at an angle and split up about one half inch. She pulled a sheet of paper in front of where she was sitting, opened the ink bottle and dipped the big end of the feather that had been cut into the ink. She started to write. Great Spirits of the mountains. I thank you for fulfilling your promise to me to see my Rosa. Then she signed it, Anita Yellowhair. She opened the door and took a look at the sky. Very clear, "This will be a good time," Pupa said to herself. She then went to her kitchen and got a book of matches, grabbed her jacket and headed to the stables on a slow trot.

"Hello Pupa," Jode said as soon as he saw her. "Do you want me to get Baroka for you?" He asked.

"No, I'll go get him," Pupa said. With that she went into the stable, got her strap and headed for the pasture where Baroka was grazing. When she got within sight of him, she gave a scream that is best described as a cross between an eagle's scream and a horse's whinny. As soon as Baroka heard this, he raised his head and looked around to find Pupa. Spotting her, Baroka trotted over to Pupa and put his head down to nuzzle her. Pupa put her arms around his neck and nuzzled him right back. She pulled his head down and whispered in his ear, "Tika tika oo forca tee zaoo." Translated, this was, tika tika (you are) oo (my) forca, meant (ride, carry, or transportation.) tee (to) zaoo (spirits or, the spirit). Baroka let Pupa put the strap in his mouth and tie it around his chin. This made the rein that she would guide him with. With a handful of mane Pupa gave a fling upward with her right leg and jumped up on the back of Baroka, all the time talking to him in both Socike and English. This she had done almost every day since she was four years old, but quite a feat considering her age. Baroka was so accustomed to her doing that, that when he felt her leg going up his side he would step into her to help get her up. When he felt that she was in her usual position on his back he would start walking and waiting for her clue to him on how fast he should go. They were so accustomed to each other that she seldom used her reins. He could tell how fast she wanted to go by how much she leaned forward. She would also lean to the right or left and he would know to turn into her lean. If she needed to make a sharp turn or stop then she would use the reins. This afternoon Pupa and Baroka moved out in a gallop.

By late afternoon Pupa had reached her destination at the base of a mountain with steep sides. She rode to the lowest point in the area which was in a dry arroyo with a few trees. She dismounted in a clear spot and let the reins drop so the ends touched the ground in a clump of grass so Baroka could graze if he wanted to. She then went about gathering dry wood and some dry leaves. This she stacked in the middle of the arroyo on the gravel away from anything that might catch on fire. It made a pile about the size of a bushel basket. She then went about gathering branches with green leaves and placed them a little ways away from her pile of dried wood and leaves. Pupa was ready to give thanks to the great spirit. She lit the small pile of dried wood and leaves and made sure it was going to stay burning. Taking two hands full of green brush and leaves, Pupa started to dance around the small fire. She started a hum through her nose in a beat like a drum, keeping in time with her hum she danced around the fire. As she danced her head and upper body would bow down, then arching her back and turning her face to the sky, she kept time with the music coming from her. Besides the circle she was making around the fire she would spin her body, making small turns as she danced a circle around the fire. Her whole body kept time with the music as she danced. She was consumed in her dance not conscious of her surroundings. Pupa lay the green leaves and branches on the fire as she danced. The green leaves made the fire smoke very heavy. This was to attract the great spirit. When the smoke got the heaviest Pupa took out the note of thanks she had written with the turkey feather and laid it on the green leaves. All the time she kept up the humming and dancing. In a few minutes the heat from the fire caused the note to burst into flames. This caused Pupa to dance even harder with more movement and a faster beat. She danced in and out of the smoke, breathing in lots of smoke. She kept dancing faster and faster, getting very light headed and after a time she fell exhausted to the ground. The whole area was spinning around to Pupa as she laid there on her back exhausted. This had completed her dance of thanksgiving to the great spirit. She lay there feeling sick from all the smoke. The sun had moved far to the west and Pupa knew that it would get dark in a short time. She knew that she should start back but felt sick from the smoke and decided to lay there for a while. Pupa shut her eyes to try to make the queasiness disappear. In a minute, she felt a hot breath on her face. She opened her eyes expecting to see Baroka, but there was the biggest bear that she had ever seen, looking her in the face. She lay there frozen with fear. The bear didn't make a move, but stared her in the eyes. In a minute Pupa managed to get out, "Are you going to eat me, Mr. Bear?"

"No, I wouldn't do that," the bear said.

Pupa couldn't believe the bear was talking to her. Maybe it was her imagination going wild from the smoke. "What do you want?" Pupa squeaked out.

"I want to help you get your granddaughter to her ancestors," the bear said.

Pupa noticed that the bear wasn't moving his, or her lips, but the bear was talking to her, she could hear it as plain as anything. "How are you going to help me?" She asked.

"To find the answer you are seeking, you must ask the Peyote plant." the bear said.

"Peyote!" Pupa exclaimed. I should have known, she thought to herself, and closed her eyes for a moment with disbelief that she had not thought of that. When she opened them, the bear was gone.

Pupa turned her head from side to side to see where the bear was. There was no bear, just Baroka standing a few feet away. "I must have fallen asleep and dreamed the bear," Pupa said to herself. "But, the Peyote cactus is the answer!"

*I'd better get going, it's going to get dark before I get home,* Pupa thought. She got up and dusted herself off. That was when she saw the prints in the sand. Four bear paw prints right where she had been laying. No prints leading up to the four in the sand, but four definite bear prints. Two on each side of the indentation of where she had laid. Baroka was very close to where she had laid. If there had been a real bear he would have made a fuss. *Was that a spirit bear?* She wondered. *If it had been a spirit bear, why did it leave prints?* This was confusing to Pupa.

Pupa walked over to Baroka and picked up his reins. "Did you see the bear?" she asked Baroka. "It sure was huge. It was so big I'm sure it was a male. I know it was a male." Pupa grabbed a handfull of mane, swung her leg up and over Baroka's back and off they went on a fast gallop. She thought she would go as fast as she dared while there was still light. By the time it was dark, Baroka was walking and they made their way to the stable a little past ten p.m. Pupa was surprised to see a light on in a small room where Jode had a table, chairs, and an old sofa. When Pupa led Baroka in the stable to make sure that he was dry and not wet with sweat before she turned him out to pasture, Jode stepped out of the room. "Jode, I thought you would be gone by now," Pupa said.

"I would have, but I was kind of concerned about you when you didn't make it back by dark," Jode said. "You usually come back before dark."

"I'm sorry I should have warned you, I didn't know when I'd get back," Pupa said.

"Well, you are okay, that's what matters," Jode said.

Pupa led Baroka to the pasture, let him go, and shut the gate behind him. As Pupa walked through the stable Jode said, "I'm going past your house. Can we walk together?"

"That would be great, we haven't talked in a long time," Pupa said. Pupa and Jode used to talk to each other a lot because of their mutual love of horses. After Maria's death Pupa rode, but she just didn't feel like talking to anyone about anything. She had gone through the motion of her duties like keeping the council doing their job, because that was her way. But, now it would be nice to have the company on her walk home.

The two started off on their walk to pupa's house. "I had to pull a nail out of that white mare's hoof the other day. It was one of those roofing nails that has a big washer on the head. I have no Idea where she picked it up." Jode said.

"Was it where it bothered her?" Pupa asked.

"No, I wouldn't have even noticed it if she hadn't been standing on the concrete by the side of the stable. I was hearing this clicking sound and went around to see what was making it. There she stood tapping her hoof on the cement. The nail was making the tap, tap, tap. I think she liked the sound. First time I had ever seen a tap dancing horse, so I renamed her dancer. Of course, I pulled it out so it wouldn't come out and one of the other horses pick it up in the wrong spot," Jode said.

"You never shoed her?" Pupa asked.

"No, If I shoed her she would probably spend all her time out there on that cement slab tap dancing," Jode said.

"That would be something, a dancing horse, wouldn't it?" Pupa said.

"I guess it would," Jode said. "I could charge for people to see the dancing horse."

"Instead of working the stables you could manage Dancer, the dancing horse." Pupa said. They both laughed, then walked on, not saying anything.

In a few minutes Pupa ask, "Jode, is your friend, Big Crow, still selling the plants of the Gods?"

"Peyote?" Jode asked.

"Yes, the Peyote cactus," Pupa said.

Jode was hesitant to answer at first. The Peyote had been used by many Indian tribes since the beginning of time for religious ceremonies, but it was against the white man's law, because it is a hallucinogen. Then he thought to himself, this is Pupa. "Yes, he still sells it." Jode said.

"How long would it take him to get me three plants?" Pupa asked.

"He just got back from Mexico with a load. I could get you some tomorrow or even tonight if you wished," Jode said.

"Tomorrow would be great," Pupa said. "What time would you want me to pick them up?" Pupa asked.

"I'll call him tonight and put it on your porch tomorrow when I go to work," Jode said.

"That would be great, and if there's a light on, knock on the door and we will have coffee," Pupa said.

"Sounds good, I may see you tomorrow then," Jode said and the two said good night, they were at Pupa's house. Jode walked on.

# Chapter 14

The next morning, Pupa was up bright and early getting coffee ready. She was anxious to start her quest to get answers from the peyote plant. She felt really lucky that Big Crow had just gotten back from Mexico, because he didn't always have the little cactus on hand and she was afraid she would have to wait to start her quest. Pupa sat there drinking her coffee and mentally planning her trip out in the wilderness where she would go to turn her life over to the peyote plant. She would allow it to take her to where she needed to go to get the answer she so desperately needed. As Pupa sipped her coffee, she was beginning to wonder why Jode hadn't knocked on her door yet, she knew that he would have to be at the stables pretty soon. Those horses wouldn't feed themselves.

She got up from the table, paced back and forth a few times, then went to the door, opened it to see if Jode was anywhere in sight. The sun hadn't come up yet, but she could see the light in the east and she knew that Jode was always at the stable before daybreak. Pupa stepped out on her porch so she could look down the street to see if he was on his way. Straining her eyes to see as far as she could, she spotted a stray dog scavenging the streets but no Jode. Disappointed Pupa hung her head and turned around to go back inside when she spotted a brown paper sack on the porch setting next to the door. Stepping over and picking it up, she noticed it was about the right weight to be what she was waiting for. Hurrying into her house, she went to the kitchen to get a better look. Pupa tipped the sack and out rolled three fat healthy Peyote cactus on her table. She examined them and saw that the roots had not even dried out yet. They were very good samples of the plant of the Gods, very juicy and fresh. *Jode is a true gaucho,* Pupa thought.

Gaucho to the Socike didn't just mean cowboy, but it meant cowboy with manners and a person that had respect for other people and their property, especially older people.

Pupa started to put the little cactus back in the paper sack when she noticed writing on the sack.

> *Dear Pupa, I received a call early this morning that one of the horses has his leg caught in the fence and is just standing there. I knew you would probably still be in bed, so I didn't knock. Big Crow said he was honored to furnish you with the trip. There is no charge for the Peyote. Big Crow said to be careful and watch out for Sand Walkers. Please watch your step and do be careful of Sand Walkers. Jode*

"That Jode is a real Gaucho. Yes sir, a real Gaucho," Pupa said out loud. Going about her normal morning chores, she started thinking about the Sand Walkers. They are the evil spirits that hang near the same plane as the ancestral spirits, but not on the same plane. It is a plane that one has to go through to get to the ancestral spirits. The Sand Walkers are wicked spirits that can take any shape or form. They can travel in their plane or in mortal man's plane, but by all accounts are too afraid to travel in the ancestral plane. Pupa starts to think about the weapons that she needs to take on her journey, in case she has to battle the Sand Walkers. She will take her war club and fighting knife. These are weapons that were made for her when she was a young woman and had passed the test to become a brave. These weapons she trained with, as all her ancestors did when they were young. When they got older then they taught the younger men and women how to fight.

In an hour she had all of her chores done and had even managed to have breakfast. Pupa opened the trap door to her root cellar, went down and brought up her war paint. This was something that she thought she would never have to do again in her life time, but here she was, once again taking the walk of the warrior.

She never had to fight flesh and blood as her ancestors did, all her battles were with the Chief of darkness and his braves.

The paint was all dried and cracked, but Pupa wasn't worried, she added a little water and let the jars set on her kitchen table to get soft. Next was to get her traditional winter brave uniform ready. This done, she went in and showered. By the time she was finished the paint was soft so she took a butter knife out of the kitchen and stirred them. They had softened nicely and were ready to apply.

Pupa took them in her bedroom and started applying them. When she finished her face she had two straight yellow lines on the left side of her face starting at the corner of her eyebrow running at a forty five degree angle down passed her chin line. Red paint circled her left eye to make her eye look big. The right side of her face and neck was covered all white with a circle of red paint around the eye to match the left side. She was surely a frightening sight.

She felt that just the sight of her would keep the Sand Walkers away from her. She then put on her winter uniform added her black headband and the eagle feather. The nights got very chilly at this time of year, so she rolled a blanket and tied the ends together enabling her to carry it draped over her shoulder and across her chest.

Next, she got a frozen plastic jug of water out of the freezer and tied the two ends of a strap to it so she could carry it like the blankets. Putting her weapons in her belt she then got a sack with a long strap and placed Maria's ashes in it still in the box and plastic bag just as it came from the funeral director from Benson.

She was now set to start her quest. On her way out, she put a small tin of matches in her blanket roll and grabbed the small sack of Peyote. Walking across the reservation she was about to reach the edge where the small market is. Everyone who saw her would greet her, even the ones that didn't recognize her. They all knew she was a brave in good standing because of her dress.

She decided to stop at the market to pick up some beef jerky for her trip. Pupa walked in the market and grabbed a half dozen sticks and went to the head of the line, showed the clerk what she had and the clerk wrote it down. This was one way people at the store and the store owners showed respect to a person on a quest like Pupa's. Any tourist that happened to be in the store at that time, would find their view blocked by the Indians getting in their way of sight. God help anyone who pulled out a camera for any quest that required a uniform and war paint was sacred to the Socike.

Pupa walked out of the store into the bush and headed for the wilderness. After walking for about an hour, Pupa started to look for a sign of some kind. She sat down on a large rock when a ground squirrel ran down a tree, moved a small rock and disappeared in a hole under the small rock. The small rock fell back into place when the squirrel went in the hole. She wondered if that was the sign she was looking for. Pupa sat down her jug of ice and blankets to gaze at the sky, no sign there. Taking the water, she sipped the liquid that had melted and pulled out one of the beef jerkies and started chewing on it, when she saw the crow, actually a raven, the largest of the birds in the crow family. She had missed the Raven before because it was sitting in a shadow of a large rock.

Getting eye contact with the crow, Pupa concentrated her thoughts. "Mr., Raven, are you my guide?"

The crow just stared back.

Pupa got nothing, back. Then in a moment she received what the Raven said.

"I beg your pardon, (Mrs. Raven)! — Are you my guide?"

With this, the crow flies straight up and circles above, until Pupa put the blanket and the strap to her ice jug back on, then she flew off.

Pupa walked after her. The crow flew ahead a ways, then waited for Pupa to catch up. This went on for an hour and Pupa noticed that the crow flew in one direction, then headed off in another, and all of this had been up hill. Pupa was in good shape for her age, but this was getting irritating.

She had been on many quests, most of them when she was quite a bit younger. She had never had a guide that changed directions on their path to the Gate Of The Planes before. They had always gone in a straight line.

Pupa had many different guides before, sparrows, blue birds, and once even a rabbit, but this crow was getting on her nerves, zigzagging like she did. Pupa sat down on a rock about twenty feet from the crow. They both just looked at each other. *What are you up to, crow?* Pupa wondered. Then it crossed her mind that this crow might be a Sand Walker.

Pupa turned her head to look at the path she had been taking up this hill. She studied the landmarks that she took a mental picture of, as she walked this not so steep hill. Yes, there is the big oak tree and the clump of willows before that, there's the Huge rock that looked like a giant's head, Pupa thought. With her eyes she followed the path she had taken and noticed that the crow had showed her the easiest path to where they were at this time, not the shortest. *Sorry to doubt you Raven*, she thought. Pupa got up and headed toward the raven.

After about fifteen minutes more, the Raven headed up a steep cliff and landed on a dead limb on a small tree hanging over the top of this cliff.

Pupa looked up. *That's a steep cliff*, she thought. "Oh well," she said, and started to climb. In another ten minutes she was at the dead tree. Pupa sat down to rest a minute, and in a few minutes she caught her breath and looked around to find the raven. The raven was gone but there was a cave with an entrance about the size of two horses. *This must be the Gate To The Planes*, she thought as she walked around the entrance. Unloading her ice jug and blankets, she started gathering wood and made a pile by the side of the entrance of the cave. This she did in preparation for her journey. She kept the sack with Maria's ashes in it on her at all times. After all, that was the reason for the trip, to help Maria find her ancestors.

Pupa made a small pile of wood at the cave entrance and lit it. She stood there in the smoke, to purify her soul, or spirit. To the Socike, they are the same. In a few minutes, she took out the Peyote cactus and flattened the paper bag they came in, and then laid it on a rock. Taking one of the cactus, Pupa peeled and sliced it. She ate it and drank some water, then went to the cave and sat cross-legged at the entrance. She was waiting for the Peyote to take her on her journey.

Pupa started to get up to peel another cactus when she heard a buzz coming from the cave. Slowly turning to see what was causing the buzz, she came face to face with the biggest rattle snake she had ever seen. As she watched the snake it seemed to swell even larger. The snake was coiled in a defiant position with it's head reared above her. Pupa inched away from the snake, trying to get out of striking distance. The snake lunged at her face, she could see the fangs coming for her, they were six inches long if they were an inch. Pupa Blocked the strike by lifting her left arm, catching it under the chin and straightening her arm and swinging it to her left. This deflected the snakes strike, and Pupa managed to scramble to her feet. They both stared at each other, not moving, when Pupa heard the distinct evil voice of a Sand Walker.

"I know why you are here, and I was sent to stop you," the snake said, not moving his mouth except enough to flick his tongue in and out in a rhythmic way.

Pupa concentrated and with her mind asked the snake his name.

"I am Kiki, the great brave of the Toto's, and I command you to go back, do not try to go forward or I'll kill you," the snake said.

"Your are a Sand Walker," Pupa said with her mind.

"All Totos are Sand Walkers, except Brava, that traitor that married your ancestor, Eagle Woman."

"O, great ancestors, give me strength to defeat this evil spirit!" Pupa said out loud.

"That will never happen," Kiki said, and once again he delivered a strike at Pupa's throat.

She grabbed the snake by the neck and squeezed, pulling it down with her left hand and grabbing her knife with her right she stabbed him in the head. The snake was flopping and trying to wiggle loose. She noticed that her left hand that would have been too small to reach around his neck and her arm which would have been too weak to hold him had turned into a giant eagle leg. The talons dug deep into the snake, holding it steady, her ancestors had answered her prayers. She squeezed and worked the knife back and forth in his head until the snake lay perfectly still. As pupa watched, the snake vanished while still in her grip and her arm and hand turned back to normal.

Pupa stepped over to the paper sack wiped her knife off and started peeling another peyote. In a minute she had it peeled and sliced. Just as she was chewing the second slice she felt a sharp pain in the middle of her back and she was knocked forward on her face.

Pupa turned over on her back and saw a male brave standing straddling her legs, with his war club raised ready to bash in her skull. His face was painted all black with white lightning bolts painted on each side of his face. "I'm back," he said to Pupa, not moving his lips. Pupa swiftly kicked him in the groin and followed through with a kick to the chin, knocking him backwards and down. Pupa was on her feet with her war club in hand swinging at his head.

Kiki, the same spirit that was in the snake, rolled to his right, making Pupa's war club miss him by inches. With his left hand he back-handed her on the left side of her face knocking her over. He raised his war club to strike, but Pupa struck first. In a minute, the brave vanished like the snake.

*They come back stronger than before,* she thought. I had better get going or the first Sand Walker is going to finish me before I even get started. Pupa grabbed the cactus, put it in the paper sack, tucked the top of the sack up into her belt and pulled the top of the sack down over the belt so it would stay there. Pupa started on a slow trot into the cave. Her eyes had become like the eyes of the cougar, being able to see in the dark.

"I didn't know the plane of the Sand Walkers was that close to the plane of the humans," Pupa said out loud as she walked.

"It's not," a sinister voice bellowed from ahead. "But, we thought we'd give Eagle Woman's daughter a welcome she would never forget before we kill her."

"Kiki?" Pupa asked.

"Kiki, is a mouse, you are dealing with Kota the bravest of the Toto's Braves. And I'm going to kill and eat you, Eagle Woman's daughter," the booming voice said.

"Why do you call me 'Eagle Woman's daughter'? Eagle Woman is way up my ancestors' line. You are too stupid to even know who you are dealing with," Pupa said.

"You are the stupid one. You only think you know the spirit world. Well, I'm going to give you some lessons. First lesson—you are Eagle Woman's Daughter just as your mother is and as your daughter is, and as your granddaughter would be if she could find her ancestors," the voice said, starting a sinister laugh over the thought of Pupa's granddaughter being lost in the spirit world.

This made Pupa mad that a Sand Walker would laugh over her granddaughter being lost. "If you were as brave as you claim, you would show yourself."

In a minute Pupa was kind of sorry she had said this. she had just stepped into a big cavern in the cave and she could see what was talking to her. She had no words to describe what she was facing. As big as the cavern was, she could not get past the thing that awaited her. It had no legs and was a purple being with eighteen arms and hands. In each hand was a weapon. Four had war clubs, four had knives, four had tomahawks, four had wooden clubs and two had spears.

"What in the world are you?" Pupa asked.

"I'm not of this world, daughter of the despised Eagle Woman. I told you I would give you lessons in the spirit world," the being said. "Now either go back or come and let me kill you, then I will eat you and your spirit will become one in me to make me even stronger and you will not join your ancestors but become one with me."

Pupa looked this being over, she could see no eyes, but as she moved from side to side, the arms that were closest to her would become active, it was if they sensed where she was at all times. Just as she was about to attack with her war club Pupa screamed with pain. There was a spear sticking through her calf, the pain was as if it was red hot steel.

The being began to laugh, "I got you, Oh despised one's daughter. That's another lesson for you, never stick around to visit with a Sand Walker! They will kill you!" The being had thrown one of it's spears and it went through the lower part of her leg.

Pupa grabbed the spear and pulled it out, The burning stopped after it was removed. She jumped forward and swung with her war club, it sank into the flesh of this being, but her hand was hit with a wooden club causing her to loose her grip and the war club disappeared into the being.

"I've got your war club," the being laughed out at her, and continued to laugh after he had gotten the words out. Come on try your knife.

Pupa had only her knife. She stepped back keeping an eye on his arm with the spear, making sure he didn't throw it. She picked up the spear and ran forward with it, ramming it into the being up to three-fourths of the shank. In a moment, it sank in further and disappeared all together.

"You killed me, you killed me," the being screamed with pain!

Wham! The being hit Pupa at the back of the knees causing her to fall and to drop her knife. She grabbed her knife and rolled back away just as the being came down with the tomahawk where she was laying.

"Ha, ha, ha, ha," the being was cracking up, he tried over and over to talk, but lost his words in his laughter. "You should have seen your face when I said, 'You killed me.' You actually gave me my weapon back." With this, his hand that had held the spear reached into himself, pulled out the spear and held it in a threatening manner.

*He can see me*, Pupa thought.

"Well, sort of."

"What?" Pupa asked.

"Oh, a, nothing."

"You said, 'Sort of,' You said, 'Sort of'," Pupa said. "You can't see me."

"Well no, but you can't get by me either."

Pupa stepped back out of the larger cavern and kneeled. "Great spirits of all spirits, I ask you to give me wisdom to fight this monster."

She heard in her head, "You have purified yourself, use holy water."

"What the heck does that mean?" Pupa asked herself. "I don't have any water here, it's outside, besides it's not holy, just drinking water," Pupa said to the great spirit. This holy water must be something I thought up, not what the spirit actually said to me. It doesn't make any sense. "No" I have to believe or I will die on this quest. What did the Great Spirit say to me? "I had purified myself." I did, I did that with the smoke. "Use holy water."

Pupa rushed into the great cavern with her knife drawn above her head like she was going to strike the monster with it, but she just spat on the monster.

Immediately, the monster started to scream, then Pupa heard a sizzling and saw smoke coming from the monster. It was dissolving. In a few minutes all that was left was Pupa's war club.

Pupa picked up her club and started on her way further into the cave. The color of the cave walls started to change. They became a bright red, then changed to green, then blue, then yellow and then the colors started to mix and there were streaks of these colors mixing and swirling constantly changing. All of this motion was making Pupa dizzy and she closed her eyes to get her balance. After she had steadied herself against the cave walls Pupa opened her eyes. The colors were still there, but everything was still now. Pupa continued on her walk down the cave.

She had been walking now for quite awhile and Pupa was getting tired, she had been on quests before, but none of them had been this hard. The thought had entered her mind to take a rest, but she thought it would be better to keep going. Pupa was starting to turn a corner in the cave when out stepped a brave holding a tomahawk and a large shield. Pupa rushed forward and spat on him.

The brave threw down his shield and his tomahawk. "That's disgusting! — Why did you do that?" the brave asked.

"Aren't you a sand walker?" Pupa asked.

"No!" he answered. "I'm Bo-ox, your guide to your ancestors."

"Oh..., I'm sorry, I didn't realize," Pupa said.

"Follow me." Bo-ox picked up his tomahawk and shield, then walked further down the cave.

Pupa followed behind, feeling a little sheepish. In a few minutes they reached a bend in the cave. After the bend, the cave opened into an area so open that there was blue sky with white clouds, green plants, trees, and the richest greenest grass Pupa had ever seen. She couldn't help but think Baroka would really like to graze here.

A voice ahead of the brave said, "Thank you Bo-ox."

Bo-ox nodded and made a sharp right turn, revealing a woman standing in traditional Socike war uniform. Pupa wasn't able to see her before Bo-ox had taken the turn. She was even wearing a black head band, the same color as Pupa's headband.

Pupa walked closer and recognized the woman as her mother that had passed away twenty years ago. "Mama!" Pupa shrieked and rushed to the woman standing there. "Mama," Pupa said again when she reached the woman.

"Anita," the woman said and gave her daughter a hug. The two women stood there hugging each other for the longest time, her mother whispering secrets in her ear. In a minute, they separated and Pupa's mother said, "We don't have much time. We know why you're here, we learned right after you entered into the Gate To The Planes. I'm very proud of you, my daughter, and I want you to meet another mother and father of yours." She raised her arms to the sky. There came a swish sound that reminded Pupa of the sound she had heard once, that of a hawk when it dove at another bird very near her. It was the same swish sound.

In a mater of seconds, two people on horses were standing in front of her. A beautiful woman dressed in beautiful clothing on a black horse and a very well built man on a snow white horse. They both dismounted and stood in front of Pupa. "We are very proud of you, also, daughter."

Pupa's mother introduced these people as her mother, Eagle Woman and her father Brava. Both people nodded.

The two mounted their horses, "Give me my daughter, Maria," she said in a firm but gentle voice and held out her hand. "We must hurry."

Pupa took the box out of the sack she was caring, and handed it to Eagle Woman.

Eagle Woman took out the plastic bag, dropping the box and taking a knife cutting the tape that held the bag shut. She smiled at Pupa and, at once, both she and Brava were riding in the sky in a huge circle. As they passed overhead, Pupa could hear that swish sound. On the third circle that they passed over head, Eagle Woman started to pour out the ashes of Maria. The ashes shown as little specks of gold, floating in the air. On the sixth pass there were three horsemen instead of two. One white, one black, and one spotted horse that reminded Pupa of a horse that Maria had as a child, but was as big as the other two horses. On the ninth pass, the three horse men were standing in front of Pupa.

The face of the rider on the spotted horse was blurred and Pupa strained to see what he or she looked like.

In a minute Pupa heard the familiar words, "Nana, thank you."

The face became clear, it was Maria. "Maria," Pupa got out.

Then Brava broke in, "We must hurry," and his horse stepped forward next to Pupa. He reached down grabbed Pupa's arm, lifted her up behind him, and off they went, so fast that Pupa blacked out.

# Chapter 15

Mary Smith was home fixing her breakfast, mentally going over the events of the last few weeks. Chief Blight had pressured her heavily into admitting that she had lied to Captain Yellowhair, about Jack knowing that Maria was at her grandmother's. After Jack had confessed, she had finally admitted to Chief Blight that she had lied. Fully expecting to be arrested for lying to an officer, she was surprised when Chief Blight offered to drop all charges if she would sign a statement that said, that Jack was no where in sight when Maria had caught the bus and Maria had told her that she was leaving Jack to go to her grandmother's and not coming back.

She signed the statement because it was the truth. In fact, if it hadn't been for her, Jack wouldn't have found out where Maria was so soon. She even felt partly responsible for what had happened. She had always been jealous of Maria and had called Jack that morning and had told him what Maria had said, hoping that he would let Maria go and let her move in with him, in Maria's place. She hadn't been afraid of Jack, she knew that he had hit Maria once or twice, but it had always been because Maria had hit him first. She knew that to be true because that was what Jack had told her. The people that said Jack was mean, just didn't know him the way she did. She loved him so much, and missed him terribly. He had always promised her that he was going to leave Maria and marry her. Why did he kill Maria, if he did?

He had told Mary that he was innocent of the charges. That he went to the reservation to tell Maria that he didn't want her back because of her use of drugs and he was going to divorce her and marry her cousin. But, when he got to the reservation he had found Maria and her Grandmother dead already. He believed, that Maria double crossed a drug dealer and that was the person that killed her. After that, he drove back home. When he realized that he needed an alibi, he got a hold of her and asked her to lie for him. She had no idea why Jack had confessed to something he didn't do. In her heart she knew he was innocent. Maybe he was afraid of whoever killed Maria or maybe he was afraid of the police. She had to find out.

Mary Smith grabbed her car keys and headed out the door. She popped the hood on that old clunker, checked the water, then the oil, a quart low. "Sure wish I could afford a new car," she said out loud. Reaching under the front seat, Mary pulled a quart of oil out, and at the same time she felt to see if there was any more under there. Only one more, that would get her to Bisbee and back, but she needed to pick up some more, when she got back.

Mary headed east on Fourth street. Right before she got to the underpass, she took the fork to the right that headed to Bisbee. Five miles down the road Mary slowed down to drive through St. David, a small town which only takes about three minutes to drive through, and then she resumed her original speed.

Right after she left St. David she looked over at the two round houses on the left. They were very attractive to her because of her Indian heritage. One reason was the round shape, but the main reason was that they were made from the earth. They were made of rammed earth. The contractor used the dirt from the lot they were standing on, then stuccoed both inside and outside. Mary knew that because the contractor sometimes ate at the Horseshoe and she had talked to him about the houses.

It was about a thirty minute drive to where she was headed, which gave Mary time to think over the last couple years of her life. She had met Jack O'Reily at the Horseshoe where she worked two years ago right after her divorce from Harry Smith. He had been so kind and nice to her after her bitter divorce. Harry Smith had been a big mistake, he had been so abusive to her. Everyone had warned her about him, but she had been so in love.

Jack, on the other hand, had always been a perfect gentleman. Yes, he had been married to her cousin, but that Maria had never treated him right, always belittling him almost every night. Not in public, but in the privacy of their home. They hadn't even made love for over three years. He only stayed with her because she had threatened suicide if he ever left. Jack had such a good heart. She was sure there was more to this story than what Chief Blight had told her. Chief Blight might even be in cahoots with the drug ring.

As she drove, Mary noticed the railroad tanker that a rancher had moved out to a windmill in the middle of nowhere. This had always been a landmark to her that she was getting close to Tombstone the town that was advertised as, the town too tough to die. Around a small hill, Tombstone was in sight. Once again she slowed down and breezed right through that town, too tough to die.

It won't be long now, Mary thought to herself. Mule Pass was coming up. Mule Pass was a long tunnel that was drilled through a mountain for the wagons to go through to Bisbee when it was a booming mining town. Now the road she was driving on went right through it and it was even lit up with electric lights.

Mary exited that tunnel and decided to keep going straight, and bypass the main business district of Bisbee. The road she chose went around the side of the mountain, and the main town was below, sitting between the mountains. At the bottom there was very little flat land, so most of the town was built on the sides of the mountains. It was like building a town in the middle of a large bowl with a small base. In a minute she was headed down to the bottom, just at the end of the business district. Next, she was driving around a mammoth hole where they used to mine copper. Straight ahead on the left was Yaford hospital.

Mary pulled into the parking lot and headed for the front door. As she went up the front steps she heard the loud scream of a hawk. She looked up, and there sat a red tail hawk looking down, then it screamed again. "What's wrong with him?" Mary said out loud, and walked on through the door. There was a woman dressed in a nurse's uniform at a desk "I would like to visit with Mr. Jack O'Reily?" Mary said.

"Jack O'Reily?" The lady asked, not believing she heard right.
"Yes, Please," Mary said.
"Who are you...?" The lady asked.
"I'm, Mary Smith."

"Are you a relative?" The lady asked.

Mary thought for a minute, "Yes, a… yes, I am."

"And what relation are you, to him?" The lady asked.

"He is my cousin's husband," Mary said.

"Just a minute," the lady said and got up from her desk and walked to Dr. Gonzales's office. In a minute, the lady returned with a man.

"I am Dr. Gonzales," the man said and held out his hand to Mary. "How may I help you?"

"I would like to visit Mr. Jack O'Reily." Mary said.

"Step into my office," Dr. Gonzales said. With this, he turned and walked to his office.

Mary followed, when they got to his office he turned back to her and with his hand gestured for Mary to have a seat that was in front of his desk. He then proceeded on around to his chair behind the desk, and sat down.

"Why do you want to see Jack O'Reily?" Dr. Gonzales asked.

"He is my cousin's husband. Do I need more of a reason than that?" Mary asked.

"In this case you do," The doctor said. "You do know that Jack has been accused of killing his wife, Maria, don't you?"

"Yes, I know, but he didn't do it," Mary protested.

"He has confessed to me and to Chief Blight of Benson, many times," Dr. Gonzales said.

"I don't care, he didn't do it, I know him, and that is something he couldn't do," Mary said. "He has been framed for this, and I know that he has confessed, according to Chief Blight and now you tell me that he has confessed to you. But I know he didn't do it."

"Maria was your cousin?" the doctor asked.

"Yes, she was my cousin," Mary said.

"And you believe he didn't do it?" the doctor asked.

"I know he didn't do it," Mary said.

"What about Maria's grandmother, well she would be your grandmother, too?"

"Maria's Grandmother, My Grandmother by adoption only, I'm not related by blood to Anita Yellowhair," Mary interrupted.

"I see… well, Anita Yellowhair, according to Chief Blight, was there and witnessed the murder," Dr. Gonzales said.

"I wouldn't count on anything Anita Yellowhair would say, she's a notorious liar," Mary said.

Dr. Gonzales sat back in his chair thinking, "Hum," he said under his breath. Then he came out with, "Were you Jack's lover?" He asked.

Mary turned red, "Is it, that obvious?" she asked.

"Educated guess," He said.

Mary hung her head, "Am I going to be able to see him?"

"I don't see what it would hurt and maybe it might be good for him to see some one that believes in him so much," Dr. Gonzales said. "But, I must warn you, the dreams have taken a terrible toll on him."

"Dreams!" Mary burst out. "Dreams, what dreams, what do you mean?"

"Didn't you know...? Dreams, that's why he's in here. He has these dreams that torment him constantly. Didn't Chief blight tell you that?" Dr. Gonzales asked.

"The only thing Chief Blight told me, was that he had confessed to the murder of Maria and he was in here for observation." Mary said.

"Do you still want to see him?" Dr. Gonzales asked.

"More than ever," Mary said.

Dr. Gonzales, smiled. "This way." He got up and headed for the door.

Mary walked with Dr. Gonzales through two locked doors and then stood in front of another locked door. "This is where he is, I must warn you again, he will not be what you remembered him as. We bathe him once a week, but we don't shave him, it's two dangerous for the staff." Dr. Gonzales said.

Mary nodded her head and Dr. Gonzales opened the door.

The man strapped to the floor was half naked with the smell of urine in the room. He had pants on, but no shirt. Mary could see the wet stain around the pelvic area.

"This happens a lot, he will wet himself to get attention," Dr. Gonzales said.

Mary looked at Dr. Gonzales with suspicion. Then turned her attention back to Jack lying on the floor. His beard was about an inch long and his hair and beard had been combed recently. His head was laying on it's side and Mary could see where he had worn the hair off the back of his head, like a baby sometimes does when he has been lying on his back too long. Mary kneeled down beside Jack. "What have they done to you, my darling? What has that witch done to you?"

Dr. Gonzales took all this in. He was an optimist when it came to mental health and willing to try about anything for the sake of science. "I'll leave you two alone," The doctor said, then turned and walked out. He didn't tell her that someone else was observing them.

"Jack," Mary said. "Jack, talk to me, Why are you here?"

Jack turned his head toward Mary, "Mary?"

"Yes, it's me, my darling, I'm here for you."

"Mary, I keep having these dreams, that Anita turned loose on me," Jack said.

"Yes, I know. I'll get them out of your head if it's the last thing I do." Mary said. "Pupa's not the only one that can manipulate dreams. I'll save you," and Mary started stroking Jack's hair. Then she ran her finger over his chest and lightly circled each nipple and down the front of his body from his shoulder down to his navel. All the time she was kissing his face and whispering things into his ear.

"Mary, thank God you came. Bring me some poison so I can be free of these demons!" Jack whispered.

This was the first time since Jack had arrived at Yaford that he had responded to an outside stimulus, and Jane Weiman was writing it down frantically. She only stopped momentarily to acknowledge Dr. Gonzales' arrival in the room above the glass ceiling.

"He's reacting to her, he's responding," Jane said excitedly. "Who is she?"

"An old girlfriend," the doctor said.

"Interesting," Jane said. "For a minute I thought you might have brought in a prostitute."

"No, but that's an idea," Dr. Gonzales said. "I'd better stop her before she short circuits his brain. With that, he left to go back down to Jack and Mary.

Entering the room, Dr. Gonzales noticed that Jack was following Mary with his eyes even after he asked Mary to please get up and let Jack rest. The two gazed at each other as he escorted Mary out of the room. "I'm very glad you came Ms. Smith, Jack responded well to you. I was wondering if you could make it a regular visit. Maybe we could increase the time spent with him as time goes on. Depending on how Jack takes your visits. If I know what time you are coming, I'll make sure that Jack will be cleaned up. Of course we clean him regularly but Jack fights us, trying to manipulate us. But I think you made a genuine difference in him."

Mary was asked to fill out some personal information about her and Jack for his records, then she left for home.

Dr. Gonzales was delighted about the small response that Jack had shown before Mary left, and had one of his sessions right after she left. In the session, Jack asked to get a shower and clean clothes. Dr. Gonzales was ecstatic at the request.

# Chapter 16

Pupa woke up at the caves entrance, it was starting to get dark. She felt the ashes of the previous fire and they were cold. She had no idea how long she had been gone or even if she had gone anywhere. Kind of groggy, Pupa dragged the remaining wood and brush she had gathered and piled it on top of the ashes of the previous fire. Digging around in her clothing, she found her matches and lit her fire.

Her mouth was dry and her stomach seemed empty. She took her water and beef jerky and sat down for a meal when she noticed that she still had the sack hanging around her shoulder that contained Maria's ashes. Taking the sack off her shoulder she opened it and pulled out the box and opened it. Inside was the plastic bag, but no ashes. Pupa gave out a loud eagle scream and started to dance her dance of victory. She had done it, she had made contact with her ancestors and had gotten Maria connected with them. It had not just been a vision, but the real thing. She had walked the three planes of the worlds, and lived! After her dance she sat down for more water and a bit more jerky. It had gotten dark and she could hear the call of the coyote. A chill set in, so pupa unrolled her blanket, rolled up in it and laid down for the night.

Early the next morning pupa woke up with first light. She sat up in her blanket, looked around and got to her feet. Grabbing the bag that she carried the ashes of Maria in, she checked it once more. There was the plastic sack with the paper the funeral home had put in with the remains with her name, age, and date of birth, and date of her death, but no ashes. "It was real, it was real," Pupa said with real conviction. She felt so relieved and delighted that she had managed to get Maria to her ancestors.

This experience was going to have to be written in the *Great Book Of The Living Souls* to help others in similar situations. It would first have to be told to the Women Council and if they believed her and thought it worthy, then it would go to the men council and the male Chief. Pupa was excited about telling the council about her journey.

She picked up her paper sack and looked for the Peyote that was left, but it was nowhere in sight. She found the peelings of the other cactus she had peeled and eaten and it looked like that there were enough peelings to make three cactus, but she couldn't remember peeling or eating the third. "Strange," she said. She then rolled up her blankets and started home. She was in a hurry, she wanted to tell someone about her experience. This was big. Her mother had whispered many secrets in her ear when they stood and hugged each other. Secrets that she was to share with her people. Secrets that would give them hope.

After walking all morning and part of the afternoon, Pupa saw the reservation ahead. There was a gathering of people by the grocery store where she bought the beef jerky. Pupa walked towards the people when she started to recognize some of them, they all started to walk towards her.

Jode came running towards Pupa. He reached her before the rest of the crowd did. He wanted to blurt out (Where have you been?) but knew better. He managed to say to her before the rest of the crowd got there, "We were concerned about you, we were going to start a search party and look for you, you've been gone so long."

"What do you mean, I've been gone so long?" Pupa asked. "I told everyone I was going on a trip. Everyone saw me leave yesterday with my war paint on."

"Pupa, that wasn't yesterday that was three days ago. That's a long trip for anyone. We had a right to be worried," Jode said.

"Three Days?" Pupa asked.

"Yes, three days, some of the men are out on horseback, looking for signs of you, but these people and I were waiting for Joe Tracker, we thought we'd have a better chance if we tracked where you went. Your tracks are three days old now and he's the only one that we thought had a chance of following you. We would have started this morning, but Joe is in Flagstaff with his wife having a baby. He should be here any minute now," Jode said.

"Just then, the crowd that was with Jode reached them. "She's all right people, we need to let the searchers on horses know," Jode said.

Pupa held up her hand for silence. "I thank all of you, for being concerned, but I was on a mission and I had no idea how long it would take. It evidently took much longer than I believed it would. But the mission was very important and I learned many secrets of our ancestors that we did not know. I must go home right away and write them down before they leave me."

Pupa was starting to forget some of the secrets her mother told her and she was desperately trying to remember all of them. In a minute, there were several automobiles honking their horns. That was the signal for the horsemen to come back. Some of the horsemen were women, but to the Socike, horsemen meant either men or women. The horns were making more of the secrets leave Pupa. She covered her ears, trying to concentrate on remembering. As she walked on, more were leaving every minute. They were flying out of her head like a flock of birds flying out of a barn after they had been startled. Pupa was beginning to wonder if there would be any left by the time she reached home.

Jode saw Pupa's flight and wanted to help. He was aware of what Pupa was going through. Others had gone through the same thing. The Peyote plant would take them on a trip and they would receive much knowledge, but when they returned they would forget most of it, if not all they had learned. Jode got a friend to drive up in his pickup to give her a ride home so she could get home faster.

As soon as Pupa got in, she immediately got back out. "It'll leave too fast when I'm in there," Pupa said to Jode.

"Would it help if we rode in the back?" Jode asked, as he let down the tailgate.

Pupa started to sit on the tail gate, but as soon as she touched the pickup she immediately stepped back, shook her head and started to walk as fast as she could to her home.

Jode ran to catch her and then walked in front of her to make sure that none would delay her in anyway.

When they reached her house Jode knew that she needed to go

right in without delay. He opened the door for her and closed it behind her. without either of them saying a word.

Pupa grabbed a pen and paper and started to write. She wrote for about fifteen minutes and then could remember no more. "Think, think," she said. "Think, damn it, think." But it was no use, some of the things that she had written down had already left. There were some things that she could remember that her mother had said that she thought she would never forget, for they kept popping back in her head. But some of the things that she wrote she had already lost the memory of, and only had the written words she had scribbled. She tossed down the pen in frustration. She folded her arms on the table and laid her head on them, trying to remember more. In a minute, she was fast asleep.

## Chapter 17

The drive back home from the hospital after seeing Jack O'Reily seemed like the longest she had ever made from Bisbee. The thought of him in that hospital in that condition made her sick to her stomach. The man of her life, the man of her dreams, was being treated like an animal. He was such a kind and gentle person and Pupa and Maria had always treated him like dirt. Why did Maria ever marry him if she was going to treat him so badly, Mary wondered.

As she drove, she rested her head on her hand with her elbow on the window sill of her car, with that window down and the rest up, there was a slight breeze flowing through her black hair, making it flow behind her. Her thoughts were running wild, how did Pupa get that dream in Jack's head?

Mary had spent her childhood on the reservation and had learned the ways of the Socikes Indians, like all the children of the reservation. Pupa had remarried after her first husband's death, she had a child who was Maria's mother. She married Mary's grandfather after he had gotten a divorce from his first wife who had a child, Mary's mother. This was how Maria and Mary became cousins. The two girls didn't have a lot to do with each other as they were growing up, even though they were cousins. Maria was four years older than Mary and had older friends. Mary always wanted to hang out with Maria and became jealous of her when Maria didn't want to spend all of her time with Mary. Mary was actually more Rosa's age, Maria's little sister, being only one year older than Rosa.

But Mary always thought she was too old to hang around young Rosa, so those two girls never became friends, either.

To make matters worse, Pupa and Mary's grandmother, Graybird Yellowhair, were never friends because Pupa had married Graybird's first husband after they had divorced. Later, Graybird Yellowhair became Mrs. Graybird Bluesky after she remarried. Mary had left the reservation for college and had married Harry Smith who was from Benson, Arizona. It had just been a coincidence that Maria had married Jack O'Reily from Benson.

When Mary got home she was all fired up to find out how Pupa had managed to put the dream in Jack's head. She immediately called her mother, Redbird Bluesky, at the reservation. After dialing her number she heard the phone ring four times before someone answered.

"She's not home now," the voice on the other end said. Her mother was on a party line with three other people, and each had their own ring. When the phone of one person would ring, they all rang. Redbird's ring was two short. Another person on the party line was two long; another three short; the other was a long and a short. Each person would have to listen to see when the phone was ringing if it was their ring. Sometimes people would get irritated hearing their phone ring when it wasn't for them and would answer it anyway if it rang too long, as this person did. Or they would just pick up their phone and hang it back up to break the connection, so it would stop ringing. If either case happened and the person making the phone call was on a pay phone, they would loose their money they put in the phone. So the caller sometimes would get very irritated at this practice.

"Where is she?" Mary said in an irritating voice.

"I don't know," The person on the other end of the line said, sounding very young.

"Then how do you know she's not there?" Mary asked.

"Well, it rang a long time," the voice came back.

"Well, she might be outside, you think?" Mary asked.

"Maybe," the voice said back.

"Since you decided to answer her phone for her, then why don't you go over to her house and see. If she is there, ask her to call her daughter," Mary said.

The voice said, "Okay." Then they both hung up.

This really irritated Mary. "That kid won't go over there, I'll just have to call her back later."

She was really getting antsy. Mary paced back and forth. "This isn't doing me any good," Mary said out loud.

Mary sat down to wait and see if her mother was going to call her. She picked up a magazine and started thumbing through it. An article caught her eye, the name *How To Know If Your Man Is Cheating On You,* Mary got half way through the article when her phone rang.

"Hello," Mary said.

"Mary?" The voice on the other end of the line asked.

"Mama? Is that you," Mary asked.

"Yes, I'm sorry, it didn't sound like you," Redbird said.

"That kid did go get you," Mary said.

"Yes, I was out in the yard talking to Blossom. Gladys's little girl came over telling me, you had called. I can't remember her name. But, anyway, I was talking to Blossom. You remember Blossom next door?" Redbird asked.

"Yes, I remember Blossom," Mary said.

"Is everything all right?" Redbird asked.

"Yes, everything is all right. I just wanted to ask you a question." Just then the phone had a hollow sound, which meant that someone was probably listening in on Redbird's party line. "I want it to be private, though. Could you go to the store and call me on the pay phone? Call me collect, and use the phone outside so no one can listen in on your conversation."

"Okay, I'll go right now," and both women hung up.

Mary waited by her phone patiently. After about twenty minutes she was starting to get antsy, why isn't she calling, Mary wondered, it doesn't take that long to walk to the store. In another ten minutes the phone rang. "Hello," Mary said.

"I'm sorry it took me so long, but when I got here there was a tourist on the phone," Redbird said. "Now, what is it that you need that is so secret?"

"Mom, I need to know if you wanted to make someone have terrible dreams, how would you do that?" Mary asked.

"Mary, you know that I can't talk to you about that, until you are reinstated back into the tribe. You got a white man's divorce, but you haven't gotten a Socike divorce, and then I must get permission because of that lie in high school. Until then, I can't talk to you about tribal secrets," Redbird said.

"Mom, please, you know I'm going to do that. I just haven't had time. But I need to know about those bad dreams, terrible dreams," Mary said.

"Why do you need to know that?" Redbird asked.

Mary had no qualms about lying, even to her mother. She had no intention in getting a Socike divorce, and she didn't mind taking advantage of her mother, either. "Mom, please tell me, that is why I had you go to the store and call me, so no one would know. That party line of your... anyone could over hear us. No one would know," Mary said.

"Mary, why do you need to know?" Redbird asked again.

"Mom, I think Maria did something to me to make me have bad dreams before she died. They're terrible, I think I'm going crazy. I've been to three doctors and they can't find anything wrong. I didn't want to say anything about this, but Maria got mad at me before she went to the reservation. She thought that I was flirting with Jack when he came into the Horseshoe. I was just talking to him. After all, he is my cousin's husband. She wouldn't listen. The last time I saw her she said, she would get even if it was the last thing she did," Mary said.

"Maria?" Redbird asked.

"Yes, Maria, she isn't the person everyone thought she was," Mary said.

"I'm sorry, Mary, I didn't know... There are two ways to cause a person to have bad dreams, even nightmares. One is to make a standard Socike dream catcher that is all black. I mean all black. When you do the webbing leave the center hole three times as large as a regular catcher. You then hide the catcher in the room where the person sleeps. This kind of catcher attracts evil spirits. They enter the catcher and the extra large center lets them go right through. They like the catcher so they hang around until they find a human to enter. If more than one person is sleeping in the same room it could enter either person. The other way to make a person have a bad dream, and this is a surer way, is to have caught an evil dream, and then take the catcher to where you want to hide it. Don't cut the center because it will let the evil spirit right out. If you cut it to soon, it will go into you. So you cut the first and second string next to the center. It will take the spirit awhile to find his way out, and it will go into whoever sleeps in the room where you hide it. That's it, those are the only two ways to make a person have bad dreams, that I know of," Redbird said.

"Well, how do I get rid of it?" Mary asked.

"You could try to make a dream catcher that is all black, hang it in your room, just in case it is a stray spirit. But if it is a dream that was let out on you like you think, then it won't go into another dream catcher for several years. You would have to find the original catcher it came from, and make the hole smaller or repair it, whichever it needs. The spirit has become accustom to their dream catcher and will return to it, you know it can be more than one spirit. It can be many spirits," Redbird said. "But, You must use the very same webbing to repair it or it won't work, I mean you have to get it off the same spool or ball that the original webbing came from, unless you use a special webbing you would have to make."

"How would I make the special webbing?" Mary asked.

"You have to make it from a virgin female feline's gut. It doesn't mater if it is a mountain lion, bobcat, or just a house cat. But it must be a virgin feline. You kill the cat, take out the guts, clean them, cut in strips, and twist them into a long string and dry in the sun until ready to use," Redbird said. The best bet is to look around your house and see if you can find a dream catcher that she hid in your home, most likely it would be in your bed room. If she removed it, you will have to find out where she left it. That is, if she didn't destroy it," Redbird said. "Good luck, dear."

"Thanks, Mom. I really appreciate this and don't worry, I won't tell anyone that you discussed this with me. I'll let you go now, thanks again," Mary said.

"Mary if you don't have any luck with the dream that is bothering you, I'll come down and help you," Redbird said.

"I'll call you and let you know if I need any help," Mary said. "Goodbye now."

"I love you, Mary, goodbye," Red bird said.

It was getting late and it was time for Mary to get ready to go to work at the Horseshoe. After she was at work for a while and Mary was into her regular routine, she let her mind wander to the conversation she had with her mother earlier. If someone had left a dream catcher in Jack's house who would have it now? She noticed Bob Atkee sitting at the counter, drinking coffee. She knew that he was Jack's landlord, because Jack was always complaining about him.

Mary took a fresh pot of coffee over to Bob, "Hey, Bob, how you doing?" She asked as she freshened his coffee.

"Doing good, how you doing?" Bob asked.

"Oh, I'm doing alright," Mary said. "You know, we sent the ashes of Maria to her grandmother's on the reservation. They had the services there. I wanted to go, but I couldn't get off work."

"Old Bill wouldn't let you off work so you could go to your own cousin's funeral?" Bob asked.

*Uh- oh, I shouldn't have said that. I didn't know Bob knew my boss,* Mary thought. "Well, I'm sure he would have, but it was going to cut us so short-handed here, that I didn't want to do that to the other girls, besides, my car was broken down at that time," Mary said.

"Oh," Bob said. "I was wondering why there wasn't a funeral here. So her folks on the reservation had the funeral there?" Bob asked.

"Yes," Mary lied.

"I only saw her a few times when I went to collect the rent. She seemed to be very nice, not like her husband Jack. That sure is something about him being in Yaford, isn't it?" Bob asked.

"Yea, something," Mary said. "Bob…, I gave Maria some trinkets, I sure wish I had one or two of them. You know for a keep sake, especially because I didn't get to go to her funeral. You wouldn't know who has her things, would you?" Mary asked.

"Well, yes, I have their furniture and household items, holding them for the rent money Jack owes. I was going to auction it off at the end of this month. But if you want to come by, I'll let you look through it, and see if there is something you want," Bob said.

"That would be great. How about tomorrow?" Mary asked.

"Tomorrow morning would be fine. Tomorrow afternoon I have to go to Tucson," Bob said.

"How about nine o'clock?" Mary asked.

"That would work out fine. Why don't I just meet you at Jones's Self Storage, number six? That's where I have it stored," Bob asked.

"Great, I'll see you tomorrow morning at nine," Mary said, as she turned and walked back to her side of the cafe to wait on her own customers. As she walked, she gave a little more wiggle than usual, for Bob's viewing pleasure.

Early the next morning, Mary was up getting ready to go meet Bob. She decided to wear something that would reveal her figure, she knew her charms helped her get what she wanted and she used them to her advantage often. This morning she wore tight jeans and a midi blouse that showed her navel and some mid section of her hourglass figure. Mary strutted in front or her full length mirror. *Not bad for my age,* she thought.

Mary arrived at Jones's Self Storage fifteen minutes early. Bob Atkee was already there waiting for her. "Oh, I hope I didn't make you wait long, I thought I was early," Mary said as she stepped out of her automobile.

"No, I just got here. In fact, you are early. Something I admire in a woman," Bob said, and started walking towards her. He bumped his knee on the bumper as he stepped around his truck because he had his eyes on Mary's mid section instead of where he was going.

Mary saw this and wanted to laugh, but she didn't dare. She was on a mission and she didn't want to spoil it by making Bob angry or embarrass him. Mary bowed her head to hide her true feelings and tried to keep the smirk off her face. When she got it together, she lifted her head and smiled at him.

Bob's knee really hurt, but he let on that it didn't. He couldn't help but be a little embarrassed, but he tried not to show it. This didn't keep him from admiring Mary's figure. "It's right over here," he said, as he walked to number six. Mary hurried up to catch up with him. As Bob was fumbling with the lock, Mary stepped right in front of him and very close, then leaned against the over head door, so when he got the lock opened he was staring right into her eyes. This made him nervous, so he dropped his eyes and was starring into her open neck blouse, which revealed two very shapely breast. This made him even more nervous so he lifted his eyes and he was once again staring into her dark eyes. Mary smiled at him and tilted her head. Then she stepped to the side so he could open the door.

Bob reached down grabbed the door and lifted it up. It was dark inside, he had to step around Mary to reach the other end of the door where the light switch was. When he flipped the light on, the whole room was illuminated. There were beds, dressers, a television and other furniture and boxes crammed in up to the ceiling. "This is it, their furniture and everything they had in the house. I really don't know how you can find any thing in this mess. You might want to look in that box over there, it seemed to have some of Maria's things in it," Bob said.

Mary was overwhelmed with what she saw. There was no way she could go through all of this, her heart sank. She turned her eyes to where Bob pointed out a box. "It seems to have some of Maria's things in it," he said.

There it was, the dream catcher sitting right on top. Mary gasped, then tried to cover it by coughing. Her heart was beating so fast, she could hardly get her breath. Mary slowly stepped over to the box and picked up a small jewelry box and pretended to be interested in it, then she lay it down and just looked over the box for a moment. She reached down and picked up the dream catcher. This was it, the very sight of this evil thing gave Mary butterflies. All black and old, *I'll bet it was Pupa who turned those dreams loose on Jack,* Mary thought. Mary fingered the cut place in the web. This was it.

Bob stared at Mary as she was transfixed on the dream catcher, oblivious to every thing else in the world. After a minute, "Are you all right?" Bob asked.

This snapped her out of her trance. "A... yes, I'm fine. This, I gave to Maria," she lied. "How much do you want for it?" Mary asked in a very serious voice and manner.

"I wouldn't charge you for that. Why don't you look through the rest of this stuff and see if there is something else you want?" Bob asked.

"This is all I need," Mary said, still serious and not doing any flirting any more.

"Well, okay. I'll tell you what, when we get everything spread out for the auction, I'll let you know so you can come over before anyone else gets to see it, okay?" Bob said.

Mary was holding the dream catcher close to her in a manner that no one could grab it out of her grasp, if they had a mind to. "Thank you very much, Bob. You are so kind." With this she went to her car and drove off, leaving Bob staring after her.

*That old dream catcher must have meant a lot to her,* Bob thought. *I'm* glad I didn't throw it out. He closed the door and locked it, then headed off to his own business.

Mary got home so excited she could hardly contain herself. "This is it, this is it!" She said. She took the dream catcher and studied it carefully. The webbing was thin and black. She wondered if she should die her webbing black also. "Dang! I wish I had asked Mom if it had to be the same color," she said to herself. It hadn't crossed her mind, that it wouldn't be like most dream catchers and be a yellowish brown like ninety nine percent of them. *I'd better call her*, she thought. No, I can't do that, if I mention a color she'll know it's more than what I told her.

A dream catcher this old was more than just a regular dream catcher. A dream catcher this old was something special and the color was something out of the secrets of the council. If her mother suspected that she had something that the council should know about she would have the council come down and take her back to the reservation whether she wanted to go or not. Most people didn't know that some of the Indian tribes had their secret service just like the U.S. Government did. And they were not to be dealt with lightly. The Socike nation was a very proud and patriotic people. That was why when a woman married out of her nation she was no longer a citizen. This was something she was just going to have to figure out herself.

There was certainly no way to get the webbing from the original source, so she was going to have to get the virgin feline some place for the webbing. If I get a cat, how am I going to know if she is a virgin? Mary wondered. Then it hit her, a female kitten. she could go to the humane society. That would delay it a day or two because she knew that before they adopted animals out they spayed them first.

Mary picked up the paper and looked for the pets section. There it was, pets for free. Her eyes wandered down the column until it stopped on an add that read, free to good home, eight week old kittens. Mary picked up the phone and dialed the number that was in the ad. After a brief conversation Mary made an appointment to see the kittens.

Mary drove to the house right on time for the appointment to see the kittens. It was in an old part of the town and at a run down house. As Mary walked up to the house there were three cats that ran across her path. *This place must be full of cats,* Mary thought. She didn't like the looks of the place, but she figured, I'll get the cat and get out of here. After knocking two times, an old woman dressed in rags came to the door. "What do you want?" The old woman asked.

"I'm Mary. I talked to you a few minutes ago about the kittens you have to give away."

"I didn't talk to no one, and I ain't got no cats to give away," the old lady said.

"Not cats, ma'am, kittens," Mary said.

"I ain't got none of dem eater," the old lady said.

"Grandma, that lady is here to see me," a voice behind the old lady said.

"You... then why didn't she say so?" The old lady asked, and stepped back out of the way.

A pretty young lady stepped to the door. "I'm sorry about the confusion, I'm Gloria," the young lady said. "I'm the one you talked to. This is my grandmother's place and I come over and try to help her with some of her affairs, please come in."

Mary stepped in to the dark room. It took a minute for her eyes to become accustomed to the darkness. The stench hit her as soon as she stepped in the doorway.

The place was filthy, there was a sofa with newspapers piled on one end. A coffee table piled high with mail and other things, two chairs were there each with stuff piled on them. The old woman sat down on the sofa that was covered with cat hair.

"The kittens are back here," Gloria said as she stepped to the kitchen.

Mary was glad that she wasn't offered a seat. In the kitchen things were worse. Two cats were on the table that was piled high with open cereal boxes and open cans along with dirty dishes. On the floor was a box with kittens.

"There are two males and four females," Gloria said. "They are a little wild, but I think they would calm right down with a little human interaction."

"The gray one, is that a male or female?" Mary asked.

Gloria reached down and picked up the gray kitten, that gave a hiss out at her. Turning it over to look at the area below the tail. "I think this is a female, yes it's a female," she said after careful examination. "Did you want a male or female?" she asked.

"A female," Mary said.

"Do you want this one?" Gloria asked.

"Yes, I like that one," Mary said.

"Good, I'll get a box for you," Gloria said, and went to a corner of the kitchen where there were several boxes for this purpose. She put the kitten in one and folded the top over, interlocking the four flaps so they would stay shut. "Would you like another?" She asked, hoping that Mary would take more off her hands. "They really get along good when you have two."

"No, I only need one, I mean, I only want one. Thanks anyway," Mary said, relieved she wouldn't have to touch that kitten to get it home. "Thank you very much," Mary said again, and reached out taking the box with the kitten in it. As she walked through the living room the old lady mumbled something about her granddaughter giving away all of her cats. After she was outside she almost ran to her car. She was never so glad to get out of a place in her life.

Driving home, Mary could hear the kitten trying to get out of the box. "Feisty, aren't you? Well, I chose you because you were the ugliest of all," Mary said to the kitten.

When she reached home Mary was pondering whether to kill the kitten now or wait until tomorrow when she would have more time. As a child growing up on the reservation she had to catch rabbits, kill, skin and gut them for fur and meat. But it wasn't something she liked to do. It crossed her mind to simply put the box in the freezer and take it out after work when the kitten was dead. If she did that, she would put herself behind another day and Jack was depending on her to help him. "Oh… what the hell, it's not like I haven't killed an animal before," she said.

Mary took the box out to a tool shed that was in her back yard; looking around she found a hammer. "This will work," she said. Mary very carefully opened the box and started to grab the kitten. The kitten arched her back and gave a hissing sound. "It's like you can read my mind," She said. "Don't worry, I won't hurt you," Mary said, as she stroked the back of the kitten near the hind legs so she wouldn't get the business end of the sharp claws. After doing this a little while the kitten quieted down and Mary was able to pick it up. She placed it on a bench, took a firm hold of it's neck and lifted the hammer to smash it's head. Just then the kitten turned in it's own skin and managed to sink her claws on all four feet in deep and started ripping the skin on Mary's arm. Mary let go of the kitten and let out a few choice swear words. She looked at her hand and arm, the blood was rushing out.

The kitten headed for the door which was shut, but clawed at the bottom where she managed to spread the doors apart enough to squeeze out.

Mary gave out with some words that would make a sailor blush. "I should have frozen you to death," she yelled. "You little bastard."

As she walked out of the shed she saw a car parked in the street with a lady at the front wheel kneeling down. Mary walked out to the street and then she saw her kitten on the street by the front wheel. The head was smashed. The lady was crying. When she saw Mary, she looked up, "It just darted out so fast, I didn't have time to stop," she said.

Mary looked at the woman, and wanted to tell her she had done her a favor but didn't dare. "That's all right the cat was very wild; and it isn't your fault. I'll take care of it for you." Mary picked it up like she really cared for it and as soon as she was out of sight of the lady she then held it by the tail and dropped it into the box she had brought it home in.

Mary looked at her arm and the blood had stopped but there were some deep scratches. She went inside and washed her arm off in the kitchen sink. After she got her hand and arm cleaned off Mary went into the bathroom and got a bottle of alcohol and some cotton swabs. When she applied the alcohol to her arm and hand she could feel the burning going deep. Being a true Socike she didn't let it show even in private. Her mother used to tell her that, "It was more important to be brave in private than in public. Anyone one could put up a front in public, but a true Socike lived the life of bravery."

Mary noticed it was getting time to start getting ready for work. I'd better wait until tomorrow to do this, so she went and got the dead kitten in the box and put the whole thing in the freezer. She had already taken a shower that morning right after she got out of bed so she just needed to wash up, put on fresh clothes and make up and she would be ready for work.

In a few minutes Mary was on her way to work in her old clunker.

She had plenty of time so she stopped off at the local auto parts house and picked up four more quarts of oil and put them under her front seat.

When she arrived at the restaurant Mary was thirty minutes early for her shift so she went behind the counter and got herself a cup of coffee and sat at one of the empty tables in the dining room. She was there contemplating the day's events when she noticed that she was scratching herself a lot. It felt like a bug bit her in her arm pit and she put her hand inside her blouse and put her finger right on the spot where it felt like she was getting bitten. It felt like a small hard grain of sand so she pinched the small hard thing and pulled it out to take a look. She had it pinched between her index finger and her thumb. As she spread them apart she noticed a small brown thing about a third the size of a tiny bead. She lifted her hand closer to her face to get a better look and the speck jumped. "Fleas," Mary said. Then she looked around to see if any one had heard her. *That damn cat gave me fleas*, she thought.

She went through her shift itching and scratching trying to pick off fleas that were not really there. She never found another flea, but her skin felt like she was crawling with them. She had been off the reservation too long to put up with fleas. As a child her family lived in a house with dirt floors, as many of her friends' families did. She and some of her friends would get fleas once in a while from the many dogs that roamed free there because people aren't covered with hair the fleas would leave of their own accord in a very short time. She wasn't a child now and she hadn't been an outdoors woman since she left the reservation. She did not like fleas or any other vermin, little or big.

First thing Mary did after she got home was take a shower and use lots of soap. Next thing was take out the frozen kitten and put it on the back screened porch, to thaw out. She then hit the bed and went right to sleep, she was worn out.

## Chapter 18

Pupa woke up the following morning after she had gotten back from the trip. She was still at the table where she had been writing down the things that her mother had revealed to her. She was trying to remember the things her mother told her when she had fallen asleep.

Pupa got up from the table and looked outside, it was dark. She assumed it was that evening. Then she saw the glow from the sun in the east. Checking the clock in her kitchen she realized it was the following morning. "My God," She said. "I've slept through the rest of the afternoon, evening, and the night." This was something that she had never done before and would have never dreamed of doing, wasting a whole afternoon and evening.

Pupa sat back down at her table where the paper was that she had written down the things that she remembered that her mother had told her. Before looking at the paper she tried to remember the things that her mother revealed to her. She could remember that in the afterlife all power was given to you to do good, within the boundaries of the spirit world, if you were a true Socike in the mortal world. She couldn't remember what her mother said was a true Socike. After all the Socike's took in many outside the blood line to help build up the nation and keep it strong. They were even big on adopting children from other Indians tribes or nations and raising them as Socikes.

Pupa tried to remember what her mother had said about the boundaries of the spirit world. As hard as she tried, she just couldn't remember.

Next, she remembered that after you go to your ancestors you can change your looks to a certain extent. Like her mother was more beautiful than when she had ever seen her before, she didn't have the birth mark on her chin anymore and she seemed taller than she remembered her, but Pupa recognized her. Her mother had told her what the boundaries of the changes were, but she just couldn't remember what she had said about it.

She remembered that her mother said that all good and honorable Indians went to the plane of the ancestors, but all evil and cowards went to be Sand Walkers and live on their plane.

She could remember that a person whom most people, both white and Indians alike, did not respect at first, would rise to lead the Socike nation to great glory.

This was all that she could remember of the secrets her mother told her. She studied the paper that she wrote the day before of the secrets. On it was everything she could remember and after the sentence about a person who would rise to lead the nation to great glory was a sentence that stated, "That person will be a descendent of Eagle Woman, and female." Also was written was that Sand Walkers never live longer than one thousand years, where the ancestors lived forever. Then followed was that ancestors or Sand Walkers could go into any bird or animal and become them. The last thing that was written was, if a woman or man married out of her race that they were still Indian and should be able to have the same rights and same funeral as any Indian of good standing, according to the traditions of their tribe.

This was all important and Pupa had to get this information to the Women Council right away. Pupa went about her kitchen making herself coffee and getting herself breakfast. After eating she got out her calendar and figured out what day it was now, by what Jode had told her and to see when the next council meeting was. If her calculation was right there was a meeting that would start early this afternoon.

It was light now and Pupa heard a knock at the door. She opened the front door and there stood Jode smiling. "Good morning, Pupa," he said.

"Good morning, come in. Do you have time for coffee?" Pupa asked.

"Yes, thank you. I went to the stable early so I could come back here and maybe get a chance to talk to you," Jode said as he walked into Pupa's kitchen and sat at her table.

Pupa poured him a cup of coffee. "Is there something in particular you wanted to talk about or did you just want to visit?" Pupa asked.

"I just wanted to make sure you were alright and to visit," Jode said. "Are you alright?" Jode asked.

"Why... yes, why do you ask?" Pupa asked.

"Well, for one thing you still have on your war paint," Jode said in a soft timid voice. Even though he was speaking to Pupa his friend, she was still Pupa, chief of the Women Council. She held the highest and most honorable office any women could hold in all of the Indians nations anywhere.

Pupa instinctively put her hand to her face. She could feel the harden paint. "After you left me yesterday, I came right in and started to write down the things that I had remembered. I laid my head down to try to think more clearly when I fell asleep. I just woke up a few minutes a go."

"Wow, that was some nap, I'm sure you deserved it, after the journey you took," Jode said.

Pupa smiled, "It was, some journey, and I couldn't have made it without the help of you and your friend Big Crow. Be sure and thank him for me, will you?"

"I will, and it was our privilege to help you with something so noble," Jode said.

"Would you help me with something else?" Pupa asked.

"Sure, anything." Jode answered.

Pupa put the calendar in front of him. "What day is it?" She asked, with a big smile.

Jode put his finger on the number sixteen, "This is where we are today."

"That's what I thought, from what you said yesterday," Pupa said. "I have a council meeting today."

"Yes, you do, and that's all I've heard talked about, yesterday. I'll bet you don't have one absent member today. Everyone wants to know about your trip and the knowledge you bring back to them," Jode said.

"I can't remember as much as I'd like, I was told so much, and most of it left like a covey of Quail that has been spooked by a coyote," Pupa said.

"Yes, that's what I've always been told happens about those trips," Jode said. "I've never been on one. My mother and father always told me it was a trip to only take in an emergency and never to take it lightly," Jode said.

"Your mother and father told you right. It is not something to take lightly," Pupa agreed.

Their conversation went on about small parts of the trip, but Pupa never got into any important parts of the trip. Jode was a friend, but he was too young to hold a high enough position in the tribe to be told the more important secrets of the Socike nation.

After Jode finished his coffee he went back to the stables and Pupa took a shower and washed off the war paint. Pupa put away all of the things she had gotten out for her trip and straightened up the rest of the house. She then ate an early lunch and left in her traditional Socike dress to walk the six blocks to the Women Council meeting.

Pupa was early for the meeting, but to her surprise, the lodge was full. When she came through the front door a cheer went up and all the women clapped their hands to greet her.

Rose Bud, the one every one called Bud, was the person who presided over meetings when the Pupa was not present, she stood up and spoke after Pupa had gotten to her seat. "Great Pupa, we the council, stand to pay you kudos. Anita Yellowhair, we are proud to have you as our Pupa. When we elected you Chief Squaw we thought you would do us proud and now we know it." The council stood and applauded.

After the applause stopped and everyone took their seats, Rose Bud went on. "All fifteen members are here, you can start the meeting whenever you like."

Pupa was still standing, "Members of the Women Council, I am honored by your kind words. I promise to do all in my power to be a leader that you can be proud of." With this, there was another round of applause. "Keeper of the book, you may start the meeting" Pupa sat down.

A younger woman in her fifties stood up and addressed the council, then read from the book the events of the last meeting. They went through the rest of the meeting in a hurry, not bringing up any unnecessary things that would prolong the meeting. Everyone was anxious to hear about Pupa's trip and the knowledge she brought back to them.

When it was time for Pupa to speak she stood and again addressed the Women Council. "As you all have probably heard, I went on a trip courtesy of the Peyote plant. This trip was advised to me by a bear spirit. It was to find out what to do with the ashes of my granddaughter who had been cremated off the reservation. She was no longer considered a member of the Socike nation. I was concerned that she would not find her ancestors. This concern was reinforced by a visit from my granddaughter, Maria. I am here to report that she is now in the care of her ancestors." This being said, there was applause from the council.

"On my trip I encountered three forms of sand walkers. Two were the same walker but in a different form, the third was a different walker," Pupa said.

There were two women writing this all down. One was the woman that read out of the book in the beginning, called the Keeper of the Book. The other was a person who had been a keeper of the book, but after her term she would write in a second book to compare with the writing of the keeper of the book. This was to make sure there were no mistakes on something this important. She was only called on to do this on special occasions.

Pupa went on, "I saw many wondrous things. I saw Eagle Woman and her husband Brava. By the way, Eagle Woman is beautiful, I know there has been some discussion on this part, whether she was beautiful or ugly, there was never an option that she was half way, just average. Anyway, she is beautiful now. I found out that after we die we can change our looks to some extent. But your ancestors will always recognize you and your children, your grandchildren, your great-grandchildren, your great-great-grandchildren will always recognize you. Those of you who knew my mother, she doesn't have that birth mark on her chin now. Everyone is in good health and great shape. They never lose a battle with the sand walkers." Pupa went on about all that she had seen and what she could remember of what her mother told her.

After Pupa told about all of her experience and what her mother told her that she could remember, Pupa gave the paper that she had written down what she had remembered when she returned home to the council, and left for home.

The council then discussed the things that Pupa had told them and looked over the things that the paper had written on it. Rose Bud took the place of Pupa for this matter, because Pupa was who took the trip, so someone else had to handle the rest of this matter. In this matter, Rose Bud was in the acting role of Pupa. Pupa (Anita Yellowhair) had done all she could do. The rest of this matter was left to the Women Council and the Men Council, then the chief of the nation.

The Women Council discussed everything pertaining to this and then after everyone who wanted to say something had their say and then they voted. Rose Bud chose someone to help her with this matter. Everyone else left, but the Keeper of the Book and the one keeping the second book stayed and went over what each person wrote. The two books were almost identical. Rose Bud and the woman she chose to help her, took the opinion of the council to the Men Council. This was to set up a meeting to present them for consideration to be entered into the *Great Book Of The Living Souls*.

Pupa had finished her mission of getting her granddaughter to her ancestors. She had brought back knowledge that her nation may use in their *Great Book Of The Living Souls*. She was very disappointed that she couldn't remember more, but what she did remember was more than any other Indian had remembered since the starting of the Great Book. Pupa couldn't help but wonder how much of what she brought back, if any, would be entered into the Great Book. It was not easy to get anything entered. The men council scrutinized everything that was proposed to be entered. So did the Chief. They didn't want anything that was not absolutely right going into this holy book. Pupa had done all she could do now. Now she could concentrate on seeing her granddaughter, Rosa.

Pupa spent the next few days getting the yard cleaned up and all the bushes trimmed. She made sure everything was picked up around her house then she concentrated on the inside. She cleaned and cleaned again. She took all of the bed clothing and washed them. She took potpourri and put in some of the drawers and out in a small bowl. All of this to make the house feel like home to Rosa.

Rosa never had her own room, she had to sleep on the living room sofa as a child because Maria was the oldest and the oldest always was the one to get things first. She left home about the same time Maria did, so she never had her own room. So Pupa took out the things that used to be Maria's. Then she put some of Rosa's things that she still had, in Maria's old room. She was hoping that Rosa would feel welcome and stay with her a while. Finally, Pupa felt she was ready for a visit from Rosa.

# Chapter 19

Mary woke up late, after a night of tossing and turning. She had a hard time getting any real rest and was still tired. She got her coffee and sat down to think over the way she should do the cat's guts to make a string out of them. She finally decided that she had done it to rabbits and squirrels as a child and she even had to skin them for fur and meat. This was no big deal.

She got up from the table, took a sharp knife, the dead kitten, and a mop bucket out in the yard where she opened the kitten's stomach up and pulled out the insides. The stench went up into her nostrils and she almost gagged. Mary had forgotten how much this sort of thing stunk. She then separated the rest of the insides from the intestines. Next she stripped out the food that was in the intestines and took them to the outside water Faucet, filled the bucket and washed both the inside and outside of the guts. She found a cardboard box, cut down the side and laid it out flat. There she stretched the gut out to visualize the size of the string it would make if she twisted it whole. It would be way too big, so she had to cut it into strips. After she had a strip she thought would be just about right, she tied one end to a twig about the size of her middle finger on a tree. Next she dug out a Popsicle stick from the trash. She then tied the Popsicle stick to the other end and started twisting it as she also stretched out the strip of cat gut. As she was twisting the strip she ran her hand up and down the string to keep it uniform. It was getting disgusting to her on how long it took to make a string, but she stayed with it. After a while it looked like a string. To make sure it was uniform Mary dipped her hand in the bucket of water and ran her hand over the string harder to make it smooth. When she let up on the string it would twist around itself, so she stretched the string out, putting pressure on the green twig, bending it. She then reached another green twig that had a fork near the end, she pulled it towards the popsicle stick. Putting the popsicle stick behind the fork in the twig with the string going through the fork, she let up on the two twigs and let the small branches stretch the string out straight. This kept tension on the string but would give when the string shrank. It was done. She would get the string after the sun dried it. Getting some newspapers she cleaned up her mess and threw it in the trash.

After washing off the blood and gunk she sat down for another cup of coffee. She deserved it. She felt like she could still smell stench from the kitten. She sure didn't feel like eating anything after that. As Mary sat there having her coffee, she started trying to think of a way she could get the dream catcher in the room with Jack. Maybe if she took it in there in her purse enough times the spirit would go into it and get caught. It was a long shot, but she couldn't think of anything else she could do. She even thought of telling Dr. Gonzales that Jack believed in dream catchers and maybe putting one in with him might help him. But she was afraid that he wouldn't go along with that and might be on the lookout for her trying to sneak one into his room.

Mary got up and started getting ready for work. She still hadn't thought of a good way to get that dream catcher in Jack's room for any length of time. She changed her clothes and was brushing her hair in front of the mirror in her bedroom when she noticed a large picture of herself she had hanging in her bed room. Excitedly, she took it down and got the dream catcher. Laying the picture face down on her bed she laid the dream catcher on top of it. She then folded the beads and feathers that normally hung straight down from the catcher back over the catcher. It would fit if she could get the dream catcher to fit behind the picture. Mary finished getting ready for work, grabbed the picture and headed for work.

On her way to work Mary stopped at a large shop that sold souvenirs, leather goods, and pictures. They made their own frame work for the pictures they sold. Mary took the picture of her in the shop. In a few minutes she was leaving the shop without the picture.

She went on to work, knowing she had found the answer to her problem.

Two days later, Mary went back to the shop where she had left her picture and picked it up in a new frame. The frame was very plain but deep. This was what she wanted. They made it so it could be hung or set up on a table. After getting it home she took off the back and used it for a pattern to cut out a piece of cardboard that size. She then took the cardboard and put it behind the picture. Then she took the dream catcher and put it behind the cardboard and folded the feathers and beads upon the dream catcher. She then took the back that she had taken off and placed it over the dream catcher. She held it all together and held it up right to see if her idea would work. She decided it would. She would only have to move the little nails that held the back on, further out. She then took off the back and got out the dream catcher. Laying out the dream catcher on the table as she slowly shook her head, she murmured, "How evil this looks."

Going outside she got the string that she had left to dry on the tree. It had been drying for two days. Mary took it inside It was too stiff to be of much use as a string. She had two options, one was to mix a concoction of oils and herbs and soak the gut for two days. That way it would stay flexible. The other way it would be flexible for only a day or two, but it would be much faster. That way was to steam the string. She decided to steam it. Mary put a pan of water on the stove then placed a screen on top. When the steam started she rolled up the string and placed it on the screen. Mary kept checking it and turning it over several times until it was flexible.

Mary studied the knots and she was sure she could tie it the same. Armed with a pair of scissors and small pliers she took the cat gut string and mended the dream catcher. The new string looked so light; almost white, compared to the black mesh. Mary decided to take some black shoe polish and wipe on the new string to make it blend in. She didn't know if this was necessary, but she didn't figure it would hurt anything. Pretty soon she had it looking like it was all the same. She took the dream catcher and placed it back in the picture frame the way she just had it. Then, taking the small nails, she moved them back, so anyone who might examine it, wouldn't suspect that there was more than just a picture. She set it on her dresser and it stayed standing up like it was supposed to; *success*, she thought.

Mary then called Dr. Gonzales at Yaford hospital and made an appointment for her to see Jack tomorrow on her day off. After that she got ready for work.

It was the first good day, or rather night, she had at work in a long while. She had been so worried about Jack, but now she had the answer to all of their problems. She just knew it, somehow, in her heart she new this was the beginning of her happiness with Jack, her beloved. "Don't worry, darling, the cavalry is coming," She said in a low voice, that no one else could hear.

Mary arrived at Yaford hospital in the beautiful town of Bisbee, Arizona, at around ten the following morning. *What a beautiful place,* she thought as she ascended the front stairs of the hospital. The sun was up and she knew the day would get warm even though winter was approaching. Just as she stepped onto the stoop she was startled by a loud screech. Just a few feet above the top of the door perched on a window sill of the second floor was a red tail hawk, making threatening jesters at her. His mouth was open and Mary thought he would attack at any moment. She put her large bag she was caring for a purse over her head and rushed through the door. Then she walked over to the receptionist, "You people should do something about that hawk you have stationed at the front door!" Mary said.

"What...? Hawk...? What are you talking about?" The lady sitting behind the desk asked.

"The hawk right outside your front door, I thought it was going to attack me," Mary said.

"It's there now?" The lady asked.

"Yes..., now," Mary said.

The lady got up from her chair and went to the door.

"Be careful," Mary said.

The lady stepped through the door, walked out on the stoop and looked up, then came back in. "I don't see a hawk or any bird of any kind. Sometimes there are pigeons that roost out there, are you sure it wasn't a pigeon?" The lady asked.

It infuriated Mary for the lady to ask such a question. She went back outside and looked for the hawk she had just seen moments earlier. It was gone, it was nowhere to be seen. She came back in to where the woman was standing. "It's gone, but it was a red tail hawk,

I know the difference between a hawk and a pigeon. It probably has a nest on the roof. It was there the other time I came. You should have someone check it out," Mary said.

"I'll have Max take a look. You're here to see Jack, aren't you?" The lady asked.

"Yes I am," Mary said.

"I thought I recognized you. You are Mary Smith, right?" The lady asked.

"Right," Mary said.

"I'll let Dr. Gonzales know you are here," and she walked off to Dr. Gonzales' office. In a minute, she stepped out of his office, "He can see you now," She said and walked back to her desk.

When Mary walked into Dr. Gonzales' office he rose, "So good to see you again, Ms Smith. Did you have a good drive down from Benson?" he asked.

"Very good," Mary answered. "It's a beautiful day out there."

"Well, Jack is expecting you, but don't expect too much, he really hasn't changed any that I can tell. I'm hoping that your regular visits will help. If you are willing to take your time to help us help him, we will be forever grateful," Dr. Gonzales said.

"I'll do whatever I can," Mary said.

"If you are ready, shall we go see him?" Dr. Gonzales asked.

Mary followed the doctor to the room where they kept Jack. There were two chairs there now and Jack was sitting in one. There was an orderly standing nearby, to make sure that Jack didn't hurt himself as he had so often tried.

"Jack?" Dr. Gonzales said.

Jack looked up at him, but didn't say a word.

"Jack, Mary Smith is here to see you. We are going to leave you alone, but we will be right outside the door and if you try anything, you know what I mean. If you do anything that you're not supposed to, we will cut the visit off, right then. Do you understand?" Dr. Gonzales asked.

Jack looked up at the doctor, he didn't want to say anything but he knew that he had better. The good doctor was not adverse to using an electrical cattle prod on his more stubborn patients. "Yes," he murmured.

The doctor nodded to the orderly and they both left.

Mary moved her chair over to where Jack was sitting. Then sat down and put her large bag down next to Jack's chair. The chair was a little wobbly because the whole floor was covered with a padded mat. Mary put her arm around Jack's shoulder, "Darling, listen to me carefully, your dreams are going to stop soon, believe me," Mary said.

Jack turned his haggard face to Mary and smiled. "You brought me some poison!"

"No..., No, I didn't bring you any poison, but your dreams will stop, I promise," she said.

"I told you to bring me poison, that's how you could help me," Jack moaned.

Mary started rubbing his shoulder and back. She got real close and kissed his ear. "Listen to me, Jack O'Reily. I came to rescue you from the demons that haunt you in your dreams," Mary whispered in his ear. She then took the picture out of her bag and stood it up on the mat so Jack could see it. "Look at my picture, Jack." Mary said.

Jack looked at the picture she sat up on the mat, then turned back, not at all interested in it.

Dr. Gonzales left the orderly at the door and he went up to the room above them. There he watched what was going on below with Jack and Mary. "She brought him a picture of herself. He doesn't look too interested in it. In fact, he doesn't look too interested in her on this visit," he said to Jane, who was sitting there, taking notes.

"Give her a chance," Jane said.

"Oh, you think she's going to win him over with her womanly charms, huh?" Doctor said.

"Maybe. Don't under estimate a woman's charms," Jane said.

"You listen to me. I'm your only hope! I love you and I know that you love me, too. I know what is causing your dreams. You were right, Anita was the one who caused this, I'm sure."

"I know you can't understand this, but your only hope is that picture. Look at it and keep it near. Don't let them take it away from you. JACK! LOOK AT IT!" Mary said, very firm.

Jack turned his head and looked.

Mary was kissing his face and running her hands over his back, shoulders, and arms. "That's it, keep looking at the picture," Mary said. She pulled his head down on her shoulder.

"Why couldn't you just have brought me the poison? This would have all been over," Jack moaned, rocking his head back and forth on Mary's shoulders. "I don't want to live any longer, I can't stand the horror."

All the time Mary was rubbing his back and shoulders with one hand and his chest with the other. "Trust me, Jack. Trust me," she whispered in his ear.

Dr. Gonzales and Jane were taking all of this in. After thirty minutes The doctor went down to get Mary out of the room. The attendants came in and strapped Jack to the floor just as Mary was leaving the room. "Please set my picture where he can see it," Mary said. Dr. Gonzales nodded to one of the orderlies and the orderly put it about three feet away.

Jack remembered Mary's words to look at her picture, so he kept his eyes on it, as she and the doctor left. This impressed Dr. Gonzales.

When they got to his office, Mary turned to him. "You saw the picture I left for Jack. I was wondering if you would be so kind as to leave it with Jack for a few days?" Mary asked.

"Because I think it might help, I'll leave it for now. But, if I think it should be taken away, for Jack's health, I'll remove it. Right now he couldn't be much worse than what he is, I can't see how it can hurt. I thank you for coming; will I see you again next week?" Dr. Gonzales asked.

"I'll be here, but I'll call again first. I was wondering, do you think I might be able to stay longer?" Mary asked.

"Let's wait and see how things go this week. Then we can decide next week when you come," Dr. Gonzales said.

Mary nodded, and left.

# Chapter 20

The following week Mary went to visit Jack and was informed by Dr. Gonzales, that Jack was getting better, and he believed it was the picture of her that was helping him. When Mary was escorted to his room, she noticed that there was no longer a pad on the floor. There was a bed, a small desk, and two chairs. Dr. Gonzales had explained to Mary, that Jack still had bad dreams but not as many, and each day seemed to be getting better. Jack even smiled at her when she entered the room. Jack was clean shaven and sitting at his desk.

"Mary!" Jack said excitedly, as she walked into the room. "Dr. Gonzales told me you had been here to see me, but I couldn't remember if you had, or if you had just been in some of my dreams."

"I was here," she said as she bent down and kissed him.

Jack was embarrassed because it was a long, loving kiss, not a kiss you give your cousin's husband.

Mary read his mind, "Dr. Gonzales knows all about us. I'm so glad, you are better. I was so worried." Then she bent down and kissed him again.

"I'll leave you two alone," Dr. Gonzales said. Then he turned and went out the door. Mary or Jack didn't know it, but he hurried upstairs to watch them through the glass ceiling.

Jack stood up and Mary stepped into his arms. "I'm so glad you are getting rid of your dreams," Mary said.

"I still have some, but they aren't as bad as they were," Jack said. "But I know they will be back, I just know it."

Mary wondered if she should tell him about the dream catcher in the picture frame, behind her picture. *Why should I do that? Let him think it's my picture that he needs,* she thought. "It's our love for each other that's getting rid of the demons, Jack! You need me, It's our love that's getting rid of them," she said. "If you keep my picture near, you will get rid of all of the dreams." All this time she had her arms around him and was pressing her body against his. "Just believe in me, Jack. I'll set you free, I promise." Mary was hoping she was right. She was getting the teaching of the dream catcher as a child, as all Socike Indians did, when the teacher caught her in a lie. That was something that Indians, and especially the Socike Nation, did not tolerate. They wouldn't teach her anymore because of the lie. They let her learn other things but what they considered sacred they kept from her and anyone else that was considered a liar. She thought that the reason that Jack hadn't stopped the bad dreams was because all of the evil spirits hadn't gone into the dream catcher yet. But she was pretty sure that they would. Her mother had told her that there could be more than one spirit. She was hoping that was the case with Jack.

"Jack, we've got to talk serious for a minute." Then she started to whisper, When you stop having any dreams at all, don't tell anyone."

"Why?" Jack asked.

"Because, if they know, they will call the cops and you will be tried for murder," She whispered.

Jack's eyes got big. It just now sunk in. He was going to be charged with murder if he ever left this hospital. He didn't know why the dreams were leaving him, but anything would be better than those awful dreams. He did believe that it was evil spirits that were haunting him, but he didn't think it was Mary's picture that was getting rid of them. After all, he didn't love her, he had just told her he did. Everyone knows that men tell women they love them when they don't. *Oh well, I'll go along with her, what do I have to lose?* he thought. Jack hugged her a little tighter. Jack couldn't let himself believe that he was going to be rid of the dreams, it was just too much to hope for, but for now he would go along with Mary.

Mary was so delighted that Jack was getting better, she let herself think of getting him out of that place and being with him for the rest of her life. "Jack, just do what I ask, please," she said. "We can be together for the rest of our lives." The two of them sat there hugging and kissing, Mary being the aggressor.

Dr. Gonzales and Jane Weiman were intensely watching all that was going on in the room below. "I wouldn't believe a picture of a woman could make this much difference if I hadn't seen it with my own eyes," Jane said.

"You believe the picture made the difference?" Dr. Gonzales asked.

"You don't?" Jane asked.

"I told Mary that I thought it did, but I can't really see how it could. It might just be that Jack finely started to respond to the therapy we've been giving him," Dr. Gonzales said.

"I guess that could be it, after all we've been at it a long time and he should have responded to your treatment by now," Jane said. "I wonder what would happen if we didn't let him see Mary or her picture for a while?"

"That might give us the answer," Dr. Gonzales said half out loud and half to himself, as if he was lost in his own thoughts. "That just might give us the answer... if it sets him back we can always put her back into the picture, so to speak." After about thirty more minutes Dr. Gonzales went down and ended the visit.

Mary and Dr. Gonzales were in his office. "Mary, I really appreciate your help with the treatment with Jack. I'm sure you will understand when I tell you that my colleague and I believe that we should slow down the visits so we can delve deeper into his subconscious to make his healing more permanent."

Mary looked at the doctor with contempt. "What are you saying? You're saying I should stop visiting Jack?"

"Not stop visiting him, just suspend them for a while. Just until we are sure that they are the best thing for him." The doctor said.

"The best thing for him? You had him for months, and he only got worse, Your words, not mine. I came, after two visits and he makes great improvements and you want to suspend my visits?" Mary said with great sarcasm in her voice. "What are you up to?"

"I understand your reluctance in suspending your visits when he is doing so good, but you've got to understand that we only have Jack's best interest in mind. We don't want this to be only a temporary remission, but a honest to goodness cure. Can you understand that?" the doctor asked.

"Suspend? How long?" Mary ask.

"I'm... we aren't sure, maybe two or three weeks," Dr. Gonzales said.

"Can I go back in to tell him goodbye?" Mary asked.

"I don't think that would be wise. When I have my regular session with Jack, I'll explain it to him. We will keep in touch with you and let you know how he is progressing. Now, if you will excuse me, I have other patients to see." Dr. Gonzales said. He then turned and went behind his desk and sat down and started looking at the papers on his desk.

Mary slowly walked out of his office, out the door and down the front steps. On the roof of her car perched a Red Tail Hawk. As Mary approached her car it gave out a screech that startled Mary, then took to the sky. "What's with that hawk?" Mary asked out loud.

# Chapter 21

Pupa kept her house and yard up for Rosa's visit, which would be any day now. She stayed at home most of the time just to be sure she would be there when Rosa showed up. Pupa knew that when Rosa came she would stick around, but she wanted to be there when she did come. Pupa had her commitments to the Women Council so she had to make all of those meetings and anything else that she had to do as Chief Squaw. She also went almost every day to visit, if not ride Baroka, her horse. Other than that and getting groceries she stayed home.

Pupa still had her occasional gatherings at her house on Friday and they had been getting bigger and more regular since Shosho showed up. But, no one new yet if Black Feather was going to get the high school principal job or not.

Pupa hadn't heard if any of her writings were going into the Great Book Of The Living Souls. The Women Council voted for all of the writing that she had written after her Peyote trip to go into the book, but they had not heard from the Men Council or the chief yet. Maybe she would hear today there was a council meeting that she had to go to. Maybe the Men Council had let Rose Bud know if any of the writing was going into the Book, and she would hear today.

Pupa had dressed in her traditional Socike dress for her part of Chief of the Squaws and had left for the meeting when Rosa arrived at Pupa's house. Finding no one at home she left her suitcase on her porch and went to one of her neighbors to see if they knew where

Anita Yellowhair was. After being informed that she was at her council meeting and would be there most of the afternoon, Rosa decided to put her suitcase inside her Grandmother's house and go over to Maria's old friend Rita's house. She hadn't seen her since high school when Maria hung around her. She was wondering if she still lived there or if she was gone. *Anyway, I'll see her parents if Rita is not there*, she thought.

Rosa reached Rita's parent's house, walked up the front steps and knocked. *Looks about like it used to*, Rosa thought. In a minute she knocked again. Rita opened the door and stood there studying Rosa's face. "Rita," Rosa said.

"Rosa......, Rosa, my gosh it's you! Come in," she said and opened the screen door to let her in.

"I didn't know if you still lived here, Rita," Rosa said. "I was hoping you did, but I wasn't sure."

"Well I'm here now, I did move out after I got married, but I got a divorce last year and have been living with my parents since," Rita said.

"I'm sorry your marriage didn't work out," Rosa said.

"Oh, he was a jerk, what can I say. I've heard he's living with some bimbo in Flagstaff now, good riddance," Rita said.

"Jerks, I know about, I've met a few," Rosa said. Both girls laughed.

"Come on in the kitchen," Rita said. They both walked into the kitchen where her parents sat having coffee. "You know my parents don't you, Rosa?"

"Yes, I do, how are you, Mr. and Mrs. Small?"

"Little Rosa!" Mrs. Small said as she got up and gave Rosa a hug.

Mr. Small got up, "Rosa, we are so glad to see you. What have you been up to these last few years?" Mr. Small asked.

"Well, I've been trying to get my act together and I just got here to see my Nana. But she's at a council meeting, so I haven't seen her yet. I thought I'd come over here to say hello to you folks," Rosa said.

"Rosa, have you been in touch with your Grandmother, recently?" Mrs. Smith asked.

I haven't been in touch with Nana, but I've been in touch with Shosho who has filled me in on some of the things that have been going on at the reservation. I've learned about the death of Maria, which I wish I could have seen her before it happened. I heard about Nana being elected Chief of the Squaws, but not much more than that though," Rosa said.

"We are so sorry about Maria, she was such a nice girl," Mrs. small said, and both Mr. Small and Rita were nodding their heads yes.

"Thank you, I hadn't seen her for a while and that I'm sure I'll always regret," Rosa said. "Sit down and have some coffee with us," Mrs. Small said.

Both Rosa and Rita sat down and Mrs. Smith got them each a cup of coffee. They sat and talked about the events of the Reservation that had taken place since Rosa had been gone. Rita caught her up on the last celebration of Eagle Woman that had just passed a few weeks back. Pupa Played a big part in it, but not as much as usual because of all the things that were going on in her life. The tribe understood and didn't ask a lot from her, but went about the celebration and everyone had a good time.

"How long are you going to stay here on the reservation?" Rita asked Rosa.

"I'm not sure yet, that's something I'll have to work out with Nana," Rosa said.

"I wish both of you Girls would consider making a life for yourself on the reservation. You two could do a lot worse," Mr. Small said.

"Rosa," Mr. Small continued. "The elders would give you special help, being you and Pupa are the last decedents of Eagle Woman."

Both Rosa and Rita looked at each other with kind of puzzled looks on their faces. Neither had thought of making a permanent life for themselves on the reservation as their parents had done. They, like a lot of young people had dreamed of leaving the place they had been raised, and going out into the world where there was excitement, and making their mark. They both had done that, and now they were both back. Granted, Rosa had just arrived, and Rita hadn't made an effort to do anything since she had arrived, but Mr. Small had planted the seeds in their mind now.

After spending the afternoon with the Smalls, Rosa and Rita agreed to meet in the next few days for lunch. Rosa said goodbye to the Smalls and headed back to Nana's house.

When Rosa reached her Grandmother's house, Nana had not come home from her meeting yet, so Rosa sat on the front steps. There were a lot of things that she was going to have to work out in her life. She was an alcoholic, and she was not sure that she could stay away from this awful drink. Even as she sat there thinking of her problem she was wanting a drink. She was determined to stay sober while she was visiting Nana. If she could, she would stay sober for the rest of her life, but Rosa was not sure she could do that. Like they taught her at the clinic she was going to take it one day at a time and take baby steps for now, so her goal for now was to stay sober for the rest of this day. She would not make any long term plans that she may not be able to keep, but only short term plans for now. *Short terms and small steps,* she thought.

Pupa saw someone sitting on her front porch, but couldn't make out who it was from that distance. Expecting Rosa any day now, Pupa picked up her pace so she could make out the figure. When she could make out a young woman's figure she started to run, which wasn't easy for a woman her age. Rosa had her head down so she didn't see Nana coming. By the time she reached her yard Rosa looked up to see Pupa heading straight for her. Both women spoke at the same time.

"Nana!"

"Rosa!"

Rosa stood up and both women embraced two feet from the steps.

"Rosa, my Little Rose, It's so good to see you," Nana said. When Rosa was little Nana always called Rosa, Little Rose.

"Nana, it's good to see you, too." Rosa stepped back to get a better look at her Grandmother." You are beautiful, dressed in your leadership attire!" Rosa said.

"Thank you, Little Rose, and you are beautiful, too," Nana said. "I am so happy to see you, You are beautiful. You remind me of your mother," Nana said.

"Really, I don't remember much about my mother. It all seems so long ago, but I remember staying with you," Rosa said.

The two women sat on the porch and talked until it started to get dark. "Let's go inside and get something to eat, I'll bet you are starved after your trip here," Nana said.

The two women got up and headed inside. "I hope you don't mind, Nana, I put my suitcase inside when you weren't here," Rosa said.

"Of course, I don't mind. You could have made yourself at home and helped yourself to the food," Nana said.

"I found out from your neighbor that you wouldn't be back until later, so I set my case inside and went over to Rita and her Folks' house. We got in some good visiting and I got caught up on some things that have happened here. I understand you have some messages that will be put in the *Great Book Of The Living Souls*," Rita said.

"I don't know if any of them will go into the Book, but I did bring back some from my trip that I think should be entered into it," Nana said.

Both women went into the kitchen and Nana started coffee and frying up some pota. Pota is Potatoes, onions and scramble eggs mixed together. First the potatoes go into the skillet. When they are almost done, the onions go in. When they are tender, the eggs are stirred with a little goat's milk and poured over the potatoes and onions and cooked until done.

Rosa sat in a chair at the table and the two women kept their conversation going.

"From what I heard you brought back more than anyone else has ever brought back in one trip," Rita said.

"You know what they say... don't count your quail until you've caught them. Like I said, I did bring back some messages, but it is anybody's guess, if any will go into the book. I was pretty sure some would, but the Men Council is taking a long time to send it on to the Chief," Nana said.

"From what the Smalls said, the whole Women Council is for it, they said it's all over the reservation that they want all of it entered," Rita said.

"That's one bad thing about taking so long to approve or disapprove of anything. Things leak out, and it really should be secret between the Men's and the Women Council until the ruling. But that's the way it is. And people take sides before any decisions are made," Pupa said.

"You are very wise, Nana. I wish I had a tenth of your wisdom," Rosa said. "I'm so proud of you."

"I'm very proud of you, Little Rose, and when you are my age you will be much wiser than I," Nana said.

"Me, I'm afraid not, I've made some pretty dumb choices," Rosa said.

"Rosa, you are in your twenties. You haven't been an adult very long. One must make decisions right or wrong before they can do anything worth doing. You know there are lots of people that go through life making no decisions at all, except to not make a decision. You might have made some bad decisions, but you have made some very good decisions, too," Nana said. "I would count on a person that makes decisions, good or bad, before I would count on a person that has never made a decision at all."

"Look at us, we haven't seen each other forever, and we are discussing philosophy of life, like we used to. I think we started in where we left off. Only I might be a little wiser than I was when we left off," Rosa said. "I'm listening now."

The two women laughed at that last statement and Nana was putting two cups of coffee on the table along with cream and sugar. "It'll take a few minutes for the Pota to get cooked," Nana said as she sat down to enjoy her coffee.

"Is this cow's cream or goat's cream?" Rosa asked. looking in the creamer.

"What difference does it make?" Nana asked.

"I was hoping it was goat's cream. I haven't had goat's milk or cream since I left the reservation. It just tastes better than cow's," Rosa said.

"It's goat's cream, I still get it from the trading store," Nana said.

The trading store is the name the Indians gave to the only grocery store on the reservation because it started out in frontier days as a trading post.

"Does the milk still come from Gray Coyote's herd?" Rosa asked.

"No, it's his son, Joe Coyote's herd now. He took his father's place and herds the goats now," Pupa said. "Gray had a stroke and just sits at home now. Joe has built the herd to twice the size and uses two more dogs to keep them together."

"Jim Walter had to buy a truck twice the size to pick up the milk from him. Jim pasteurizes most of it and sells it to one distributor in Flagstaff the rest he bottles and delivers to three reservations. Joe made him sign a contract that he wouldn't cut off the reservations if he increased his milk production. From what I hear, Jim liked dealing with Gray Coyote better than Joe because Gray made all his deals by his word, but Joe makes him sign a contract," Pupa continued.

"Joe...? I know him from high school. He always said that he wouldn't take his father's place, herding goats. He used to be so embarrassed that his father was a goat herder. Joe always said he wanted to be a lawyer," Rosa said.

Nana got up and finished making the Pota, then set the table and brought the Pota dish to the table. "That must be where the contract idea came from, him wanting to be a lawyer and all," Nana said.

"I suppose so, it sure is strange that he wound up herding goat's like his father did, though. He always said that was something that he was never going to do," Rosa said.

"Like his father and his father before him. Some say it's his Navajo ancestry, I know we are all Socike, but some have a longer ancestry in the Socike nation than others. We all tend to act and do like we were taught by our father and mother and their father and mother before them. Joe's ancestors were Navajo and Navajo's are good herders. They herd lots of sheep and goats and since the white man, they do a good job raising cattle," Nana said.

The ladies started eating and didn't say much, while they enjoyed their Pota and coffee. "I didn't think..., would you like some goat's milk instead of coffee, I have some?" Nana asked.

"No thanks, not now. The coffee is good and the Pota is delicious, I haven't had Pota since I left," Rosa said.

"We could go see Joe Coyote while you're here if you like," Nana said. "He sure has a large herd now. He's probably the richest man on the reservation, that is if you consider money making you rich."

"It would be fun to see some of my school mates. Are there many that stayed on the reservation after graduation?" Rosa asked.

"There are actually quite a few," Nana said. "Rose Bud's granddaughter... I can't think of her name."

"Ruth?" Rosa asked.

"Ruth, yes, Ruth. Funny her name just slipped away from me for a minute. Anyway, Ruth is a first grade school teacher now at our grade school." Nana said.

"Good for her, she was always smart and loved school," Rosa said.

"My good friend, Jode Black Horse, runs the stables now. He was in your class.

"Do you remember, Bob Yazzie? I think he was a grade or two ahead of you," Pupa asked.

"I remember him, I had a crush on him since I was five. I think he had a crush on and off on, Maria," Rosa said. "He was two grades ahead of me."

"He's a policeman here now, and doing well," Nana said. "There are more, but I don't know all of their names."

"That's great that so many young people are staying on the reservation," Rosa said. "From the way everyone talked at school I didn't think that anyone would be left here."

Nana got up and started clearing the table. "A lot did leave, but a lot didn't and a lot that left are coming back. Both the women and the Men Council are trying to do things to make the reservation more attractive for young people to stay here. We've been trying to form an industry here to make more jobs for everyone, young and old alike," Nana said.

Rosa got up and started helping Nana with the dishes. "That sounds great, I'm glad to hear the councils are starting to take an interest in creating jobs for everyone here. I hope they get that task done," Rosa said.

"Well the spirit is willing, but the flesh is weak. There is plenty of good intention, but not much is happening. Every time we look into something, either one of the council persons wants to nix it, or the U.S. government doesn't want us to have it. The last time a well-known politician wanted us to pay him, he called it a campaign contribution. Only thing is, there was no campaign going on at the time, it was his last term in office," Nana said.

"I'm afraid that's what the world is like off the reservation," Rosa said.

The two women finished their dishes and had them put away.

"Let me show you the room I have made up for you," Nana said as she led Rosa to Maria's old room. It was freshly painted and made up, but no smell of paint. Instead, there was the faint scent of herbs and lilacs. The only rug in the house was on this floor. At the far wall was a double bed made up with a white bed spread with the likeness of an Indian woman from the waist up holding a war club in the center. When you stepped into the room you stood at the foot of the bed facing the headboard. On each side of the head board, about five feet up over night stands two dream catchers hung on the wall. One was bright red, the other had three colors—black, white and blue.

Rosa stepped into the room and immediately felt the spirit of love in the room. "It's beautiful," She said.

"I was hoping you would like it," Nana said.

"Like it? I love it," Rosa said as she bent down and felt the bed spread.

"Let's get your suitcase and when you unpack please use the dresser and closet. This room is yours as long as you want to stay," Nana said.

"Thank you, Nana, I'm not sure how long I can stay," Rosa said. She went in and brought back her suitcase and sat it on a small chair in the corner of the room. The two women went into the kitchen and sat at the table and visited for the rest of the evening.

Early the next morning, Nana was up fixing breakfast when Rosa woke up. Rosa could hear Nana in the kitchen shuffling around in the cupboards. The thought of breakfast made her nauseous, what she needed was a stiff drink. She had slept well, but she couldn't get that thought out of her mind, that she wanted a drink. Rosa lay there a minute, trying to think of the conversation she had with Nana last night. She thought that if she could concentrate hard enough she could shake that craving of wanting a drink. Maybe some coffee, she thought, and got up, and put on a robe she had gotten from the clinic that she had just left.

"Good morning, Little Rose," Nana said, bright and cheerful.

"Good morning," Rosa said, not so cheerful.

Anyone could see Rosa was having a hard time. Nana put a cup of coffee in front of her. "Maybe this will help," Nana said.

"I hope so," Rosa said as she took a big gulp of black coffee. She thought she could handle a few days of not drinking with Nana after her stay at the clinic, but without the medication and the support of the staff she didn't know.

Nana went about her toil at the kitchen counter. In a minute, she set a glass of light green liquid in front of Rosa. "This is one of my special teas, give it a try and tell me how you like it.

"Thanks, but I'll stay with my coffee," Rosa said. This was being rude to Nana according to Socike tradition, but Rosa was never, even as a child, concerned about tradition or being rude.

Nana took it in stride and only said, "Please taste it for me and tell me what you think."

Rosa took a sip then another. "This is good, what is it."

That statement, was rude too, but Nana just said, "Tea, Indian style."

Something about that drink made Rosa drink it right down and start back sipping her coffee. After a few minutes she started feeling better and was even getting hungry. "I don't know what got into me this morning," Rosa said. "I was as grumpy as an old bear."

"You feel like breakfast, yet?" Nana asked.

"I could eat something," Rosa said. "Can I help you make it?"

"That's all right, I've got it." Nana said, and sat down two bowls of steaming hot oatmeal. She also sat out two drinking glasses, a pitcher of goat's milk, and a bowl of brown sugar. Nana put four slices of toast on a plate along with goat's cheese. She then topped off their coffee, and sat down to join her granddaughter with breakfast.

Rosa had already put brown sugar and milk on her oatmeal. "This is delicious," she said, after her first bite. I don't remember oatmeal being this good before.

"Maybe it's because you haven't had it with the goat's milk for a while," Nana said.

"Maybe," Rosa said.

The two women finished their breakfast. Nana did the dishes while Rosa took a shower. After they were both dressed in blue jeans and Indian shirts the two sat and talked for a while. "I've got to go to the stables this morning. Do you feel like going with me or would you like to stay here?" Nana asked.

"I'll go with you," Rosa said, and noticed that her craving for a drink was gone. Strange, she thought. This was the first time that she had not wanted a drink since she could remember. *I can't be this lucky, it will come back,* she thought.

On the way to the stables, Nana pointed out things that had changed since Rosa had left the reservation. Rosa pointed out things that she remembered. The two walked along talking like school girls. Rosa would lean down and pick up a small rock and toss it like she did when she was a kid, trying to skip it off the ground. She could get it to skip about three times and that was the max. She kept trying for four, but never made it.

The two were greeted by Jode when they reached the stable. "Good morning, Pupa and Rosa!" he said.

Rosa had gone to school with Jode, but at that distance she wouldn't have recognized him. When they got a little closer she could make out the features on his face. He was recognizable, but he had filled out since high school and was really good looking now, she thought.

"Hi, Rosa," he said.

"How did you know it was me?" she asked.

"Pupa and I talk a lot, and the last two months have been mostly about you coming for a visit," he answered. "I know she is really glad to have you here."

That last statement brought a twinge of regret for being so rude to Nana, that morning when she was having her craving for alcohol. "I'm really glad to be here with Nana, I hope my being off the reservation so long hasn't made me so rude that she can't put up with me." She looked over at Nana to see if she could read anything in her face, but all she could see was a loving grandmother.

"It won't take you long to get back into our customs. I know, I too left the reservation for a while, but when I came back it didn't take long to fall back into the Socike tradition," Jode said.

The three walked into the stable where the hay was stacked in square bails. Rosa sat down on one, "I'm not used to this much walking, I don't know if I'll be able to keep up with Nana," Rosa said.

"I don't think I could keep up with Pupa," Jode said. "She is an amazing woman."

"I've got to go check, Baroka. If you want, you can stay here while I go do that," Nana said to Rosa.

"Sounds good to me, I'm not used to this much walking." Rosa said.

"Okay, I'll be back shortly. I dug a small stone out of Baroka's hoof two days ago and he still had a slight limp yesterday. I need to check him today." Pupa walked out the door and into the pasture.

"Your grandmother is sure a great leader," Jode said.

"Really?" Rosa said.

"Yes, she has done more as Chief Squaw since Eagle Woman, than anyone before her, so much, the Men Council is seen as a little jealous," Jode said. "She is a great woman."

"You seem to be impressed," Rosa said.

"I am. She has done a lot for this nation and a lot for many individuals as myself," Jode said.

"Oh, what has she done for you?" Rosa asked.

Jode looked a little perturbed. "Well, after high school I left the reservation like a lot of our classmates."

"Classmates, I haven't heard that term since grade school," Rosa interrupted. There was a silence, "Well, go on."

"Like I was saying, before I was so rudely interrupted." Rosa looked a little sheepish at that remark. "I left the reservation, to do big things, I made it as far a Flagstaff and found the bottle. That was all I could think of and I did a lot of cleaning bars and sleeping in the streets to scrape up enough money to buy my next drink. I also learned to beg. I always asked for enough money to get a meal. But, when I got enough to get a bottle I'd get a bottle instead. I could always get enough to eat from the dumpsters in town."

Rosa was starting to look interested now, this was sounding like her life.

Jode saw the interest Rosa was giving him and went on. "One day when I was really sick from a week of drinking and needed a drink, I was on the street begging for some money. I stopped this Indian Woman and asked for help. To my surprise, she stopped and put her hands on both of my shoulders and looked deep in my eyes. I tried to look away, but each time I did, she shook me and I had to look at her."

"Studying of the face and eyes," Rosa said low under her breath, not wanting to interrupt Jode.

"Yes, studying the face and eyes," Jode acknowledged. "Anyway, she said, 'You need a drink.' I had never had this happen to me before. To be begging for money for food and someone telling me, I needed a drink. I didn't know what to think. Was she going to give me money for a bottle or what? Well, it didn't take long for me to find out. That woman was your grandmother, and she grabbed me by the arm and half walked, half dragged me into the nearest liquor store and asked me what I liked to drink. I thought, this is my kind of woman. After she bought a bottle of what I told her, we left. I could hardly wait to have a drink, but she wouldn't give me a drink, she kept the bottle. It was a whole quart of my favorite whiskey. She had business in Flagstaff and she told me I'd had to wait until she finished her business, then she would open the bottle. Well, I didn't want to wait, so I grabbed the bottle away from her. That was the biggest mistake I had ever made in my life. One jab in the throat and I was out like a light. When I came to, she was bending over me holding that bottle in a sack and told me I was going to have to wait."

Jode had Rosa's undivided attention now. "Anyway, I stayed close to her as she finished her business. When it was time for her to go back to the reservation she took me to the bus station and bought me a ticket. I thought she was buying herself a ticket, but she already had a ticket to go back. We were sitting in the bus terminal and I was wondering when she was going to give me the bottle. Then she told me that I was going to have to share the bottle with her. Well, I'd spent all that time waiting for that bottle, I wasn't going to give up now. I decided to wait longer. When they called for the boarding of the bus to the reservation she got up and told me to come. Before she stepped on the bus she opened the bottle and poured half of the bottle out on the ground. My heart sank, I thought she was pouring out all of it. I tell you, I wanted that drink so bad, I was about to bend down like a dog and lap it up with my tongue. But after she poured out half she put the cap back on the bottle, turned to me and said, 'That was my half the rest is yours,' and stepped onto the bus."

"I followed. When she got to the seat where she wanted to sit, she told me to get in first. That put me on the seat next to the window and her on the aisle seat, blocking me from getting up and leaving. When the driver got on the bus and started to leave she handed me the bottle.

"I sat there nursing that bottle to about Willows Flats where I finished the last drop. The bus didn't even slow down at Willow Flats or anywhere else as far as I know. Sometime after Willow Flats I fell asleep. The next thing I knew Pupa was telling me to wake up, we were there. We got off that bus and we walked to her house where she let me sleep in her spare bedroom for the night."

"The next morning I woke up with vomit on me and the bed that I had slept in. The door and windows were all closed. The stench was so bad I couldn't stand it. When I opened the door, Pupa was standing there and told me to go into the bathroom and clean up. When I went into the bathroom there was a sack with clothes in it. On the sack was written a note, Take a shower, Jode, and put on these clean clothes."

"So Nana knew who you were?" Rosa asked.

"She not only knew who I was, after I had fallen asleep the night before, she had gone to my parent's house and told them what was going on. That's where she got the clean clothes for me. The clothes were some of my old clothes that I had left here. I even learned later, my parents had come over that night just to see me sleep."

"Anyway, I'm getting off the subject. After I took a shower and put on clean clothes, I went to the kitchen where Pupa was, she had already poured me black coffee and there was a glass of bright green something. I drank some coffee, but wanted some more whiskey and I told her that. She told me to drink the Indian Tea and if I still wanted the whiskey we would talk about it. She didn't make any promises about the whiskey, she just said we'd talk about it. Well, that was all I was interested in, something to drink that had alcohol in it. I drank it right down. "I drank it," I told her, "Now lets talk about the whiskey." She told me to drink my coffee and we would talk later. The next thing I knew she had eggs, hash browns, and toast in front of me."

"She was true to her word, after I finished my breakfast she told me I had to clean up my own mess and she wanted it cleaned up then. She said it in such a way that I knew that I had better do it. I took the sack that the clothes wherein and put all my soiled clothes in it. I opened the windows to the bedroom to let in some fresh air, then scraped up as much of the vomit as I could. She had me lay the blankets and sheets on the drive way and hose them off. Then she got me a basket and had me put everything in the basket. We walked to the laundry mat with me carrying that basket full of wet blankets. I was pooped by the time we got there. She didn't let up, I had to load the washer and wait for them to dry. I don't know why I stuck around, it was like that was where I was supposed to be. The craving for the liquor had left me temporarily."

Rosa was still listening to his story intensely and paid particular attention to the words 'Craving left temporarily'.

"After we left the laundry mat we went back to her house. She made me make the bed and fold my clean clothes."

"Then, true to her word, she made me more coffee and some more of that green drink. I've learned not to ask what's in her drinks, because it's not only impolite, she calls everything Indian tea that she doesn't want you to know what's in it. We sat down at her table and she asked me what I wanted?"

"I asked if she was asking me what drink I wanted? She said, 'No, I know what drink you want, you told me yesterday.' I was lost, what did she mean by 'what did I want'?"

"Then she laid it all out for me. She recognized me the minute she saw me. She used to change my diapers when I was a baby. She was one of my grandmother's best friends as a teenager. She changed my mother's diapers when she was a child. She told me about going over to my parents the night before and bringing them back to see me sleep. She told me they were going to be here in about an hour and it was my choice whether I greeted them drunk or sober. 'That green drink will take the edge off the craving for the liquor and you can talk to your parents sober, or I'll go get you some liquor and you can get drunk. The choice is yours, but make the right decision,' she said."

"Well, I made the right decision, I've been sober from that day to this," Jode said.

"That's quite a story, I had no idea you had a drinking problem. I just got out of detox and I'm not sure I can stay sober," Rosa said.

"Well, you are the only one who can decide that, the choice is yours. If you ever need to talk to someone who knows what you are talking about, come over and see me. Drink that tea that Pupa makes, it will take off the edge. It won't do it for you, but it will help you do for yourself," Jode said.

"Nana gave me some of that drink this morning, but it wasn't bright green, it had a green tint," Rosa said.

"As the cravings get less severe she weakens the tea until it's just water. Because you were in detox before you came, she probably didn't make it as strong as she started me out on . It all comes down to the person that's trying to quit booze," Jode said. "She's done this for several people, but never talks about it. If you decide to stay off the booze, good luck."

Nana showed up and the ladies said goodbye to Jode. They talked all the way home, chattering like teenagers. When they arrived, Rose Bud was waiting for Pupa.

"Rose Bud, is anything wrong?" Pupa asked her friend.

"No, I just wanted to see you for a minute. I didn't know you had company," Rose Bud answered.

"I see your granddaughter made it."

"Yes' she got here yesterday. You remember Rosa don't you?" Nana said.

"Of course, I do. Hello, Rosa," she greeted.

"Hello," Rosa said back.

"I've heard from the Men Council. I thought you would like to know."

"Yes, I would. Did they decide to put any of my messages in the book?" Nana asked.

Rose Bud looked at Rosa as if to ask if she could speak in front of her.

"It's alright, Everyone on the reservation knows what the messages are by now," Nana said.

"Well, They decided to put everything in the book that you could remember and was backed up by being written down, but not what was just written down and you couldn't remember later," Rose Bud said. "They have sent it to the Chief for ratification."

"Well that's something," Pupa said. "Bud, why don't you come in and have some lunch with us?"

Rose Bud was surprised that Pupa wasn't upset about not having everything on her trip written into the *Great Book Of The Living Souls*.

Rosa looked at Nana, "Is this good?"

"Very good," Nana said to Rosa.

# Chapter 22

Mary Smith was home when she got a call from Dr. Gonzales, asking her to please start visiting Jack O'Reily at Yaford Asylum again. *It's about time*, she thought, it had been a long time and she was sure that his dreams had all stopped by now. She was the only one that knew the picture she left in his room was concealing a repaired dream catcher in it. She had tried to mislead both the doctor and Jack that it was her that was curing him of his dreams. Mary made an appointment to see Jack the following Friday.

Friday morning, Mary was up early and took a shower before breakfast. She went into her bedroom and finished drying off. As she stood in front of the mirror she noticed the curve from her shoulders down her sides to her waist and over her hips. "Not bad," she said to herself. She turned to take a side view. Her breast were still standing out without much sag, flat stomach with just a small amount of fat that gave a nice curve to it and her thighs were nice and firm. "Jack, you don't realize how lucky you are to have this waiting for you!" She said to herself. After getting dressed, she had a light breakfast, and in a few minutes she was on her way to Bisbee to see Jack.

Mary pulled in the parking lot of the Yaford Asylum and headed to the front door. As she headed up the front steps she heard that hawk screaming at her. Mary looked up to see the bird diving at her. She burst through the door just in time to avoid a collision with the bird. "Did you see that?" She yelled to the receptionist as she walked double time to the desk where the receptionist was seated." She repeated, "Did you see that?"

"See what?" The receptionist asked.

"Did you see that hawk attacking me?" Mary asked.

"You're Mary Smith," The lady said, as if she had just come to a great conclusion.

"Yes," Mary said in exasperation.

"You're the woman who had trouble with a bird when you were here before."

"Yes, and I thought you were going to do something about it!" Mary said.

"Mary, we did something about it. We had Max go on the roof and look for any birds or signs of birds, like nests. There were none. He stayed up there almost all day. He even ate his lunch on the roof and he never saw any birds at all."

"He never saw any other bird because hawks keep other birds away, because they eat other BIRDS!" Mary said, shaking her head.

"Mary, people go in and out that door all day long. Even sometimes at night. You are the only one who has ever seen a hawk or any other bird at all. I think you called it a Red Hawk?"

"A Red Tail Hawk," Mary corrected.

"A Red Tail," the lady repeated. "Well, you are the only one who has ever seen it."

Mary gave up, "Dr. Gonzales is expecting me, is he in his office?" Mary asked.

"Yes, he said to send you right in," the lady said.

Mary walked over to Dr. Gonzales office. "Good morning, Mary," Dr. Gonzales said in a cheerful voice.

"Good morning," Mary said, holding back what she really wanted to say.

"I wanted to talk to you before you went to see Jack," Dr. Gonzales said.

"Oh"

"Yes, I'm afraid that Jack hasn't been doing so good," Dr. Gonzales said.

"I was afraid he was getting over those dreams too soon, and I was right. His dreams have increased. They have changed, but they are getting worse since you quit coming to visit him," Dr. Gonzales said.

"It was your idea that I didn't see him anymore, remember," Mary said, glaring at him. "You're the one who put a stop to me seeing him."

"Yes..., Yes, we did. We wanted him to recover on his own without the crutch you are to him. But..., I am afraid I was wrong. I'm thinking that he needs that crutch, for a full recovery. Psychiatry is not an exact science. We just have to try to do our best," Dr. Gonzales said. "So, if you will resume the regular visits I'd be very grateful."

"My picture, did you leave it in Jack's room?" Mary asked.

"We took the picture out after your last visit. Like I said, we wanted to take his crutch away, so he would heal by himself," Dr. Gonzales said.

"But now you want my help again?" Mary asked.

"We would like you to start your visits again," Dr. Gonzales said.

"Like I said, now you would like my help?" Mary said.

"Yes, we would like your help," Dr. Gonzales said.

"If I help you, will you promise not to stop my visits?" Mary asked.

"I can't promise that I will never stop visits. I have no intention to stop them, but I must do what I think is best for Jack."

"Do you still have my picture?" Mary asked.

"It's in my closet, I'll put it back in Jack's room like you asked me to when you first came," Dr. Gonzales said. "Do we have a deal?"

"If you put my picture back today I'll start my visits again," Mary said.

Mary knew why Jack didn't stop dreaming. But she wasn't going to tell Dr. Gonzales why. She had learned, as a child, if there were several bad dreams together and you caught some, but not all in a dream catcher, the others would get bolder and get worse. That was why you had to leave the dream catcher in the room of the person it was made for until all the bad dreams had stopped.

"We've got a deal, I'll put it back now," Dr. Gonzales said. "Are you ready to see Jack now?"

Mary nodded her head and said, "Yes."

They walked down the hall to the same room that Jack had stayed in since Dr. Gonzales found him to be such an interesting subject. When Mary entered the room she was surprised to see Jack looking so bad. She couldn't believe that the doctor had waited so long to send for her. Jack was lying in bed and had refused to eat because he was determined to starve himself to death. He looked up at Mary and didn't recognize her at first. When he did, he didn't seem happy to see her and just turned his face away and looked at the wall. Mary walked over to him and sat on the edge of his bed.

"Darling, what have they done to you?" she asked. She rubbed his back as she talked. "I am here now, my darling. I won't let them hurt you anymore."

"I'll leave you two alone," Doctor Gonzales said, and left the room.

Jack turned to look at Mary. "Why did you leave me to those awful demons?" Jack asked.

"What are you talking about?" Mary asked.

"The dreams," Jack said. "You said you would get rid of those awful dreams for me. You lied, you got rid of the big one, but two of the little ones have grown and are as bad as the first one."

"What are you talking about, Jack.?"

"The dreams, that's what I'm talking about, the dreams," Jack said.

"Some are gone, but some are still there?" Mary asked.

"Yes"

"That's good, we will get rid of the rest," Mary said.

"We, who is 'we'?" Jack asked.

"You and me, that's who! You and me," Mary said. "You need me, remember that, you need, me."

"Then why did you leave for so long?" Jack asked.

"Dr. Gonzales told me I couldn't come and visit you. I tried, but they refused to let me come," Mary said. Mary was rubbing Jack's back all this time and Jack was responding.

"Mary, the dreams are terrible, I can't stand them, These two toad-like beings tear me and my mother apart, and my mother hated me for that. She absolutely hated me. Those toads tear the flesh from me and her. And they do other disgusting things to her, and make me watch. She says it is all my fault. They say they are never going to leave me alone, never." Jack talked as if these dreams were real, and to him they were real. "The only way I'm going to get rid of them, is to kill myself. I've tried, but I can't. The doctor says if I don't eat, they are going to force feed me intravenously. Mary, would you please bring poison, please," Jack said, "Please."

"Jack, you would be rid of those dreams by now if you would have listened to me before, and not let them take my picture away. I told you to not let them take my picture away. I told you that if you stayed by my picture I would save you. You let them take my picture away and those dreams got stronger. Now listen to me, do not let them remove my picture," Mary said.

Dr. Gonzales knocked at the door then entered and put Mary's picture on a small stand. "I told you I'd make sure that your picture got back in Jack's room," He said to Mary.

Mary took the picture and examined it after Dr. Gonzales left. She made sure that no one had tampered with it. She had noticed the glass ceiling in the room and wasn't sure that there wasn't someone watching them, so she didn't do anything that would tip them off to the truth about the picture, and that was that there was a dream catcher behind her picture. She wanted everyone, including Jack, to think that he was getting better because of her, not because of a dream catcher.

Mary was rubbing his back, "Sit up, Jack," and helped him to sit up with his feet on the floor. She sat beside him, with her arm around his back. She unbuttoned his shirt and started running her other hand over his chest, while kissing his ear and neck. She started whispering in his ear, "I'm going to save you, Jack, I promise." Mary was rubbing his chest as she whispered other things in his ear. She kept this up quite a while and then started rubbing his stomach all the while either whispering things in his ear or kissing his ear and the side of his face and neck. Her hand ran down over his trousers and onto the front of his thigh. She slowly ran her hand up and down his thigh and then to the inside of his thigh, being careful not to touch his crotch.

Jack started breathing heavy and in a minute he was forgetting about his awful dreams. He started responding to Mary. "I wish I could get rid of these dreams, but it seems like too much to hope for," Jack said.

"Jack, I promise, you will get rid of those dreams for good if you will just listen and do what I tell you. Jack, do not let them move my picture." Then Mary leaned real close and whispered in Jack's ear. "Jack, when you don't have any more dreams don't tell anyone here. Pretend that you still have them. That's real important, not to tell anyone you no longer have dreams, no mater how much you want to. Can you do that, for me?"

Jack nodded his head affirmative. "That's a good boy," Mary said. *If he just doesn't screw up, we will be together forever, I have a plan,* Mary thought.

## Chapter 23

Rosa awoke early and got up and fixed coffee. Nana was still sleeping, which was unusual, for Rosa to rise before Nana. This morning was special to Rosa, it was the day of Kee. The day of Kee was something personal and something different to every Socike. To Rosa, it was the day of great decisions. This was the day Rosa had picked for herself to decide the path she was going to travel for the rest of her life. This was Kee to the Socike. To the Socike there is a path that is dictated to everyone that is born. We travel this path until we can make decisions. No one can decide who their parents are, as a baby we have no choice of what we eat, or when we have our diapers changed. We can not decide where we will go. We go where we are carried or when we start to walk, we go where we are led. When we are teenagers we come to forks in the road that we must decide which to take. When we take the wrong fork there will be other forks to decide on. Depending on which we take will determine what kind of life we will have. Some will take us back to where we should be, or take us further away from where we should be. In other words, we can take two or three bad roads in a row, or choices. Or two or three good roads, or choices. But, Kee is a time when one must decide to right the wrongs we have made in our life to this point, and to make the right decision as much as possible in each decision we make for the rest of our lives. Kee is a time of not one fork in the road, but an intersection of many roads. Some people will make no decision at this time, but they are the ones that never make any decisions of any importance ever in their life. Today was the day of Kee to Rosa.

Nana had heard from the Chief and he had gone along with the Men Council about what was going to be entered into the *Great Book Of The Living Souls* and Nana was alright with that. As long as Nana had something pending that was that important, Rosa had decided not to interrupt her life by making waves. But that was over, and now Rosa could make her decisions without fear of causing more trouble than necessary to Nana.

Today was the day of decision, Rosa's day of Kee. This was something that she would have to do on her own, no one else could help her. Rosa finished her cup of coffee and then found paper and pen. She wrote a note to Nana, so Nana would know why she wouldn't be there when she woke up. When she finished her note she poured herself a half cup of coffee and set the note under it. She then grabbed a warm jacket and headed out the door.

Rosa found herself walking in the dark toward the stables, all the time thinking about the last two weeks here on the reservation. She was thinking of things she never thought she would think of. She was actually thinking of staying on this reservation, something that she said would never happen up to now. But until now she had not seen the reservation as any kind of a future. In the last two weeks she had seen the reservation through many eyes. She saw it through Nana's eyes as a grandmother and as Pupa, a great leader of the Socike Nation. She had seen it through Jode's eyes as a person in love with the horses that he keeps for others. She learned that he had no horses of his own, but saw beauty in the horses he cared for. She saw the reservation through the eyes of the people living on the reservation that came and went through their daily living there. But what stood out most in her mind was Joe Coyote. When Nana and she rode out to see him and his large herd of Goats just two days earlier, she spent quite a while talking to him. Rosa had felt like he had given up quite a bit by taking over his dad's herd and not pursuing his dream of being a lawyer. But after talking to him she saw things differently. He explained that there were no law offices on the reservation and he now thinks his calling is to be the best herder in the world. He had plans to start a sheep herd for meat for the Indian people and maybe someday to even have a herd of cattle. He said that he looked forward to each morning so he could get out and look after his herd. He also said he had plans to have others herd for him and to even teach herding in the high school. This was a great dream of his. Rosa really admired him for that. She even thought she could see herself as one of his herders, but for the smell of goats that was ever present. As she reached the stables Jode was just getting there, also. Jode was surprised to see Rosa there that early. "Got a mare to rent me for awhile?" Rosa asked.

"Why a mare?" Jode asked.

"I seem to get along better with them for some reason. They seem to understand me better," Rosa said.

"I understand that, I get along with either gelding or stallions and Pupa only rides stallions," Jode said. "I'm sure we can find you a mare to your liking, how about the one you had last time you were here," Jode asked.

"She would be alright, but if you had one that was a little more spirited, she would be better," Rosa said.

"A spirited mare, and not a stallion?" Jode said in a teasing way.

Rosa just looked at him in a flirting way and smiled.
"Okay, I've got just the one for you," and he went to the very back stable and brought back a high stepping golden palomino with white mane and tail. "This is New Start," Jode said.

"New Start?" Rosa said. "Not an Indian name?" Rosa asked.

"No Indian name, her name is, New Start," Jode said. She is going to be my first breeder.

"She's yours?"

Jode nodded yes.

"She beautiful," Rosa said.

"Thank you. She is, isn't she?" Jode said, grinning from ear to ear.

"And you are going to rent her to me?" Rosa asked.

"No, I'm going to let you ride my horse as long as you like, she's not for rent," Jode said, smiling. I'm letting my friend that I trust, use my horse. I have complete confidence in you, Rosa. I'll put a saddle on her for you," Jode said.

"No, just put a bridle with a straight bit on her, I'm riding bare back," Rosa said.

Jode smiled, and handed Rosa the halter rope that was on her. In a minute Jode was back with a bridle with a straight bit. Jode was very skillful with horses and slipped the halter off and the bridle on New

Start in a few seconds. Then he handed the reins to Rosa.

"Thanks Jode," Rosa said, as she grabbed a handful of mane and swung her leg up and over the back of New Start. She started out at a fast gallop. The sun was up now and Rosa gave New Start her head and she went from a gallop to a dead run with no urging from Rosa. Rosa headed for a section of wilderness on the reservation where no one went much. It was full of wildlife, even cougars and bears. It was absolutely off limits for non-Indians. The reservation police, had arrested more than one poacher there.

The sun had risen up and was beginning to give it's lifesaving warmth to Rosa and New Start. Rosa started thinking of the schooling she had received as a child. The Socike believes that the sun is a gift of the Great Spirit. The spirit that the white man calls God. Rosa turned her face to the sun to feel the warmth of it's rays on her dark face. "I thank you, Great spirit, for your gift of the sun and of the moon and of the stars and of all living things." Then she started to ride in to a heavy brushy area and spooked a male dear who jumped up and headed off away from her. He had been so close that she was surprised that New Start hadn't jumped, but she hadn't. "Good girl," Rosa said as she patted New Start on the neck.

*The males must be coming down for the breeding season*, Rosa thought to herself. They are usually up higher in the mountains and come down to find the females during the breeding season. As she rode in the heavy brush she was glad that she was wearing jeans to keep the brush from scratching her legs. In a few minutes she was out of the brush and headed for a place Maria and she went as children. It was by a stream that had both red clay and white clay banks. New Start had been walking since they first entered the brush. Now Rosa noticed a large oak tree and steered to it. As they got to the tree, Rosa slid off and led New Start to a low branch and tied the reins to it, then started picking up acorns. After she had about ten acorns she sat at the base of the tree and started to eat the acorns. They had a bitter taste, but as a child she had acquired a taste for them. As she sat under the tree she started to think about her future. Was this really the life she wanted for herself? If she married and had children, was this the place she wanted to raise her children? If she stayed on the reservation and got married would she really want to marry an Indian. If she married a non-Indian she would loose her citizenship and everything she had on the reservation like land or a business. They wouldn't take any of her personal things like an automobile or anything that she could take with her. If she stayed on the reservation she could start any business that she could save the money for. The Men Council may even give her a grant or loan for a business that they thought would be successful.

If she left the reservation she could make a life for herself. She could marry anyone she wanted to and not lose anything that she worked for if she married a non-Indian. All these things she thought over in her heart.

But all these questions meant nothing if she couldn't kick the booze for good. It wouldn't make any difference what she chose if she went back to the booze that she thought that she could never kick. She had talked to her friend, Jode, these last two weeks and heard his success story. Now she was thinking that maybe, just maybe, she could do it, too, if she stayed on the reservation and off the booze. If not, she would have to leave to save Nana the embarrassment of having an alcoholic granddaughter.

Then Rosa said, "What do I want? What—do—I—really—want?" This said, Rosa put down the remaining acorns and went over to New Start and untied her. A handful of mane and a swing of her leg and she was on her way again. When she was at the banks where the white clay met the red clay, she slid off New Start. This time she just dropped her reins Most horses stay where you drop their reins and won't run. She then removed her clothes and moccasins. The sun was warm now—almost like summer. She then went to the bank where the red clay was and covered her legs and stomach with the red clay then she waded across the stream which was ice cold and dug out some white clay and covered her breast arms and shoulders and neck with the white clay. Rosa was starting to shiver from the cold water she was standing in. She took the white clay and made stripes across her face and then waded back across the stream where the red clay was. When she stepped out of the water she had lost some of the red clay from her ankles so she covered her feet and ankles again with the red clay. She then stood in the sun until her body absorbed the heat from it. When she was warm she took the reins and was on New Start's back again. She rode like she was part of the horse, and was determined to stay there until she had her answer, should she stay or should she go. Rosa could feel the muscles of this magnificent steed working under her bare legs and let her go as she wanted while Rosa tried to keep every thought out of her head until she received her answer.

New Start started with a fast walk then a gallop, then in a minute they were covering country so fast that it seemed as if they were flying. In a minute, New Start was headed straight toward a ravine and the next moment they were air born and Rosa felt that she was no longer Rosa a person, but Rosa a part of New Start. In seconds, they were on the other side of the ravine and were still going. The air and the heat from the sun had dried the clay and Rosa was warm and comfortable. "This is me," she said to herself. "This is me, descendent of Eagle Woman, I belong here." She had her answer and she knew what she must do. Rosa turned her steed around and headed to where her clothes were.

When she got to the place where she left her clothes she slid off New Start and frantically started scraping the clay off her. It was taking too long, so she got in the ice cold water and scrubbed off the clay. By the time she was clean again she was shivering so much that her teeth was chattering. She moved New Start so she could lay up against her for her body heat and at the same time have the sunshine directly on her and the side of the horse that she was leaning up against. In a few minutes she stopped shivering and was dry. This was a trick she had learned from watching the lizard get warm as they lay down on a rock in the sun that is absorbing the heat from the sun. But there were no large rocks around so she used a horse as a rock. As soon as she was dry and she had put her cloths back on, they were off for the stables.

Jode saw them coming at a slow gallop. He watched his new horse and his friend coming and he thought the way they look together is one of the most beautiful sights he had ever seen. *Now that is what I call poetry in motion,* he thought; nothing fancy, just the horse and rider moving as one in every move they made.

The next minute, Rosa was standing in front of Jode holding the reins of New Start. "How was your ride?" Jode asked.

"Fantastic, I don't think she would even need a bridle to ride, just a halter or a strap like Nana uses. She is the best horse I think I have ever ridden. Rosa said as she reached for the halter on the wall that she had on before. "This is her halter, isn't it?" She asked as she took it off the wall where Jode had hung it.

"Yes, that is her halter. I'll put it on her," Jode said.

"That's alright, this will give me a little more time with her," Rosa said as she slipped the bridle off and held up the halter and slipped it over her face then over her ears and fastened the strap under her neck. "She's great, a real sweetie."

"Sweetie? Bold, courageous, or magnificence is what I want, not sweetie," Jode said.

"She's that, too. I just love her," Rosa said. "I'll wipe her down and put her back in the stall."

"I'll help you wipe her down, but I want to put her to pasture," Jode said. With this, he got two towels and tossed one to Rosa. The two wiped New Start down more for the grooming and bonding with the horse than that she actually needed it. Jode thought to himself, this is the life, wiping my own magnificent horse down with a beautiful woman helping me. After they finished and said their goodbyes Rosa left and Jode led his horse out to pasture, feeling like he was ten feet tall after this interaction with Rosa.

Rosa headed for the only grocery store on the reservation. It took a few minutes before she reached it, but once she got there she wasn't disappointed, there were several cars and two pickups. This next part of Kee she was not at all sure of, and she dreaded it terribly. If there was a way she could skip this she surely would. Rosa went inside and looked around to see how many Indians were there, to her surprise there were many more Indians than tourists. Rosa stood by the register and asked so everyone in the store could hear, "Is any one headed to Roy's?"

The tourists looked at her curiously, but one Indian lady said, "I'm going that way, I could drop you off."

"Great," Rosa said. "I'll wait outside for you." This was a way that the Indians had of getting around when they didn't have a car or truck to drive. It is very acceptable to come in to any public place on the reservation and make an announcement that you needed a ride to some place and if anyone in there is going that way, most likely, they will give you a ride. This was a way that the Indians had of helping each other.

In a few minutes, The lady came out of the store carrying a small sack and pointed to an old pickup. Both ladies were soon in the truck, headed down the road. The lady looked familiar to Rosa, but she couldn't remember who she was. "I'm Rosa Yellowhair Reed. I know that I know you, but I just can't place you right now," Rosa said.

"Anita Yellowhair's granddaughter," The lady said. "I thought I knew you also, but like you said, I couldn't think who you were, either. I'm Morning Sun Blackfoot. Your Mother and I were good friends in high school and we kept in touch after we got married. I used to come over to your grandmother's house when you and your sister were staying with her. You have grown up to be a great looking woman."

"Thank you, you look very good yourself. What have you been up to lately? Are you married?" Rosa asked.

"No, Ray Blackfoot died last year and I haven't been doing much since then. I've looked for a job but you know there aren't many jobs on the reservation. The ones that are there are taken up by younger people. So I get my monthly government check and live on that," Morning Sun said.

"That's too bad, it's a shame that there aren't more jobs on the reservation. Has anyone tried to bring jobs here?" Rosa asked.

"I don't know," Morning Sun said. "It sure would be nice if someone would bring industry here."

*Industry, that's interesting that's what Nana said the councils were trying to get started and couldn't,* Rosa thought.

The two women rode on, talking back and forth. Then they pulled into Roy's parking lot. "I wish you were going to Flagstaff, I really enjoy your company," Morning Sun said.

"I enjoy yours, too," Rosa said, then slid out of the truck and Morning Star drove on.

Rosa stood there in the parking lot, wondering if this was the right thing to do. Her plan was to go into Roy's and eat lunch and not have any alcohol. Up to now she had stayed away from any place that served alcohol after she had gotten out of the clinic. They told her not to tempt fate. The tea that Nana had been giving her was helping to take the edge off the desire to have a drink, but it had never taken it completely away, and besides, Nana had been making the drink weaker these last few days and Rosa didn't know if the drink was helping now at all. She did know that right now, standing there at

Roy's, that she wanted a drink now, worse than she had for several days. She was hoping, that coming to Roy's and having lunch would let her know if she could go for the rest of her life without a drink. She knew that she couldn't have just one drink, she had tried that too many times before. She could hear the music from the juke box and smell the beer. It smelled so good that it made her want a drink more than ever. Maybe she was putting herself to the test too soon. Maybe she should wait and try this later because right at this moment, the only thing she could think of was a drink. She had twenty dollars in her pocket she had been saving. Her plan to go into Roy's have a sandwich, then leave the bar and grill and catch a ride back to the trading post, seemed like too big of a task now. But if she could do that, then she thought that she would be ready for the next step, whatever that would be. But standing there outside this place, she wasn't at all confident that she had the fortitude to do this. Rosa stood there trying to decide whether to go inside or to catch a ride back to the trading post. She had stood there for over fifteen minutes, but what seemed like an hour to her. Just as she was about to turn and walk out to the road and thumb a ride back, she was startled by a loud screech that made her jump. A large shadow passed over her and as she looked up she saw a large Golden Eagle gliding right over her.

The spirits had shown her a sign, she thought. Rosa turned back and walked into Roy's. The light was dim and at first she couldn't make out anything except the lighted signs because the sun had been so bright outside. In a minute, her eyes had become accustomed to the dim lighting and she made her way to a little table with two chairs. In a minute, a waitress came over and asked if she needed a menu. "That would be great," Rosa said.

The waitress took a few steps back and grabbed a menu, then asked what she wanted to drink. Rosa told her a water and started looking over the menu. In a minute, the waitress was back to get her order. After the waitress was gone, Rosa was left there alone with her water. She looked around the bar and noticed a clock on the wall that said two. That explained the reason why there weren't many people in the bar. She had missed the dinner crowd and it was too early for the crowd that came in after work. There was an Indian woman at the bar with a drink in front of her and she didn't seem too steady. She had just lit a cigarette and seemed to have had a hard time doing that.

There were two guys at the other end of the bar that kept looking at the woman and doing a lot of giggling. Rosa could tell they were drunk along with the woman. Rosa was relieved that they hadn't noticed or even seemed interested in her. One older man was sitting at a table alone and he seemed to be having a drink and minding his own business.

In a minute, the waitress came back with Rosa's order and set it in front of her. "Will there be anything else?" she asked.

Rosa wanted to order a beer so badly, but resisted the temptation and said, "Not at this time." She had ordered a grilled cheese sandwich with fries. It wasn't her favorite meal, but it was the cheapest thing on the menu and she was trying to conserve her money. Rosa put some ketchup on her plate so she could dip her fries in it.

The juke box started playing, a slow song. One of the guys that had been giggling so much, earlier, was standing at the juke box feeding it. In a minute, he turned and went to the woman at the bar and she got up and they were trying to dance.

Rosa was watching them stumble on the dance floor and for the first time in a long time she was so grateful that was not her out there making a fool of herself because of drink. She was eating very slowly and enjoying the view from her table. The food was tasting so good that Rosa became lost in the role she was playing of watching the drunks instead of being one. A bang on her table brought her out of her fixation on the two on the dance floor. Startled she looked up to see the waitress setting two glasses in front of her. One was obviously a beer and one looked like whiskey. "What is this?" she demanded from the waitress.

"The guy at the bar sent them over, he said he knows you," the waitress said. "I told him you weren't drinking, but he insisted on sending them to you."

Rosa looked over to the guy at the bar and he held up his glass to her as to say, 'salute'. She studied his face but she didn't recognize him. "Well, I don't want them, so take them back," Rosa said.

The waitress shrugged and picked up the two glasses and carried them over to the guy at the bar and set them down in front of him.

Rosa thought that would be the end of that, and went back to her watching the two on the dance floor. The first song was over and another had started. The two dancers had decided to stay on the dance floor for this song, too. Rosa was wondering how the woman managed to stay on her feet because anyone could see she was the worst of the two and Rosa was expecting her to drop any second now. But she managed to stay on her feet with the help of the guy she was dancing with.

Rosa was aware of someone standing next to her and she looked up to see the guy who had sent over the drinks standing there holding the same two drinks. "You sent back my gift to you?" He asked.

"Yes," Rosa said.

"Why?" He asked.

"Because I'm not drinking," Rosa said, politely.

"You too good to drink with me?" He asked.

"Look," Rosa said, "it's not that, it's just that I'm not drinking," hoping that answer would suffice.

"You not drinking, since when?" He said sarcastically.

"Since I decided not to. Do I know you?" Rosa asked.

"I bought you a bunch of drinks in Flagstaff one night and the next thing I knew you disappeared, remember?" He asked.

"No, I don't, I'm sorry," Rosa said. "And it must have been a long time ago, because I haven't been in Flagstaff for years."

"Well, it was a few years back, but I still remember, and you are not going to do that to me again," he said, and set down the two drinks on her table.

"I have no intention of doing anything to you," Rosa said. "If I was that mean to you, why did you send over the two drinks?"

"I just wanted to see if you were going to try to pull that trick again," he said.

"Well, you know I'm not going to try to trick you, so please take your drinks and go," Rosa said.

He grabbed his drinks and went back to the bar. After he sat down he tipped up his whiskey and drank the shot down, then used the beer for a chaser.

Rosa was relieved that the argument hadn't gone any further. The waitress noticed that Rosa was finished with her meal and came over to clear away the dishes. Rosa ordered an iced tea so she could sit there a while longer. The juke box was playing and Rosa saw that the Indian woman was back at the bar with another drink. Rosa was thinking of getting up and leaving, hoping to catch a ride back to the Trading Post by using her thumb. She started to get up and pay when she notice that the two guys and the woman were getting ready to leave, so she sat back down and waited until she thought they had left.

Rosa paid for her lunch and left the waitress a one dollar tip. This didn't leave her much from her twenty dollar bill, but it was worth it. Rosa learned that she could be around drinking without taking a drink herself. At first, it was very hard. She wanted to grab the drinks and thank the waitress for them, but she didn't. Then when the guy brought them back over it was even harder to resist but, thanks to the obnoxious jerk, it got easier.

She felt good, this day of Kee. She had faced her fear and had conquered it. She had made her decision to stay there on the reservation and continue in the tradition of the great Socike nation and Eagle Woman. As she stepped through the door, the sun's warmth hit her face and blinded her for a few minutes. Before she could see very well because of the brightness, she heard this faint voice saying, "No... please, no." Rosa put her hand over her eyes to shield them from the sun. She could make out a truck with a man in it. She moved around to get a better look to see what he was doing. The man in the truck was holding down a woman and another man had the door on the other side of the truck open and had his pants down and was trying to rape the woman, but the woman was thrashing around and trying to get away. Rosa recognized the men and woman as the three that were in Roy's a few minutes earlier. *That poor woman,* she thought, she could see her trying to fight them off, but they were too much for her and she was so drunk. Rosa looked around for a weapon and saw a few rocks lining the parking lot along one side. Rosa ran over and picked up a rock about as big around as a lemon and twice as long. She rushed back to the man with his pants down and hit him on the back of the head. He went out like a light and lay on the woman unconscious. The guy holding the woman's arms so she couldn't move hadn't realized what was going on yet. The woman had kept her protest up even now. Rosa crawled right on the back of the man she had beaned just as the man holding the arms of the lady looked up. "What the?" was all he got out when Rosa hit him in the eye with the rock. Because of the confinement of the truck she couldn't get a good swing with the rock, but she got in a few more punches with the rock in her fist. Most of the punches landed on his hand and arms. The man cursed a few times and opened his door, and when he got out, he met Rosa standing there with her rock. One swing and he was out, flat on his back. She went back around and grabbed the first man's legs and pulled him out and off the woman. As she pulled, he slid off the woman. His head went between her legs, then off the seat, hitting the body of the truck on his way down to the ground.

Rosa helped the lady up to see if she was alright. The woman was very drunk, but she insisted on putting her panties back on under her dress. The woman was drunk, but she knew that Rosa had helped her and she kept thanking her for helping her. Rosa inquired if she lived on the reservation. The lady said she did. Rosa looked around to see if anyone was around to help them. There was no one else and at this time of day there wasn't much chance of anyone coming either. She thought of going into Roy's and asking for help, but thought better of it. Two Indian women complaining about two white men off the reservation. She decided to look for the keys to the truck and when she didn't find them in the truck she went through the men's pockets and found them. She put the lady in the truck and got in and drove off toward the reservation.

As they drove, Rosa kept an eye on the woman to make sure she was alright. Several times, Rosa thought she was going to have to stop for the lady, she didn't look good. She thought she would drive the woman to Doctor Cook's office. That way she could tell the Doctor what went on and he could check her out. After all she didn't know what went on before she came out and found the lady in her plight. Before she got to Dr. Cook's office, a reservation patrol car came up behind her with it's lights flashing and Rosa pulled over to let him pass, but he didn't pass. The patrol man walked up to them and ordered them out of the car. Rosa told him that the lady was sick and she was taking her to Dr. Cook's office. The lady started throwing up from all the alcohol and Rosa scooted out to keep from getting it on her. Rosa put her hands on the hood of the truck and told the officer to go ahead and help the lady out if he wanted to."I won't go anywhere," Rosa said.

The young officer didn't know what to do. He had gotten this call from the county sheriff saying that a truck by this description was stolen and that was why he stopped them. Now there was a sick woman making a mess in the cab and he didn't want to get all that stuff on him. "You can help your friend out of the cab, ma'am," the officer said.

"Not me," Rosa said, "You want her out, you get her out." Rosa stood there with her hands on the truck's hood.

The Officer was at a loss as to what to do. They hadn't taught him anything like this in the academy. "What the...," the young officer said. *How dangerous can two women be*, he thought. He stepped over to the passenger side of the truck and opened the door, the stench hit him in the face. He turned his head in disgust, then he helped the woman out of the truck. She stumbled and got against the officer. "Aaaaa...," was all he said as he looked down at the stuff he got on his uniform. The lady sank to the ground as the officer held onto her arm to keep her from falling and hurting herself. She was sitting there with her knees bent and her head was between them, her hands were flat on the ground. The officer stepped back to his patrol car and took out a box of Kleenex and started to wipe off the vomit he had gotten on his uniform. "What is going on?" he asked Rosa.

"Can I turn around?" she asked.

"Yes..., turn around," he said.

Rosa turned around and recognized Bob Yazzie as the young officer. *He's filled out since high school*, she thought.

"Now, what is going on here?" Officer Yazzie asked.

*He doesn't recognize me*, Rosa thought. "What do you mean?"

"I think you know; whose truck is this?" he asked.

"Oh..., the truck..., that's what this is about," Rosa said.

"Yes, the truck, whose is it?" he asked again.

Rosa shrug, "Beats me..., I assume it belongs to those two rapists I took it away from." Rosa said in a manor of fact tone.

"Two rapists? What are you talking about...? Just tell me what happened and how you got this truck?" He said.

"I was at Roy's eating lunch and there were these two guys and that lady over there drinking at the bar."

"They were together?" He interrupted.

"I don't know if they were together or not. I don't think so, but they left together. When I came out of the bar I heard this call for help and saw one man holding this lady down and the other one with his pants down trying to rape her. I picked up a rock and helped this lady to get loose from them. We had no way of leaving the place, so I borrowed this truck to get this lady to Dr. Cook here on the reservation. I don't know if one of them raped her before I got there, or not. But she needed help, so I helped her," Rosa said.

"Where were these men when they were raping or trying to rape her?" He asked.

"One man was in the truck holding her arms and the other one had the other side of the truck door open and had his pants down trying to rape her. She was moving and bouncing around, so I don't think he managed to penetrate. But, they had been out there quite a while before I came along and I don't know if anything happed before that," Rosa said.

"You didn't ask her if anything happened to her before you came along?" He asked.

"No I didn't, what happened before isn't my business, it's something she can tell Dr. Cook when he sees her," she said.

"Do you know this woman?"

Rosa shook her head.

"Do you know her name?" He asked.

"I don't know her and I don't know her name. She told me that she lived on the reservation, though," Rosa said.

"Stay here," He said as he walked around the truck to check with the woman sitting on the ground. He didn't know what to think about Rosa's story, it was getting pretty bizarre. He walked up to the woman. "What is your name?" The officer had a note pad out ready to write down her name. The woman lifted her head pointed to her mouth and upchucked again, only this time she hit his shoes. "Oh… no," he said, and shook his head. Officer Yazzie walked over to his patrol car and got that box of Kleenex again. He took several out and went back over to the lady and handed her one. Stepping back so he wouldn't get hit again, he bent down and wiped his shoes off the best he could and put the Kleenex in a plastic bag he had in his patrol car. After the woman cleaned her mouth, Officer Yazzie started again. "Ma'am, do you know that woman standing over there?"

The woman looked up at officer Yazzie, then at Rosa, then back at officer Yazzie and nodded her head yes.

"Who is she?" he asked.

"She is the lady who gave me a ride."

"I know that, do you know her besides her giving you a ride?" he asked.

The lady nodded again.

"Ma'am, I need you to say yes or no, not just nod your head. Okay."

The lady said, "Yes."

"Where do you know her from?" he asked

"She is the lady who beat off those guys who were trying to rape me." she said.

"Did you know her before that?" he asked.

The lady shook her head again.

"You didn't know her before today?" he asked.

The woman gave out with a loud noise when she exhaled, like she was perturbed, "No."

"Thank you," he said.

Officer Yazzie was glad to finish the questioning. The lady was so drunk that it was such a chore to get anything out of her. He walked back over to Rosa. He saw no reason to keep the two ladies apart anymore. "Come on over here with me so we can keep an eye on this lady to make sure she is alright."

Rosa walked over with him, but didn't get too close. "What is your name? he asked.

"Rosa Yellowhair Reed," Rosa said.

Officer Yazzie's mouth dropped. "Pupa's granddaughter?" he asked.

"Yes, Pupa's granddaughter, Officer Yazzie," Rosa said.

"You know me?" he asked.

"Yes."

"I'm sorry I didn't recognize you. Why didn't you tell me who you were when I first pulled you over?" he asked.

"You didn't ask," she said.

"Your right, I didn't, and I should have recognized you. You haven't changed that much. A little older and a little taller. But your face is still as beautiful as ever," he said.

"You are thinking of my sister, Maria," Rosa said. "She was older than I."

"No, I am talking about you. I knew Maria and I also knew her little sister, Rosa. I knew who you were anyway. What I mean is that I knew you when I saw you, we only spoke once or twice. I knew Maria from school. But she hung with a different crowd than I did. I was what you call a nerd," he said. "Let's sit in the squad car so we can talk." Officer Yazzie was helping the woman up and Rosa walked over to help. The two walked the woman over to the squad car one on each arm. Before he opened the door for her he opened the trunk and got a blanket. This he spread over the back seat and let the woman sit on the blanket then he wrapped it around her. He opened the front door and let Rosa get in. Officer Yazzie could smell the vomit on the woman so bad he went to the truck and got the keys out of it. When he got in his squad car the stench was so bad Rosa was rolling down the window. The officer started the car. "Let's take her to the doctor and then I'll get your statement," he said.

After they took the woman to Dr. Cook and he examined her. Officer Yazzie got Rosa's statement about what happened. Bob Yazzie and Rosa were talking when Dr. Cook interred the room. "They didn't manage to rape her, but she has so much alcohol in her that I want to keep her for two or three days to dry her out," Doc said.

"Did you get her address, Doc?" Bob Yazzie asked.

"Yes, we finally got it out of her that she is living with her mother. Stop at the desk and they will give it to you," Doc. said.

"I've got your statement about what happened. That is all I'll need for now.

The county sheriff called us with the stolen truck report, and I'll have to call him back and tell him we have the vehicle on the reservation. If he pushes the stolen truck charge I will probably need you to tell your story again and maybe go to court," he said.

"That will be fine, I'm planning on staying on the reservation for now, maybe forever," she said.

"By the way, that lady you helped was White Owl. You've probably heard of her work with the youth on the reservation. She used to be a mover and a shaker for the young people here before she started drinking so much. I've never met her before, but I heard a lot about her," he said.

"White Owl, I knew her years ago, I had no idea that was her, what a shame," Rosa said.

"Yes, it is a shame what drink can do to you, a real pity," he said.

Rosa felt a pang of guilt with those words, they could have been for her benefit, she didn't know. She didn't know if he knew about her drinking.

"Can I drop you off some place, Rosa?" Bob asked.

"Would you mind dropping me off at Nana's?" Rosa asked.

"Certainly," Bob said.

The two walked to his squad car without talking. Rosa thought of asking him if he knew of any job openings, but she was afraid that the remark about the drinking was meant for her, so she didn't say anything.

When they reached Pupa's house it was getting dark and Officer Yazzie insisted on walking her up to the door. Rosa was planning on telling him thanks and goodbye. But when they reached the front door he knocked on the door, to Rosa's surprise. When Pupa came to the door Officer Yazzie nodded his head as a sign of greeting and respect to Pupa. "I insisted on walking your granddaughter to the door, so I could tell you of the great deed she has done this day," he said. This was an old tradition that the Socikes had when they told a family of some brave deed another family member had done. No one did it much anymore, but Bob was doing it tonight.

Pupa was very pleased to hear this greeting said once again and opened the door wide, "Please come in and tell me of this great deed, Officer Yazzie."

"Thank you, I will come in and tell you of the great things your granddaughter has done this very day." Then officer Yazzie proceeded to tell Pupa what a brave granddaughter she had and how she fought off two men to save the honor of a Socike woman.

After he finished the story, Pupa thanked the officer for not letting this act of bravery go untold. That ended the old ritual.

Officer Yazzie excused himself and said goodbye to the two ladies.

As he was leaving, Rosa mouthed the words, 'thank you'.

After he left, Pupa said to Rosa, "I think he likes you."

"Why would you say that?" Rosa asked.

"I can tell. That was quite an adventure you had today, Rosa," Pupa said.

The two ladies walked into the kitchen where Rosa's half-filled cup of coffee was still on the table. Rosa sat at the table and drank the cold coffee while Pupa started to cook them some dinner. The half filled cup of coffee was the Socike way of making a promise that they would return soon.

# Chapter 24

Mary was on her way to Yaford Asylum to see Jack. It had been a week since her last visit and Mary was anxious to see if Jack was still having dreams. When she arrived at the asylum she was aware of her surroundings at all times. She was on the lookout for that hawk, she didn't want any more surprises. Mary walked through the front door without any sign of the hawk that had given her trouble before. She let out a sigh of relief after she entered the door. *I must be going bonkers, letting a bird shake me up like this,* Mary thought.

Mary heard her name being called out, so she turned to see Dr. Gonzales coming her way. He was all smiles, "It's so good to see you, Mary. I think you will be surprised when you see our boy, Jack. Come on to his room, I'll show you."

*'Our boy Jack,' He's not a boy and he's not yours,* Mary thought. But she forced a smile and went along with Dr. Gonzales. When she got to Jack's room, Jack was sitting there and smiling at Mary when she came in.

"Mary, I'm so glad to see you," Jack said as he got up and went over to her. He took her hand and led her over to a small sofa that he now had in his room. This took Mary by surprise, because he never acted like that, ever. "Mary, I'm so much better all because of you. Dr. Gonzales explained everything to me. He said that I was so infatuated with you, that me thinking of you constantly has caused me to get better."

*Right..., the doctor thinks he knows everything,* Mary thought. Then she looked around to see where Dr. Gonzales was, but he was gone and the door was closed. "Well, I'll be."

"What?" Jack asked.

"Nothing…, I was just wondering where the doctor went," Mary said.

"He left when he brought you in," Jack answered, matter-of-factly.

"Jack, listen to me," Mary said in a low tone. "Jack are you still, having those dreams?"

"No!" Jack said in a low voice. "I haven't had a bad dream since you left the last time you were here."

"Have you told Dr. Gonzales, this?" Mary asked in a whisper.

"No!" Jack whispered back. "I only told him that I wasn't having as many as I was and that I was feeling better. He said that I must have a fixation with you, and I think of you constantly. I've got to agree with him."

Mary smiled and put her arms around him. "See, I told you we were meant to be together," Mary said. *Why not use Dr. Gonzales for my benefit,* she thought.

"I can't wait until we can be together," Jack said. "Dr. Gonzales said that I could get out of here if I quit having bad dreams. I know he would release me right into the arms of the law. He keeps talking to me like I'm a little kid and don't know anything. I know what he's up to."

"Well keep him guessing, and don't let him know you are over those dreams," Mary said. "Is there a time when they aren't watching you constantly?"

"Only when I'm showering." Jack said.

All this time the two were whispering and Dr. Gonzales and Jane couldn't hear what they were saying in their observation room above them. "I wish we could hear them better, what do you think they are talking about?" Dr. Gonzales asked Jane.

"Your guess is as good or better than mine," Jane said. "But, I think, they are not telling each other how much they love one another. Their body language would be different if they were doing that. They may be planning something. I think we'd better watch her carefully."

"You think she'd try to get him out of here?" Dr. Gonzales asked.

"Oh, I don't know, I just don't trust her for some reason," Jane said. "I really don't know why,"

"I think he will be safe here as long as he's still having those dreams. If he quits having those dreams he might try to leave, but he says he still has bad dreams almost every night." Dr. Gonzales said. "Jane, have your notes changed recently for when he sleeps?"

"You know, he hasn't been having those distortions when he dreams like he did when he first came here," Jane said. "But it hasn't been very long since he's had some pretty bad dreams. I'd have to check my notes to tell you exactly when was the last time he showed signs of having bad dreams."

"I'll tell the orderlies to really watch him just to be on the safe side, but I think we're okay," Dr. Gonzales said. "Captain Yazzie from the Reservation called me to see if Jack was any closer to being able to stand trial. I lied, and told him that he wasn't at this time. That's the same thing I've been telling Chief Blight from Benson. He calls every couple of weeks. I just want to get Jack cured of those dreams for both our sakes. We would both be admonished if we managed to cure him in such a short time. We'd set the mental health profession on it's ear, so to speak. Let's not blow it. After Mary leaves I'm going to drill Jack to make sure he's telling me the truth."

"That's a good idea," Jane agreed.

Mary started to pet Jack and kiss him. "Jack, I need you," Mary said.

"I need you, too."

"Is there any time you could get out of this place without being noticed?" Mary asked.

"No, The only time that I'm alone is when I take a shower and there are no windows and an orderly is always standing outside waiting for me." Jack said.

"What about when Dr. Gonzales has his session with you. Where does he talk to you, in his office or here in your room?" Mary asked.

"He sends for me and his orderlies take me to his office," Jack said. "Why?"

"Keep your voice down, Jack," Mary whispered.

"Sorry," Jack whispered back.

"What happens then?" Mary asked.

"The orderlies leave me, and Dr. Gonzales and I talk, mostly about you now. It used to be about the dreams I had," Jack said.

"How long does he talk to you before you have to go back?" she asked.

"Oh, I'd say about from thirty minutes to an hour," he said.

"When he is talking to you has he ever left for a minute or have you had to go to the rest room?" she asked.

"One time I had to go to the bathroom," he said.

"What happened then?" she asked.

"What do you mean? I went to the bathroom," he said.

"I mean did he go with you or did he let you go alone?" she asked.

"Oh... a... he sent for the orderlies and they took me," he said.

'They took you. Did it take a little while for them to come or were they right outside the door?" she asked.

"I don't know, at the time I was really having bad dreams and I wasn't aware of what was going on around me even when I was awake," he said.

"Think, Jack. Did they come right in or was it a minute or so after he called?" she asked.

Jack sat there with his head in his hands, trying to think.

Mary started to rub his back and whispering in his ear. "Relax, Jack. Just go back in time and try to remember that time. You had to go to the bathroom, you must have asked to go, right?" Mary asked.

"Yes, I was sitting in Dr. Gonzales' office and that policeman was there, he wanted to talk to me, but I had to pee bad, so I said I had to go to the bathroom. Dr. Gonzales called for the orderlies and I thought I was going to pee in my pants before they got there," he said.

"Then they weren't just standing outside the door!" Mary said.

"Yes, it did take them a while to get there," Jack said, surprised that he could remember that much of that time.

"You are doing great, darling. I love you," Mary said as she laid her forehead against the side of Jack's head and put her arms around him. He was doing so great she wanted to go to bed with him right then and there. Mary kissed his ear and ran her tongue in his ear until Jack started to squirm around. "Jack, listen careful," she whispered again, "Is there a time when you know that Dr. Gonzales is going to have you in his office?"

"Yes, right after you leave today," he said. "He'll have me brought right into his office and ask me what you said, what I said, what I thought you meant, how I felt about everything that went on in here," Jack said.

"He has you come in his office after every meeting?" Mary asked.

"Yes, after every meeting and after every bad dream, he sees me and asks me all kinds of questions," Jack said.

Mary thought for a minute. "That's it. Next week when I come, you be ready to run. After we have our visit and he takes you into his office and you are in there about fifteen minutes, give the orderlies time to leave, just get up and run out the front door. I'll be waiting there in a car for you. Then we will be together forever," Mary said.

Jack looked worried. "I'm not sure."

"What are you not sure of, Jack?" You're not sure whether you want to be here or with me?" Mary asked, and took her arm from around him and scooted back away from him.

"It's not that, it's if I get caught, it's what they may do to me," Jack said in a timid voice like he had when he was having those bad dreams. I've seen what they can do to someone they get mad at. They used electric shock on me when they were trying to get rid of those dreams, before you started visiting me. And when I displeased those orderlies they could get pretty brutal when no one can see them. Sometimes at night, I hear screams from others in here. They have those cattle prods that they use freely on anyone they want to.

Mary didn't like this kind of Jack, she liked the Jack that was strong and a little brutal, himself. "Who said bang and taught you to play dead?" Mary asked.

"What?" Jack asked in a tough voice.

"I said who..."

"I know what you said," he interrupted, and glared at her.

*That's better,* she thought. "Take it easy, big boy, I just meant that wasn't like you. I mean — the you — the real man I fell in love with. The man that didn't take crap from anyone. The real you. The one that wasn't afraid of anyone or anything. The man that took what he wanted," Mary said with a smile as she put her arms back around him and started kissing his ear again.

In a minute, Jack had forgotten all about what Mary had said, and was starting to squirm around again. Mary was playing him like a fiddle. "Okay... I'll do it," Jack said.

Mary squealed like a pig and laid on Jack, pushing him down. They both started to laugh. After they both straightened up. Mary went on. "You just run out, I'll be there."

"Next week?" Jack asked.

"Yes, next week, I promise," Mary said. "When Dr. Gonzales asks you about what we were talking about, tell him I wanted to bed you down here and now." Then she gave Jack a kiss that was only meant for lovers.

The two got so steamy that, they both thought they should separate. "Jack, I can hardly wait," Mary said in a low steamy voice.

"Me either," Jack said in the same low voice they had been talking in. Then the two started talking in a regular voice about the weather and how things were in Benson.

The two talked until it was time for Mary's visit to be over. She kissed Jack goodbye and left. All the way to her car she kept an eye out for that pesky hawk, but not a sign of it.

After Mary left, Dr. Gonzales had Jack in his office over an hour, drilling him about what Mary and he were whispering about. After spending about forty-five minutes on what went on in the room, he spent another thirty minutes on dreams that Jack had the preceding night.

Jack hadn't had any bad dreams for a week so he just made up a dream to tell his doctor. After Dr. Gonzales was satisfied that Jack wasn't hiding anything he let Jack go back to his room. As Jack was walking out Dr. Gonzales door, he paid particular attention to where the front door was and how he was going to make his escape the following week.

When Mary got home she couldn't believe she was finally going to be with the man she had loved for years. Oh, she had slept with Jack many times, but then he would have to go home to his wife. Now it was going to be different, she was going to be with him forever with no other woman in the picture, and Jack was in love with her. He was so grateful that she had gotten rid of those awful dreams. Mary was amazed how Dr. Gonzales had played into her plans of making Jack believe that it was her and his love for her that rid him of his dreams. Mary was so delighted with how things were going.

Mary had a busy week. She went to the local bank and took out as large of a loan as she could qualify for. Then she went to Tucson and went to three loan companies and tried to get more loans. She managed to get one and also a new credit card. She thought of going to a car lot and getting another car, but thought better of it. What she had would do, just as long as she keep plenty of oil in it. The next part of her plan was to call on some friends she had in Mexico. This family had once been in Benson and she had helped them with food and later, also, with money. When they got back to Mexico, the family sent her some money to pay her back for her kindness. It turned out the Mexican people that she helped were rich, very rich, and had simply had a string of bad luck when they were in the U.S. They had once insisted that she come to Mexico for a vacation which she accepted. They met her at Naco the small town on the border and took her to their ranch in the mountains in Mexico. Once they had her there they had a fiesta that lasted a week. Before she left, they told her that she was welcome to come back at any time since she now knew the way.

Mary's plan was now set to go, and she was very eager to put it into place.

On the other hand, Jack was getting cold feet about running away after Dr. Gonzales had drilled him unmercifully and let Jack know that if he did something that displeased him the consequence would be severe.

Finally, Friday arrived and Mary was on her way. She had bought a case of oil for her clunker and she was confident that her plan was foolproof. The sun was high and warm on her face as she arrived at Yaford. She got out of her car and looked around to see if she could spot that hawk. As she walked to the front door, Mary looked all around to make sure that hawk didn't attack. As she walked up the steps she kept an eye up, making sure she wouldn't get attacked. Just as she entered the front door she saw him, that hawk was sitting just above the door jam. He didn't attack, but with his mouth wide open he did give a threatening hiss at Mary as she went through the door. The hair on Mary's neck stood straight up and she could feel shivers go through her. "That damn hawk," she murmured.

As Mary walked through the front door, the receptionist saw her and stood up. "Dr. Gonzales is expecting you, Mary. You can go right on in," she said.

Mary nodded and went straight to the doctor's office.

"Mary, I'm so glad to see you and I know Jack is looking forward to your visit. You will never know the help you've been to him, and us, too. I've never seen anything like the transformation he has gone through since you started your visits. Not in all my years of practice. It is absolutely amazing," Dr. Gonzales said. "I'm in great hopes that he keeps this progress up until he is rid of all the bad dreams that haunt him. There is a reason that he isn't rid of all the bad dreams, and I think it is because he will not talk about what happened to his wife and her grandmother anymore. For the last few sessions, he has refused to talk about it. Before, he wanted to tell everyone that he not only killed his wife, but he insisted that he also killed her grandmother, even though everyone told him that she wasn't dead."

"Maybe it's because he didn't kill anyone, have you thought of that?" Mary asked.

"If he didn't kill anyone, then why did he confess to killing his wife?" Dr. Gonzales said.

This kind of questioning was making Mary extremely angry and she could feel her face getting red. She turned away from the doctor and took a couple of steps back. Cool down, she thought to herself, then she turned back towards the doctor. "I only know what he told me right after the death of Maria and that was that he had nothing to do with the death of his wife. She was into drugs, and I think that one of the drug dealers killed her," Mary said.

"That could be," Dr. Gonzales said. "But I can't get to the truth if he won't talk to me about it." The doctor took a few steps away from Mary and looked out the window. "It would be a shame if I cured him and then he was convicted of a crime that he didn't do."

Mary couldn't help but get furious. *That pompous ass,* she thought. *It was me who cured Jack not him,* "Yes, it would be a shame for Jack to be cured and then have him convicted of a crime he didn't commit," Mary said, trying not to let her anger show in her voice.

Dr. Gonzales turned from looking out the window and to looking back at Mary, "Then it's agreed, we need to help Jack clear himself of this crime," he said.

*What kind of gobble goop, double talk is this?* She thought.

Mary, not wanting to show her hand for the plans she had for Jack, but not wanting the doctor to think that she was a pushover either, put her lips together in almost a pucker and wrinkled her brow. "It's agreed that we want the best for Jack," she said in a very deliberate and stern voice.

"Good... good, then Maybe you could talk to Jack about talking to me about everything he knows about the killing of his wife," he said. "Maybe if he opens up to me, then he can rid himself of the last remaining dreams he is having."

The doctor said nothing more, but was in deep thought. *Then I can turn him over to the law where he belongs, and I can finish my book on healing the most severe schizophrenic in the history of mental illness without drugs*, he thought.

"Sure, Doctor, I'll talk to him," she said, thinking all the time, *I'll talk to him about what I want to talk to him about.*

"Good," he said. "Well, I guess we'd better not keep our boy waiting," then started moving towards the door.

Mary started walking with him towards Jack's room. When they got there Dr. Gonzales excused himself and Mary went in by herself. Jack was standing there pacing back and forth, when Mary stepped in. "What are you doing?" she asked.

"I didn't know if you were coming for sure," Jack said.

"And why wouldn't I come?" she asked.

"I was just worried about you, that's all," he said.

"Look Jack, don't do anything suspicious to ruin our plans for today," Mary said in a low voice.

"About our plans," Jack whispered, "Maybe we should wait."

"Wait? What the hell for?" Mary asked in a very low voice.

"Dr. Gonzales is acting so strange, I think he knows," Jack whispered.

"He doesn't know shit, just do as we planned and everything will be alright," Mary whispered back. "Now come over here and kiss me."

Jack obeyed Mary's command. It wasn't very long until the two were making out, and only stopped after they were having trouble putting a limit on it. "Just relax, Jack, we will be together soon, but don't let me down, okay?" Mary asked in a low voice.

Jack was starting to be encouraged by Mary's gutsy way. "I won't let you down," Jack whispered.

"Great," Mary said.

The two sat there talking about everything under the sun. All the time Dr. Gonzales and Jane were watching every move. And listening to every word that they could hear. Fortunately for Mary and Jack they couldn't hear unless they were talking pretty loudly. After the time was up for Mary's visit, the two kissed and said goodbye.

Like always, Dr. Gonzales sent for Jack. The two orderlies took Jack to the doctor's office and sat him down on the couch that was there. Jack was nervous and the doctor could see it. "Jack, that was quite a visit you had with Mary."

Jack didn't say any thing at first. Then he said. "How so?"

"How so?" The Doctor repeated. "You two talked for a long time and most of it was whispering."

"Do you get your kicks by watching Mary and me?" Jack asked, getting some of his nerve back.

"Jack, I'm surprised.... you talking to me like that and all," Dr. Gonzales said, looking straight at Jack. "After all I've done for you. We only observe you to make sure that you don't hurt yourself, or maybe... Mary."

Jack lowered his eyes and bowed his head, losing his nerve now and wishing that he hadn't said a thing.

"Maybe you don't feel like talking to me now. I'll tell you what, I'll let you skip this session, and you can go back to your room," Dr. Gonzales said, as he picked up his phone and started to dial the extension to get the orderlies to come and get Jack.

"No!" Jack interrupted. "I... mean... I do feel like talking."

The doctor stood there with his phone in his hand, looking at Jack curiously.

"I'm sorry, I don't know why I said that. I know that you are here to help me and I'm very grateful for the help." This was as close to an apology as Jack could think of.

The doctor hung his phone back up. Not that he believed Jack, but Jack was acting differently than he ever had since he came to Yaford, and the doctor was wondering where it was going.

Jack silently sighed a sigh of relief. Then the doctor walked around to the front of the desk and sat on the front edge. This was too close for Jack because he was afraid that the doctor could grab him when he got up and ran. It wasn't that he didn't think that he couldn't overcome the doctor, it was that he was afraid that the doctor would slow him down long enough for the orderlies to get there.

"Tell me, Jack, what do you and Mary have planned?" The doctor asked.

"What do you mean?" Jack asked.

"Come on, Jack. Don't play games with me," Dr. Gonzales said in an angry voice and stood up, leaning right into Jack's face.

Jack pushed the doctor back, at the same time he stood up. The push and Jack standing up startled the doctor enough that he stumbled backwards, hitting the edge of the desk then falling to the floor. Jack bolted out the door and made a b-line to the front door. When he burst through the front door he hesitated a little because of the bright sun blinding him for a few seconds.

Mary had pulled around where she could pull up fast and have the passenger door closest to where Jack could reach it first. She had kept the motor running so in very few seconds she had pulled up and stopped just a few feet from the front steps where Jack was standing. She leaned over and opened the passenger door for Jack.

This was the first time that Jack had moved faster than a walk in a long time and he had a little trouble going down the steps at any speed. When he got to the bottom, he ran the short distance to the car. Just as he reached the open door and was about to set his rear on the seat, a hawk hit him in the face full force digging in with his talons. Jack screamed with pain as the bird hung on putting more pressure on and sinking his talons further into Jack's face.

Mary screamed and, through the panic and confusion, took her foot off the break and the car rolled forward leaving Jack there screaming and fighting this bird that had a hold of his face. Mary slammed the gear shift into park, got out with her purse, ran around to Jack and started swinging the purse wildly at the bird, hitting both the bird and Jack. After a few swings the bird was knocked loose and down on the drive. Mary pulled the bleeding Jack to the waiting car and pushed him into the seat. Getting his legs in, she slammed the door, and in a minute she was behind the wheel and they were on their way.

It took a few seconds for Dr. Gonzales to realize what had happened, and by the time he got the orderlies there, Mary and Jack were gone. The two orderlies and the doctor were standing on the front stoop and didn't see a trace of Jack anywhere, but their attention was drawn to a floundering bird that was flopping in the drive. In a minute, it stopped flopping around and was very still. Then in a split second it was on the wing and headed high into the sky. This snapped the three out of their trance and they went back into the clinic. After a few minutes the city police were there, taking a statement from Dr. Gonzales about the escaped mental patent.

"What the hell was that thing?" Jack asked, as they drove through Bisbee at normal speed.

"A Red Tail Hawk." Mary answered.

"A hawk? Why would it attack me? God, look at my face," Jack moaned. Blood was streaming down his face.

"Mary took a quick look at Jack, then went back to her driving. "I have no idea why it attacked you," she said. She had an idea, but she didn't want to spook Jack, so she didn't mention what she thought caused the hawk to attack. "Jack, they are going to be looking for you very soon, so scoot down so no one can see you in here with me." Jack scooted down and Mary drove right past the police station, then took a right. She stopped as soon as she got to a spot where no one was going to see them. Mary got out and opened the trunk, took out some boxes, and told Jack to get out and climb into the trunk. "Scoot way up in there, Jack." When Jack was as far up as he could get, Mary put a blanket over him. Then she put the boxes in, took a last look, and shut the trunk.

Mary got back in her car and headed for Naco, a border town about ten miles from Bisbee. They were traveling on a well-graded dirt road to Naco and Mary had time to think about that hawk. In her mind she thought it must be Maria's spirit in that hawk, that caused it to attack Jack. That would explain why it was so aggressive to her. Mary didn't know that Maria's spirit hadn't found her elders until after the hawk had given her trouble, but in Mary's mind that was the only logical explanation.

They had reached the city limits of Naco, although Jack had no idea of where he was or where they were going. *City limits,* Mary thought. There wasn't much of a city there. On the American side there were no stores, just some adobe homes and the border crossing was just two small buildings, both about the size of an outhouse. One on the American side, the other on the Mexican side. Mary pulled up to the first, and an American border guard came out of his little shack, "How far are you going into Mexico and for what purpose?" The guard asked.

"To see some friends just across the border, a couple blocks away," Mary said. The guard waved her on, and the Mexican side didn't even bother to come out of his shack. They were used to seeing old cars crossing at this point. There were no big houses on either side of the border, just small homes, most made of adobe, and there were four small stores on the Mexican side, two of which were food stores — one regular grocery store, one a fish market. Mary sighed a sigh of relief as she drove over the border.

She pulled around the corner to a spot where no one could see them and got Jack out of the trunk. By this time his face had quit bleeding. Mary took the jug of water she had in case the car overheated and a handkerchief, and cleaned his face. When she got the blood off she examined him and decided that he wasn't too bad just a few puncture wounds.

When she was satisfied, they headed to her friend's ranch. They drove down a dirt road for a few miles then the road started to climb. They were in the foothills and soon they would be in the mountains. The road was rough and the driving was slow. As they got to a higher elevation there were trees on both sides of the road. After about an hour of driving on this road, they reached a clearing and the place looked like a tropical paradise. There was a large hacienda with four small houses close by. There were stables and a corral about three hundred feet from the largest house. There was a jeep and a sedan parked next to the big house. Mary pulled up to the house and parked.

"Where are we?" Jack asked.

"This is where some friends of mine live and they've invited us to stay with them for a while," Mary answered.

"They know that I've escaped?" Jack asked.

"No, they just know you are a very good friend of mine, and we plan to marry," Mary said.

"Plan to marry?" Jack said in surprise.

The expression on Mary's face turned to hurt. *After all I've done for him*, she thought. "That's what they think, and I'm not telling them any different while we are here and don't you tell them any different, either."

"I won't," Jack said.

By that time, people started coming out of the large house. One old lady that was leading the group came up to Mary. "Mary, we are so glad you could come and bring your fiancé. We have two rooms ready for you in the main house," she said. Then she turned to Jack, "I'm Lisa, Mary's friend," she said, and put out her hand to Jack. As Jack took her hand, her face dropped and as soon as Jack no longer had her hand in his, she quickly turned and walked away.

The rest of the people that were there, looked on with surprise. Then one middle-aged man stepped forward and shook Jack's hand. "I'm Jesus, Lisa's son. "Welcome to my hacienda."

Jack was abashed from all the attention from these strangers. Each one introduced her or himself to him. Everyone of these people spoke perfect English. After all the introductions, they all moved inside. Jesus offered them drinks and informed them that dinner would be ready soon. Mary explained to Jack who all of the people were, and how they met. Pedro, one of Jesus' sons, showed them to their rooms. They were across the hall from each other. After all they were not married yet and Lisa would never hear of unmarried couples sleeping together in their house. Technically, the house belonged to Jesus, but Lisa ruled the roost. She was the boss of the family.

Pedro took the car keys from Mary and went out to her car and brought in the boxes that were in the trunk. They were full of clothes for Mary and clothes, shaving gear, soap, and a toothbrush for Jack, as well as presents for the family they were staying with.

Mary took the presents back to the living room and gave them out to the family—one to each family member. As Mary handed one to Lisa, Lisa took hold of her hand and wouldn't let it go for a minute or two. She was looking deep into Mary's eyes and then Lisa started to cry silently and Mary saw the tears. Then Lisa turned and excused herself and went into the kitchen, without opening her present. This was rude to Mary but no one dared to say a thing to Lisa about it. In a bit, Lisa came back in and apologized to Mary and opened her present, which was a white silk scarf. "Thank you, Mary. It is beautiful. I'll cherish it always."

The maid came and announced that dinner was ready. Jesus seated both Jack and Mary, everyone else automatically took their regular seats. This evening meal was a tradition with the Rodriguez family and Lisa sat at one end, and her son, Jesus, sat at the other. Next to Jesus was an empty chair that belonged to his wife. After everyone was seated, Jesus said a prayer of thanks and everyone at the table except Mary and Jack made a sign of the cross. *Catholic,* Jack thought.

The family was passing around food and Mary was having a good time at the table of her friends. There was a lot of small talk, mostly including Mary, not paying much attention to Jack. Lisa was caught by Jesus several times glaring at Jack. Jack wasn't aware of the special attention he was receiving from Lisa, but the dinner went off without a hitch. After dessert most of the family went their own way, but Jesus invited Jack and Mary to the living room for some conversation.

"Jack and Mary, we are honored by your visit. I want you to feel at home while you are here with us and have the best vacation you have ever had in your life," Jesus said. "We have over a dozen horses here and if you feel like you would like to take a ride, please let one of us know and we will have two horses saddled for you. There are some great trails here, even one of your presidents went riding on our ranch a few years back. If you want someone to go with you, please ask. One of the girls will be glad to show you around. I wish that I could accompany you, but my sons and I have to go on a short business trip tomorrow. Please make yourself at home and if you want something to eat or drink you know where the kitchen is."

"Are you going to be gone long?" Mary asked.

"Only two days, then we will be back," Jesus said. "Lisa has a plan for a fiesta in your honor after we get back. Don't be surprised if it lasts several days. Some of my wife's relatives will come to meet you and they, most likely, will stay several days. As long as they are here, the fiesta will go on. I'm sure you will enjoy it. So if you want to take a ride in the next few days, I'd suggest you do it tomorrow or the next day, because I think the fiesta will begin after that."

"You are so kind, I really appreciate your hospitality, Jesus," Mary said. "I'm looking forward to seeing your wife again. She is such a sweet lady."

Jesus was beaming because of the flattery Mary was saying about his wife. He had told her and Jack earlier that his wife was with her mother. "Thank you for your kind words, but I'll have to agree with you about my wife being sweet. I'm very proud of her."

"I know you are, Jesus," Mary said.

"I thank you, too, Jesus, for letting me, a... us, stay here with you for a few days," Jack said.

"You both are quite welcome. Mary was so kind to my wife and my son when they were in Benson. She is a good friend for life, and any friend of hers is a friend of ours," Jesus said.

In a short time, Jesus left Jack and Mary alone to do what they wanted to do. They decided to take a walk and see some more of the ranch. "It's beautiful here, isn't it, Jack," Mary said.

Jack agreed that it was beautiful, but out in nature wasn't his favorite place to be, a dimly lit bar would have suited him better. "What's your plans after we stay here for a few days?" Jack asked.

"Does it matter?" Mary asked. "You're with me, isn't that what's important to you?"

They walked down a path where they heard roosters crowing and in a minute they came into a clearing where there were small barrels spaced evenly apart, each barrel had a hole in the side and a rooster on a tether at each barrel. Mary noticed that they had very short combs, almost none, and she mentioned it to Jack. He explained to her that they were fighting cocks and the comb was amputated so the opponent wouldn't have a target to catch hold of.

"Interesting," she said. "If you have a weakness, amputate it so the enemy won't have a chance to take advantage of it."

"I guess so," Jack agreed.

"I didn't know they had fighting cocks, very interesting," Mary said.

"I didn't know you were interested in that sort of thing," Jack said.

"I admit it, I'd like to see a fight," Mary said. "I'll have to ask Jesus about these fighting cocks."

Jack could feel a warmness going over him, a feeling of jealousy. He turned his face away so Mary couldn't see him getting mad. He wanted to slap the snot out of her for bringing up Jesus' name while she was in his company. But, he had enough sense to know that if he showed the least bit of anger towards Mary, that family would make sure that he would pay for it. In a minute he could feel the anger subside. "If you like, I'll ask him for you," Jack said.

"No, that's all right, I'll ask him," Mary said.

"Okay," Jack said, reluctantly.

Jack and Mary walked around looking at other things, Jack not saying much, he was kind of pouting, and Mary didn't realize everything wasn't okay. She put her hand on his arm at the elbow and pulled him close. This made him smile and the anger left him for the moment. "You know, just because we have two different bedrooms doesn't mean that you can't come visit me during the night," Mary said.

Back at the house Jesus was talking to his mother. "Mama, why were you so rude to Jack and Mary?" he asked.

"He is going to kill her!" she said.

"What?" he said.

"He's going to kill her, I saw him—then I saw her dead," she said.

"You saw this? Are you sure?" Jesus asked.

"Yes, I'm sure," she said.

Jesus sat down, not knowing what to say to his mother. She was one half Haitian and one half Mexican, her father was Mexican. Her father and family were Catholic and Lisa was Catholic, but she learned a lot of Voodoo from her mother and she practiced it sometimes. "You know, Mother, that I believe what you see, but I must ask you again, are you sure?" Jesus asked.

"Yes, I am sure," Lisa said.

"What should we do?" Jesus asked.

"Let me handle it," Lisa said. "I don't know if I can save her life, but I know he won't get away with it. Please treat them normally, and let me take care of this thing.

"Okay, I'll let you handle it as you wish, Mother," he said.

"And treat them as if you know nothing about this," she said, looking him in the eyes.

"Yes, Mama, I'll do as you say," Jesus said.

It was getting late and Mary and Jack entered the living room where Jesus and Lisa were. "Hi," Mary said. Jack just nodded.

Lisa and Jesus said, "Hi."

"Jesus I noticed that you have fighting cocks," Mary said.

Jesus smiled, "Yes we have fighting cocks. Do they interest you?"

"Yes, they do, you must think me awful, but I'd like to see a fight," Mary said.

"Then you will, actually during the fiesta, we were going to have some sparring, to get them ready for the meet that's going to go on two weeks from now in Naco. When we have the sparing, we will have a couple fight to the death, so you can get a feel for it. Then, if you like, you can join us when we go to Naco for the meet. There will be some of the best fighters in the country there. There will even be Americans from Arizona and Oklahoma there with their cocks.

Mary looked at Jack. "That would be great, won't it, Jack," she said.

Jack nodded. "Sparring?" He asked.

"Isn't that the word for it?" Jesus asked, thinking that he might have his English wrong. "You know when two boxers practice."

"Yes, that's the word for it," Jack said. "I wouldn't think those chickens would need to practice though."

"But they do, they need the experience or they will loose. Just like the gladiators of old, they have to practice to be the best or they die," Jesus said.

"Will there be other women at the meet?" Mary asked.

"Oh, yes, lots, and children. It's a family affair. Cockfighting is a great sport and a great tradition here in Mexico, and some of the states in America also," not wanting Mary to think that Mexicans were the only people who enjoyed cockfighting.

"I know, they had them in Arizona, but I never got to see one," Mary said.

"You will get to see one now," Jesus said.

This had been a great day for Mary and she was looking forward to the night. "I really appreciate all you and your family are doing for us, I hope we can repay you someday."

"There is nothing to repay. We are friends and, besides, you showed kindness to my wife and boy when you didn't even know them, this kind of kindness can never be repaid," Jesus said.

"Anyway we really thank you, don't we, Jack?" Mary said.

"Yes, yes, we really appreciate all your hospitality," Jack said.

"Well, gentlemen, I'm getting a little sleepy, so I think I'll go upstairs to my room." Mary said.

"I think I'll do the same, " Jack said.

"When you get up in the morning my sons and I will be gone, so enjoy yourselves and we will see you when we get back. Please ask for anything you want, I'm sure we can accommodate you. Have a good night's sleep. Good night," Jesus said.

"Good night," both Jack and Mary said at the same time, as they headed up the stairs. As they reached the top of the stairs they met Lisa starting to descend the stairs. She greeted them cordially, and went on down the stairs. "Wonder why she was up here?" Jack said when Lisa was out of hearing distance.

"Who knows? After all, it's her house," Mary said.

"I know it's her house," Jack said. "But, she seems a little hostile towards me."

"How so?" Mary asked.

"She's always giving me the evil eye," Jack said.

"Evil eye?" Mary said laughing.

Mary's remark made Jack both embarrassed and mad at the same time. He just turned away from Mary and went into his room. Mary followed him into his room. "I'm sorry, Jack, I didn't mean to laugh." She almost tackled him and they fell on the bed with Mary on top, laughing. Then Jack started to laugh, too. "The evil eye," Mary said, teasing and opening one eye wider than the other. Then she kissed Jack a long hard kiss before Jack could get mad. After the kiss he had other things on his mind and forgot all about getting mad. "I want to take a shower and brush my hair, by then everyone should be in bed. After you get ready for bed then come into my room," she whispered. With that she jumped up and went to her room.

Jack lay there on his bed thinking of what was in store for him tonight. He couldn't believe his luck. Just last night he was in a mental asylum, and just a few weeks ago he was having dreams so bad that he wanted to commit suicide. But tonight he was a free man in Mexico with a woman who was in love with him. And in a few minutes he would be making love to her. He could hear the shower running in the bathroom and he could imagine what Mary looked like taking her shower. After he heard the water stop and the door from the bathroom open and close, Jack grabbed his toothbrush and toothpaste. Then he noticed a hair brush laying there on his dresser. *That brush wasn't there earlier,* he thought. *Or was it?* He picked it up and examined it. It looked new. Maybe Mary did leave it there for him and he hadn't noticed it. He picked it up and brushed his hair a few times and then headed for the bathroom to brush his teeth. When he finished brushing his teeth and put on some deodorant, Jack went back to his room and changed into a robe.

In a few minutes he was trying Mary's door and let himself in. It was totally dark inside her room. He was wondering why it was dark, but in a minute his eyes became accustom and he could see Mary lying on the bed with nothing on. Jack stopped in his tracks and just stared at the form on the bed. After not being with a woman for so long he was fixated at the form lying there. He could make out the figure by the moonlight now and it was the most beautiful thing he had ever seen. It was truly a shame that he could not express his feelings, it would have meant so much to Mary. But, it just wasn't in Jack O'Reily to say anything to anyone like that. In a minute, Jack could see Mary holding her arms out beckoning him to her bed.

Both Mary and Jack awoke to the crowing of a rooster then another rooster started crowing and then others joined in. Mary got up, put on a robe and checked out her door. When she saw it was all clear she motioned to Jack so he could go back to his room without being noticed. After Jack got his shower and dressed, both Mary and Jack went downstairs to breakfast. It was different not having any males there except Jack. Lisa was at the head of the table, and was quite cordial to everyone, including Jack. *No evil eye*, Mary thought. They had a large breakfast of eggs and tamales with salsa, quite tasty.

"Did you both sleep well?" Lisa asked.

"Yes, very well," Mary said.

"Yes," Jack said, as he nodded his head.

"Jesus said that you two might like to do some horseback riding," Lisa said.

"We haven't talked about it, but it does sound like fun. What do you think, Jack? Want to go horseback riding?" Mary asked.

Jack was kind of in a bind, he had never ridden a horse before, but he didn't want to admit it. "I guess... it's been years since I've ridden, but we can give it a try if you want."

"Great," Mary said and clapped her hands with joy. "It'll be fun."

"Then it's all set, I'll have one of the girls saddle two horses for you," Lisa said. "They should be ready in about thirty minutes."

After they had finished breakfast, Jack and Mary went upstairs to get ready for their ride. Jack wished that he had a hat, but Mary didn't think of bringing him one, so he was going to have to go without one.

When they went outside, Christina, one of Jesus' daughters, had two horses saddled and waiting. She handed the reins to Jack and stepped back. "Have fun," she said. "We will expect you back for lunch."

Jack handed one set of reins to Mary and watched what she did, then he tried to imitate her. Mary first patted the face of her horse and went around to the left side of the horse and put her left foot in the stirrup, grabbed the saddle horn and swung her right leg up over the saddle.

Then it was Jack's turn to mount his horse. He did go to the left side of his horse. But, putting his left foot in the stirrup was more of a job than it looked like. He got his foot in the stirrup and grabbed the saddle horn, but instead of swinging his right leg up and over to the other side of the saddle, he stood straight up. He was standing straight up next to the horse with all of his weight on the one stirrup. This made the horse move to the right trying to get away from the uncomfortable feeling. This made Jack feel like he was going to fall away from the horse, so he leaned over the saddle. There he was with the top half of his body on one side of the saddle, the bottom half on the other side. He then managed to swing his right leg over the saddle. Then he sat up. Mary and the young girl took all this in. The young girl had her hand over her mouth to keep from laughing. Mary felt sorry for Jack and asked if he was alright.

Jack was just glad he was finally on the horse. "I told you, it was a long time since I was on a horse." He still wouldn't admit that he had never ridden. Jack took the reins, kind of kicked the flanks, and they were off.

Christina went inside and giggled from the sight she had just seen. Lisa saw her giggling and asked her in Spanish what she was laughing about.

Christina answered her in Spanish that she was sorry to laugh at their guest.

Lisa pressed her for more detail.

Christina explained how Jack had mounted his horse and when he finally managed to get on the horse that he took off in another direction because he didn't know how to make the horse go where he wanted it to go. Lisa and Christina started giggling and Christina told Lisa that Jack was bouncing so high that she was afraid that he was going to bounce off. Lisa had a good laugh then straightened up and said. "We really shouldn't laugh at our guest."

"Yes," Christina said, then went on to do her chores.

Lisa could hear her giggle again. Then she went up to the room that Jack was staying in and found the hair brush she had placed on his dresser the evening before. Lisa picked up the brush and examined it careful. There on the brush were four hairs. She could tell they were not Mary's because Mary had coal black hair like most Indians. These hairs were brown. They were most likely Jack's, but to be absolutely sure she would test them. Lisa carefully removed the four hairs, being careful not to break any of them. She then went to her own room and took a small cloth doll that she had made the night before. Lisa took a small needle and threaded all four hairs through the needle. Using the hair as thread she sewed the hair through the scalp of the doll and tied them there. She then put the doll in her top dresser drawer for later use. "Tonight, I'll try you out Señor O'Reily," she said to the doll.

Jack and Mary returned back before they were expected, and it was clear to the Rodriguez family that the couple had been arguing. Jack was walking funny and they presumed that was because of the bouncing he did in the saddle. Mary said that they had a wonderful time and excused herself because she was tired and was going to take a nap before lunch. Jack just wanted to sit down but that even proved to be somewhat precarious because he couldn't get comfortable even in the softest chair.

The Rodriguez girls would check on him every now and then to see if he wanted anything. One of the girls was upstairs and heard Mary crying through her closed door, which she reported to Lisa.

Jack, in the meantime, decided to go upstairs and draw a bath so he could soak his sore bottom in the warm water. After soaking about thirty minutes he got dressed and came downstairs.

Mary was there and told him that the girls had lunch ready for them. Lunch was not like their dinnertime. Everyone ate their lunch when they felt like it. But for Mary and Jack, because they were guests, the girls had fixed them some tortillas, beans with meat and

Spanish rice for their lunch. Then asked what they wanted to drink; tea, water, or milk. Jack actually wanted a beer, but was afraid to ask for it. He settled for the tea. Mary took the tea, also, and found it very good.

After lunch the two went for a walk and, by the time they returned, everyone could tell that the couple had made up. It was all that Lisa could do to stay out of Mary's problems, because she liked Mary so much. Even though she had only known Mary since her daughter in-law and grandchild had trouble in Benson, Lisa had taken a liking to her. When Lisa took a liking to anyone, everyone that knew her, knew they had better like them also. The Rodriguez family was well known in that part of Mexico. They had a hand in everything in that part of the country, both Mexico and America. They were a family that no one in that part of the world that knew who they were, messed with, not even the police. They owned ten bars along a strip just south east of Naco that a lot of Gringos from across the border visited, and some young Mexicans went to for fun and frolic. There were about twenty bars and a couple houses of prostitution. The Rodriguezes owned more than anyone else on that strip. They also owned several massage parlors in Tucson. Every bit of dope that went across the border had better pay the Rodriguezes a toll or they would wind up in a Mexican jail or dead. The police and border patrol were invited and went to a lot of celebrations at the ranch. Jesus was expecting both the police chief and a border patrol Captain to be at the fiesta they were having when they got back.

The evening meal went very well with Mary and Jack getting along with no hint of the disagreement they had during their riding adventure that morning. Lisa touched Jack one more time to make sure that what she had seen was still there. It was even stronger now. *This man is pure evil and Mary has no hint of it*, Lisa thought. *He must be stopped.*

After dinner Jack and Mary went for another walk and Mary was enjoying her time with Jack immensely. Jack, on the other hand, was getting bored. He wasn't used to all of this nature and longed for the adventure of the bars and the women that hung out there. He was forgetting that Mary was the one who saved him from the terrible dreams. It was starting to seem like that all had passed and he was starting to think of going into the Naco strip and spend some time in the famous bars of Naco. He had no idea that the Rodriguez business was the biggest part of that strip. The Bars were well known across the border and a lot of young men lost their virginity there. Jack decided to mention to Mary about going there for a few beers. "What do you think about us going to Naco for a few beers?" Jack asked.

"When?" Mary said.

"Tonight or maybe tomorrow night," Jack said.

"Jack, I don't think that would be smart, us leaving our host and going off drinking. The fiesta will start sometime tomorrow and there will be all kinds of beer, tequila, and anything else that you could want," Mary said.

Jack was disappointed that Mary wasn't wanting to go off and go bar hopping with him, so he decided to pout.

Mary took hold of his arm and got closer to him. "Besides that, I have plans for tonight, that don't include anyone else but you and me." With that said, she grabbed him between the legs and gave a slight squeeze, then pulled his head down and kissed him.

This shut Jack up for the rest of the walk. He didn't even think of going out drinking, let alone talk about it.

After the long walk they came back to what seemed like an empty house, so they went upstairs and got ready for bed.

Lisa waited until late that night when she knew that everyone in the house would be asleep. Then she took the cloth doll with the four strands of hair sewn in the head and headed outside to the barn. There, in the corner where there was an electric light burning, was a rooster tethered to a post. Nearby was a water tray for the rooster to get a drink. Lisa held the doll up, muttered some words. laid it by the rooster and sprinkled cracked corn on it. The rooster started to peck at the corn on the doll. Lisa started to dance and turn and twist in a rhythmic form to a beat that only she could hear.

Jack was sound asleep next to Mary and all of a sudden he started to thrash about and hit Mary with all of the thrashing he was doing. Then he started to scream and twist. Mary tried to wake him to no avail. After about ten minutes of this, Jack woke up. "My God, Jack, you scared me to death. Are you okay?" Mary said in a panic.

"They're back, they—are—back!" He screamed.

"Sh—sh," Mary said. "Who's back?"

"Those dreams! Those damn dreams," he said.

"What dreams?" Mary asked.

"Those damn dreams, those dreams, you know what dreams, those damn dreams!" Jack shouted.

"That's impossible, Jack, those dreams are gone forever," Mary said.

"Don't tell me those dreams are gone, I just had one. A giant bird was picking my guts out. He pecked a hole in my stomach, pulled out my guts, and was eating them," Jack said.

Mary was sitting up and got out of bed, put on a robe and turned on the lights. Jack was sitting up in bed and was sweating profusely. The color had drained from his face. He had thought that Mary had gotten rid of those bad dreams forever, but she hadn't. There was nothing that Mary could say to convince him that the dream he had tonight was not the same that he had before. Jack got up and paced the night away and no amount of coaxing could convince him to come back to bed.

The following morning, Jesus and his boys were back and the atmosphere was jubilant around the breakfast table. Jesus had brought back presents for everyone, including the maid. She had been with them for a long time and she was now considered one of the family. Jesus' girls helped the maid with the breakfast, and the chores around the house. The Rodriguez family believed that everyone should work regardless of how much money they had, and they didn't believe in spoiling their children. Jesus noticed that Jack was very sleepy at the table and he figured that it was because of something his mother did. He had seen her magic before work on their enemies, and he knew that she believed that Jack would kill Mary if she didn't intervene. He gave out all of the presents. Jack's was a cowboy hat and, surprisingly, it even fit. Mary's was a bright red dress, which she loved.

After breakfast Mary learned that Jesus' wife and relatives would be there between lunch and dinner time. Jesus and his boys had brought a lot of things back for the fiesta that would start that afternoon, as soon as his wife and in-laws showed up. The boys spent some time unloading things from their car. The maid and the girls started making something to eat. They even brought back a pig prepared to roast and the next morning the men would dig a pit to roast it.

Lisa went to her room and unwrapped the doll she had made the day before. She had tested it the night before and she had heard the screams that came from upstairs and she also saw the lack of sleep that Jack had shown at breakfast. She was set, the doll had been proven. At the first sign of trouble she would strike.

There was a small alter in her room that she knelt at and placed the doll between two candles. She said a short prayer, then got up and blew out the candles. As the smoke from the candles came off the wicks as a ribbon and went up to the ceiling, she continued to pray. After the candles stopped smoking she then quit her praying and got up, took the doll, wrapped it back up and put it in a drawer.

Jack was sitting in the living room when he fell sound asleep. Mary explained to everyone that Jack had a hard night and it would probably be best to let him sleep. The guests were visiting with each other and Mary was very happy to see Jesus' wife, Juanita. Mary and Juanita got together and were doing a lot of visiting with each other while Jack slept for a couple of hours. When he did wake up, only he, Mary, and Juanita were in the living room. All the men had gone outside and started digging the pit to roast the pig in, the following day. All the women and girls were in the kitchen, either cooking or just talking.

"Hi, honey," Mary said to Jack when she saw that he had woken up.

"Hi," Jack said back. "How long have I been asleep?" He asked, embarrassed that he fell asleep.

"Oh, not too long," Mary said. "We thought you could sleep until dinner, but you didn't last that long."

"You should have woken me," he said to Mary.

"I would have, but I thought you needed the sleep," Mary said. Then she walked over to Jack's chair and leaned down and whispered in his ear. "Did you have any dreams?"

"No," he said.

"See, I told you they were not back," She whispered.

Then a smile came over Jack's face.

"Jack I want you to meet my friend, Jesus' wife, Juanita," Mary said as she straightened up and walked back over to Juanita. "Juanita, this is my Jack, who I've been telling you about."

"I'm very glad to meet you, Mr. O'Reily," Juanita said, smiling at Jack.

*Gorgeous*, Jack thought. "I'm very glad to meet you," Jack said, and stood up.

"You might like to join the men outside digging the pit for the pig," Mary said, smiling at him. "They got beer."

"Sounds good to me, but first I'll go upstairs," He said. Jack excused himself and went upstairs, first to the bedroom to pick up his hair brush and his tooth brush then to the bathroom to brush his hair and brush his teeth. He wanted to make a good impression on Juanita. When he came back down he noticed that Mary and Juanita were deep in conversation, so he went outside.

Outside, the men were digging a hole for a pig roast. Most of the digging was being done by the young men and the rest were drinking beer. They were speaking in Spanish, but when Jack came out everyone started speaking in English, except to one old man who they had to translate for. So for most of the rest of the day they were speaking in English and also in Spanish to keep the old man interested in what was being said. Jack spoke little, but did a lot of drinking.

# Chapter 25

It had been several days now since Rosa had been on her day of Kee and her quest had gone favorable for her to stay on the reservation. Nana and she had discussed what she would do to establish herself on the reservation, but had not came up with a job for her yet. She had thought of asking Joe Coyote for a job as a goat herder for him. After all he had mentioned that he had plans to get herders working for him. But, Nana thought this was not her calling and she reminded Rosa she was a descendent of Eagle Woman, she was not a goat herder. There was nothing wrong being a goat herder, but that was not in her family tree. She was a true lineage of Eagle Woman and as such, was a true warrior. Because of this, Rosa thought of applying to the academy to become a police officer, but for two reasons she thought better of it. One was, she was a woman, on the reservation there had never been any women police officers. The other, was with her history of alcohol, they wouldn't hire her knowing this. So things were pretty much at a stand still now. Nana told Rosa, "When thing's are not going as they planed or wished, to just wait, and give the ancestors that have gone on before them time to work things out."

Rosa and Nana had been up now for about an hour and both had gotten dressed and had breakfast. They were enjoying a cup of coffee when there was a knock at the door. Nana got up and went to the door and there stood Sergeant Blackwood.

"Good morning, Pupa," Sergeant Blackwood said.

"Good Morning, Sergeant Blackwood," Pupa said. "Please come in."

Sergeant Blackwood stepped into the room and removed his hat.

"I'm glad I caught you at home Pupa."

"Would you like some coffee, Sergeant Blackwood?" Pupa asked.

"No, thanks, Pupa, I can't stay but a minute, but I wanted to talk to you before I leave for a short trip. I had a call from Chief Blight of Benson. He informed me that Jack O'Reily escaped from Yaford and they have no idea where he is right now," he said.

Pupa had a strange look on her face, *How could he escape from those dreams,* she thought. She knew the secret of the dream catcher, but it was not common knowledge—even on the reservation—how to catch those dreams again. He had to have help from someone of the inner circle of the reservation, to have gotten rid of those dreams.

"Are you all right, Pupa?" Sergeant Blackwood asked.

"Yes, I'm all right," Pupa said. "I thought that Jack was having such bad dreams that he couldn't function. In fact, you told me that he kept trying to commit suicide. How could he have functioned enough to escape?" Pupa asked.

"That's why I'm taking the trip, I'm going to Benson to talk with Chief Blight and then to Yaford to talk with Dr. Gonzales. I don't know what has happened, but I'm going to find out," Sergeant Blackwood said.

Rosa heard what was being said and went into the living room to see what was going on.

"Sergeant Blackwood, this is my granddaughter, Rosa," Pupa said.

"I'm very glad to meet you," Sergeant Blackwood said and put out his hand to shake hands with Rosa.

"I'm very glad to meet you, too," Rosa said, as she shook hands with Sergeant Blackwood.

The two stood there and looked deep into each other's eyes, not thinking of what was going on around them. In a minute, Sergeant Blackwood started stuttering, not knowing what he just said. "I... I... I'm, sorry, I heard about the problem you had a few days ago." Sergeant Blackwood was taken by Rosa's good looks and Pupa could see this.

"Are you sure you won't have some coffee with us?" Pupa asked the Sergeant.

"I didn't realize that your granddaughter was here, so I guess I could stay long enough to have coffee, I need to talk to her, also."

"Good," Pupa said. "Come on in the kitchen and let's sit down."

The three went in and sat at the kitchen table and Pupa got Sergeant Blackwood a cup of coffee.

"I wanted to tell you, Rosa, that we have cleared up the problem you had the other day. The county sheriff called me and said that the owners were going to file a complaint on you and the other lady, White Owl, for stealing their truck. I told the sheriff to have the men come to the reservation and sign a complaint, and we would be glad to take care of the incident, and give them back their stolen pick-up. When they showed up, the sheriff was with them. We immediately arrested the two men and charged them with attempted rape. When the sheriff objected, we arrested him for interfering with the investigation. This put us in the driver's seat, so to speak, but White Owl refused to press charges, so we had to let them go, but only after they agreed not to press charges on the stolen vehicle. Anyway, I thought you would like to know what happened," he said.

"Yes, thank you. I appreciate your taking care of that in such an efficient manner, and then letting me know," Rosa said.

"Believe me, it was my pleasure. We have had trouble with that sheriff trying to run this reservation along with the county," he said.

"Well, I appreciate it Sergeant," Rosa said.

"Officer Yazzie said that you were planning to stay on the reservation, now that you are back."

"Yes, I have decided to stay here, but there aren't many jobs on the reservation, and I'm having a hard time finding any work here," Rosa said.

"Maybe I could help," Sergeant Blackwood said. "The tribal chief has authorized a small group of young Socikes to form a committee to do some brainstorming to bring prosperity to the reservation. Right now it is all voluntary work, but the chief wants this group to eventually form a political force for the reservation. Would you be interested in coming to one of our meetings?" He asked.

"Well, yes, I'd be interested in that, but I still need a job," Rosa said.

"Some of the business people and reservation leaders have heard of this group and they sometimes come to the meeting, also. I thought this would be a good place to meet some of the people that could hire you, and I think you would be an asset to the group, not to mention the fact that you are a direct descendent of Eagle Woman," he said.

"Sounds good to me. My plans are to stay on the reservation, so I need to get involved in its business," Rosa said.

"Great, the next meeting is at the activity center at seven o'clock this Tuesday evening," he said.

"Now, about the escape of Jack O'Reily. Please lock your doors, just in case. We don't think that he is headed this way, but we can't be too careful. Our officers are checking all vehicles that enter the reservation, but it's conceivable that he could get past them without being detected. Just be extra careful until we have caught him. If you like, I'll have an officer stay here with you or out front in his squad car," Sergeant Blackwood said.

"That won't be necessary," Nana said. "As long as we know that he has escaped we can take precautions. After you return from your trip, please come by and let us know what you have found out."

"I will do that," Sergeant Blackwood said. "And, I'm glad you are coming to our meeting, Rosa."

After Sergeant Blackwood left, Nana started getting dressed in her traditional Socike war uniform and putting on war paint. Rosa asked her what she was doing.

"Taking care of business," she said.

"Don't you think you should be teaching me some of this business?" Rosa asked. Then she didn't say another word, terrified of what she just said and how she said it. This was Pupa, leader of the women Socikes, as well as her grandmother. "I'm sorry, Nana, I didn't mean to speak in such a tone to you."

Nana smiled, "You are right, it is time for me to teach you the secrets of the daughters of Eagle Woman. I have been praying for the great spirit to show me who I should trust with these great secrets. First, we will paint your face with war paint then we will pick a weapon for you. For now you can wear jeans and a shirt, later we will get you a traditional war uniform a lot like mine. But because you are not me, your uniform must be a little different. That is one of the small secrets. I have learned on my last trip that there are no granddaughters or great-granddaughters of Eagle Woman. They are all daughters of Eagle Woman regardless of how far down the line she is on the genealogy scale." Nana went on about other small secrets and facts, in general, about Eagle Woman and her daughters to this time. She also told her about her last trip and the things that she could remember that went on during that trip. Nana showed her a copy of the writing of what she had written that the Women Council had voted to go into the *Great Book Of The Living Souls*. But the Men Council voted to not put in the book because she couldn't remember them after she had written them.

After Nana had finished telling Rosa everything that she thought Rosa would be able to remember at this time, she showed her the box that had once held Red's dream catcher. She told her how she had released the spirits to go into Jack O'Reily and that he should not be free from them, without interference from someone high in the Socike ruling body. She explained that she was going to the wilderness to try and get answers from their ancestors spirits, and now she would take her along to teach her the thing, that she could legally do so.

Nana and Rosa stopped on their way to the wilderness at Lonesome Bear's place. He had a small shop where he made Indian artifacts to sell to the tourist. But in his back room he had the real stuff. Pupa and Rosa entered his shop and greeted Lonesome Bear.

Lonesome Bear greeted them back and then he locked his door and put a sign in the window that read closed. The three proceeded to the back room where there were all kinds of weapons and shields. There were other things also that would customize whatever they wanted. Like horsetails, dear skins, and feathers of all kinds, even eagle and turkeys. There were even several turkey beards from the tom turkey. "What are you needing today?" Lonesome Bear asked the ladies with war paint on.

"We need a weapon for Rosa," Nana said.

"I see, any particular kind of weapon?" he asked.

"I mean, she needs a weapon," Pupa said.

"I'm sorry, Pupa. I didn't realize who she was. This is your granddaughter?" he said. "She is the Chosen One?"

"I believe so, we shall see," Pupa said.

Maria looked at Nana and mouthed, "Chosen one?"

"I'll talk to you about it later," Nana said.

Lonesome Bear got a big grin on his face. "I'll be right back." He left and in a few minutes he came back with a roll of leather. He cleared a place on the table and laid the roll on the table. Very carefully he rolled out the leather, revealing three war clubs. The first was decorated with leather and silver with a gray stone. The second one had a black stone with eagle feathers. The third had a round stone covered with rawhide that made it look like a baseball without the stitches and decorated with leather only. Lonesome Bear arranged them in a row with all the handles facing in one direction.

He then placed Rosa in front of them, facing the war clubs. "Now don't touch them, but open your hand and slowly move your open hand over the handles like this." He demonstrated by moving his hand over the handles of the war clubs.

Rosa moved her hand over the war clubs and all of a sudden let out with a scream. She was holding the war club with the raw hide stretched over the stone. "It jumped in my hand!" she screamed, and was shaking the club.

Both Lonesome Bear and Pupa were yelling and dancing for joy. "She's the one, she's the Chosen One!" Lonesome Bear was yelling.

Pupa was giving a Socike yell of thanks giving and doing the thanks giving dance.

Rosa was just standing there looking at the war club in her hand, not believing what had just happened.

Both Lonesome Bear and Pupa were laughing and crying with joy and they both were dancing around the room.

"The war club will pick you if you are the Chosen One. That club will always stay with you. You can put it down and leave it some place, but you will never loose it accidentally. Or it will never slip out of your hand during battle," Lonesome Bear said. "Now you need a knife."

Pupa helped Rosa put the club in her belt where it would be comfortable.

Lonesome Bear went over to a show case that had a blanket draped over it. He took off the blanket and a spotless showcase emerged, and in it was a selection of knifes. Pupa and Rosa walked over to the case and looked at the knives.

"Will one of these jump into my hand too?" Rosa asked.

Both Pupa and Lonesome Bear smiled at that remark. "No, you must choose the knife, but choose one that is comfortable in your hand, and fits your personality," Lonesome Bear said.

"How am I going to know if it fits my personality?" Rosa asked.

Lonesome Bear took out two knives and handed one to Rosa. Is that comfortable to you?" he asked.

Rosa shrugged.

Lonesome Bear took that knife back and handed the other one to her. She took it and balanced it on her first finger, opened and closed her fingers around the handle. "This does feel better than the other," she said.

"Good, good. Now look them all over, including this last one and keep your mind blank, don't look for any particular thing, Just look them over until one comes to your interest, then we will try it for a fit," Lonesome Bear said.

Rosa did just that. She scanned the three rows of knives in the case several times. Then she asked to see one that had a curved blade. She placed it in her hand and turned her wrist in several directions. She then felt the sharpness of the blade and discovered that it was sharp on both edges of the blade. "This is it," she said.

"Great," Lonesome Bear said. He then reached down in a drawer below the showcase and took out the sheath it fit.

Rosa threaded her belt through the slits in the sheath and buckled her belt back. All the while she was doing this, her war club stayed on her hip where it was put under her belt.

The two women were now ready for their quest. They both thanked Lonesome Bear and left his shop. As they left the shop two tourists were there with their cameras taking pictures of them. "You know if we charged them to take those pictures, it would help the reservation," Rosa said.

"That's an idea," Nana said, as the two walked out into the wilderness. "We are looking for a hill that is out in the open so we can make contact with one or more of our ancestors."

After walking for about forty-five minutes they saw a small hill in a valley standing alone. The two were kind of drawn to that hill as they walked along not saying anything, just listening to the sound of nature as they walked.

As they started up the hill Rosa could hear the wind saying, "This is the way." She looked at Nana as to ask, if she had heard it too.

Nana just nodded.

As the two reached the top of the hill they both sat down and waited, not saying a thing, Nana knowing what she was doing, Rosa just going along trying to learn from Nana and not getting in her way.

They must have sat for forty minutes when a crow landed in their midst. "Who are you?" Nana asked aloud.

Then came this voice, crystal clear. "I'm Yellow Light, daughter of Eagle Woman. Why do you seek me?" The crow asked without moving its mouth.

"We want to know why and how Jack O'Reily got loose from the dreams?" Nana asked aloud, this time not moving her mouth, but Rosa could hear her as clear as rain water.

"You will know soon, as to how, and as for why? It was love. This you will also understand by the power of our new sister." Yellow Light said, then flew away.

"That's that," Pupa said.

"What do you mean?" Rosa asked. "Did that make sense to you?"

"Just because we don't understand now, doesn't mean we didn't get our answer. Let's take the answer in reverse. Yellow Light said that the reason he quit having dreams was because of love. That could mean many things. It could mean he loved someone or something. Someone else loved him, or it could mean something else that we can't see right now. But then she made a promise that our new sister would reveal it to us. That part I think she was talking to me, and she meant that you would find the answer and reveal it to me, but it might mean someone else like your sister, Maria," Pupa said.

"This is very confusing," Rosa said.

"Sometimes it can be, confusing," Nana said. But she said new sister would reveal it to me. You are the only one that is new in receiving her weapons as Eagle Woman's daughter. But on the other hand, it could mean Maria, because she is new in the spirit world. Right now that is the only thing that makes sense to me," Pupa said.

"Well, how am I going to get the answer?" Rosa asked.

"Don't worry about that, it will be revealed to you or me, or Yellow Light wouldn't have said it," Nana said.

"Now, as for the first part of the answer, it will be revealed to us. It means that it will be revealed," Pupa said. "We are not in danger at this time or Yellow Light would have warned us. Now let's get started back home."

The two women got up and started back, but on the walk back the two talked about everything from when Rosa would get fitted for her traditional war uniform to what they were going to eat and drink when they got home. "Will I ever have to use these weapons that I just got?" Rosa asked.

"Oh, yes, many times. But most likely you will be in the spirit when you do. Nowadays we usually don't have to use our weapons in the flesh. But if we did they would be just as true to us as they are in the spirit world. With that war club there are many responsibilities that go with it. I know that you are up to them. There are things that you will learn in the next few years."

When Nana and Rosa got home each took a shower to get the war paint off their faces and the dirt off their body. When Rosa got out of the shower, Nana had dinner ready and the two ate very heartily. Rosa was very excited about everything that had happened that day. She kept looking at and feeling the war club and the knife. "Where do you keep your weapons?" she asked Nana.

"I keep them with my uniform in the closet," Nana answered.

"Oh," Rosa said. She had expected an answer more exciting than in the closet. Getting up from the kitchen table, Rosa took her new weapons and put them on a shelf in her closet, and then returned to Nana at the kitchen table. "I can't believe that all this has happened today. I could hear that crow speak clearly. Then I heard you speak to that crow without moving your mouth."

"Yes, yes... and you could have spoke to the crow also as I did, if you tried. But... it wasn't the crow we heard or talked to, it was Yellow Light who had entered into the crow to converse with us. She is a great-granddaughter to Eagle Woman in our world. But in the spirit world, she and all descendants of Eagle Woman are daughters. Even you and I," Nana said with a great big smile.

"That is amazing, isn't it?" Rosa said.

"Yes, it is," Nana agreed.

"I haven't talked to you about the responsibilities of being the Chosen One, and I guess this is the time to tell you all about it," Nana said.

"Oh... yes... I guess I should know what this is all about, I might not want it," Rosa said.

"Yes, you will want to be the Chosen One. The spirits have already searched your heart and have found you to be the desirable one. That means that it is the life that you were destined for. If you had not found it, you would have spent all of your life looking and not being satisfied. No, this is the life you will love, I promise. Do not doubt. This was the life that the Great Spirit had chosen for you since before you were born. Many bad spirits will come to you and will try to tell you that you are wrong in what you are doing. Don't believe them. Keep your eyes on the prize, which is honor and dignity in the eyes of your ancestors," Nana said.

When Nana finished speaking she had a look on her face as if she had been in a trance and her words were not in the same tone of voice or in her usual speaking manner. It was as if someone other than Nana was using her voice.

These words put goose pimples all over Rosa's arms. Rosa reached across the table to put her hand on Nana's arm to thank her for these words, but quickly withdrew her hand, being startled that Nana's arm was so cold. Her arm and hand were cold as ice. She touched Nana's hand again and by that time her hand had started to warm up. Rosa had a surprised look on her face. In a small voice she asked Nana, "What was that?"

Nana smiled, "That was the great spirit, with a message for you."

"Were you aware that you were speaking to me?" Rosa asked.

"Yes, I was aware, but it was more like I was watching, rather than speaking," Nana said.

"Have you done that before?" Rosa asked.

"Only a couple of times before and the messages were never that long. You can be assured that you are the Chosen One. Don't doubt it," Nana said.

"But, chosen for what?" Rosa asked.

"To be a leader and you will be a great one. I know it," Nana said.

"This is all overwhelming for me," Rosa said.

"I know it is, but don't be afraid. You have great things that you must do, but you will take them one at a time. You will take baby steps at first and the spirits and our ancestors are here to help you. They will lift you up on wings of eagles and you will fly higher than you can ever imagine. The wind will speak to you, as well as all of the animals and birds. Lightning and thunder will be your partner for fighting your enemies. There is nothing in this world or in any other world that can stand before your advances. I have spoken!" Nana was sitting there with the same look on her face as before. All of this had come out of her mouth, but Rosa could tell it was not Pupa talking.

Rosa reached back across the table to feel Nana's hand and it was as cold as ice, as before. This time Rosa could feel the goose bumps over her whole body. She had never felt anything like this before.

In a few minutes, the two ladies were back to talking about other things. This evening had been too much to continue on the subject of Rosa's new life. It had taken a lot out of Pupa and Rosa alike. They decided to retire for the night and both thought they would sleep well.

Nana fell asleep, slept well all through the night, and didn't wake up once. Rosa, on the other hand, had fallen right to sleep and then started to dream. In her dream she was standing in the center of the reservation and there were dark clouds rolling in, covering the whole reservation. Rosa was standing there dressed in a traditional war uniform that looked just like Nana's uniform except that at the collar it had feathers on each side. She had her war club in her belt and her knife on her other side. The clouds were dark, thick, and were at about the height of a person's head. They were so thick that they choked people when they tried to breathe. To keep from choking, one had to stoop over so they wouldn't breathe in the cloud. Everyone on the reservation was walking around bent over so they wouldn't choke on the cloud.

Rosa took her knife and tried to cut the cloud. As she sliced the cloud it would part and she could stand up straight and breathe the fresh air. But after the clouds moved away from her it would come back together, and everyone else would have to stoop over but her. As she walked she would take harder swings at the cloud with her knife and the clouds would part further away from her. A few people would step into the clearing she had provided with her knife and stand upright with her and could breathe without stooping over. As she walked she would swing as hard as she could with her knife and try to make a bigger opening, but after she went on the clouds would close in behind her and the people would have to stoop over again. It became frustrating trying to clear the clouds for everyone with no one else helping her. Her strength was about to give out when she grabbed her war club and began to swing at the clouds and knock them down to the ground so the people could trample them with their feet. At first, she could knock down small parts of the cloud and a few people would rush in and start to stomp them and pulverize them. They would disappear as the people stomped on them. This gave her encouragement and she forgot about being tired. She would swing harder, knocking bigger chunks of the cloud down so the people could stomp on them. Other people saw what was going on and they, too, pulled out their war clubs and started knocking down the clouds and stomping on them. After a while, all the clouds disappeared and the people were walking upright again.

In the morning, Rosa woke up tired from all of the fighting she had done in her dreams. She had a lot of questions to ask Pupa that morning and was anxious for them to sit down to breakfast so she could talk to her. She arose early and got coffee ready while Nana was getting up and getting dressed. After they had their breakfast and coffee with the dirty dishes still on the table, the questions started. Rosa explained her dream to Nana and was wanting to know what it meant.

"I Don't know what it means, but it was not an ordinary dream," Nana said.

"What do you mean, it wasn't an ordinary dream?" Rosa asked.

"If it had been an ordinary dream, the dream catcher in you your room would have caught it and not let you dream it. A dream like that would have never gotten through. I think it was a leaka," Nana said.

"Leaka, I remember the word, but I can't remember what it means," Rosa said.

"It means a messenger spirit that was sent to deliver a message. They just dance around the edge and across the webbing without being caught. They can go through any dream catcher without even being slowed down," Nana said

"Oh, that's right, I remember now. They are sent from the great spirit," Rosa said.

"You remember," Nana said. "You always paid attention when you were in school and learning about the traditions and spirits of the Socikes. I was always so proud of you and your grades in school. You took everything seriously when you were in school."

"I seem to have forgotten much of what I learned then," Rosa said.

"I know, but it will all come back to you, especially if you go to the refresher course being offered by the Women Council," Nana said.

"Refresher course, huh," Rosa said. "I don't know, this is all coming so fast and so much at a time and I really do need a job and a place to stay. I can't mooch off you for the rest of my life," Rosa said.

"It's a very good class, I've sat in on several classes and they are very good," Nana said. "But, if you feel that this is all going too fast, or you just don't want to do it right now I understand."

"As far as a Job, I'm sure something will come along soon. As for mooching off me, you are not. You've been such a lifesaver to me. I was so down after Maria was killed. When I learned that you wanted to see me. It was like a great rock had been lifted off my shoulders. I enjoy you staying with me very much and I have more than I could ever use," Nana said.

"Thank you, Nana," And Rosa got up and went around the table and gave her Nana a big hug.

"Thank you, Rosa, I need a hug once in a while. I'm so glad you have decided to stay home on the reservation. This is where you belong. I just know that you will come to love the choice you have made," Nana said.

"Yes, I feel that I have made the right choice and that there is a job waiting for me. I thought I'd go out this morning and look some more," Rosa said.

"If you really feel you need to, alright, but if you just want some spending money I can let you have some," Nana said.

"No, you've done enough, by letting me stay here and letting me eat here," Rosa said. "I really feel like I need a job, though."

The two women got up and did the dishes, then Rosa got ready to go look for a job. As she was leaving Nana called out. "Remember I'm going to a council meeting this afternoon."

"I'm glad you reminded me of that. I forgot your meeting. I might have remembered it when you weren't here, but I might have forgotten and wondered where you were," Rosa said as she went back and gave Nana one more hug.

Rosa headed for some of the shops that she had approached earlier to see if any would hire her with her persistence. About noon, she headed to the stables to talk to Jode. On arrival, she caught Jode starting his lunch which he offered to share with her. She accepted to share only after he agreed that she could buy him lunch after she found a job.

"Too bad I don't have enough work here to hire you. You would make a good horse person," Jode said.

"I'd make a good horse person? I am a horse person! I ride and when I get settled I'm going to have a horse," Rosa said.

"You know what I mean, a professional horse person," Jode said.

"A professional horse person?" Rosa asked.

"Someone that makes their living by taking care of horses," Jode said.

"I know what professional means," Rosa said.

"I know that you know what professional means, I didn't mean anything by it," Jode said, afraid that he had insulted Rosa, which he didn't want to do. "I'm not good with words."

Rosa started to laugh. "You are very good with words. I was just teasing you and, by the way, this sandwich is very good. Did you make it?"

Jode was relieved that she was just kidding, so he thought he'd kid back. "Yes I did, I made it from smoked skunk."

Rosa looked at her sandwich, then smiled. "I had that coming. My guess is it's smoked turkey, am I right?"

"Yes, it's smoked turkey," Jode said.

"Well, it's very good," Rosa said.

"Why hasn't some girl made you her brave by now? You being such a good sandwich maker and all," Rosa said.

"I guess that all of them got tired of eating sandwiches, and I don't know what you mean by, 'and all'." Jode answered with a laugh.

"I did let myself in for that last remark, didn't I? The, 'and all'." Rosa said.

Jode nodded.

"I'd better get back to my job looking, and thanks for the sandwich," Rosa said. Then she left but after she went about ten feet she turned and waved to Jode.

Jode waved back. He wanted to call out to Rosa and ask her for a date, but he didn't.

Rosa went to more stores and the three schools to apply for a job without success. By the time she went home to Nana's house she was worn out. She went right into her bedroom and lay down on her bed. She lay there thinking about the day she just had. It was nothing like the day before. Today was dull with no excitement, unlike the day before. The only highlight of the day was lunch with Jode. Jode, at least, understood her and her plight. At least she thought he did. He was really sweet and was her friend. She didn't have to worry about him wanting anything from her, he seemed to be all giving and no taking, not like the boys and men who had been in her life before she returned to the reservation. *He is a true friend,* she thought as she lay there almost asleep.

Pupa had been at her meeting and it turned out to be a very lively meeting. Pupa told the Women Council about the day before, and how Rosa was the Chosen One. Everyone accepted her story except Redbird who wanted proof.

"Lonesome Bear was there. I can have him come and speak to the council and tell you what he saw," Pupa said. "Would this satisfy you?"

"I won't be satisfied unless I see something with my own eyes," Redbird said. "Sometime back, you told us you went on a trip and you brought back only a piece of paper with things that you said the spirits told you, and you couldn't remember many of the things that you wrote. You gave them to us to consider if they should be put in the *Book Of The Living Souls*. Everyone in the council thought that they all should be put in the Great Book. I went along with everyone else without question. Now you come to us, saying that your granddaughter should be recognized as the Chosen One without any proof except your word. I will not go along with this."

Bud stood up. "Redbird, and other members of the council. Many people have gone on trips and could not remember what the spirits told them. Some couldn't remember anything. Others could remember some of the things that were told to them, as Pupa did, but Pupa had the good sense to write them down as soon as she could get to a pen and paper."

"As for Rosa being the Chosen One, there are three facts that we should consider. First is the fact that Rosa is the only and last descendent of Eagle Woman after Pupa. Second is the fact that we can talk to Lonesome Bear as he was there and can answer our questions. The third, is we have Rosa here on the reservation that we can question," Bud said. With this she sat down.

After Bud, others rose to speak. Most spoke the praises of Pupa and of Eagle Woman and her descendants. Only one stood up and backed Redbird on her accusations. At the end of the meeting they had not made a decision as to whether to recognize Rosa as the Chosen One. This didn't bother Pupa because she had faith that Rosa was the Chosen One and she had only to trust the spirits for the Chosen One to do the work she was destined to do.

When Pupa arrived she found Rosa had arrived home before she had and was sitting at the kitchen table, drinking coffee. Nana poured herself a cup and sat down with Rosa to talk about their afternoon. Nana didn't mention what went on in the meeting of the Women Council but just said that things went on as most meetings.

Rosa just said that she went around to the businesses that she had visited earlier and as yet there was nothing open. She didn't mention how discouraged she was getting about getting a job there.

Nana had just taken her first sip of coffee when there was a knock at the door. She got up from her seat and started to the door. "I can't imagine who that could be at this time of day." When she opened the door, there stood Sergeant Blackwood smiling. "Come in," Pupa said.

"Thank you," he said, as he stepped in and saw Rosa peering around the doorway of the kitchen to see who was at the door. This brought a big grin to his face.

"Sergeant Blackwood, so good to see you again," she said.

"Good to see you again so soon, also," he said. "I thought you two would like to hear what I found out in Benson and Bisbee."

"Yes, we would," Pupa said. "Please come into the kitchen and have a cup of coffee with us."

This invitation, Sergeant Blackwood jumped at. Anything to spend time with Rosa. Her beauty had struck him so hard that he couldn't get her off his mind. "Thank you very much, I'd love to have some coffee," he said, as he walked into the kitchen.

Rosa hadn't notice at first, but now she saw a paper sack that Sergeant Blackwood was caring. *Wonder what's in the sack,* she thought as he entered the kitchen. In a minute, all three of them were in the kitchen having coffee and Sergeant Blackwood, almost all the time, had his eyes on Rosa, only occasionally looking at Pupa to be polite.

After a few minutes he took his eyes off Rosa to get down to business. "Pupa, Rosa." He addressed them this way to give respect to Pupa. This was very important to the Socike, Pupa being Chief of the women. "I wasn't sure what had happened in Yaford yesterday when I talked to you. Now I know quite a bit more than I did then," he said, as he tried to keep his eyes off Rosa so he could keep his mind on what he was saying.

"First thing I did when I got to Benson was to talk to Chief Blight. He filled me in on what he knew about Jack O'Reily and the case. Then I went on to Yaford and talked to Doctor Gonzales. This was where I got most of my information about the case, and I'm going to need your help about some things that are very sensitive. I hope I can be very frank and candid with both of you," Sergeant Blackwood said.

"Certainly you may be candid with us," Pupa said, as Rosa nodded yes.

Sergeant Blackwood went on. "Chief Blight informed me that when they arrested Jack O'Reily he had already caught Jack and Mary Smith staying together for the night at her place. He had interrogated Mary very intensely, she admitted that she had been having an affair with Jack for quite some time, and she lied for Jack about knowing that Maria came to the reservation. This was important because, at the time, Jack said that he knew that Maria caught that bus to the reservation when in fact he didn't, and that was why he lost his temper when he finally found her."

"Jack started having those dreams, and he confessed he killed Maria. At the time he even thought he killed you, too, Pupa. Which he almost did, but you were too tough for him. Chief Blight saw no reason to bring out to the public anything about the affair. He wanted to save the family from any gossip that might arrive from this knowledge. He kept in touch with Dr. Gonzales at Yaford to see how Jack was, just in case he was getting over those dreams and could go to trial. We also kept in touch to see if we could bring Jack to trial, but we were happy with the dream spirits punishing him and hoped to let them continue," Sergeant said.

Both Pupa and Rosa were listening intently and didn't interrupt the Sergeant's story.

"After I talked to Chief Blight, I went to Dr. Gonzales' Office at Yaford and spent some time talking to him. At first, he told me every thing like Chief Blight had told me, but after I caught him in a couple of lies, he confessed that Jack had been getting better after Mary started visiting him every week. He showed me this picture of Mary that she had insisted on him leaving with Jack at all times." With this, Sergeant took the picture of Mary Smith—still in the frame she had placed it in—out of the bag. "Now I don't know as much about dreams as I should, as a true Socike. I think I must have been asleep during that class when I was in school," Sergeant said as he lay the picture on the table. "I don't remember any way that a person could get rid of the dream spirits with a picture of his girlfriend. This is the part that I was hoping you could clear up for me."

Both Pupa and Rosa looked at the picture of Mary Smith, Rosa's cousin, and both were perplexed to why Mary had insisted on it being near Jack at all times. Then Rosa took the picture and examined it closely. "The frame is sure thick isn't it?" she said. Then she turned it over, got a kitchen knife, straightened out the nails and took off the back. There was Red's dream catcher laying there mended.

There was a slight shriek from Pupa as she lifted out the dream catcher from the frame. Rosa and Sergeant Blackwood looked on in silence. Pupa fingered the mended section, not saying anything.

There was a long silence, then Pupa told the Sergeant and Rosa all about Red's dream catcher, Pupa even went and got the box that Red's dream catcher had stayed in for many years. Then she told them how she had hitched rides to Benson and waited until Jack was out of the house, then cut the dream catcher and slipped it between the mattress and the box springs. She then hitched rides back to the reservation.

"Well, that explains why Jack started having those awful dreams, but how did you get past our officers at the road blocks we had set up?" Sergeant Blackwood asked.

Pupa just looked at him and he knew that she could go about anywhere she wanted to without being detected. She had spent a lifetime walking in and out of the spirit world and she could certainly do a simple thing like getting passed some officer on a road block. Besides, they were looking for someone who was being abducted not someone that slipped out on their own.

The Sergeant bowed his head, ashamed that he asked such a stupid question. "Sorry," he said.

"This is what is perplexing," Pupa said, as she fingered the repaired place. "This is top secret, how to repair a dream catcher that would work. Mary didn't have that knowledge. She was removed from class as a child because of her lying. I remember her mother telling me this because she was so ashamed that her daughter had lied. Especially in class where the punishment was so severe. I can't imagine anyone telling her how to do this. But who else would repair it for her?"

"I'm glad your faith in the Socike nation is so high, but in the job I have, I have lost some of that faith in the people," Sergeant Blackwood said. "I remember how to repair a dream catcher, though I don't speak of the secret, but I can imagine someone else doing it, especially if they were drinking. Drink impairs one's ability to think clearly."

Rosa looked at Nana with a sorrowful look, knowing that she had faith in the old ways of the tribe. "I'm sorry, but Sergeant Blackwood is right," Rosa said. "I'm sure there are many who might reveal secrets of the tribe. There is just not the pride of the Nation as there used to be."

"You have certainly cleared up a lot of the mystery in this case," Sergeant Blackwood said. "It is a case that I can't reveal to any of the officers off this reservation, though. They would think me crazy. I can hear them now. 'Silly superstition,' they'd say. Now, what should I do with Red's dream catcher?" Sergeant Blackwood asked.

"Put it back in it's box and let me worry about it. It's something that I wouldn't wish on anyone, but we have our obligations that we must face up to," Pupa said.

Sergeant tightly closed his lips and nodded. He then placed the catcher in the dust covered box. "I'm sorry to leave this responsibility with you, but you are by far the most qualified person to handle it. I'm thinking that we should keep this between the three of us for now."

Pupa closed the box and took it downstairs in the cellar where it had been for many years. "I was hoping I had seen the last of you," Pupa said to the dream catcher, as she walked down the cellar steps.

"Do you have any idea where Jack O'Reily or Mary Smith is right now?" Rosa asked.

"I have guesses, but no proof of where they are. Mary has disappeared, hasn't shown up for work since Jack escaped. No one has seen her around Benson. Bisbee is so close to the border, I think they are probably together in Mexico. From what I've learned from Chief Blight neither of them could have too much money, so it will be hard for them to stay in Mexico very long without help.

Pupa came back from putting away the dream catcher and was listening to Rosa and Sergeant talk.

"Do either of you know of anyone they may know who they may be staying with?" Sergeant Blackwood asked.

Rosa and Pupa looked at each other, then shrugged and both said, "No"

"Chief Blight has put an A. P. B. out on them and has asked the Mexican Police to watch for them, so the only thing we can do now is wait. I'm sure they will show up sooner or later. Chief Blight is furious at Dr. Gonzales, about how he let Jack escape because he didn't think he was that much of a risk. I don't know whether he's going to ask the medical board of psychiatry to do anything about not telling him Jack was getting better," Sergeant said. "But don't worry, he will show up. We will get him for what he did to Maria and you, Pupa."

*Not if I get to him first, the old ways are still the best way to treat your enemies,* Pupa thought. "Don't worry too much about revenge on Jack O'Reily. The spirits will make sure he doesn't escape his fate for too long," Pupa said.

"I suppose you're right, but I'd still like to see the law lock him up and make him pay for what he's done," Sergeant Blackwood said. Sergeant Blackwood believed in the spirit world but had no real knowledge of what it was or what it could do. After all he was of another generation than Pupa, and had not grown up around someone like Pupa that traveled in and out of the spirit world as she had all of her life. "I'll leave you Ladies now and I'll see you Tuesday evening, Rosa," Sergeant Blackwood said. Leaving, he turned and took one more look at Rosa. *She is so beautiful,* he thought.

# Chapter 26

The first big day of the fiesta was the roasting of the pig and it wouldn't be done until tomorrow, but there was a lot of other food for everyone. There was a lot of beer and tequila being drunk, a lot of music and there was dancing all day long. Mary enjoyed the party and spent a lot of time talking with Juanita, Jesus' wife. Jack just spent the time drinking and flirting with the other women. Jesus came in to where Mary and Juanita were. "Mary, the boys have been sparring the cocks, and we are going to have a fight. You mentioned you'd like to see a fight," Jesus said.

"Oh… yes, I'd love to see one," Mary said. "What about you Juanita, want to see the chickens fight?"

Juanita laughed. "Yeah, I'll watch the chickens fight. But we'd better stop calling them chickens. The boys get upset when I call them chickens. They are their gladiators, to them, so they insist I call them cocks or fighting cocks or birds, but never chickens. I can't tell you how often they have corrected me on that point, huh Jesus?"

"Well, they have a point. After all, they spend a lot of time raising them, training them, and taking care of them. Then one of you women comes along and calls them chickens like Colonel Sanders," Jesus said.

"I'll remember that," Mary said. "No more Colonel Sanders. They are cocks… fighting cocks." Then she burst out in a giggle, and Juanita joined in on the giggles. "Juanita, let's go see the cocks — fight," and the giggles started in again.

"I think you two have been hitting the margaritas," Jesus said.

"I think you're right," Juanita said, and Mary nodded her head. Then they stood up and followed Jesus out the door to where the cocks were going to fight.

The boys were waiting for Mary before they started getting the birds ready to fight. There was a black and white one in one pen and a red one in another pen. The pens weren't much bigger than about two feet by one foot. It was just for holding them before a fight, or to transport them from one place to another. "I made sure that the boys picked two opponents that you could differentiate. If the color was similar, it was sometimes hard to remember which was which. I remember when I was a boy and my dad took me to a cock fight. The first few fights I couldn't tell the difference. I'd made a small bet and I didn't know if I had won or lost until the owner picked up the winner. I knew whose bird I had picked, but when it was on the ground with another, I couldn't tell them apart, so I thought I wouldn't put you through that," Jesus said.

"Well, did you win?" Mary asked.

"No, my bird was laying on the ground dead," Jesus said.

"Your cock was laying on the ground dead?" Juanita said.

"I appreciate you thinking of the two color cocks for my first time," Mary said, and the two women burst into laughter. "Any more margaritas and I won't be able to tell the difference in the two colors."

"I really should go get Jack, I'm sure he'd like to see the fight," Mary said, just now thinking of him.

"Stay and watch the boys get the birds ready for the fight. Pedro will go get Jack. Won't you Pedro?" Juanita said.

"Sure, mama," Pedro said, and off he ran to find Jack.

Two of the boys took out one cock each and held it while their partner started working on the birds' legs. Jesus took Mary close to the cocks so she could get a good look at what was going on. "This fight will be with long knives like this one and Jesus took out a small blade with a U welded on the end of it. Sometimes we use a short knife." He held up a short blade like a long blade, but shorter. "Or we sometimes use a gaff like this, and instead of a blade it has a round needle longer than the long knife. Show Mary the spurs," Jesus said to the boy holding the bird.

The boy held the legs of his bird up and one spur was sharp and the other one was sawed off flat, about three quarters of an inch from the leg. Further down in Mexico where the people are poor and can't afford all this fancy equipment they just take a pencil sharpener and sharpen the spurs that God gave the bird.

The boy's partner put a hard rubber block with a hole in it over the spur that was sawed off. Then he placed the U part of the long blade over the hard rubber. Next, he took a long ribbon about one eighth of an inch wide and what looked to Mary to be about ten feet long, and started to wind it over the U part of the blade and hard rubber, and around the leg.

"You have to be careful not to get it too tight or it will cause the bird trouble in the fight. You can tell if you get it too tight because it will cause a slight limp in the bird when you put it down. If you get it to loose, the blade won't stay straight. In other words, you need to know what you are doing." Jesus said.

"These boys know what they are doing. They have had birds since they could walk. We think it's good for them to have the responsibility," he said, as he put his arm around his wife.

Pedro showed up with Jack in tow. "Hi honey," Mary said. "We thought you would like to watch the cock fight."

"Sure, do we bet on the outcome?" Jack asked.

"Why not, a cock fight isn't a cock fight without bets, even if it's a few coins, that's part of the sport," Jesus said.

"Well, I'll bet on the red one," Jack said. "Wait, I don't have anything to bet," and he turned his pockets inside out.

*What's the mater with Jack, acting like that,* Mary thought. *Why is he acting that way?*

In a minute, people who didn't want to watch the preparation of the birds, showed up for the fight. "We're here, you can start the fight," one boisterous guest said.

The two boys with the birds held them close together and let them peck at each other. Then they parted them and put them on the ground and let go. The two birds rushed at each other and leaped into the air about two feet off the ground trying to strike the other bird with it's spurs, which on one leg was a razor sharp knife that was about two inches long. This was repeated over and over. Mary was surprised there didn't seem to be any blood. The men started to make bets by calling out how much they wanted to bet. Then someone else would call out they had that bet. The two cocks jumped at each other until they got weak and no longer were jumping. The boys picked up their birds and both boys blew on the head of the bird they were holding to warm him up. They then placed them back on the ground and the two birds jumped at each other again. The crowd would call out words of encouragement for the bird they had picked to win. Pretty soon the red one fell over dead. As Mary looked closer she then saw the blood. The feathers had been soaking it up, so it didn't show until the bird was saturated in it. The one boy picked up his live bird and held it up above his head and the people cheered the winner. This boy kissed his bird on the head and started examining him for wounds. If he had any deep wounds then they would have to be sewed up. The men and one woman went to the individuals that they had bets with, and collected their money.

The other boy picked up his dead bird removed the metal spur and took it out to the manure pile and threw it there to rot in the sun.

Mary took all this in and thought, *what a shame, you don't win so you get thrown on the manure pile.*

# Chapter 27

It was Tuesday evening about six o'clock and Rosa had just finished getting ready for the meeting that Sergeant Blackwood had invited her to. She had just sat down to wait for another fifteen minutes before she started walking to the community center where the meeting would take place. There was a knock at the door. Pupa doesn't usually get company this time of the day, so Rosa was curious to see who was at the door. When she opened it, there was Sergeant Blackwood.

"I thought we might as well ride together to the meeting," he said, with a sheepish smile.

Rosa was glad to see him, but she didn't want to look or act too eager to go with him, with a last minute invitation like this was. "Were you just in the neighborhood, and decided to give me a ride or—?" Rosa asked.

Sergeant Blackwood looked embarrassed. He just realized that he had taken Rosa for granted and should have dropped by earlier to ask if he could give her a ride to the meeting. Maybe she had changed her mind and wasn't even going to the meeting, or maybe she just wasn't interested in riding with him. "I'm sorry, I should have dropped by earlier, and asked if I could drop by and give you a ride to the meeting. I'm sorry… I hope you still come to the meeting. I really do think you will be a big asset to the group." Then Sergeant started backing off the porch and was about to turn and leave.

When she first opened the door he looked like a fox in a chicken house, but now he looked like a whipped hound. She liked the fox look better. "I would, appreciate a ride, Sergeant Blackwood. It was nice of you to think of me, but my question remains, were you just in the neighborhood?" Rosa asked.

"Not really, I just thought I'd like to give you a ride, so I acted like a foolish school boy and came over without getting permission first. Not thinking of my manners or your feelings by first coming by and asking you, I apologize," he said, and nodded his head to her.

"Let me tell Nana that I'm leaving and we can go," she said.

Just then, Pupa came around the corner and saw Sergeant Blackwood. "Sergeant Blackwood," she said, acknowledging his presence. "To what do we owe the pleasure of this visit?"

"Sergeant Blackwood was in the neighborhood and he thought it would be nice to give me a ride to the meeting, being he was the one who convinced me to attend. Wasn't that nice of him, Nana?" Rosa said.

"Very thoughtful," Pupa said, looking straight at Sergeant Blackwood.

"We were just going as soon as I let you know," she said to Nana. "Shall we go," she said to Sergeant Blackwood.

In a minute Rosa and Sergeant Blackwood were on their way to the activity center. "I thought if we got there a little early I could show you around in case you haven't been to our new center yet," he said. In a few minutes he pulled into a nicely paved parking lot next to a new building. Rosa was impressed with the architecture of the building. It had a south western look to it with stucco, Santa Fe style walls. When they entered, the ceilings were high and the place looked and smelled new.

"When did they replace the old Activity Center?" Rosa asked.

"They tore down the old center after school was out last year. The new center has been up and running for a month now. We don't have the volunteers to do what we would like to do. We have a full-time coach for the sports played in the gymnasium, a teacher for the preschool children, and a superintendent to run the center. That's all of the staff right now, except for the cafeteria and it's staff," he said.

"Who cleans the place?" Rosa asked.

"The superintendent and I do," Sergeant Blackwood said.

"You do? I'm impressed! I'm also impressed with the

superintendent. You must really think this center is important," Rosa said.

"I think it's important. I believe if we, as Socike, don't help each other we will no longer be a tribe, let alone a nation. I think we should be growing, not shrinking. That's what this meeting is all about. We must build up this reservation and every other Socike reservation. Well, not just the Socike, but every Indian reservation. The way I think we can do that is by first, building this reservation, then concentrating on helping others—first the Socike, then other tribes," Sergeant Blackwood said. "I'm sorry I didn't mean to preach to you."

"I think you're right," Maria said.

"You do?"

"Yes, I think you are absolutely right," she said. "I feel the same way."

"Really, I usually get a hundred reasons why we can't do that. That is why we have these meetings to try to figure out how we can help the community. I really appreciate you coming tonight. Again, I apologize for how I just came over without checking first with you about giving you a ride," he said.

The two walked around the community center until it was time for the meeting to start. Then they went to the auditorium where there was a stage, and seating out where there would have been an audience if this was a play or a concert. On the stage there was a long table and chairs around the table. "Well, I can see everyone is late as usual," Sergeant Blackwood said. "Pick a seat, others will arrive soon."

"Where are you going to sit?" she asked.

Sergeant Blackwood got a smile on his face. *She's going to sit next to me*, he thought. "Right here," he said, and pulled out a chair. So Rosa pulled a chair next to him. By this time he was grinning like an opossum eating cow patties. In a few minutes, four more people arrived and sat at the table. "Everyone is here now," Sergeant Blackwood said. "Before we start this meeting I want to introduce Rosa Yellowhair Reed to you."

"Rosa Yellowhair Reed, Pupa's granddaughter?" one of the young ladies at the table asked.

"Yes," Sergeant Blackwood answered.

Everyone said hello to Rosa and Rosa was introduced to everyone at the table.

Sergeant Blackwood started the meeting by saying, "Last week we ended the meeting by discussing ways we could raise money to help the reservation. Someone mentioned sending a delegation to Washington and lobbying for more money. Someone else suggested we get investors to build a casino to give people jobs on the reservation. Doesn't anyone else have any suggestions."

"We could have a carnival, with rides and concessions stands. We could advertise in Flagstaff to get people to come and spend their money," Tom Big Horn suggested.

"That's an idea, but what we need is something that would bring in money on a regular basis," Sergeant Blackwood said.

"We could have it on a regular basis, say once a month," Tom said.

The meeting went on like this for about thirty minutes and Rosa didn't say a thing, just listened to the suggestions. Then Sergeant Blackwood asked if she had any suggestions to help the reservation.

"I know I'm new to this group and I'm not sure if I will be asked back, but what I would like to see on the Reservation would be a bustling economy of what we already have and not have strangers building anything that would belong to them and not to us. My suggestion would be to help the people that are already here trying to make a living, to help them expand their existing business," Rosa said.

Everyone started listening to her. "Can you give us any examples of the businesses that you think we could help?" Sergeant Blackwood asked.

"Joe Coyote, for one. His father had these goats that he struggled with for years to sell us milk. Joe was raised with these goats, he knows these goats and when he took over the family business he created a vision to increase his father's business and he did it very efficiently. But he has not reached his full potential or his full vision. Now Joe doesn't have the collateral to go to a bank to take out a loan to increase his business, he has the knowledge. The Reservation has the collateral to get the loan and to guarantee the loan. With time and help, Gray Fox, Joe's father's little goat herd could evolve into a huge milk dairy, including goats and cows and even expand into a meat producing company. We have the land to do this and we have a very qualified person, to oversee it and teach it," Rosa said.

"Another place we could help is at the stables. We have a young man there with a dream. His dream is to breed the best horses in the land. He gets up early and goes to bed late, all for the love of his horses. He watches them closely and acts as a doctor for them. He's the one who shovels the stalls and keeps them clean. He feels he is blessed to be able to do something he loves in life even if he's barely make enough to get by. I could see the reservation getting the school children to help with the cleaning of the stalls and the caring of the horses. We could finance better stock for him to work with."

Rosa was interrupted by Terry, the girl, who the week before had suggested going to Washington asking for money. "How would that make any money? People who rent the horses don't know if they are good horses or bad horses, so he's not going to get more money, he would just spend money," she said.

Rosa went on. "The better horses wouldn't be for rent or for sale. They would be for racing."

"You mean thoroughbreds," Terry interrupted again.

"No, I mean Indians horses. Thoroughbreds, we wouldn't have a chance against the horses that the white man has been breeding for years," Rosa said.

"I mean to build a horse track here with stands, a restaurant, concessions, and race Indians horses. What some people call *Indians Ponies*. I'm talking about a clean place. A place people can take their families to have a family day. It would be a day of celebration for tourists."

"It would be a day for a lot of the Indian businesses to make money, like Lonesome Bear could sell more Indian artifacts. Snack stands could be set up all over the reservation. Before and after the races we could rent horses for short rides, give children rides, for a fee, of course. We could open the races to all Indians of all tribes. We could make it a bareback race like our ancestors rode and maybe have the riders dress in traditional Indian garb. The programs sold could have pictures of the riders and explain what tribe they came from. This would all have to be worked out by people that would be overseeing this. To keep the tourists around longer, spending their money and having fun, we all could wear traditional garb," Rosa said. "I'm sure there are a lot of other businesses that could be expanded with a little help, or a lot of help. We would just have to keep it all under control."

"Those are some great ideas. We really need to explore them further," Sergeant Blackwood said.

The meeting went on with other ideas being tossed around, but none on as grandiose a scale as what Rosa had come up with. A few mentioned what other businesses on the reservation could be expanded, like the local bakery. When it was time to close the meeting, everyone got up from their chair and some came over to Rosa and told her what great ideas she had and they were glad that she attended the meeting. Some told her to please come to the next meeting.

After most of them were on their way out of the building, Sergeant Blackwood excused himself for a minute. "If you will just wait for me a minute I'll drive you home, I must talk to someone before I leave," Sergeant Blackwood said.

Rosa nodded her head.

Sergeant Blackwood walked out into the area where the audience sat. There he walked to a dark corner and Rosa could barely make out some figures. She hadn't even noticed there were four figures sitting in the shadows. In a minute, Sergeant Blackwood returned. "Chief Crowfoot would like to speak to you a minute," he said.

"The Chief?" she asked.

"Yes, Chief Crowfoot. He wants to talk to you a minute," he said.

Rosa followed Sergeant Blackwood over to the four people sitting in the shadows. When she got close enough to recognize the people, she recognized Chief Crowfoot and three men from the council. First, Chief Crowfoot stood up to greet Rosa, then the other three men stood. The Chief held out his hand to Rosa. Rosa didn't know what to do at first, because the Chief didn't hold his hand out to anyone to shake hands. This was extremely unusual. Rosa just stood there until the Chief nodded his head and made a beckoning gesture for her to extend her hand. When she did, he grasped it, closed his eyes, and tilted his head upward. He stood there with a tight grip on her hand for a good two minutes. No one said a word while he held Rosa's hand. Then he opened his eyes and looked into Rosa eyes and smiled. "You are the Chosen One!" he said. "I heard, and I came tonight to see for myself. After I heard your ideas, I knew you had much knowledge, but after I held your hand I saw you lead your people into prosperity. Like Eagle Woman did that winter when our people were starving and she ran the enemy over the cliff so our people would have horse meat to eat all winter. Come to my office tomorrow, we have much to talk about. I'll be there all morning, will that suit you?" he asked.

"What time in the morning?" she asked. Then immediately knew she should not be talking about hours with the chief. "Early or late?" she asked. This was acceptable with tradition.

The Chief smiled and said, "Anytime, Rosa, anytime in the morning will be fine."

On the way home Sergeant Blackwood asked Rosa if she knew why Chief Crowfoot wanted to see her in the morning. She said she didn't, but she was going to be there early in the morning. After all, this was quite an honor for her, to meet the chief and then meet with him in the morning.

"I think he's going to offer you a job so good you can't refuse," he said.

"If he offers me a job washing dishes, I'll take it," she said.

"I'm sure it won't be washing dishes," Sergeant Blackwood said.

"Well, if it is a job, I'll be forever grateful to you for asking me to the meeting," Rosa said.

"It wouldn't have mattered if I had asked you to the meeting or not. Ever since he's heard there was someone that Lonesome Bear thought was the Chosen One, he has been intrigued and he would have managed to meet you somehow. It wasn't by accident that he was at the meeting tonight. You heard the others' suggestions we got tonight. None of them were anything that would have made a difference to the reservation in the long run. But everything you suggested will make a great deal of difference," Sergeant Blackwood said.

Rosa wanted to ask him what he meant by, "Will make a difference." Didn't he mean would make a difference if they used them? By now they were home and he had already stopped the car. He got out and went around to Rosa's side of the car and opened her door for her. *Gallant, this man is very polite. I like that,* she thought.

The two walked to the door and then at the door they turned and faced each other. "I would offer to come and drive you to the chief's office tomorrow, but I am on duty at eight o'clock," Sergeant said.

"That's alright. I am used to walking and besides, you can't be my taxi, every time I need to go some place," she said, as she lightly rubbed his forearm with the finger tips of her right hand.

The touch of Rosa's hand sent waves of joy over Sergeant Blackwood. He wanted to kiss her, but was afraid that he was reading too much in this slight touch of her hand. Instead he said, "Would you like to have dinner with me some time? We could go to Flagstaff, it's not that long of a drive."

"When?" Rosa asked, as she gazed into his eyes.

"How about Wednesday?" he said, dropping his eyes, not being able to hold the gaze he had looking in her eyes. It was just too intense.

"Tomorrow?" she asked.

"Yes… it would be tomorrow, wouldn't it? About five o'clock?" he asked. "I mean early evening."

"That's alright, to use the white man's time with me. I'm not Pupa or Chief Crowfoot. And five o'clock would be fine," she said.

"Good, I'll see you tomorrow, then," he said. Then he turned and walked back to his car and drove off.

Rosa stood and watched his taillights disappear around the corner. She sighed, then turned and went inside. She was surprised that Pupa was talking to someone in the kitchen. Rosa walked to the kitchen and saw her friend, Shosho. "Shosho," she cried, and Shosho jumped up and the two women embraced. The three women sat at the table and talked into the night. Shosho informed Rosa that she was moving back to the reservation. Her husband had gotten the job at the school and they had rented a truck to haul their furniture to the reservation. Her husband was staying at one of his friend's tonight and Shosho was going to spend the night with Pupa and Rosa. In the morning, they would get their new home that the reservation furnished to all the teachers and staff. This was great news to Rosa, to have her friend live on the reservation with her. "You can sleep with me, the bed's big enough for two," Rosa said.

"Sounds good to me, I'm an early riser, I hope I don't disturb you when I get up in the morning," Shosho said.

"If I'm not awake when you get up, wake me. I've got an appointment with Chief Crowfoot," Rosa said, looking kind of proud.

"Sure, you do," Shosho said.

"I do, I really do," Rosa said.

Pupa looked at Rosa, "You have an appointment with Chief Crowfoot in the morning?"

"Yes," Rosa said. "So I need to get up early to make my appointment."

"This must be very important, this meeting," Nana said. "You had better get some sleep, so you will look refreshed."

"I suppose you're right. I do need to get some sleep. Oh, just to let you know, tomorrow evening I won't be here for dinner. I have a date with Sergeant Blackwood," Rosa said.

"Sergeant Blackwood," Shosho said, smiling. "Stinky."

"Stinky, why do you say that?" Rosa asked.

"We were in the same grade all through school and in the third grade he got too close to a skunk on his way to school. The teacher sent him home to get cleaned up because he stunk up the whole class room. When he came back to school the next day all the kids called him 'Stinky'. Through high school some of the kids still called him 'Stinky'. I know now it was cruel, but I can't help but call him 'Stinky'. I never do it in public, but if I see him alone, I get him by calling him 'Stinky'," Shosho said. "He is good natured about it, and just laughs. So, if you want him to open up tell him Shosho said to say hello to 'Stinky'." The two laughed.

"I don't know if I want to open that can of worms, yet. Or should I say sack of stink?" Rosa said. All three women started laughing.

They all went to bed and Rosa told Shosho all about her day of Kee and how she decided to stay on the reservation. She also told her about Jack O'Reily and Mary Smith. Shosho was well versed on spirits and spirits' travel. She asked Rosa if she or Pupa had any plans of spirit travel to locate the two. "Not up to now, I don't know if Nana has any plans to do that. She hasn't said anything about it," Rosa said.

"Knowing Pupa the way I do, I suspect she has everything planned out and Jack O'Reily won't be on the loose very long. Whoever revealed our secrets about the dream spirits to an untrusted one, that Mary Smith, will not go unpunished, either," Shosho said.

"I suppose you're right, even though Nana hasn't said much of anything to me about it," Rosa said. "Well, I guess we'd better get some sleep."

"By the way, I know, and if there is anything I can do to help you, I will. Just let me know and your servant will do what she can," Shosho said.

"'My servant'. What are you talking about?" Rosa asked.

"I'm talking about you being the Chosen One, that's what I'm talking about. Pupa told me all about it. She said that she didn't think you were aware of the ramifications of being the Chosen One. But, you soon will. After tonight I will be able to brag of being in the same bed with the Chosen One," Shosho said.

"I don't think most of the citizen of this clan will accept me as the Chosen One. I have a hard time believing this. I know what happened, which I can't explain, but to think I'm the Chosen One. That's hard to accept," Rosa said.

"What happened," Shosho asked.

Rosa got up and got her weapons from the closet. Shosho was already in bed, but sitting up. Rosa laid the war club and the knife on the bed. "I was instructed to move my hand over all of the war clubs that were there, and this one jumped into my hand," Rosa said.

"Jumped... into your hand?" Shosho asked.

"Yes my hand was about this far from it and—" Rosa was stopped in mid sentence. The war club had jumped into her hand again. Both Rosa and Shosho jerked, then sat there not saying a word, staring at the club.

"Did you do that?" Shosho asked.

"All I did was move my hand over it as you saw," Rosa said.

"I would say you are the Chosen One," Shosho said. "Does the knife do the same thing?"

"No, just the war club. It doesn't fall from my side if my belt is loose either." Saying this, Rosa placed the club at her side and let go. It stayed on her side just laying next to her pajamas. Both ladies were amazed by this.

"It is written in the *Great Book of the Living Souls* that the Chosen One's weapon will not leave. The earlier version said 'will not leave *her*'. But the men council took out the word her, in the late eighteen hundreds. This is well known by the Women Council, but they have had no success in changing it back," Shosho said.

"How do you know all this?" Rosa asked.

"I was in the Women Council, remember? One of the things that you have to do when you are asked to join the council, is to go to a class to study the *Great Book Of The Living Souls* and pass that class before you are accepted on the council," Shosho said, matter-of-factly.

"I didn't know that," Rosa said.

"Oh, yes, you learn all about why and when it was written and how our society is based on it, how things can be changed in it. There are certain verses that one must memorize to pass that class," Shosho said. "It's quite a book. I think every high school senior should have to take that class. I think they would have more respect for our ways. Anyway, that's what I think."

"You are probably right about that," Rosa said, getting up and putting away her weapons. She got into bed and both ladies were asleep in a few minutes.

The next morning Rosa was in Chief Crow Foot's office and he was telling her why he asked for this meeting. "I asked you here today to explain to you what has been going on for the past five years. Five years ago I was visited by a spirit that claimed to be Eagle Woman's husband. I had been bothered by rheumatism for about six months and I had eaten some Peyote for the pain. I was sitting in my kitchen when I was confronted by this tall brave. He was dressed in traditional Socike war uniform. I had just started to get relief from the rheumatism and had my eyes closed, when I heard my name called. When I opened them, there stood this brave as clear and as real as you are to me now. He was an awesome and fearsome looking warrior. I'm sure he instilled fear in the hearts of his enemies just by his appearance. I tried to stand, but found my knees weak and decided to stay sitting less I look afraid to this brave. He said his name was Brava. We have a record of Eagle Woman having a husband, but we didn't have a name for him. I never told anyone ever, about this vision until now. You are the first I have ever told."

"Your Grandmother had never heard this name until she came back from her three-day trip. Her writings described this same brave and she came back with the same name he had told me. This is the verification that, by Socike law, we are obligated to act on."

"When Brava visited me, he warned me that I was lacking in leadership. He said that both Eagle Woman and he were disappointed in the leadership of the Socike for the last five generations. He told me that the battles go on in the spirit world of good and evil and they must go on in the flesh, as well as the spirit world. It was up to the leaders of this world to lead all people. To lead the good people of this world to fight the evil of this world. He warned me that I had two years to start leading this nation into prosperity or lose my seat as Chief. He told me if I did my best that he would send me the Promised One that has been written in our Book. Then he told me not to take his visit lightly, and he disappeared."

"I have done some things to try to get this reservation to be it's best, but I know in my heart that we are not where we are suppose to be. When I learned that your grandmother said she and Lonesome Bear had seen your weapon jump into your hand I knew that Brava had kept his promise to send us the Promised One."

"Sergeant Blackwood and I have been getting together now at least once a week for the past three years, trying to make things better here. When he started the meeting with the young people I took some of the men council to the meeting and sat in the shadows to hear what the young people's ideas were. Until last night I had been very disappointed. But last night I heard wisdom beyond anything I have heard in the men or Women Council." He got a map from off a file cabinet and unrolled it on his desk. "This is a drawing that I had drawn a year ago, showing what I had in mind for the reservation. We are doing the projects as we have the money for them. This is the new Activity Center you were at last night." He pointed to a building on the map. "That building is where I want to build a new grocery store with all the foods that our people go to Flagstaff to buy. This, over here, is new housing for our people, here is a park and a swimming pool for all the families here on the reservation."

"When I heard you mention that we should help the people that already have businesses, it was like I looked directly into the sun. That was the light that was going to save the reservation. I stayed awake almost all night trying to think of how I could offer you a good paying job here at my office. I wish I could tell you I figured out a way to do that. But I just couldn't. I can offer you a job as an adviser, and pay you the same as a secretary," Chief Crow Foot said. "I wish I could offer you more."

"If I agree to this job, just what would be my duties?" Rosa asked.

"Because of the low pay, you could pretty much set your own hours. You could come and go as you wished, but I would need you to be available for the men council meeting and to me when I wanted advice from you," the chief said.

Rosa was delighted to get any kind of job, regardless of the pay, but she didn't want to show any excitement and decided to try to get more. "You want me to go to the Men Council?" she asked.

"Yes, you will attend the council as my personal adviser. You will only talk to me when we are at the meeting. Women are not permitted to speak to the men council, except if they are invited to," the Chief said.

"The men won't object to me being there at every meeting?" she asked.

"They may object, but I will over rule them," he said. "Are there any more questions?"

"Yes, I know what you said about the pay, but could you see yourself furnishing a home for myself like the ones you furnish to the school teachers?" she asked.

The Chief thought for a minute. "There is an empty house that no one is living in now. It's not in the best condition and it's small. But you could have it for ten dollars a year. And I will have some high school boys fix it up and paint it for extra credit," he said. The teachers were required to pay low rent and the chief had to charge Rosa something, so he made the rent the lowest he could.

"I'll take the job," she said.

"Great, let me show you your office," he said and got up, opened the door for her and they walked down the hall to a small office.

Rosa walked in and took a look around. There was a desk with a swivel chair that was very wobbly, a file cabinet and three wooden chairs that had seen better days. Rosa walked over to the desk and sat in the chair. She leaned back in it and almost fell over. The place had been empty for quite a while and other employees of the tribe had taken the best furniture and put the worst in this empty office. It wasn't much, but Rosa thought it was the best place she had ever seen. It was her new office. "This will be great," she said. "I'll get some soap and water and have it looking presentable in a little while."

"Why don't you let it go for now, I'll have someone fix that chair. I'll have Big Joe clean the office tonight. He and his son clean the offices, they can clean this one tonight. I'll show you where the office supplies are and you can get what you need after you get a clean office. As of now, you are on the payroll. You should get your first paycheck in two weeks. Have you any questions?" the Chief asked.

"Just one, where is that house you said I could have?" Rosa asked.

The Chief was a little embarrassed, because he knew that the house was in bad shape. "I'll show you on the map," he said. He got the map and pointed to a street. "Do you know this street," he asked.

Rosa nodded her head and said, "Yes."

"You go to the end of this street and at the very end is a house that hasn't been painted for a few years. That's the one. You can go look at it, it's the only one there that's empty. If you don't like it, let me know, so I won't bother to have it cleaned up," he said.

"Okay, I'll look at it. When do you want me to start to work?" Rosa asked.

"You started ten minutes ago," he said.

"If you get any ideas, put them down on paper, so I can present them to the Men council," he said.

"You just want me to think of things that will improve the community and write them down for you?" she asked in disbelief.

"That's it," he said. "I know that sounds simple to you, but wait until you put something on paper and you will find that other problems will arise that will not be so simple to solve.

Rosa couldn't believe her good luck. This was like a dream, her problems were solved. She said goodbye to the Chief and started walking to the street where the house was that the chief had said was hers.

When she got there, she couldn't believe the rundown condition that awaited her. He had said that it was a house that hadn't been painted for a while. They all looked like they hadn't been painted in quite a while. She had remembered when these houses were new and they looked so pretty with their fresh coats of paint. They didn't seem like the same houses. They were all rundown and needed a coat of paint. She knew that these houses were all rented to the people here at a ridiculous low price. Not as low as ten dollars, like she was going to have to pay, but still very low payments. As she walked towards the end of the street where the Chief had said that her house was, she noticed old tires in the front yards of three different houses. There were several old trucks in the front yards that she could tell wouldn't run. The screen door was off almost all the houses. There were dogs and dog droppings all over the place. The dogs were almost wild. These dogs were not safe for the children that played in and around the yards. *This is terrible,* she thought as she walked on down the street. It was a paved street, but in some places you couldn't tell it, by all the dirt in the street. There was not one house that had grass in the yard. There were plenty of weeds, but no grass. Rosa felt a sense of shame as she walked down this street. The shame that her people would live like this. Anyone could tell that there was no pride here. A few blocks away, were houses that were kept up by their owners, but on this street there was no one to keep these houses clean. This, she was going to have to find out about. At the end of the street she saw a little house that looked even worse than the rest. *This must be it,* she thought. When she got there she walked right inside, there was no door on the front. She could tell that the roof leaked and children had been playing there. There was a broken roller skate and an old scooter in the living room. Dust and dirt were everywhere. Her heart sank, was her job going to be like this house, was it going to be as much a disappointment as this house was? Rosa didn't even look at the rest of the house. She just turned and ran. By the time she reached the end of the block she stopped running. She turned around and took another look. Rosa tried to imagine what it would be like if every house was painted and there was grass in the yards and all the junk was picked up. It would be beautiful again. Rosa pondered this in her heart and decided to talk to some of the people on that block to see why this place was like it was. She went up to the first house and knocked on the door.

Pupa had gotten up early and went to check on both Shosho and Rosa. Their bed had been made and neither one was in the house anywhere. *These girls had become women warriors already,* she thought. They are rising before the sun and are going about their business early. This is a good sign.

Pupa put on some coffee and sat at the table. Her years of hard work were catching up with her and she knew in her heart that her days as a mortal would come to an end. She was hoping that her granddaughter would learn the things from her that she could teach her before she died. If the Gods gave her the years to teach her what she could, then she knew that Rosa would be a great leader. Surely, the Gods would give her this time to pass on the secrets of the Socike. But there were no guarantees in this life and she could only hope to last as long as it would take to teach Rosa the secrets of the Socike Nation and let her get the experience she would need to be a great leader. As she sat at the table and thought of the events of the last few days, she was trying to sort out what was most important. They still needed to get Rosa a uniform. Rosa was going to have to go to the classes that would teach her the history of her nation. This, Pupa knew, Rosa would give her a hard time about. She had already mentioned it to her and she had rejected the idea of going to those classes. Then there was the problem of Maria's killer—Jack O'Reily— her husband. He had escaped the punishment that she had placed on him by the help of a traitor in the tribe that had told Mary Smith how to mend the dream catcher. This, Pupa would not let go unpunished.

Pupa walked to the next block where Rose Bud lived. She went to the door and knocked. Rose Bud answered the door and welcomed Pupa into her house. "I am calling an emergency meeting this afternoon," Pupa said.

"This afternoon," Rose Bud repeated to make sure she got the time right.

"Yes, and it is mandatory that every member attend," Pupa said.

"Mandatory!" Rose Bud repeated.

"Yes, I will see you this afternoon," Pupa said and turned around and left.

This was how the emergency meetings were called . Pupa would go to the first person and tell them when a meeting was. This person would go to the next person and tell them and so on. They could go in person, as Pupa always did because she didn't have a phone, but the members that had a phone would just call the person on their list. In the case of a person that wasn't there, then they would go to the next person on the list and both ladies on each side of the person that was left out would try to reach the person that they missed. This system seemed to work very well and almost everyone would make it to the meeting. If a person couldn't make a mandatory meeting, the meeting would go on and there would be another meeting that the person that missed it would have to attend and all the attention would be directed to that person. The women of the council were almost always available to attend a meeting. This was their lives and they liked these meetings. This was their goal in life. They were important people and none of them took their duties lightly. If a meeting was called for in the morning, the meeting would be early, six a.m. If the meeting was called for at noon, then everyone knew the meeting would be at one o'clock. If the meeting was called for afternoon, then the meeting was at three o'clock. An evening meeting would be six p.m. Pupa had started the ball rolling, so to speak, to have the meeting that afternoon. Now she had other business to tend to.

Pupa grabbed a sack and headed to the stables. There, she greeted Jode and called out for Baroka. She grabbed the strap she used for a bridle and mounted her horse and headed off toward Stone Hill, a place of many rocks. In about an hour and a half she came riding back to the stable. Riding right up to the corral, she dismounted and took the strap from Baroka's mouth and let him go back to the pasture. She walked briskly to the stable and hung the strap back in its place, greeted Jode again and walked home.

It was getting close to two p.m. and Pupa started getting dressed for her meeting. When she had finished she picked up the cloth sack she took to Stone Hill and walked to her meeting. The place was already filled when she arrived and Pupa was greeted with excitement. The women of the council were all excited to be there at an emergency meeting. It was always an important event to have an emergency meeting, especially a mandatory meeting. This was never a trivial matter when a meeting was called on such short notice. Pupa went to the center of the room and asked to have a roll call to make sure everyone was there. Before the roll call was called the group formed a circle.

The roll call began and, in a few minutes, Pupa knew that all the council was at the meeting. "Women of the council, it has come to my attention that one of our most guarded secrets was given out to an untrustworthy one. One that has been caught telling lies."

The women looked surprised because this was a serious accusation, for anyone of the tribe to tell an untrustworthy one of the great secrets of the Socike Nation.

"It has come to my attention that the traitor is most likely among the women of the council." Pupa went on.

Then the women began to look around to see if they could tell who the guilty one was. In a minute, they were all very quiet and were listening to what Pupa had to say next. They were expecting Pupa to call out a name and tell everyone why she suspected this person to be the guilty one. Pupa didn't even look at any one in particular, instead she reached into her sack that she had in her hand and pulled out a rattle snake. "Mr. Snake will reveal who the culprit is," she said. She held the snake in the middle and let it coil around her arm. It coiled around her hand and tried to go up her arm, all the time his tongue flicking in and out.

The women all watched the snake as it moved in her hand and Pupa stepped in the middle of the circle. She slowly turned and held the snake out, letting it look at all that was present and let everyone see the snake. "Is there anyone here who does not want to go through the circle of truth?" she asked.

There was no answer, so Rose Bud went to Pupa and took the sack. She left the room and in a few minutes returned with the sack filled about one third of the way up with small one-half inch hard clay beads, about three times as many as there were women in the group. The group started to move in a clockwise direction. They started to hum a song and then started a song that, when translated, went like this. *We the Women Council always tell the truth and the snakes of the land know we do. They are here to protect the innocent but the guilty will be punished.* The ladies sang this song and the tempo picked up. Pupa put the bag in the center of the room and placed the snake in the open bag of beads. As the women danced, the vibration made the snake move inside of the bag as if he, too, was dancing. Pupa was first to dance to the bag and pick out a bead. Then Rose Bud moved forward and picked a bead out of the bag. The idea was that each woman would go to the bag and take out a bead and keep it in their hand as she danced. They believed that the snake would bite the guilty and not the innocent.

As the dance went on, the ladies, one at a time, would go forward and take out a bead. Redbird knew she was guilty and couldn't decide whether to let the dance go on or to stop it and confess that she had told her daughter the secret of how to mend a dream catcher. As she was trying to decide, the women were getting caught up in their dance and each went forward and picked up their bead. After everyone had picked a bead except Redbird, the women thought that all had picked a bead because no one was going forward now. No one was bitten and the dance came to an end by a shout and everyone held up their beads and turned to look at each other's beads. This was part of the dance and as they turned to Redbird and saw no beads, everyone stared at her.

"Do you want everyone to start the dance, so you can pick your bead?" Pupa asked Redbird.

Redbird hung her head. "No," she said. "It was me." Then she told the whole group why and when she did it. They all went home and were to think over Redbird's reason and come back in one week to vote whether she would be punished or not. After the council decided they would call Redbird to the council and tell her what her punishment would be. It could be as severe as banning her from the council.

Pupa took the snake out of the bag and emptied all of the beads into a clay pot, then put the snake back, so she could return it to stone hill.

Pupa was bothered that she had to do this to Redbird, but she was Chief of the squaws and she had a job to do. Telling a non-trustworthy person of the secrets of the tribe, even a daughter was treason to the tribe. In the old days a person found guilty of treason would either be thrown off a cliff and killed or banned out of the tribe and would have to live far away from the tribe. If that person was seen again, the tribe would hunt them down and kill them as an enemy. What Redbird did was serious even in this day. She would not be killed or even banned from the tribe, but Pupa was afraid that her punishment would be severe.

Redbird went home in shame. She could feel the hurt in the pit of her stomach. Why had she told her daughter how to mend that dream catcher? She could have easily gone to her daughter and mended it for her, and not told her about how it was done. If only she would have insisted on doing that, she wouldn't have broken any laws. *Why, why, why*, she thought to herself. When she got home she lay on her bed and sobbed for hours.


Rosa got home about the same time that Nana did. They both were worn out from what they both had been through. Rosa went through how she was now working for Chief Crow Foot in an advisory capacity. "Is this the weirdest thing you have ever heard of? Me being an adviser to the Chief." Rosa said.

"I don't think it's weird at all. I think that you have shown exceptional ability in seeing things that others don't see. That's what the job is about anyway. I think that you will look back on this as your destiny. Have you started work yet?" Nana asked.

"The Chief said that I started about ten minutes after I got there," Rosa said.

"That's not what I mean. I mean, have you come up with any suggestions about improving the reservation?" Nana said.

"I interviewed everyone that was home on the block where the house is that I was offered for my own. I asked them what it would take for them to clean their yards and paint their houses. Most said that they were not interested in living in a clean neighborhood. Some said if they had the money they would. Everyone, without exception, admitted to either drinking on a regular basis or taking dope on a regular basis. I think I will start in my new neighborhood by getting these people cleaned up and then cleaning their houses," Rosa said.

"That house won't be yours," Nana said.

"What do you mean? The Chief offered it to me, and he offered to have it cleaned up for me," Rosa said.

"I know, but when you take him up on that offer he will find another house for you. He won't let his adviser stay in that awful neighborhood. Chief Crow Foot is a good man, but he will try and bluff you when he can. He's betting on you not wanting to live there and decide to stay with me. This would be all right with me, but I know how much you want your own place and I don't blame you. You need your own place sometime, so you can have your own identity. This is how it was planned by the gods, for the children to grow up and start new families and reproduce. Have their own den like the coyote or their own nest like the bird. But first they must move out on their own so they can get some experience in living in this world, so they can teach their children when they come along. So just hang tight on the idea that you will take that house and he will offer you another," Nana said.

"I will hang tight on the idea that I want a home and if he offers me another one I will insist on the first one he offered me. I want that home, and I'm going to change that neighborhood starting tomorrow, wait and see," Rosa said.

Nana laughed, "Chief Crow Foot doesn't know what he has let

himself in for by trying to bluff you. I know what you say will come to pass. He will regret that he offered you that house, but after a while he will be glad he did, for I know what you say is true," Nana said.

"Not to change the subject, but don't you think you should be getting ready for your dinner date for tonight?" Nana asked.

"Oh, my god, I forgot all about Sergeant Blackwood coming tonight. I've got to take a shower," Rosa said as she headed off to her room.

By the time Sergeant Blackwood arrived, Rosa was ready and the two headed off for Flagstaff in his patrol car. "I don't want to take advantage of our friendship, but if I knew of drinking and taking of illegal drugs going on in homes on the reservation, could I get the police to raid the homes and take the stuff away from them?" Rosa asked.

"It's against the law to have alcohol or illegal drugs on the reservation except for some of the natural high one can get for medication and religious reasons. I could never get the Captain to agree to raiding a house for Peyote, for instance. But that junk, the white man sometime sells to us, I would certainly take that away. What do you have in mind?" Sergeant Blackwood asked.

"You know that area on Foxwood road that's so run down?" Rosa asked.

"Yes, we've raided it so often the people just hand us their whisky when we go to their doors. Once in a while we do get some drugs out of there, but mostly whisky. The chief has been trying to figure out how to straighten those people out. But as yet, he hasn't come up with anything. Was that what he wanted to see you for?" he asked.

"No, he offered me a job like you said last night. He offered to rent me a house there and I saw the plight of the people, when I went to look at the house," she said.

"You're not going to rent the house there are you?" he asked.

"Yes I am. He promised to fix it up and I'm going to hold him to it," she said.

"What kind of a job did he offer you anyway?" he asked

"I thought you would know, you being such good friends and all. I'm going to be his adviser. I will even go to the Men Council meeting with him," she said.

"Really...! He offered you a job as an adviser?" he asked.

"You didn't know?" she asked.

"No, I had no idea what kind of a job he was going to offer you. You must have really impressed him," he said.

"Actually, I think I had the job before I walked into the interview with him," she said.

"I think you should know I'm not friends with him. I met him and we work together on different projects, but I can't actually claim to be his friend. But I'm very glad to hear that you got the job. It sounds important," he said.

"I think it is. I still can't believe he thinks I can be his adviser. I'm going to go all out on this job. I don't know how long I will last, but I'm going to say and do what I think is best, regardless of who gets in my way," she said. "I'm not even going to let myself get in my way." Then she gave out with a small laugh.

"You're not even going to let yourself get in the way," he said. Then he gave a short laugh, too. "I've never heard it said that way before, but I think I know what you mean." Then he looked over at her and smiled.

She smiled back and thought to herself. That's nice he said that he knows what I mean, most guys would just laugh. "Are you going to tell me where we are going to dinner?"

"Do you like Italian?" he asked.

"Yes, I do," she said.

"Tony's, that's the place. Have you been there?" he asked.

"Tony's," she repeated. "No, I've heard of it, though."

"I think you will like it. I used to go there at least once a week when I went to college here. It's just a little further," he said.

The sun was starting to set and Rosa could see the lights of Flagstaff straight ahead and wondered what life would have held for her if she had gone to college when she graduated from high school. "Did you like college when you went?" she asked.

"I guess, I was a lot younger then and didn't actually know the importance of schooling. I wish I had taken it seriously. But, I did like everyone else, I went to parties and even did some drinking then. I should have taken advantage of the opportunity I had at the time. But I guess everyone has regrets of things that they didn't do. What about you, did you go to college?" he asked.

"No, I went out on my own right after high school and didn't do too well. I went to a lot of parties and did a lot of drinking. In fact, drink became the only important thing in my life. I'm an alcoholic. I don't drink a drop now, and that is how it's going to stay. Does that surprise you?" she asked.

Sergeant Blackwood looked over at Rosa. "No, I knew about your drinking. I was just wondering about your schooling. I didn't mean to pry into your personal life. I was just curious about what you did as far as work and your social life, besides the drinking," he said.

"I had a job right after high school working as a waitress in a bar in Flagstaff and then went to Albuquerque. I did the same thing and made very good money. But, people would buy me drinks and I got to liking the alcohol better than the work, and the rest is history. Anyway, I went to a hospital and dried out and came to see Nana and then I got this revelation of staying on the reservation and making my life there.

"I've had my day of Kee, and I'm convince that I can live up to it." she said.

"You've had your day of Kee. I'm impressed." he said. "You are quite an impressive woman, Rosa."

"Thank you, sir," she said.

They reached the restaurant and Sergeant Blackwood found a parking place. When they were in and seated, Rosa decided to order the spaghetti and Sergeant Blackwood had lasagna. While they were waiting for their meal they did some more small talk. "I think it's time you quit calling me Sergeant Blackwood," he said. "Please call me Robert or Bob."

Rosa was feeling a little ornery. "You want me to call you, Robert or Bob? Not Stinky?" she asked.

"Who told you about that?" Bob asked in surprise.

"I'm good friends with Shosho," Rosa said, laughing.

Bob gave out a sigh, "I don't think I will ever live down that time with the skunk."

Rosa was still kind of giggling. "No one would call you that if they didn't like you. Besides, I think it's kind of cute. After all, you didn't get teased because you stunk. It was the skunk that gave you that name," she said.

"I guess you're right, no one was mean about it. At the time I sure didn't like it, but I really don't mind it now," he said.

"Then it's settled, I can call you Stinky," she said, laughing.

"I didn't say that."

"Oh, you're no fun," she said. "You're not going to let me call you stinky, poo."

By that time the waiter came with their salads and they stopped their talking. Then their main meal and it was silent through the rest of the dinner.

"I must have been hungrier than I thought I was," Rosa said. "I usually don't stop talking during a meal, but this one was delicious."

"Good, you liked it," he said.

"It was fantastic, I could get used to this place," she said.

They sat there and talked and had coffee for quite a while before starting home.

# Chapter 28

Pupa had been tired and after Sergeant Blackwood and Rosa had left for Flagstaff, she got some Indian tea and was sipping it in the living room and thinking about Jack O'Reily. How he killed her granddaughter, Maria, and had escaped her punishment. *I wonder what Eagle Woman would do in this situation*, she thought. She dozed off and was awaken abruptly by a figure standing in front of her. At first she thought it was Rosa who had returned from dinner, but when she got her vision, she realized it was Maria.

"Maria!" she exclaimed.

"Nana," the spirit said to her. "I was sent to show you some things. Come with me." She held out her hand.

When Pupa took her hand she immediately left her body and could look at herself from a distance. Maria and Nana moved through the roof of the house. They moved by floating and they could move very slow or as fast as lightning. They moved high in the sky and Pupa felt warm and comfortable as she moved with Maria. They moved over Phoenix and Tucson, then in a southeast direction and Pupa could see the lights of Benson, then Sierra Vista. They came down lower as they zoomed passed Bisbee and Naco and then to the mountains. They landed by this big house with little houses by it. There were cars and trucks parked by.

The two walked into the big house where there was a party going on. Pupa was wondering if the people could see them. It didn't take long for Pupa to realize that no one could hear or see them. They even walked through two people that were talking and went upstairs and into a room. There they saw a lady laying on a bed crying and pounding her fist into a pillow. Pupa recognized the lady as Mary Smith, Maria and Rosa's cousin. Maria told Pupa to shut her eyes and turn her back to the lady.

Pupa complied. She shut her eyes and turned around.

"Now open your eyes," Maria said.

Pupa opened her eyes and it was daylight.

"Now turn back around," Maria said.

Pupa turned back around and they were standing in the hall. There was Mary bent down, peaking through a key hole in the door. "Lets see what she is looking at," Maria said. The two ladies walked through Mary and the door. There on a bed was a naked lady with Jack O'Reily on top of her.

Pupa picked up a lamp by the bed and started to hit Jack on the head when Maria stopped her. "Let them be," Maria said.

The lamp was put back on the stand and the lady on the bed looked up because she saw the lamp move. "What the hell!" She said and pushed Jack off.

"What's going on?" Jack asked.

"That lamp moved," the lady said.

"What... what are you talking about?" Jack asked.

"That gald damn lamp moved. I am saying it moved by itself, Jack," she said.

"You are seeing things, Darla," Jack said.

"Close your eyes" Maria said to Nana. "Now open them."

"It was night again and Mary was back on the bed crying. The two women were once again standing by the bed. "I wanted you to see why Mary was crying. The time we were in, was late this afternoon," Maria said to Nana.

"Come." Maria took Nana's hand and they went through some other walls and into another bedroom with some candles and an alter. There was an old woman kneeling on a small alter and saying words in a language that Pupa could not understand. Put your hands over your ears for just a moment, Maria said.

Pupa did as she was instructed by Maria and she could then understand what the old woman was saying.

"God of darkness, I come to you, to offer you a mortal to be tormented by you and your army of servants in the deep pits of hell. I release his soul to you for your pleasure," the old woman said. Then she picked up a long needle and held it high above her head and brought it down and stuck it into something on the alter. Pupa looked closer and she could see a cloth doll on the alter with a needle sticking in its chest.

Pupa closed her eyes and opened them again and she could see some grotesque figures sitting around the alter. She jerked back in shock at the sight of them.

"They are of another plane," Maria said to her. "They can neither see nor hear us."

Pupa looked on in amazement at the creatures. They had fat, round bodies, short. skinny legs, and oversized heads with huge mouths with drool coming out most of the time. Their arms were long and skinny and when they walked they rocked from side to side. It reminded her in some ways of the Sand Walkers she had encountered on her three day trip. But they were definitely different. As the beings moved about, if one would get to close to the other they might get a hit or bite from the other. They were constantly bickering and snarling at each other.

"Let's go see what the doll represents," Maria said and took Pupa's hand. They walked through two walls and saw Jack standing there clutching his chest. He was bent over leaning up against a wall. There were some of the grotesque creatures excitedly standing there. They were looking on and drooling even more than they had been doing in the other room. Jack didn't look like he could see the creatures and, in a minute, he fell to the floor. The creatures circled around him and waited for a minute, then one of the creatures reached into Jack's body and yanked his spirit out of him and bit into the spirit. The rest of the creatures attacked him by biting and pulling him in all directions.

Jack's body was laying on the floor looking peaceful while Jack was trying to fight the Demons and get back into his body. The Demons were too strong for him and were pulling him through the floor. Jack was screaming something, but Pupa could not hear a word. She covered her ears with her hands and then uncovered them. She could then hear Jack screaming with fear. The screams got to be too much for Pupa. She covered her ears with her hands again and she could not hear the screams coming from Jack any longer. She took her hands from her ears and the room was still quiet, but she could see Jack still screaming and fighting the demons. They were making progress pulling him through the floor and just the top of his head was showing. In a few seconds his head disappeared through the floor.

The two women stood there in the quiet room with Jack's body laying on the floor, not moving. "They are taking him to a plane that they are from, and we Socike do not go to this plane. It is for another race of people. We will never see Jack again, Maria said. Then Maria told Pupa to keep her eyes open and turn around three times.

As Pupa turned, she could see people come and go into and out of the room at different times. She saw Mary come in and lean over Jack's body and bend down and give him a kiss. On the third turn the two were once again alone in the room with Jack, but now the door of the room was open. In a few minutes, three men came into the room. One older one told the younger ones to take the body and drop it on the street across the border. Then the older one left, and the two young ones picked up the body and carried it out of the room.

Pupa looked at her granddaughter and Maria said, "Let's go," then took her hand. The two moved across the sky like the lightning that flashes from one cloud to another, no stops or slowing down this time.

Pupa could hear her name being called and opened her eyes. Rosa and Sergeant Blackwood were looking down at her. "Nana, are you all right?" Rosa said.

Pupa sat up and looked around and Sergeant Blackwood was standing there white as a ghost. "You gave us a fright," he said.

Sergeant Blackwood had felt for a pulse and couldn't find one, and he felt her cold body. Rosa had called after him to come into the house after he had walked her to the door and was on his way back to his squad car. They had been standing there thinking she was dead until she opened her eyes.

"You will not have to worry about finding Jack O'Reily," Pupa said to Sergeant Blackwood. "He is dead."

"How do you know that?" he asked, even though it was impolite, it was something he had to ask.

"Maria showed me," Pupa said.

Just then Sergeant Blackwood felt a cold shiver go up his spine. He didn't know what to think of her words or the shiver that went through him. He didn't say a thing, but only nodded.

"I must have fallen asleep," Pupa said as she got to her feet. "How was the dinner?"

"Very good," Rosa and Sergeant Blackwood said at the same time. They both gave out with a little laugh when they realized that they had said the same words at exactly the same time. "We had a wonderful dinner," Rosa said.

"I'd better be going," Sergeant Blackwood said. Then he headed for the door.

"I'm going to walk him out," Rosa said to Nana. Then she headed for the front door that he had already opened and she stepped out. Sergeant Blackwood followed and shut the door behind him.

"Thank you very much for coming in and checking on Nana for me," she said as she placed her hand on the crook of his arm and walked to his squad car that way.

When he reached the car he turned and thanked her for the great company that evening. "I really enjoyed your company. I don't remember ever having such a good time."

"I enjoyed it, too, Robert," she said as she stepped up close to him and tilted her face up to his.

The two stood there a few seconds. Robert could feel the blood rushing to his face and he could feel himself getting very warm. He bent his face down to hers and the two kissed as they stood there in an embrace. The kiss lasted longer than he expected, but he wasn't complaining. He had never felt excitement like this before. *Surely this woman is my soulmate*, he thought.

Rosa stepped back still looking into his eyes. *That was nice*, she thought. "Thanks again," she said and started to walk back to the house, then stopped, turned, waved and then turned and went into the house.

After entering the house and watching Sergeant Blackwood drive off, Rosa went to Nana and saw that she was okay. "You said you saw Maria tonight?"

"Yes, she came right after you left and we went on a trip into Mexico," Nana said. Then Nana went into details of her trip with Maria. She told her things that she would have usually left out of the story because she wanted Rosa to learn all the secrets of the Socike, especially secrets of the spirits, and how one travels with them and how they can help her with her work.

Rosa went to bed that night thinking about the things that Nana had told her. She had many dreams that night about the spirits of the reservation and received instructions on how to walk with them.

Early the next morning, Rosa got up and was on her second cup of coffee when Nana entered in her night gown. "Couldn't sleep?" Nana asked.

"I slept good, I just woke early and was wanting to get started on my new job," Rosa replied. "I think I can do some good if Chief Crow Foot goes along with my suggestion."

"The chief is a good man, if he can see your vision and he can raise the money for the project I think he will do what is possible," Nana said.

"I hope so," Rosa said. "I need to get an early start, so I can get to all the places that I need to go to this morning." With this, she headed out the door.

Rosa walked to the stables and found Jode cleaning out the stalls. Jode whirled around in surprise, not expecting anyone to come to the stables that early. "You startled me," he said.

"Sorry," she said.

"Don't be sorry, I'm always glad to see you. Needing another horse this morning?" he asked.

"No, I came to see you. To ask you about something," she said.

This intrigued Jode, he was infatuated with Rosa since the first day he saw her after she had returned to the reservation. "What do you want to ask me?" he asked. He was hoping that she would reveal that she felt the same way about him as he felt about her.

"If I could get your help here to clean the stalls and take care of the simpler work. Could you start breeding the best horses in the nation as far as Indians ponies?" she asked.

"I'd need a good stallion, like Pupa's Baroka. To get any quantity I'd need a lot more mares of good quality, like my New Start. It'd take several years before we would see any really good results," he said.

If we had a race track and we could get the equipment what would it take to have horse races on a regular bases?" She asked.

"Why are you asking all these questions, this morning?" he asked.

"It's just something I need to know. What would it take?" she asked again.

"It would take a lot of work. So to have—say—a ten horse race I'd need about four good handlers and maybe seven or eight other people to assist the good handlers to act as handlers. Then I'd need, say, three or four people to clean stalls and feed and water the horses. I would need at least fifteen people working on the day of the race. They could handle a race of ten horses racing at a time. Then if you wanted to race, say, several times, they could handle each race. Then, of course, you would need the riders. Riders are like horses, they get tired, so you would need a fresh rider with each race. I ask you again why do you ask?"

Rosa explained what she had in mind. She wanted to have a race track that would draw people from off the reservation to watch the races to help make money for the reservation.

"Why have the horses going around in a circle like the white man does? Why not have a cross country relay race where they have gullies to go over and brush to jump, maybe even short cuts if they are rougher than the regular route? Make the race interesting, not just a smooth path that the thoroughbred horse would win if he was in the race. Make it a tough race. Only one that the best Indian pony can endure," he said.

"That's a very good idea, we could have races that people couldn't see anywhere else in the world. They would have to come here to see them. If we got busy, how soon could we have enough people and horses to ride in, say, eight races?" She asked.

"Well, let's think about what kind of race we want. Do we want only Socike Indians or do we want it open to all Indians. Then saddle or bareback?" he asked.

"Let's open it to all Indians, bareback and dressed in their traditional dress. No one can race if they are not dressed like an Indian in traditional dress. Open it to any person who has Indian blood in them and can furnish themselves with an authentic traditional uniform," she said.

"Okay, then they could bring their own horses, and we wouldn't have to furnish anything except the handlers to get them started and judges to declare the winner," he said. "We could get started anytime and we would only have to map out a route for the race."

"I'm going to talk to the Chief this morning and see if I can get you the mares you would need for the breeding program you were talking about so we will have the most winners," she said. With that said she turned and started to run off.

"What, hold on," he said.

Rosa stopped and turned back to face Jode.

"What are you talking about? One minute you are talking about breeding and the next, racing. I don't get what you're talking about," he said.

"Don't worry you will," she said as she ran off.

Jode shrugged and went back to work.

Rosa got to the office and found the building locked. "Wonder what time they open this building," she said to herself.

"Right about now," a voice said behind her.

Rosa whirled around and saw an old man. "I didn't hear you come up behind me," she said.

"I'm Big Joe. I open the building every morning at this time, but I'm afraid that there won't be anyone else here for another hour, and most won't be here for at least an hour and a half," he said.

"I'm Rosa and I just started working here for the chief," Rosa said and held out her hand to shake big Joe's hand, a habit she had picked up from the white man after high school.

Big Joe looked at her hand being held out and then shook it.

Rosa was a little embarrassed because she had used a white man's custom to an old Indian. "I'm sorry, I picked up that habit living off the reservation for a while. I guess I'm a little nervous this morning," she said.

"Ah... yes, I did the same, when I lived off the reservation. All white man's customs are not bad. I don't mind shaking hands with a pretty girl. In fact, I like it," he said.

"Thank you, sir. I was hoping that the chief would be here," she said.

"The Chief, he won't be here for at least another hour. You are the one the Chief calls the Chosen One, aren't you?" he said.

This remark embarrassed Rosa and she bowed her head, not knowing what to say.

Big Joe could tell he embarrassed her. "I'm sorry, I didn't mean to embarrass you. I have your office clean and I even replaced that chair with a brand new one. I hope you like it," he said.

"I'm sure I will," she said.

"You know if you work early or late at night, and need a key to get in the building, I'm sure the Chief will give you one. He sure likes it, when anyone takes their Job seriously enough to work extra," he said.

"I wouldn't want to be presumptuous enough to do that," she said.

"Presumptuous…, big word, but I do know what it means. I think you are going to do a good job at what the Chief has appointed you to do. I want you to see your office and tell me if you need anything other than what I have furnished you with," he said as he walked her to her new office.

When they got to her office, she got out her key to unlock the door. "Allow me," he said as he stepped in front of her to unlock the door with his key.

Rosa stepped into the office and was shocked. "I think we have the wrong office," she said, as she stepped back out to see if they had gone to the wrong office.

"You like?" Big Joe asked.

"It's beautiful. How did you do this?" she asked. The old desk didn't look old anymore There was a new chair behind her desk that was padded leather, and there were four chairs at the wall for anyone that was to see her to sit in. The old file cabinet looked new now.

"It's my job," Big Joe said with pride.

"And an excellent job you did," she said, as she walked behind her desk and instinctively ran her hand over her desktop to feel the smooth finish Big Joe had put on it the day before. "I love it," she said as she sat in her new chair. She switched a light on that had been set on her desk. "I love it, I absolutely love it."

"I'm so glad you like your new office," Big Joe said. "I don't usually get to hear that my work is appreciated. I appreciate being able to hear that you like my work. If there is anything else I can do for you just call extension nine, or leave me a note on your desk at night. I'll see it."

"Dial extension nine?" she asked as she looked for a phone.

"Oh… I'm sorry, I'll have you a new phone in this morning," he said, then he started to leave.

"Big Joe," she said.

Big Joe turned around to see what she wanted.

"Have you a minute?" she asked.
"Sure, what can I do for you?" he asked.
"Please have a seat," she said.
Big Joe sat down.
"Do you like to be called Big Joe or Joe?" she asked.
"People call me both ways. I really don't have a preference," he said.
"Then if you don't mind, I will call you Joe. I think it's friendlier," she said.
"What do you want me to call you?" Joe asked.
"Just Rosa," she said.
"Okay, Just Rosa, that's what I'll call you," he said.
This made Rosa laugh and she noticed the sparkle in Joe's eye when he said it. It was nice to have a little levity in their conversation.
"Joe, if we had horse races here on the reservation, would you go see them? I mean the kind the Indians have, like they do in the training for Braves," she asked.
"Sure, I'd go, my family and I would go," he said. "I love the races. I, especially, would love to see the ribbon race run."
"What is a ribbon race?" she asked.
"It's something that started way back in Eagle Woman's time. When our tribe captured another warrior, and they were either too much of a vicious enemy, or wouldn't join our tribe, they would give them a slow horse and give them a head start. After they were out a ways, the other braves would chase them on horseback and the first to catch him would club and kill him with their war club," he said.
"After we became more civilized, we quit killing people and we would have a person carry a long ribbon and then we would all race after him or her and grab the ribbon. The person that was carrying the ribbon would try to keep them from grabbing it. Whoever got the ribbon would win the race. Sometimes the horseman who carried the ribbon, had leather coverings on the front legs and sides of their horse so they could ride through heavy brush that would cause the other riders to have to go around. It was great fun. I don't know why we stopped having those races. Ask your grandmother about it. She and I used to ride in some of the same races," he said.
"Oh, you know who my grandmother is, I didn't realize that you were aware who I was," she said.

"Yes, Little Rose, I've known you a good many years, and I'm so glad to see you doing the work you are doing," he said.

"I guess you do know me, if you know the name Little Rose," she said. "You know the job I'm to do for the Chief?"

"Yes, I know, and I think you will do an excellent job. Well, I had better get your new phone. I'll see you later," he said. He got up to go.

"Joe... thanks," she said.

"Anytime I can help, just call me," he said. Then he left.

Rosa sat there thinking for a while. *Should I stay, waiting for the chief or should I go get something done,* she thought. *I think I'll go out to see Joe Coyote and see what he can do to help himself and the reservation. If I walk, it'll take me all day to do that. If I go back to the stables and get a horse, it will still take me all morning and part of the afternoon.* "I wish I had a car or truck," she said to herself. I guess I'll wait for the chief, *I can't do everything in one day,* she thought. Then she leaned back in her chair to enjoy her new office. In a little while, Rosa could hear someone walking down the hall, and a little later several people were moving about. She went out to see who else worked in that building.

Rosa went from office to office to introduce herself to find out who else worked in the offices of that building and what their jobs were. Some didn't like her asking what they did for the reservation, but most were anxious to meet her, and were not worried about their jobs. By the time she had met everyone who was there, the Chief walked into the building. Rosa met him in the hall. "Good morning Chief Crow Foot," she said.

"Oh, good morning," he said. He wasn't used to anyone being so happy and peppy this early in the morning. "We have coffee over here in the break room," he said and gestured to a small room.

"Do you drink coffee?" he asked.

"Yes, I do," she said as they walked into the small room. It had coffee and some vending machines in it. One had candy bars and the other sodas. There was no place to sit down so everyone had to take their drinks and candy back to their offices.

"I'd like to talk to you this morning," she said.

The two were walking towards the Chief's office. "I figured you would," The chief said. "I know that house I sent you to look at is not fitting for the Chosen One to be living in. If you give me some time I'll have you a house, I promise."

"It's not that," she said. "I think that house will be perfect for me. It is about one of my ideas to help raise money for the reservation and help restore some of their pride that they had when we ruled this part of the country.

By this time they were in his office. "Pull up a chair," he said as the Chief sat in his own chair.

Rosa pulled up one of the chairs that the Chief had by his wall and couldn't help but notice that the chairs were not in as good of shape as the ones that Big Joe had put in her office. This was a small puzzle to her, but she wasn't going to bring it to his attention.

"Did Big Joe clean up your office for you, like I told him?" He asked.

"It is very nice," she said.

"Good," he said. "Now, what can I do for you this morning?"

"I want to talk to you about having horse races here on the reservation and getting Jode the help he needs in starting a new breeding strain of strong and fast horses," she said. Then she went into detail about her plans for the races and the breeding of strong and fast horses. The two stayed there in the Chief's office all morning, discussing all the plans of having races and getting tourist to come to the reservation and spend their money. By the time they had everything on paper that they wanted to accomplish it was noon and time for dinner.

"Why don't we have lunch together at the center and we can keep this discussion on this idea of yours going?" He said.

That would be great, but I was planning on going by Nana's house so I could let her know how everything is going. I left early this morning and I don't want her to worry," She said.

"Then why don't you call her and invite her to lunch with us? She needs to get into some of the discussions, too," he said.

"She still doesn't have a phone," Rosa said.

"Oh... I forgot. She has resisted just about every new convenience that has come along," he said. "Tell you what, why don't we drive over there and take her to lunch. I know that she doesn't like to ride in cars, but she will when it's the only choice she has. It would be a fast way of getting this thing off the ground," he said.

"If she is home, I'm sure she would be delighted to have lunch with us," Rosa said.

The two went down to the Chief's car and got in. It was a two year old Cadillac and rode very nicely. It could use a washing, but other than that, it was very nice. The chief stayed in the car and Rosa went in and got Nana to take her to lunch. The chief got out of the car and opened the door for Pupa to get in. "I'm so glad you could join us for lunch," he said as Pupa got in.

"It is always a pleasure to have lunch with the Chief of my tribe and my granddaughter," Pupa said.

When they got to the center they went into the part where the food was served cafeteria style. There was a long line of people waiting to pick up their food. As soon as the manager saw the Chief and the two ladies with him, she immediately seated them and told them what they were serving. Each told her what they wanted and the manager had some servers bring them their food. One server stayed near to make sure they had everything they needed. There was small talk for about ten minutes, then they got down to talking business.

"Your granddaughter has a wonderful plan to get tourists to spend their money here. We need more than what Washington is now spending to keep this reservation going as good as it is. Every year we send a delegation to Washington and try to get more money allocated to us for improvements and we usually don't get nearly enough. We all know that Washington requires us to let tourists come to our reservation and we cannot bar outsiders from any of our functions. So... Rosa came up with an idea that I think would increase revenue for our people," the Chief said to Pupa.

By this time the three had finished their lunch, and the server was wanting to know if they needed anything else. "That will be all for now, just get us more water and you will be finished," the Chief said.

The server picked up all of the dishes and cleaned the table, brought over a pitcher of water and topped off each of their glasses, then set the pitcher down on the table. The Chief picked up the pitcher and set it on the table next to them. He then pulled out some papers from a folder and placed them on the table. "These are the things we have come up with," he said to Pupa. "We want to have horse races here on the reservation."

Pupa was smiling until she heard that. Then her face dropped. "The Navajo tried that about ten years ago and they couldn't even get other Indians to come to them, let alone the white man," she said. "The thoroughbreds that the white man has are much faster than our

Indian horses. So no one thinks that the Indians horse is worth watching."

"The Navajo had races like the white man does. They race around in circles. We plan to have races like when we trained to be braves. Big Joe told me about a race you and he used to do, called a ribbon race. No saddles and every rider has to be dressed in their traditional Indian dress. The races would be open to any Indian, regardless of their nation or tribe. But they would have to wear their traditional Indian dress," Rosa said. "Maybe we could get a representative from each nation to help with the authentic dress of the riders. What do you think?" Then she looked at the Chief.

"That might be a good idea," the Chief spoke up.

Pupa could picture it in her mind and she could see people coming to a race like that. She began to smile again. "You might have something there," she said.

"We thought that we might start the races at about mid-morning, so people would have time to visit our shops on the reservation. We would have concessions selling all day at the races. Then we would need a cleanup crew to work the next three days cleaning all the trash. We need some sort of wagering place, so the reservation could get the profits. We are going to need help with all the details on most of this," Chief Crow Foot said.

"This is a big project that you two have worked out," Pupa said.

"It's your granddaughter that has the vision, and I think it's going to be a life-giving force to us, after it's up and running," Chief said.

"We also talked about giving Jode a hand, or foot up, so to speak, in starting a breeding strain of horses so we would be getting most of the prize money. What do you think of that idea?" Chief asked Pupa.

"I think you certainly picked the right man to handle that. I might even help him with that project," Pupa said. "We would have to buy him some good mares and if he wanted to use Baroka as a stud he would be welcome to, as long as I could approve of the mares that he would use," Pupa said.

"Have you seen the Mare he has now?" Rosa asked her grandmother.

"Jode has a Mare?" Pupa asked.

Rosa smiled. "Yes, he let me ride her and she is fast and strong," Rosa said.

"He must really like you if he let you ride his new horse that I haven't even seen," Pupa said, looking at her granddaughter intensely. She knew Jode for years and he was particular about whom he let ride his favorite rental horses, let alone his own horse.

Rosa's facial expression changed instantly. She knew that Jode might like her, but what Pupa was saying was something that she hadn't really given much thought. He must really like her. How could she have been so blind. This new declaration left her confused. She had feelings for Sergeant Blackwood, and now she felt something for Jode. Why hadn't Jode said something when they were together?

The Chief saw the expression on Rosa's face and didn't want to say anything. "I have something to ask you, Pupa," he said.

"What is it?" Pupa replied.

"Can you talk your granddaughter out of that awful house, that I so mistakenly offered her?" he asked. "It's no place for one of our new leaders to live in."

"New leader," Rosa heard. *Me, a new leader? I'm just an adviser to the Chief, that's all*, she thought.

"You offered it to her, Chief. Now you are going to have to endure the consequence," Pupa said.

"I'm glad you brought that up, Chief," Rosa spoke up, coming out of her trance of the other problem about Sergeant Blackwood and Jode. "I have an Idea how to make that street, Foxwood Road, an asset instead of a debit."

"If you could do that, it would be a miracle. We have tried everything, I can think of without results," Chief Crow Foot said.

"This is my idea, first pass some new laws."

The Chief got a frown on his face immediately. He didn't like any new laws being passed.

"Then pick up those loose dogs all over the reservation, and concentrate on Foxwood road. Haul off all the vehicles on that street that the owners don't have fixed up and running. Get that tractor with the mower on it that you use for the school and the public areas and mow the yards. Keep them mowed. If anyone has a fence, they must keep the yard mowed and if they don't, take down the fence and hall it off and mow the yard. Keep this up on a regular basis. If anyone is caught drunk, arrest them and make them pick up the trash and help keep the grounds tidy," she said.

"Then, offer anyone on the reservation free alcohol and drug counseling. If someone is caught with alcohol or drugs, make it mandatory counseling. Next, offer the people on Foxwood a free house. To qualify, they must keep up their own yards, paint all buildings, keep them in good condition and pay a yearly tax like every one else pays for property. If anyone doesn't take up the offer, give them one month to reconsider or move out and give it to someone who will take care of it" she continued.

"What will I do with the people that will move out?" Chief asked.

"Don't do anything unless they make a nuisance of themselves, then put them off the reservation," Rosa said.

"Move our own people off the reservation?" Chief Crow Foot asked. "What do you think of this plan, Pupa?"

Pupa thought for a minute. "I think it would work."

"You do?" He asked.

"Yes, I do," Pupa said.

"Wow, great eagles and bears, I don't know. I just don't know. I'll have to take it up with the men council," he said. "Is there anything else you have in mind?"

"I haven't had a chance to talk to Joe Coyote yet, but I think we should help him on his dream, and I think we should take advantage of his knowledge of the law," Rosa said.

"How?" Chief asked.

"I don't know yet, but I will let you know," Rosa said.

"I'd better get you back home, Pupa, and take you, Rosa, wherever you want to go," the Chief said.

"If you have time, we need to get you measured for your war uniform," Pupa said to Rosa.

"I have the rest of the day," Rosa said, then looked at the Chief for approval.

The Chief nodded his head and said, "You deserve the rest of the day off. You have done more work in one day, than most of our workers get done in a month."

"I'd like to go out and see Joe Coyote tomorrow instead of coming to the office, if that would be all right with you Chief Crow Foot," Rosa said.

"That would be fine, but please call me either Chief, or Crow Foot. You know me well enough for that. And, Rosa, don't forget who you are," Chief said.

Rosa looked puzzled, *What did he mean by that, 'don't forget who I am,'* she thought. In a minute, she got her answer.

"Remember Rosa, you are the Promised One, don't take that lightly. Right now there is no one person more important than you. I believe that with all my heart and soul," the Chief said, looking Rosa right in the eyes. "You are going to do great things for this nation. I think you have already come up with some real answers."

"Rosa, the day after tomorrow I'd like to call a Men Council meeting and I want you to be there with me in that meeting. Is it going to work for you?" the Chief asked.

"I'll make it work for me, what time?" She asked.

"Mid-morning," he said. Then he leaned over and whispered in her ear. "Ten o'clock."

Rosa couldn't help but laugh. The chief using the white man's time. She looked at the chief and then at Pupa. Both of them were grinning ear to ear.

"Just because we have some age on us doesn't mean that we don't take advantage of things the white man does better than us," the Chief said.

"Yes," Pupa said. "But keep this between us leaders."

"Well, ladies, where can I drop you two? I need to get back to the office," Chief said.

"If you don't mind, I think we will walk. It's just a short distance from here," Pupa said.

Pupa and Rosa said goodbye to the Chief and started walking to Wanda The Tailor's place. That was a nick name she received after she got a reputation of making clothing better and faster than anyone else, even the men who traditionally made the war uniforms. In time, people just got used to having her do all of their special clothes made by her. Wanda lived in a little house at the edge of the settlement and her backyard opened out to the wilderness.

Wanda was sitting on her front steps and greeted both Pupa and Rosa when they arrived. "I thought that I might see you two today," Wanda said.

Both Pupa and Rosa looked surprised, but before they could respond, Wanda continued. "I had a dream last night."

"What kind of dream?" Pupa asked, as she sat down next to Wanda on the steps.

"I was visited by Eagle Woman and was told that I would have the honor of designing and making the war uniform of the Promised One today. The only limitation is that I must attach an eagle feather to one side of the collar and a dove feather on the other side. The eagle feather represents the fearlessness of the Promised One and the dove feather represents the love for her people and the promise of peace and prosperity she will bring to them," Wanda said, all the time staring at Rosa who was standing facing the two women. "When I rose this morning, I put everything aside and have been waiting outside to greet you." This being said, she rose and bowed down to Rosa and stayed in that position waiting for Rosa to say something.

This freaked Rosa out, she wasn't sold on the idea that she was the Promised One. She knew that her war club jumped into her hand, but she sure didn't want anyone bowing down to her. "Please don't bow down to me," Rosa said. "I am Rosa, Pupa's granddaughter. I am not one to bow down to."

"She has not accepted that she is truly the Promised One, yet," Pupa said.

"Oh, my dear… you are the Promised One. I saw you last night. Eagle Woman showed me who you are. I will not bow down to you again, until you realize who you are. Now we must get started. Come in, please come in," she said.

The three women went into the house and Wanda had Rosa stand on a small platform so she could get some measurements. "I should be able to get this finished in about four days," Wanda said. "Will that be alright?"

"That should be just fine," Pupa said.

Wanda ignored what Pupa said and looked to get an answer from Rosa.

Rosa had been looking out the window and hadn't noticed that Wanda had actually been speaking to her. When she noticed that Wanda was waiting for an answer she then confirmed Pupa's answer. "You have a wonderful place here, Wanda, right next to the wilderness and all. Isn't that beautiful out there?"

"I enjoy it," Wanda replied. "I hope you can take the time sometime and come over and let me show you some of the wildlife I have visit me here," she said. "Well, there's one of my friends, now," and she nodded to a deer that just stepped into her yard. It was a young female and you could tell that it didn't have much fear of people because it came right up to the window and looked in. In a few minutes, Wanda was finished measuring Rosa and had her step down. When she did, the deer jumped and went about eight feet away before stopping to look back at the house. "Sometimes I give them bread and they are regular beggars. That's why she came up and looked into the window."

"Let me show you the drawing I did of your uniform this morning and see if you approve," Wanda said. She picked up a sketch pad and showed both Rosa and Pupa. The drawing was quite good and the model she portrayed in the drawing was surprisingly similar to Rosa. The hair was the same length, the build and figure, and even the nose looked like Rosa. The uniform was to be made of dear skin and of a tan color which was basic for the war uniform of the Socikes. There were ten rows of quarter inch beads that went down from the shoulders on each side and came to a point about ten inches down. These would be on the outside of her breast. It would come in at the waist to show off her hour glass figure. The pants would have only a small ridge of ruffles of leather running down the leg on the outside seam. There was no silver or other decoration except the two feathers that Eagle Woman instructed to have sewn at each collar. These feathers were small feathers no longer than two inches. They would be sewn flat on the collar and none would dangle from the collar. "What do you think?" Wanda asked Rosa.

"It's beautiful, you even drew me. How did you do that? Have you seen me before?" Rosa asked.

Wanda, smiled. "I saw you last night, Eagle Woman showed you to me."

To Rosa this was amazing, even more amazing than her war club jumping into her hand. Suddenly, Rosa felt a cold chill and the hair stood up on the back of her neck. Both Pupa and Wanda turned to look at Rosa. Rosa turned to see what was going on. She could see nothing, but could still feel the cold chill. Then the chill left and she could feel a warm hand on her shoulder. She again turned and could see nothing. Both Pupa and Wanda were staring at her. "What's going on?" Rosa asked.

"Look with your mind, not with your eyes," Pupa said.

Rosa concentrated and closed her eyes, trying to see what Nana and Wanda were seeing.

"Open your eyes and concentrate on looking with your mind, not your eyes," Pupa repeated.

Rosa opened her eyes and saw both Pupa and Wanda were staring at something by her. Rosa tried again and all at once stumbled backwards. She managed to stay on her feet when she bumped into something behind her. For an instant she had seen the back part of a horse standing right in front of her. When she looked to see what she had stumbled into there was nothing there.

Just as fast as this all started, it stopped. Rosa got her composure and asked. "What was that?"

"What did you see?" Pupa asked.

"I just saw the rear end of a horse standing there by me," Rosa said. "It was so close, it surprised me and I stumbled into something, but I didn't see what it was."

"What else did you see?" Pupa asked.

"That was it," Rosa said. "Just the back part of the horse. It was standing right in front of me and I was facing the side. The rear was to my right and the front was to my left. That was all I saw."

"What color was it?" Wanda asked.

"It was gray with white spots," Rosa answered.

"Wow, that's great. That was your first time wasn't it?" Wanda asked.

"The first time I ever saw something that was not there? Yes," Rosa said.

"But it was there. It was more real than that deer you saw earlier. What you saw will be forever, the deer will only be until it dies and is consumed by this earth," Wanda said. "But for the first time to see spirits, to tell the color of the horse you saw and to tell that it was a horse was something. My first time I only saw something like vapor or smoke, I couldn't tell what it was. I still don't know what it was. Your grandmother was teaching a class on spirits and I felt a warm breeze in the classroom. I was the only one who felt it. Your grandmother told me to look with my mind, like she did you, and I could see this vapor, but couldn't make it out. After it was all over she told the class what was going on. In my case there were three warriors riding by, she told us."

"What I felt was a chill before I saw the horse," Rosa said.

"What I saw was the back of Sand Walkers, then I saw clearly some warriors ride up and chase them away," Wanda said excitedly. Even though she had seen the warriors, this was not something that was common to her to see such action.

"What went on, was some Sand Walkers attacking you, Rosa," Pupa said. "That was the chill you felt. Then Eagle Woman and some of her band of warriors attacked them and killed them. This is very unusual for the Sand Walker to come on this plane where they are so vulnerable. They were like corn stalks before the sickle. The Sand Walkers know that you are the Chosen One and they would do anything to destroy you. Anyway they can, even to sacrifice some of their warriors, like they just did," Pupa said. "Look with your mind at all times and you can keep them at bay. They knew that you were not a spirit watcher, but this we will change, and you will be safe."

"What do you mean, they were attacking me?" Rosa asked. "How could they hurt me? They are spirit, I am flesh and blood."

"If they stay there and continually attack you unchecked by our ancestors they can kill you. But the warriors are watching you so closely that you have no problem," Pupa said. "You have heard of people that have just suddenly died for no apparent reason?"

"Yes," Rosa answered.

"Most likely that was Sand Walkers," Pupa said.

"This is really getting complicated," Rosa said.

"It needn't be, just go with the current of the river you're in now. Don't fight the current, or it will wear you out," Pupa said. "Work with the spirits not against them. They love you, and they will protect you if at all possible."

"What do you mean, if at all possible," Rosa asked.

"They are spirits, not Gods. They are very powerful, but they even have their limitations," Pupa said.

"I guess I'd better take those classes you suggested," Rosa said.

"I really think you should," Pupa said.

The three women had their excitement and they went back to their business at hand. After they finished, Pupa and Rosa walked home and found Shosho waiting to see them.

"Shosho," Rosa greeted her friend.

"Pupa… Rosa…," Shosho greeted the ladies back calling out Pupa first to give her the respect of the elder. "I was about to give up on seeing you two and was about to go back home. I'm glad I waited. I wanted to hear how Rosa's first day on the job went."

"Let's go inside and have some coffee or tea," Pupa said as she started up the front steps of the porch. Shosho and Rosa followed her into the house and they all went into the kitchen and sat at the table. Pupa put on some water to boil. "I'm having tea, does anyone want coffee?"

Both Shosho and Rosa wanted tea, also, so Pupa sat down at the table with them to wait for the water to boil.

Shosho was carrying a newspaper and laid it on the table. "I got this at the Trading Post this afternoon. I thought you would be interested in this article." She opened the paper and on the front page there was a picture of Jack O'Reily with the headlines. BENSON MAN FOUND DEAD ON BISBEE STREET.

Rosa picked up the paper and started to read the article aloud. *"Benson man, Jack O'Reily, found dead on a street in Bisbee this morning by Bisbee police. There was no apparent cause of death, so the body is being taken to Tucson's forensic pathologist to see if foul play is involved, or if cause of death is natural. Jack O'Reily had lived in Benson for the last ten years and had been accused of killing his wife, Maria O'Reily. No charges were ever brought because he had been incarcerated in Bisbee's famed mental hospital Yaford. According to Bisbee police, Jack O'Reily had escaped two weeks ago and had not been seen again until this morning when he was found dead.*

"Well at least they got part of the facts right," Rosa said. "Nana saw Jack get killed by some demons of a strange plane, right?" she said as she looked to Pupa to see if she was telling the story right.

"Yes, he was killed in Mexico by the demons, and dumped in Bisbee by some men. But they won't find any cause of death unless they call it a heart attack."

"I can't help but believe that this is the time that something is going to happen on this reservation. I'm so glad that we were able to move back here, so I can help whether it's good or bad." Shosho said. "All of the spirits are moving and shaking things up here so much it seems,"

"It certainly appears that way," Pupa said.

The whistle of the teapot sounded and Pupa got up to take it off the stove. She had already gotten the three cups of tea ready so all she had to do was pour the hot water in each cup.

The three women were making small talk when Rosa got the idea that Shosho just might be interested in helping her with getting the reservation running in a more prosperous manner. She told the two woman what she had in mind and asked Shosho if she would be interested in helping in a voluntary position for a while. To Rosa's delight she said she would. Shosho and Rosa were sitting there making plans to go out in Shosho's car tomorrow morning to see Joe Coyote. "Are you sure that Black Feather won't mind you taking your car?" Rosa asked.

"He won't mind, I'm sure. He even suggested that I volunteer helping out at the high school. I don't like to work there because those high school kids are always saying something about my height and it's hard to keep from losing my temper. I've got a good husband and he is very understanding. He won't mind," Shosho said.

The two agreed to meet in the morning and Shosho left for home and Rosa and Pupa went to bed.

That night Pupa was restless and had a leaka dream, (a dream that wouldn't be stopped by a dream catcher). In the dream, a six headed beast that had heads of a bear and a body and legs of a goat came to her. In the dream, the six heads spoke in unison, each saying one word at a time. Each one had a different pitch in it's voice, like six people talking in unison, making it hard to understand what it was saying. But the beast was talking fast as if it was natural and there were no unnecessary pauses between the words. It only took a few seconds for Pupa to concentrate on the words and not the different pitches the beast was using, so she could understand what it was saying.

"I am going to kill Rosa, the Promised One, so she will not interfere with my work," the beast said.

"Who are you?" Pupa tried to scream out, but could only manage a squeak.

"I'm legion, for there are many of us," the beast replied.

"Why do you want to kill my Rosa?" Pupa asked.

"I told you, to stop her from interfering with my work!" The Beast shouted back at her.

"You can't kill the Promised One. It is written that she will free her people from the oppression of their sins!" Pupa said.

"Oh, she will do some works, but she will not finish what she would do if I let her live. And she will not give birth to that horrid

White Eagle who would continue her works. I swear to you and all that is strong and evil that I will kill her!" The beast screamed out.

"Then I will kill you first, before you have a chance to kill her!" Pupa screamed at the beast and she then was standing in her war uniform, holding her knife and war club. She ran toward the beast screaming her war cry as she ran. The beast used his goat legs to jump up and over a great ravine that she could not cross. The ravine was too wide for Pupa to jump and too steep to climb down and back up. Even if she could climb down and back up, the beast would only jump back across. The beast was taunting her on the other side of the ravine when she woke up, sweating profusely.

Pupa sat up in bed wondering what or who that beast was, who dared enter her dream. Six heads, she couldn't remember anything about six heads in the *Great Book Of The Living Souls*. There were other writings that the Socike felt may be true, but were not absolutely believed to be true by everyone. There was the book, *Souls Of The Dead*, that was written by Half Moon, a Socike chief that lived in about eighteen eighty, according to the white man's calendar. There were several others that were written by different people that hardly anyone read, but were kept with the *Great Book Of The Living Souls*. Thin Twig, the keeper of the Great Book was well read on all of these books. If anyone would know if there were writings about the beast, he would. They were kept in the same building where Rosa worked now. Maybe she could walk to work with Rosa this morning. Then she remembered that Rosa wasn't going to her office but straight to Joe Coyote's place to talk to him about expanding his herds.

Pupa looked at the clock and realized it was only three thirty in the morning. That white man's clock was a handy little gadget and wondered why they still pretended to not use the white man hours and minutes. It all seemed a waste to keep on pretending that everything was morning, late morning, noon early after noon and so on. Why didn't the Chief just declare that from now on, the Socike Nation would adopt the use of the white man's clock. Then Pupa sort of chuckled to herself, why was she thinking about something so trivial when she had just had a dream about a beast that wants to kill her only kin, her granddaughter. She was going to have to do some serious research to get the meaning of that dream and there was nothing she could do now. She had better go back to bed and see if she could get some sleep.

Rosa rose early that morning and after she dressed Shosho showed up in her car just like she had promised. Pupa was up and having coffee in her robe, not dressed for the day yet. Rosa bent down and kissed her grandmother goodbye and went out the door.

Shosho and Rosa pulled up in front of Joe Coyote's herding shack after the sun was up an hour. Joe was out in the corral teaching three young men and a girl how to castrate the goats that he didn't want to breed with the ewes. He had them penned up separately from the rams that he was going to use for the breeders. Joe was asking the young people if they knew why he had picked these eight rams over the others from the herd. Each one called out a reason why they thought he had picked the eight from the others. Joe considered each reason as they called them out and let them know if they had hit on a good reason.

Rosa couldn't help but admire the patience he had with the young people. She hadn't realized that Joe was quite a remarkable man as far a being so good with young people. She thought he was quite good looking, too, with his long dark hair and the chiseled features of his face and lean build. She sat in the car admiring the rugged good looks until Shosho got out of the car and opened Rosa's door and asked her if she was staying in the car all morning or getting out. This brought Rosa out of her concentration and she slid out of the car a little embarrassed that she had been admiring Joe so intensely. The two ladies walked to the corral and listened while Joe explained to the young people the correct way to do the job at hand and why they must not shirk in their never ending pursuit to improve the strength of the herd. When he was finished talking, he took his sharp knife and demonstrated the correct way to do the job at hand and then put the goat out to pasture with the ewes.

Joe told the young people to catch another goat and get him ready for castration and he would be right back. He then walked over to the two women who, by this time, were leaning on the corral fence watching what was going on. "Good morning," Joe greeted the two women.

"Good morning," the two women replied back in unison.

"To what do I owe this honor of a visit of two beautiful women visiting my camp this early in the morning?" Joe said as he got closer. Then he recognized the two women. "Good morning, Rosa. Good morning, Shosho," he said, as he reached them. "I'm sorry, I didn't recognize you two at first, the sun being in my eyes."

"We would have called if there was a way to reach you with a phone," Rosa said.

Joe shrugged. "There's no way to get a phone way up here. Even the cell phones they have all over won't reach me. I sure wish there was a way to get a phone here," he said, then waited for a reply to his first question.

"Joe, when I talked to you the other day when I was with Pupa, you said you had hopes of expanding your herd," Rosa said.

"Yes, I did, that is what those kids are here for. To learn about herding. I went to our new principal at the high school, your husband," he nodded at Shosho, "and asked him to get me kids that where having a hard time in school, and might make good herders. We agreed to work together to help these young people get focused on their lives. We had more, but these are the ones that have stuck to it. The young lady over there, wasn't having a hard time in school but wants to be a veterinarian, so I let her get the experience," he said. "I think with these young people's help, and the cooperation from the high school, I will be able to double my herd by next year," Joe said.

"It sounds to me like you are very focused on what you want, Joe," Rosa said.

"Yes, I am," Joe said. "It's going to take me awhile, but I plan to make a big difference on this reservation."

"That's why we made the trip out here, to talk to you about just what you need, to hurry up your plans. To increase your milk business, to increase your herds, to include sheep and cattle, like you talked about when Pupa and I were here," Rosa said, and smiled at Joe.

"I don't want to be disrespectful, but why do you want to know?" Joe asked.

"Joe, I have been appointed adviser to the chief. I am trying to find ways to increase jobs here on the reservation and make our lives better here. I think you could do a lot to fulfill that goal. I think with your desire and ability, you could not only furnish jobs here on the reservation, but you could do a lot in helping us petition Washington to get grants for the expansion of businesses here on the reservation. Are you interested?" Rosa asked.

Joe looked dumbfounded. *Not too long ago this young lady was looking for a job, now she is asking if I want to work for the chief,* he thought. *Is she for real?* "What, are you talking about, my help with the grants from Washington," he asked.

"Joe, I can't promise anything, except that I will back you on any reasonable request you make for your business. I am asking you, if you would donate your time and talent for a chance to petition Washington for grants and, in some cases, for loans to help get businesses started here on the reservation. I'm even thinking of a meat packing company to process your meats that your herds would produce. I'm asking you, because I think you are the most qualified for this job," Rosa said.

"What do you want me to do?" he asked.

"I would like you to make an appointment with me now to talk to the Chief and present your plan to increase your herds to create a fast-growing meat and milk company. You would need to estimate what you would need, and when you would need it. That is as far as help, money for supplies and how much land you would need and when you would need it," Rosa said.

"When could you have that information to present to the chief?" Rosa asked.

"I could have that information now. I figure it and look at it every spare minute I have. What I'm saying is, if you can get me an appointment with the chief tomorrow I could present it to the chief tomorrow," Joe said.

"I can't get it tomorrow, but I think I could get you an appointment the next day, would that suit you?" Rosa asked.

"If you could, I would be forever grateful, I've tried to get an appointment with him, but could never get past the Men Council," Joe said.

"We won't have to go through the Men Council to get the appointment but we may have to sell the Men Council before we get what we want. Would morning or afternoon be best for you, Joe?" Rosa asked.

"The sooner the better. Lets make it morning," Joe said.

"Meet me at the cheif's office not tomorrow, but day after tomorrow at nine a.m., room number three in the Chief's building," Rosa said.

"I'll be there," Joe said. "Thank you."

"We will let you get back to your students," Rosa said.

"We left you out of the conversation Shosho. But it is good to see you again. Please say hello to Black Feather," Joe said.

"I will," Shosho said.

Joe waited until the two ladies left and then he jumped up in the air and yelled, "yessss!"

Joe's students all turned to look at him. Joe just smiled and went back to teaching them.

# Chapter 29

Pupa was at the Chief's building that morning waiting for someone to open it up so she could go in. The name of the of the building was Chief Hunting Panther, named after a great chief in the early nineteen hundreds. But everyone just called it the *Chief's Building*.

Big Joe arrived to open the building like he did every morning except the weekends. He greeted Pupa respectfully and asked if she was there to see her granddaughter, when he learned that she had come to see Thin Twig about the books that he was in charge of, he informed her that he usually arrived early and should be there any minute. "Would you like to see Rosa's office?" he asked.

"I'd love to see it," she said.

Joe took her up to the second floor where Rosa's new office was. After they got in her office he pointed out the things that he had done for her so she would have a nice office. Pupa could tell that he really liked Rosa by the way he was talking about her. The two of them talked for a while about the office and Rosa. Then they started talking about the old days when they used to race regularly in the ribbon race. After they had been talking about twenty minutes, Joe told her that he had better get busy and open some of the other offices. The two of them left Rosa's office and locked it back up. "I really enjoyed talking old times with you, Pupa," Joe said.

"I enjoyed talking with you, also," Pupa said. "We should do it again sometime."

Joe didn't know what to say. She used to be Anita Yellowhair to him when they were young. Now she was Pupa, the women chief of the greatest Indian nation in the land. Not only was she the chief, she was one of the greatest women chiefs of all times. "That would be nice," he said. Joe would think about that answer the rest of the day. He would wonder if he should have asked her to lunch or something. *An opportunity lost forever*, he thought.

Pupa went to the small library where Thin Twig kept all of the sacred books and books of the history of the Socike nation. This job was so serious to the Socike nation that they usually had two people on it in case one died unexpectedly. Thin Twig was training a young man for his job because the other man that worked with Thin Twig had died last year and Thin Twig was old himself. This was a serious job and the people that worked at it were respected by all the nation, even though they never got a title. Some people called them keeper of the book or books, but it was not recognized as a legitimate title.

Thin Twig arrived right before Pupa got to his office and was telling the young man to study a certain book for that day. When Pupa walked in both men stood and greeted Pupa with respect. "To what do we owe this honor?" Thin Twig asked.

"Good Morning," Pupa said. Then she held out her hand to shake hands with Thin Twig.

Thin Twig took her hand and said. "This is my new assistant, Red Leaf. He is going to be a good keeper of the books."

Pupa then held out her hand to Red Leaf and shook it.

"I am so honored to meet you, Pupa," Red Leaf said, as he shook Pupa's hand.

"Gentlemen, I came to you to find out if you knew of any writings of a goat with six bears heads." Pupa said. She was going to ask more, but she saw the color go out of Thin Twig's face. "I see, you have heard of this beast," she went on. "Also, do you know of any writing about a child or even a grown person named, White Eagle?"

Thin Twig got weak in the knees and had to sit down. "Why do you ask of these writings?" he asked Pupa.

This question shocked Pupa, because to ask a leader a question so bluntly was an insult to her. "What?" she asked in a tone of authority.

"Forgive me," Thin Twig said, as he lowered his head.

Both Pupa and Red Leaf were looking at Thin Twig in surprise that he would have said such a thing.

"I meant no disrespect to you, Pupa. I never thought that anyone would speak of that beast or of White Eagle. I thought they were writings of a mad man," Thin Twig got out as a whisper.

Pupa saw that Thin Twig was genuinely upset over this question so she gave him a few minutes to gain his composure.

In a few minutes, Thin Twig got up and went to a box of books and pick out an old book that had some dust on it, but was not covered with dust because it had been in a stack of books and not on a bookshelf. "These are the writings of Saw Tooth. He was a keeper of the books in the early nineteen hundreds of the white man's time. No one thought that his writings were of any importance at all and in 1989 were marked to be destroyed. But, as you can see it wasn't. Saw Tooth was declared to be a self-proclaimed prophet. The Men Council voted to destroy all of his writings as trash and of no importance along with some other books that were never recognized as any importance," Thin Twig said. "But the keeper of the books at that time didn't destroy them as the Council had demanded. When I became the keeper I couldn't bring myself to destroy such writings and have kept them all in that box. I have read every one of them and I just can't destroy such writings."

Thin Twig took the book out and looked through it until he came to the part he was looking for. He handed it to Pupa and pointed to the spot he wanted her to see.

Pupa took the book from him and began to read. *"In the days of the Promised One there shall be a legion of Sand Walkers that will come to the plane of the humans and shall fight with the Promised One. They will come boldly as a goat with six heads that look like bears and they will fight openly with the Promised One. They shall use every form of evil that they can call up to help destroy her. If the beast wins the fight, then the Promised One will die and not do the great works that she is destined for. But she will do some good works that will last for a short time. If she dies, there will be much rejoicing on that plane of the Sand Walkers, because the Promised One will not have a chance to give birth to—that scourge of the Sand Walkers—White Eagle."*

Pupa became very cold and began to shake with fear. These writings were of the beast that she had talked to. This was the most serious coocha that Pupa could ever get involved in. 'Coocha,' was the Socike word that meant an extremely important event, but even more important than the English words.

Pupa was going to have to go home and meditate on what she should do. "Is there any other place in this book that mentions the beast?" Pupa asked.

"No, nowhere else and I know it is not mentioned in any other book of our sacred writings even the ones that have been marked to be destroyed," Thin Twig said. "I've studied them all."

"Is White Eagle mentioned anywhere else?" Pupa asked.

"No, nowhere else," Thin Twig said as he shook his head.

"I need to study this book," Pupa said. "I need to know about this beast and I need to know about White Eagle."

"You can take that book with you. It's not considered of any importance to anyone but you and me," Thin Twig said. "I don't think you will find what you want because it's like a mad man's rambling, but take it with you."

Pupa thanked him and took the book with her as she left. If it had been like the Great Book, she could not have taken it anywhere and she wouldn't have been left alone with it, either.

"She sure was interested in that writing, wasn't she?" Red Leaf said.

"It wasn't the book, it was that paragraph about the six headed beast and that passage about White Eagle, she was interested in. That book could become very important, so treat it with respect when we get it back," Thin Twig said to his assistant, Red Leaf.

"I treat all books with respect," Red Leaf said.

"Yes, you do, and I appreciate that about you," Thin Twig said.

When Pupa got home she sat down and started to read the book she brought home. After reading for over an hour she started to realize why the men council had decided to destroy the book. It was a hodgepodge of ramblings about everything from what was going to happen in the future to how a man and woman should make love. She marked her spot with a string and turned to one hundred and three, where Thin Twig had showed her where the writings about the beast with six heads like a bear were and read the first part of that chapter to the last of that chapter without anymore information. She then put the book down in frustration.

Pupa sat there thinking of what she had learned that day and the night before. She couldn't help but wonder why the writing was so vague and why there were not any other books that would give more information how to protect Rosa. This Beast that came to her in her dreams, is he really as he said, many and therefore powerful as he said, or is he just one that tries to scare people into hurting themselves by their own fears. Next, should she tell Rosa, so she could be on guard, or should she not tell her and be watchful herself. On one hand, if she told Rosa, she could be watchful for trouble. On the other hand, if she told Rosa and this beast was only a bluff, the worry just might keep Rosa from doing her job well, and the beast would win from just a bluff. Just as Pupa was mulling all of this over in her mind, the front door opened.

"Hi, Nana," Rosa said, as she walked through the door. "This has been some day.

"We went to Joe Coyote's place and he had some high school students there teaching them how to be herdsmen. I think that his dream of being bigger and better is going to work out great, even better than the races. I can see so much for this reservation. I can't believe that I'm going to be able to help all of our people like the chief has promised."

"I have no doubt that you are going to do great things," Nana said. "Why are you home so early?"

"I am a little tired. I was having these dreams last night, I kept tossing and turning and just didn't get enough sleep," Rosa said.

"Dreams, what kind of dreams?" Nana asked.

"Oh, I had a couple of nights where I had a Leaka dream. It wasn't much at all. This big bird or bat thing came and looked at me and snarled at me, that's all," Rosa said.

"That not good," Nana said. "Leaka's are annoying spirits and are usually harmless, but they can be a warning of things to come. You say, it looked like a bird or a bat?"

"More like a bat, I'd say," Rosa said. "It's probably something I ate."

"Maybe, but if you keep having them, let me know. I'll make you some other kinds of dream catchers and I'm sure we could come up with one that even a leaka can't resist." Nana said. *At least I hope so*, Nana thought.

"Oh, I don't think it's worth spending any time on that wimp," Rosa said.

"I'm really excited in what we found out at Joe Coyote's place today. He is ready to move forward and I have already gotten the Chief to set up a meeting with him the day after tomorrow. I would have set up the meeting for tomorrow if the Men Council wasn't set for tomorrow. I wish we didn't have that Men Council meeting tomorrow. I'm kind of nervous about that," Rosa said.

"You'll do great tomorrow. The men won't give you any trouble, even though they may think they are the only ones that can come up with a new idea. The Chief will keep them in line," Nana said.

"I won't be able to talk in the meeting, I can only talk to the Chief," Rosa said.

"You won't be able to talk, but you can still say a lot by your body language and facial expressions. You will not utter a word, but I bet you'll get your point across anyway," Nana said.

"I don't know, I'm really nervous about the meeting," Rosa said.

"If they bother you too much, just think what they would look like if they were sitting there naked," Nana said.

Both women started laughing at the thought of that. Then they started talking about other things and then Nana asked if Rosa ever thought of getting married.

"Not lately, I used to think about it when I was in high school. Then I thought that marriage was the answer to everything until I got out into the real world. I guess I would like to get married when I find the right guy, but I'm in no hurry. Why do you ask?" Rosa asked.

"No reason, I was just curious. If you did get married and you had a baby, what would you name him or her?" Nana asked.

"That's easy, I always liked the name White Eagle, for a boy or a girl," Rosa said.

Pupa tried not to show any facial expression at all, but she could feel the chill go all over her.

"What?" Rosa asked. She could see that Nana was shocked or surprised.

"Nothing, that is a powerful name," Nana said.

"Do you think that it's too powerful of a name to give a baby?" Rosa asked.

"No, not at all. I think that would be a good name for your baby,"

Nana said. "You are going to leave your mark on this reservation and I'll even bet that any children you have will leave their mark on it, as their mother does."

Just then, they heard a knock on the door. Rosa went to answer it. "Hello Rose Bud, come in," Rosa said.

Rose Bud had come to see Pupa so Rosa excused herself to go take a shower to give Nana time to talk in private.

"Redbird has decided to test the wilderness to her fate, for her sins," Rose Bud said.

"How do you know that?" Pupa asked.

"Hanna told me that Redbird came to her last night and told her that she was on her way to the wilderness to have her sins cleansed from her and she hoped that the Women Council would take the answer of the wilderness," Rose Bud answered.

"How are you supposed to know if she really goes to the wilderness for forgiveness?" Pupa asked. "The purpose of going to the wilderness is for your own peace of mind not to prove to anyone else that your ancestors have forgiven you."

"I know, and I'm going to tell the Council that exactly," Rose Bud said.

The Socike's believe when someone breaks their law or commits a sin they can go to the wilderness without food or water and without weapons or extra clothing or blanket of any kind and survive for thirty days and their sins and transgressions are forgiven.

"We will still rule on her breaking the law of our nation tomorrow afternoon," Rose Bud said. "I'll let you know what our decision is after the meeting."

Pupa wouldn't go to the meeting because she was the one who called for the circle of truth that had caused Redbird to confess.

"I know the council will use wisdom on this matter," Pupa said. "I know whatever the council decides will be just."

"I'm not looking forward to tomorrow," Rose Bud said. "But I know that this matter has to be handled."

Rosa finished her shower and walked into the room where Pupa and Rose Bud were talking. "After I went out to see Joe Coyote I went to my office and talked to the Chief. He gave me an advance on my first pay check. I'd like to take you two ladies to the Center for our evening meal, my treat," Rosa said.

The three ladies walked to the center in a fast walk. It wasn't that they were in such a hurry, but for people who got around walking all the time, they were so used to walking fast that they had to concentrate on walking slow. They talked all the way there and really enjoyed the walk. When they arrived, there was a short line to wait before they got to the food. But it was a short wait until all three women got their food and were sitting at a long table. Other people were sitting at the same table and Rosa noticed that one of the people was Officer Bob Yazzie, the young officer who had stopped her in the pickup when White Owl was with her.

The young officer had noticed that Rosa was looking at him. "Good evening," he said.

"Good evening," Rosa replied back.

"Do you mind if I join you?" Officer Yazzie asked.

"We would be delighted to have you join us," Rosa said.

Officer Yazzie picked up his tray and moved over across from Rosa, next to Pupa.

They all exchanged greetings and then the officer directed his question to Rosa. "I understand that you are in a very high position in the tribal government?"

"I wouldn't say that I'm in a high place in the tribal government," Rosa said. "I have a position as an adviser to the chief."

Pupa and Rose Bud were nodding their heads when officer Yazzie had asked about her position in the government. "We think she is in a high position," Pupa said, and Rose Bud nodded her head.

"Well, I'm impressed," Officer Yazzie said.

The four people were talking about everything from acorns to why eagles give out a shriek sometimes when they fly. They had all finished their dinner when Officer Yazzie asked if he could call Rosa sometime at her office and maybe have lunch together. This took Rosa off guard and said that it would be alright for him to call. Officer Yazzie excused himself and left the three women sitting there when Wanda came over to the table carrying a tray of food.

"I see you are almost finished, but can I join you?" Wanda asked.

All three of the ladies said that they would be delighted for her to join them. "I think I'll try that pumpkin pie they had up there. Does anyone else want any?" Rose Bud asked.

"I couldn't eat another bite," Rosa said.

"I think I'll get some more water," Pupa said.

"I'll get it for you," Rose Bud said.

Wanda sat down and started eating her dinner. I stopped by your Place before I came here," Wanda said to Pupa. "I have Rosa's uniform in the car, and I wanted to have her try it on. I could give you ladies a ride home after I eat and have her try on the uniform."

"That would be great," Rosa said enthusiastically.

Pupa was anxious to see Rosa in her new uniform, but wasn't looking forward to riding in Wanda's car. "I guess that would be alright," Pupa said.

"Great, then it's settled, I'll give you a ride home and Rosa will get her final fitting," Wanda said.

*Oh, I hate riding with Wanda,* Pupa thought.

Just then, Rose Bud showed up with her pie and Pupa's Water. She set the pie down and started to set the water down, but bumped the edge of the table with the water glass and it spilled out, right towards Pupa.

Pupa slid back with her chair and let out with a small screech, then a laugh. The water made a small stream right toward where Pupa was sitting and then over the edge of the table onto the floor. The other three women joined Pupa in her laughter.

A young lady was cleaning tables nearby and came over with a dish towel and wiped up the spilled water. "I'll get you some more water," she said.

"I'm sorry," Rose Bud said, and produced four forks and handed one to each lady, even Wanda, who had not finished her dinner yet. "I thought I'd share, even if Rosa does say she can't eat another bite."

The three ladies all tasted Rose Bud's pie which didn't last long. In a minute, the young lady showed up with Pupa's water and set it down without a spill. Pupa thanked her for the water.

Wanda finished her dinner and all the women started for Wanda's car. It ended up being an old faded blue four-door Ford with the passenger side dented from the front fender all the way down to the back bumper which was pulled out at the end, showing that Wanda had snagged it on something and didn't stop in time. "You'll have to get in from the left side of the car, the right side doors won't open," Wanda said. The women stepped into the street and Wanda opened the front door for someone to slide in before she got in. Rosa slid in and Wanda slid in behind the wheel. Rose Bud and Pupa slid into the back seat. Wanda put the key in and the starter started a slow turning of the engine. It took several tries until the motor caught and the engine started to run on what a mechanic would call four cylinders, which wouldn't be bad, except that it was an eight cylinder. The car coughed, sputtered and smoked and the women were on there way to Pupa's house. The only thing worse than Wanda's car, was Wanda's driving. She started off with a jerk and sped down the streets, not even slowing down at the stop signs. When she pulled up in front of Pupa's house the tires screeched to a halt. Rosa thought, *Thank God,* and waited for Wanda to get out so she could slide out of this death trap.

The four women went into the house and Wanda gave Rosa her uniform. "It's beautiful," Rosa said, holding it up in front of herself and laying it against her body so everyone could see what it looked like. There were some 'oos' and 'aws,' as the three women looked on.

"Go put it on so I can tell if I need to do any altering," Wanda said.

In a minute, Rosa was back wearing the uniform and also had her war club and knife. "It fits perfectly," Rosa said.

"Let me see," Wanda said as she moved in close to Rosa and tugged and pulled here and there. "Lift up your arms," Wanda instructed. "Now hold your arms out straight from your body. Now bring them forward."

After Wanda put her through several movements and asked her how it felt, she was satisfied that the uniform fit as well as possible. "It looks like I won't need to do any last alterations," she said, as she stepped back and took one last look at her handy work.

"Beautiful, just beautiful," Rose Bud said.

The three women stood around and looked at Rosa in her war uniform for a while, then Rosa excused herself and went back into her room and changed back into street clothes. She laid out her new uniform on the bed with her war club and knife. She stepped back and admired it once more before she hung it up and put away her weapons.

Entering into the room where the three women were waiting for her, Rosa smiled and thanked Wanda for the fine job she had done on her uniform. Wanda told her it was a privilege to have the opportunity to serve the Promised One and if she ever needed her again to please not hesitate to ask her for her help.

"I'm so glad you said that. As a mater of fact, I do need your help," Rosa said.

"Anything," Wanda said.

Rosa explained the races that they were going to have on the reservation and the uniforms that they would need.

"And you want me to make them?" Wanda asked.

"No. That would wear you out. In my opinion, you are already overworked with the uniforms you have to make now. I was wondering if you would be interested in teaching young people your craft and let the good ones make the uniforms that our people would wear and the not so good ones make the uniforms that we would sell to the tourists," Rosa said.

"Be interested? I'd love to teach anyone how to be a uniform maker, but no one seems to be interested in it," Wanda said.

"If you are willing, I'll get you the students. Then we have a deal?" Rosa asked.

Wanda nodded her head and smiled from ear to ear. "We have a deal," she said. "I'm going to go home now. Would you like a ride home?" She asked Rose Bud.

"Thanks, but I was going to stay a little longer and I really need the exercise," she said.

"Suit yourself," Wanda said and went out the door. "Bye, everyone."

All three women said goodbye at once.

After Wanda left, Rose Bud spoke up. "I love Wanda to death, but I hope I never have to ride with her again."

Both Rosa and Pupa laughed at that remark and then Rose Bud started laughing, too. "I need to get home myself, I'll let you know tomorrow what the Women Council decide on Redbird's fate," Rose Bud said.

After Rose Bud left, the two women got ready for bed and Pupa slept all night without a dream.

Rosa, on the other hand, started dreaming right away. She was standing in a grassy field with a blue sky overhead. She was watching the fluffy clouds floating over head at a slow speed, but little by little the clouds gained speed. In a few minutes, the clouds started to turn a gray and everything started getting dark. She was watching these clouds when a giant bird or bat came floating down from the clouds. When it got close, she could get a better look at it. It was a pterodactyl and it was right above her. She could feel his hot breath on her face the beast bit at her head, but she ducked and the beast bit hard into her shoulder and picked her up off her feet. The pain was excruciating and the beast flapped his giant wings and started to gain altitude. With each flap of the wings the pain became more intense. Rosa tried to scream, but no sound came. She was dangling from the giant beast and trying to hit it, with no success. She had none of her weapons with her and she was at the mercy of this beast. It was gaining altitude when Rosa woke with a start.

She was laying on her shoulder and it was hurting terribly. She sat up in her bed and rubbed her shoulder and felt blood oozing out of it. She could feel the teeth marks in her shoulder and pulled her hand away, blood was dripping from her fingers. She started to scream when her eyes cleared and the blood was no longer there. Feeling her shoulder to see if the teeth marks were still there she could only feel soft, smooth skin. What could this be, she thought to herself. Maybe it was the result of coming off alcohol so long. But she had always heard that D.T. dreams came right after one came off alcohol, not weeks after she had stopped drinking.

Rosa got out of bed and got her war club and knife and slept with them in her hands for the rest of the night.

The next morning, Nana could tell that Rosa had a hard night. Pupa didn't say anything, but she was determined to make her a dream catcher that would catch the most allusive dream leaka.

Rosa arrived at her job in time to talk to the chief before it was time for the Men council meeting. She told him of her plan to have Wanda teach some of the school children her craft so they could make uniforms for the riders of the race and also sell to the tourists.

"I understand why our ancestors chose you to be the Promised One. You don't stop, do you?" he asked.

"Do you want me to stop?" she asked.

"No, I guess not, but it's all happening so fast," the Chief said. "Well let me make some more notes to take to the meeting."

At the meeting there were twelve old men sitting at a table. There was a man that stood up and asked who Rosa was and what she was doing at the Men Council. Chief Crow Foot got up and told everyone who she was and, that from now on, she would be with him at these meetings. There was some grumbling, but they all settled down for the meeting. Chief Crow Foot got up and told them of the plans that Rosa and he discussed and that he wanted them to cooperate with her on everything. This caused quite a stir among the men. The chief stood up and asked what plan that they were grumbling about; which of the plans that he laid out in front of them had they not liked. The men all looked at each other and no one could name one that wouldn't sound like they were against the reservation, itself.

One older man stood up. "I am Gray Owl. I don't see any of these plans to be bad, but they all depend on the white man either as tourist or as buyer of our goods. We have always tried to avoid depending on the white man. That is why I will vote against all of these plans."

The other men of the council all nodded their heads in agreement with this old man.

"You are right, Gray Owl, we have always depended on ourselves to provide for our people," Chief Crow Foot said. "Look what that has gotten us. We are far behind the white man in money, power, and in providing for our people. We need to change or we as a people will die. Our young people leave our reservations in droves. We must do something to change that. If any of you have even one idea that is better or even as good as these I want to hear them, now." Then the Chief sat down.

The old men looked at each other, but no one said anything.

The Chief got up again, "I need some volunteers that will go to Washington and ask for the money that we will need for this change. Now let's see a show of hands, of men who will be willing to do that." The Chief waited for anyone to raise their hand. No one did. "I take it no one wants to do that. But men, we need some one. Does anyone have any ideas who we could ask?"

These old men were not used to being asked about such things. They were used to being asked about whether some act or another was breaking a law or not. They were all to eager to give their opinion on anything, but to step out of that role was too much.

"Does anyone think that we should use other help, like people at the school to do jobs like this?" The Chief asked.

The men all looked at each other and started nodding their heads. One old man got up. "I believe that our great Chief has the right idea.

The teachers are used to speaking in front of people and they are familiar in the ways of the world. I think that would be a good idea." Then the old man sat down.

Other men got up and all agreed with this. Then other topics were brought up that the old Chief wanted. He played those men like a tom-tom. When it was all over the chief had mentioned everything that Rosa had asked him about and got an approval to get the other help he needed to accomplish this.

On their ride back to their office, Rosa had a new admiration for the old Chief. He went to that meeting and got everything done that he wanted. Maria was surprised how fast things were happening. The Chief drove Rosa to Foxwood road and the street was all cleaned up. The old cars were gone and she saw one old dog that a man was putting in his car. As they pulled onto the street, they passed two policemen. One stepped out to greet the chief as they pulled up and stopped. "Good afternoon," the young officer said to the Chief.

"Good afternoon," the Chief said back to the officer. "I want to introduce you to Rosa. She will be living in that last house where all the wood and men are. She is the only one that you are not to stop and question."

The young officer looked into the car and looked at Rosa, so he would recognize her. Then he called over the other officer and told him what the Chief had told him about Rosa. "There will be other officers here at other times and we will pass on the message," the officer said.

The Chief drove on to the end of the street and parked his car. The two got out and Rosa was in awe of what was going on. All of the siding was torn off. Men were knocking out windows and doors. Rosa could see new windows and new doors stacked up in two piles on pallets. Rosa walked around with awe. She couldn't believe that this was the same place she had been before.

"I took your advice about this street and I'm even thinking about changing the name of this street. The policemen that we talked to are here to stop all drugs and liquor from entering onto this street. I used some of my own ideas on this street, too. Every grownup on this street that isn't taking care of children and who is not employed has to work on the cleaning up of this place," the Chief said. "I think that we are making good progress."

"I'll say, I wouldn't have recognized the place," Rosa said.

The two walked into the house and saw that the inside had been gutted. All of the burnt floors and the trash were gone. Young men were getting instructions on how to hang a new door. Rosa recognized the man doing the instructing, he was the shop teacher from the high school. Rosa looked at the Chief. "Are these high school students?"

"Yes, they are. We are planning a new way to teach. Here, the students get six hours of shop and two hours of other studies. Later this year they will get no shop and extra hours of their other studies," the Chief said. "This way they can get immersed into what they need the most. If we can give these students what they need to learn, for a trade to survive, we are doing good. The students that are well-adapted to academics will only get one or two hours of this hands-on class and that will be only four weeks unless they want more and that will be for extra credit. We don't want to deprive any student a chance to get a good education, but we do want to get them experienced in something that they can use.

"Mr. Barns, the shop teacher has been teaching here on the reservation for eight years and contacted several contractors. He has gotten them to loan us trucks and drivers to teach the students how to drive dump trucks, front loaders, graders and the like. They are supplying men to teach our students how to be carpenters and brick layers, truck drivers and the like. We agreed to have the students help them when they need extra help. What do you think of this idea?"

"I think it's wonderful. You did all this in the last two days?" Rosa asked.

"Well, to be truthful, I had talked to Mr. Barns last year about this sort of thing and the students were getting some of these classes after the first night I met you. I called him and told him to get ready to bring his students where we would need them. You see, we had some of the basics down, we just needed someone to point us in the right direction. That's what you did, with your vision. After we clean this neighborhood up like it should be, then we are going to tackle the horse race and the horse breeding. I have an appointment with Jode this afternoon to talk to him and get his input. After I talk to him, I will decide if he should be in charge of overseeing it."

The appointment you set up with Joe Coyote tomorrow will lead us in a another endeavor. I kind of think this should be enough for a while, until we get caught up, don't you?" The Chief asked.

Rosa bit her lip, "I hate to tell you this, Chief."

"What?"

"I was thinking of helping that small bakery we have here expand," Rosa said.

The Chief sighed, looked up at the sun and saw it was high in the sky, *past noon*, he thought. "We had better go to lunch so I can make that meeting with Jode this afternoon," the Chief said.

The two got back in the car and headed to the center to catch a late lunch. By this time, no one else was there to eat lunch and the workers were taking the food off the line. "I guess we missed lunch," Rosa said.

Then the manager came over to them. "In for another late lunch, huh, Chief?"

"I'm sorry, Ruth, but Rosa and I have been working some long hours lately and we don't seem to be able to keep a schedule for our meals," the Chief said.

"You don't have to explain to me, I know how hard you work, I'll get you two something to eat," Ruth said.

Rosa and the Chief sat down at a table and in a few minutes Ruth came over with a warm lunch for both the Chief and Rosa. "I saw you here with the Chief and Pupa before. Aren't you Pupa's granddaughter, Rosa?" Ruth asked.

"Yes, I am," Rosa said.

"I'm Ruth and I've heard a lot about you lately, if you need a late lunch or dinner ever, just ask for me," Ruth said. "If you need anything, just call," Ruth said to both Rosa and the Chief, then went back to her work..

"Ruth has done a great job here since I hired her," the Chief said.

"You hired her?" Rosa asked.

"Yes, the other person who was running this place wasn't doing a good job and I fired him right on the spot. He didn't think I could, because he had gotten his job through the Indian affairs department. Ruth was one of the dishwashers here and she walked right up to me in front of her boss whom I had just fired, and announced to me and everyone around, that if I hired her to run this place I wouldn't be sorry. Before anyone could tell her that she shouldn't approach the Chief, she started pointing out things that were wrong and how she would correct them. I gave her the job right on the spot and I came back in two days to check on how she was doing. The place was completely different. She fired four people and hired two to do the work of those four people. Still, no one is overworked. The place is cleaner and the food is better. She was right, I'm not sorry," he said.

"There is so much that we can do here to make our nation better, and you are one of our leaders," the Chief said. "You wait and see. These ideas that you have come up with will bring our economy around. I just know it will."

"I just came up with the ideas, that is easy. On the other hand, you are doing the hard part, you are getting the job done. You are the one who is ramrodding everything through," Rosa said.

"It's a joint effort, I have several other people working with me, most on a voluntary basis," the Chief said. "Black Feather, the new High School Principal, is working with me closely. There are four teachers and, of course, you know Sergeant Blackwood. They are all working very hard. We will get things going. You just keep coming up with ideas and we will try to keep up."

"I'll do my best," Rosa said. "Do you want me to be here for the meeting with Joe Coyote tomorrow?"

"I think so. It sure won't hurt," the Chief said. "Black Feather will be here, too. I want him to be here to help me with any questions that I might not think of. I hear that Joe has a mind like a lawyer."

"He does, and if we could get him to oversee some of our legal work, I think that we would be ahead of the game," Rosa said. "Oh, by the way, I kind of recruited Shosho, Black Feather's wife, to do some volunteer work. She drove me to Joe Coyote's yesterday," Rosa said.

"Good thinking, Shosho is a good lady. "I've got to get going. Do you want me to drop you off somewhere or do you want to sit in on my meeting with Jode?" The Chief asked.

"If you don't mind, I'll go home and to bed, I need some sleep. I've been having some trouble sleeping lately," she said. Rosa didn't want to miss the meeting with Jode, but she was so tired that she was afraid she might do something wrong.

"No, I don't mind, I think everything is pretty much cut and dry for now. I just want to feel him out to see if he is suitable to handle everything that is required to be done in the position I have in mind for him. I'll fill you in tomorrow and get your input on everything," the Chief said. "I'll drop you off and then make the meeting."

"Thanks, Chief, I'd really appreciate the ride. I didn't know I could get so tired," Rosa said.

The Chief dropped Rosa off and Rosa walked in on Pupa and Rose Bud talking about Redbird. It seems that the Women Council had voted her out of the council and had asked Rose Bud to ask Pupa to consider Shosho for reinstatement to the council. Pupa said that she would certainly bring up reinstatement for Shosho into the Council at their next meeting.

Rosa excused herself and went into her bedroom. It had been a busy day and she was dead tired. Rosa noticed that Nana had hung a black dream catcher trimmed in silver beads. *Nana, she never fails me*, and then she laid face down in her bed. In a very short time Rosa was fast asleep.

Pupa looked in on Rosa before she went to bed, herself, to see how she was doing. Rosa was tossing and turning and making strange sounds. she would give out with a kick every once in a while. Pupa took down the black dream catcher and laid it on Rosa. This move didn't help at all. In a minute, she had kicked the dream catcher off of her. Pupa could tell that Rosa was having a bad dream. Pupa went to Rosa's closet and got down her war club. She then placed it in her right hand. Rosa grabbed it tightly and began to swing. In a few minutes, Rosa lay quietly and Pupa went on to bed.

The next morning Rosa was feeling better and was wondering how the war club got into her hand. At breakfast Rosa mentioned to Nana about the war club.

"Were you dreaming last night?" Nana asked.

"I don't remember dreaming," Rosa said, thoughtfully.

"You don't remember dreaming, that's good," Nana said. "You were dreaming. I don't know why the dream catcher didn't work. I'll try a new one today and we will see if it works. This is very strange."

"I don't remember dreaming and I feel great," Rosa said. "Are you sure the dream catcher didn't work?"

"I'll leave it up in case it worked, but I still will put up a different one, too," Nana said. Pupa knew that a war club could sometimes scare off a Leaka, but usually they would bring back friends to make the next dream even worse. She didn't mention this to Rosa, because she didn't want to worry her.

Rosa was in a hurry after breakfast, she wanted to be on time for the meeting with Joe Coyote and she was anxious to find out how the meeting went with Jode. She went to her office right after she and Nana did the dishes. *I wish Nana would get a dishwasher. It sure would be nice not to have to spend time doing dishes*, Rosa thought.

When Rosa reached her office she noticed that the Chief was already in his. Rosa grabbed a pen and a notepad and hurried to the chief's office. The Chief was on his phone and Rosa said, "Sorry," and started to back out of his office, but the Chief motioned her back in. After the chief hung up. "I'm so sorry, I don't know what I was thinking, entering your office without knocking. I'm sorry, I won't do it again," Rosa said.

The Chief started to laugh. "You are a jewel, you don't know who you are yet. Someday people will be apologizing for walking into your office without knocking. You need not apologize for that," the Chief said. "Are you feeling better today?"

"Much better, I don't know what got into me yesterday. I was so sleepy," Rosa said. "By the way, how did the meeting go with Jode yesterday?"

"It went great, I got the impression that he is the man to oversee and manage the races and the breeding of the horses. What do you think?" The Chief asked.

"I think he is the right man for it," she said.

"Good, I'll check with some other people and then I'll let you know if he gets the job for sure," He said. "This meeting with Joe Coyote is different, I have already checked him out. Now I need to see what it is that he proposes before I know if I will go along with it," the Chief said.

Joe Coyote walked into the building and knocked at Chief Crow Foot's office. "Come in," Chief Crow Foot said. Joe Coyote walked into the brightly lit office.

Rosa rose from her chair, "I'm so glad to see you, Joe," she said.

"I'm glad to see you, also," Joe said to her.

"I understand that you have had a hard time seeing me," The chief said.

"Yes, I have," Joe said

"I'm sorry about that. That is changing. I have left instructions that I am notified of anyone who requests to meet with me, so at least I will know that they want to see me," the Chief said and held out his hand to shake Joe Coyote's hand." Joe shook the Chief's hand. "We are waiting on Black Feather, before we start this meeting, in the meantime would you like some coffee?"

"Thank you, I'd love some," Joe said, remembering his Socike manners.

The Chief asked Rosa if she wanted coffee. He then picked up his phone and asked into the phone that they bring in some coffee and four cups.

In a few minutes, a middle aged lady came in carrying a tray of coffee and four cups. She excused herself and then brought in the cream and sugar. Black Feather stepped into the office right behind her.

"Sorry, I'm late," Black Feather said, "I had a little trouble starting my pick-up. I'm going to have to get a new battery for it."

"You are not really late, we are just now getting our coffee," The Chief said. The lady poured coffee from the urn that she had brought in. In a minute, everyone was settled in for the meeting.

The meeting went on until lunch and everyone went to lunch and then came back. In the meeting, everyone agreed to start the great expansion that was going to increase Joe's herd and to form a partnership between Joe and the reservation. Chief agreed to let Joe use the reservation money to buy first class beef for an expansion. The Chief agreed to increase the land that Joe controlled, as the need arrived. Everyone agreed that men that were not working now should be offered a job to help Joe. Black feather agreed to encourage more of the school students to try out for the class that Joe provided to teach them herding. The meeting was a great success and everyone went home feeling that everyone accomplished something.

Rosa went home to find Nana studying a book that she just put away when Rosa arrived. The two women sat and talked until they had dinner, which each helped to make. After they finished the dishes, Rosa filled Nana in on what was going on in the expansion of Joe Coyote's herd. She told her of a plan to have a slaughter house that would process the meat that Joe's enterprise would make, and also give a fair price for the beef and sheep that other tribes would bring to sell. Their target date was four years for completion. Both Rosa and Pupa were excited about what was happening on their reservation. Rosa's goal was to provide jobs for everyone that wanted one.

Rosa went to her room to find another dream catcher to go with the one that was black with silver beads. This new one was purple with white feathers and red clay beads. It was about two feet in size which was the largest Rosa had ever seen. *Nana sure doesn't want any dreams to bother me,* she thought, then she went to bed.

Pupa was asleep for about an hour when she was awakened by screams from Rosa's room. She rushed in to find Rosa thrashing about wildly in her bed, kicking and screaming. Pupa thought that she was too wild to put a war club in her hand. She tried to wake her, without results. Pupa could make out a word once in a while, but try as she might, she couldn't wake Rosa. She decided to take a chance on the war club. She put it in Rosa's hand and Rosa threw it and it hit the wall with a thud and sank into the plaster and stuck there. Pupa went and got a pitcher of cold water and dumped it on Rosa's face to wake her, without results. Pupa was pacing back and forth, yelling at Rosa and stopping to shake her. She had never seen anything like this in her life. Rosa was in this dream state and Pupa couldn't get her out of it. Rosa started to bleed at the nose and then at the mouth. Then she saw bite marks appear on her arm and Rosa was screaming with pain. Then Rosa started to choke and Pupa could see that Rosa couldn't get her breath. Pupa tried to wake her again by slapping her and yelling at her. Pupa was yelling and crying, she was going to lose her granddaughter if she couldn't get her to breathe. Pupa could see an indentation on Rosa's neck like an invisible hand was choking her to death and she had turned blue. Then Rosa's eyes opened and she sat up in bed, She was coughing and Pupa could see that Rosa was breathing. In a minute, the two women were hugging each other and both were crying.

"I couldn't breathe. He was choking me," Rosa said.

"Who was choking you?" Nana asked.

"That beast, that damn beast," Rosa said. "I thought I was dead. There was a big fight. We were out-numbered. I got some help, but we were out-numbered. This thing was pulled off me, but he pointed a finger and he said he was going to kill me," Rosa said. "If I go back to sleep he will kill me."

For the first time in Pupa's life she didn't know what was going on. She didn't know why the dream catchers weren't working. She didn't know why she hadn't been able to wake her granddaughter up. This was going to be a sleepless night. She needed to reach her ancestors and get the answer. But she was afraid to leave Rosa alone. She didn't know who would know about this, after all she was the expert on spirits and dreams. No one knew more than her. "What can I do? What can I do?" Pupa said to herself in such a low voice that Rosa couldn't hear her while she buried her face in her hands.

Rosa was softly sobbing, sitting up in her bed. "I almost died, Nana," Rosa said in a whisper. "I couldn't do anything."

"At first light, we are going to get dressed in our uniforms, take our weapons and go seek our ancestors," Pupa said. "Until then, we need to get up and drink some coffee and not go back to sleep."

"I'm so tired, though," Rosa said.

"I know, a dream like the one you just had, wears you out completely. But I tried to wake you, and I couldn't," Nana said.

"Gaud... I must have been sweating a lot, My face and hair are all wet. Look at my bed," Rosa said.

"That's not sweat, I poured cold water on you, to try and wake you, with no results. I couldn't wake you. That's why I don't want you to go to sleep. I might not be able to wake you," Nana said.

"How did you wake me?" Rosa asked.

"I didn't, you were turning blue from not breathing, I thought I had lost you. Then you opened your eyes and you woke up. You coughed a few times and started breathing," Nana said.

"I remember. This beast that looked like a giant bat had his claws on my neck and was choking me so hard that I couldn't breathe. I was surrounded by other beasts of different shapes and they were being attacked by our ancestors. But there were so many beasts that our ancestors were having a hard time getting to me. That thing was choking me and other beasts were looking on and chanting, 'kill her, kill her.' The one who was the loudest was a furry one with six heads that looked like bear heads," Rosa said.

When Nana heard this she felt a shiver go up her spine. "We need to get dressed in our uniforms," she said, and helped Rosa out of bed and went and got her uniform for her. In a few minutes, Rosa was in her uniform and Nana handed her weapons to her. Now it was

Pupa's turn to get dressed. The two women went into Nana's room and she dressed in her war uniform and holstered her weapons.

Then the two of them went into the kitchen and started coffee. They sat at the table, sipping their coffee. "I didn't tell you, but I talked to Jode today, and he wanted to thank you for recommending him to the chief for the job of running the races and starting the breeding research. He was really excited about it. By the way he talked, I think we will be seeing him coming over more to see you," Nana said. She wanted to keep the conversation going to keep Rosa from getting sleepy. She wanted to wait until almost daylight before they started walking out in the wilderness to hunt for their ancestors.

"He was the natural choice, for that job, but what makes you think that he will be coming over to see me?" Rosa asked.

"By the way he talked. He kept asking about you. When you were usually home? Things like that," Nana said. "So now, you will probably have two suitors coming around."

"Four," Rosa said.

"Four?" Nana asked in surprise.

"Yes, I saw officer Bob Yazzie and he asked if he could call me.

"I saw Sergeant Blackwood today and he asked me to lunch next week, he's going to call me first. Joe Coyote asked if he could call me for dinner next week when he wouldn't be quite so busy. Wow, everything happens at once," Rosa said.

"Well, of the four, is there one of them that you like more than the others?" I guess, I'm asking you if there is one that may wind up being in our family?" Nana asked.

"Could be," Rosa said. "I really like them all. Each has his own appeal. I'm very fond of Jode, but he isn't husband material... yet. I really like Sergeant Blackwood. He's a little older than I, but I don't know if that's all bad. In fact, I kind of like that. Officer Yazzie is nice and I've had a crush on him since I was in grade school. Joe Coyote, I think he is going to be the richest man on the reservation and one can't but admire anyone with such ambitions, he also has a great personality and—his build isn't bad either. So I guess you could flip a coin and maybe you could come up with a name for me," Rosa said with a chuckle.

"I could flip a coin, but something tells me that wouldn't tell me anything. I have a feeling that they will eliminate themselves as time passes," Nana says.

Rosa got up to walk around, her tailbone was getting sore and she needed to walk around.

"I need to go to the bathroom," Nana said, and got up and went into the bathroom. She took a little longer than she wanted and after she washed her hands and went into the kitchen, Rosa was nowhere in sight. "Rosa... Rosa," Nana shouted as she walked from the kitchen to the living room. There she was on the sofa with her head laid back and her mouth open sound asleep. Nana bent over and shook her, trying to wake her. "This is not good! Wake up. Rosa, wake up!" She shouted. "This is not good!"

In a few minutes, Pupa could tell Rosa was in trouble. She kept trying to wake her without success. *What to do? What to do?* She had read about this in the book, *The Sand Walkers Future*, written by Saw Tooth, that Thin Twig gave her to read. But she didn't know if he knew what he was talking about. It would be very dangerous to her and could be the death of Rosa if it didn't work. Rosa was starting to choke again. Pupa ran to her kitchen cabinet and took out a tin of dried mushrooms and other herbs she used to make the sacred Indian tea. She grabbed a spoon and went to the living room with it. She checked that Rosa had her weapons strapped on and she checked her own. Then she pulled Rosa out straight on the sofa. She then took the spoon and dipped it into the dried Indian tee and in one motion she swallowed it. It tasted dry, but the book said not to drink anything with it. In just about five seconds she started to get dizzy and she grabbed her weapons, one in each hand and lay flat on Rosa.

Pupa was falling into a deep shaft and kept gaining speed as she fell. The idea was to enter into Rosa's dream armed with her weapons and have Rosa's weapons there, also. She must reach her in time, she could see the colors of red, yellow, and blue flash as she fell. In a matter of seconds, all colors turned to gray, white and black. She found herself in a great clearing next to Rosa. Rosa was limp, held up by a claw around her throat of a beast that was huge and had wings of a bat. Pupa swung the war club at the beast's leg, breaking it. The beast screamed with pain and Pupa rushed forward at the beast and stabbed it with her knife. A frog-like creature grabbed Pupa from behind and she brought her knife down in a swinging motion, sticking it all the way up to the handle as the creature loosened his grip on her, she turned around, dragging the knife with her and cutting the creature across the stomach, letting all of his insides fall out. Another like him jumped to her and she swung her war club at his head, crushing the head, and the creature rolled over on his back dead.

The fighting stopped and Pupa looked around. She was surrounded by Sand Walkers and other beasts and creatures from the dark side and they were as deep as she could see. She looked at Rosa slumped at her feet. She wasn't moving and Pupa checked to see if she was breathing.

The beast that had six heads like bears and a body like a goat that Pupa had seen in her dream stepped forward. "She is Dead Pupa, we have no quarrel with you. You can leave without getting hurt. Let Pupa pass," he said and the Sand Walker and beast parted and made a path so Pupa could leave.

Pupa looked again at Rosa, there was no life in her that she could see. *Where are our ancestors?* She wondered, *They are no place to be seen.*

"Pupa, leave now, or I can't guarantee you will get out alive. Leave," The six-headed beast said.

Pupa bent down to pick up Rosa and leave. "Leave her, and go. She is dead, leave her," the beast said. The path made for Pupa got wider.

Pupa looked at the beast, "Well, I have a quarrel with you!" And she threw her war club at the six headed beast. The beast ducked his head and the war club sailed right passed him. The beast laughed,

"You missed," he said. The war club made a short circle and hit the beast on the back of the first head, bounced and flew back to Pupa. The other five heads screamed with pain. The war club flew out of Pupa's hand again, this time hitting the beast on two heads and then back to Pupa. As pupa stood there, she saw another war club go flying towards the beast and hitting it in the back breaking it's back, and come flying back towards her. She glanced to Rosa who was kneeling, she had come to, and had thrown her war club like Pupa had.

The beast screamed and pawed at the ground. The rest of the crowd of Sand Walkers and creatures took off in retreat in a panic. Pupa held her hand out to Rosa to help her to her feet. In a few seconds, they heard what sounded like thunder, and in a minute there was a legion of braves on horseback riding towards them with the Sand Walkers running ahead of them. As the braves overtook the Sand Walkers and the creatures, they slew them with one swipe of their war clubs or with a spear or a knife. They even shot arrows of lightning with gold bows that hit their target every time. Rosa walked over to the beast that had three heads bobbing and begging for mercy.

Rosa said, "I will show you as much mercy as you showed me." With her war club she smashed each head, killing the beast. Then she and Pupa examined the beast with bat wings. It was dead and the creatures that looked like frogs were dead. Pupa and Rosa were soon surrounded by all of the braves that came to their aid.

Eagle Woman came forward, "I am proud of my daughters," and she pointed to Pupa and Rosa. The other braves gave a victory shout that echoed through the plane of the Sand Walkers and the Sand Walkers that had escaped shook with fear and hid themselves wherever they could find to hide. "You will not have anymore trouble with the likes of them for a long time," Eagle Woman said.

Then another woman brave rode forward on a spotted horse. She was dressed in bright blue and looked like a princess to Rosa. When she got closer Rosa knew it was Maria, her sister. "I am so proud of you, Rosa," Maria said. "I pray for you each day and I sometimes watch over you when I am permitted. We were looking for the Sand Walkers after we learned that they were after you, but their plane is big and we had many places to look. They would not usually gather together like this, but because they did, we were able to slay many with them all in one spot like that. They would not usually take that chance, but they all wanted to see the Promised One killed. Nana saved you by not running when the beast told her to go. Those three creatures there should not have been involved in this," and she pointed to the beast with bat wings and the two frog men.

"Now, do you want a ride back?" Maria asked. She offered Rosa a hand to help Rosa get on her horse behind her. Rosa turned and looked at Pupa and she was getting on a horse behind Eagle Woman. Rosa took Maria's hand and swung her right leg up and over the back of Maria's horse. When she was settled behind Maria, she had the sensation that she was somehow attached there like two magnets that would have to be pulled apart. In the next moment there was a sensation of moving faster than sound and then the three of them— Rosa, Maria, and Nana were standing in Pupa's house.

"This has been one exciting time, even for us," Maria said.

"I don't understand anything about your world," Rosa said to Maria.

"I know you don't. I didn't either before I went there. But once I got to our ancestors, the knowledge came like the lightning in the sky. With one big flash and boom, I had all of this knowledge. Take the classes that Nana suggested you take, you will need them," Maria instructed. "You have a bright future ahead of you and so does your child. Now I will leave you to your real worries like who you will date next." Then Maria giggled and started to fade away.

"Wait! Do you know who I am supposed to marry?" Rosa asked.

Maria was only a vapor now "Yes, I do. But if I told you, it would take the fun out of it for you!" Maria giggled some more and was gone.

The next morning, Rosa and Pupa were having coffee and Rosa could see that something was bothering Nana. "What's wrong?" Rosa asked.

"Something your sister said, about those three creatures that shouldn't have been there," Nana said, then got up and went to the trap door in her floor and went down into the cellar. When she emerged from the cellar she was carrying the box that held Red's dream catcher. Nana laid it on the kitchen table and opened it, then took out the catcher. "That's the reason why untrustworthy people should not get information about our secrets." She pointed to the hole where Mary had repaired it. The repair knots hadn't held. "That was why the creatures that should not have been there, were there. They escaped from this dream catcher. They were the ones that almost killed you. That's why those dream catchers I made didn't work. They were too wary to get caught again so soon."

Rosa picked up the dream catcher and examined it. "These things can be dangerous," she said.

"Yes, they can," Nana said and she tossed it into the trash can. "We won't need that one again. I'm going to toss out those last two, also, so they won't attract any more bad dreams. It's not good to hang those kind up, unless you really need them.

After the two women had their coffee, Rosa went to work and later that day, Pupa showed up at the keeper of the books and returned the book, *The Sand Walkers Future*, to Thin Twig. "I will be forever grateful that you didn't destroy this book. It needs to be saved and studied. That is something that I will bring up at the next Women Council meeting," she said.

As she was leaving, she saw Big Joe sweeping the sidewalk and went up to him. "It's almost lunchtime, can an old friend buy you lunch?" she asked him.

Joe grinned from ear to ear. "I would be honored to have lunch with you," he said and put up his broom.

Two young boys that were playing hooky from school and were picking at the trash left at the dump when one spotted something. A closer examination revealed three dream catchers, one with the center broken, another which was black with silver beads and the last one was purple with red clay beads. That one he gave to his friend. The black one he held and could feel a strange vibration coming from it. "These will look neat in our rooms," he said.

**The End**